Part

Trilogy

Breaking Lies

Breaking Lies

First published 2018 in Great Britain by GoApe Books.
An imprint of:

Monkey Island Publishing
Hurgill Road
Richmond
North Yorkshire
DL10 4SZ

Design and typography by Gill McLean
1st Edition published 2018

ISBN 978-0-9930636-5-7

A CIP catalogue record of this book is available from the British library

Printed in Great Britain

Part II

1

The North Sea. November 2067

Kate came up from behind, putting her arm around her son's shoulders, as he stood on the deck of the ship. He was leaning on the rail, staring ahead into the darkness. The icy wind sliced through his hair and burned his cheeks, but he was glad of it. Kate pulled the hood of her Parka closer round her face.

'Can't sleep?'

Si shook his head.

'Me neither,' she said.

They were heading back to England, just over a year since they had fled to Amsterdam.

'Nervous?' Kate asked.

Si shrugged.

'I am,' she offered. She rubbed his back, like she used to when he was a little boy. He still didn't respond. 'You want me to go?' she asked.

He shrugged again. 'Don't mind.'

They stood in silence, allowing the blackness to slide past them. It was a strange feeling, standing here in the dark, ploughing through black water, not knowing what lay ahead of them.

'You miss her,' Kate said.

Si pursed his lips. His mother was good at reading his mind. He did miss her, but he was also angry with her. Why did she have to go back so soon? Why couldn't she have waited with him?

'No point dwelling on it,' Si said. 'Chas will always do what Chas wants.'

'Don't be angry with her. She did what she needed to do,' Kate said.

'She's selfish!' He thumped his palms on the rail of the ship.

'Come on Si. Not really. She's been through a lot and she stuck by you all that time. Saved your life and little things like that,' Kate said, trying to lighten his mood.

'She only stuck by me because she wanted to get close to her brother and take revenge. Selfish! And now that's where she'll be headed. Back to find him.'

'She said she wanted to find Ben,' Kate said.

'An excuse. Most of all - she wants to kill Resolution.'

The idea of revenge troubled Kate. 'Well, it's you and me now kiddo and we need to focus on the path ahead of us. Tobias and Mikel have been an amazing support in Amsterdam. Without their help this would have taken a lot longer. But we're on our own again now.'

'Apart from Nick of course. Is he meeting us at the port?' asked Si.

Doctor Nick Reece had helped Si and Chas when Si had nearly died from the rogue nanomedibot inside him last year when they were on the run. Nick was a friend of Peter

Marsden's and a member of the Way, a religious group that Si's mother belonged to. She and Nick had been in regular communication over the last year. Nick was keen to help them and had been fantastic at getting what they needed to get back into the country. They were wearing new phones on their wrists with fake IDs on them, courtesy of a covert operation from the UK on Nick's part.

'He should be there when we dock. He's taking us straight to one of the plague camps he visits.'

'I can't believe how much worse it's got since we've been away,' Si said.

We can't prove the Rulers are behind it... yet.'

'You will though.'

'We will. But for now, the Nanomedibots are primed and ready to help those infected. We can finally do what your father and I intended, way back. We can save people's lives.' They stared silently into the distance for a while. 'Your dad would be pleased to know that you're fulfilling his role now.'

Si hugged his mum. 'You miss him,' he said.

'Every day.' She squeezed his hand and went back below deck.

2

Eight months earlier in Amsterdam.

'You're making a big mistake.'

'Really? O Wise One!'

Si pulled a face at her. 'What good will it do? He's settled with the family now. You'll just churn it all up for him. He'll be confused. You'll just hurt him all over again.'

Chas was packing her things into her rucksack on her bed. She didn't look up or stop. 'Emotional speech, Bastille Boy. Save it for the bleeding hearts.' She always called him that when she wanted to turn the knife.

'You know I'm right. That's why you're angry with me,' Si persisted.

She stopped packing and turned to him, thrusting her face in his. 'The discussion is one hundred percent over. I can't stay here any longer. I've got to square it with Ben. Every day I see his face and the look of betrayal. I can't bear it.' She turned back to her packing.

'It won't be long until the Nanomedibots are ready. Then we can all go back together. He'll have had more time to settle then. We could visit him.'

'You don't know when the NMBs will be ready. Kate's not even certain yet. This is your quest. Yours and hers. You've found your mum. You can work with her now. You don't need me, and I've got things to do.'

'Like finding your brother, you mean.'

'That would be a bonus,' she said, shoving the last few things into her rucksack, including a new knife she'd bought in Amsterdam last week.

'He's most likely dead; the state we left him in,' Si said.

'He's not. That is not an option.' She stood with her hands on her hips. 'Killing him will be one hundred per cent my pleasure.'

'Off you go then, on your stupid selfish quest and don't be surprised if you end up one hundred percent dead!' Si slammed out of the room.

She found him a while later, sulking in the living room of the flat they shared with Kate, in the suburbs of Amsterdam. She threw herself down next to him on the sofa. Si kept his eyes fixed on the HTV. Some Dutch programme about schools. Their arms and legs touched, but neither of them spoke for ages.

Eventually Chas nudged him, keeping her eyes on the screen. 'Come on Si, I don't want to leave on bad terms.'

He shrugged, keeping his eyes on the screen also. 'You're still going though.'

'I have to. I'm restless here.'

He didn't look at her. 'When does your ferry leave?'

'A couple of hours. Tobias is taking me to the port.'

They watched the children on the HTV babble in Dutch for a while. They understood only snippets of what was being said.

Chas touched his foot with hers. 'I'm glad we met. Despite

everything.' Si didn't reply. He didn't trust his voice not to do something stupid.

Tobias came into the room. 'Chas, I'm ready. We need to go.'

'Okay. I'll be down in a minute. Where's Kate?'

'She's waiting by the car to say goodbye. Si, you want to come to the port with us?'

Si shook his head slowly and emphatically.

Tobias left the room.

Chas stood up. 'I've got to go. Please say something!'

He turned away. She grabbed his cheeks in her palms and turned his face towards her. His eyes were brimming, and he struggled to yank his face away, but she was determined and strong.

Her own eyes began to fill up. She had fought her emotions for a long time, but now she was leaving there was no containing them.

Si closed his eyes and two tears dribbled quickly down his face. He tried again to pull away, but Chas straddled his knee and pulled his face to hers. She kissed him hard and he responded, both of them in tears now. For a moment, Si thought that she might change her mind; (emotional displays were unusual from Chas) but she jumped up, heaved her rucksack on her back and was gone.

It was unlikely they would ever see each other again.

*

Chas boarded the ship, went below deck, found a sofa and slept. Sleep was good for blotting out the difficult stuff.

The ship docked that evening in Newcastle. She showed

her wrist, around which was wrapped her wearable phone with a false ID on it, to get her through customs. The official checked the projected holo-screen and let her pass. Nick Reece, the doctor who had helped them escape from England, was waiting for her. He was relieved to see all had gone smoothly. He led her to his waiting car and they drove to his flat.

'How are you, Chas?'

'I'm fine. You?'

'Fine. Si and Kate?'

'Fine.'

'How's it going with the Nanomedibots?'

'Kate hopes they'll be ready by November.'

'That's great.'

It wasn't a long journey to Nick's place, and once inside, Nick made her something to eat. He tried more conversation, but she wouldn't really engage. She told him the bare bones of what her intentions were regarding Ben, and starting a new life, but nothing of her brother. Her mind was already planning how she might find him and trying hard not to think about who she had left behind.

'I'm really tired Nick. Is it okay if I just go to bed?'

The next morning, she was keen to leave early.

'You sure about all this?' Nick asked.

'Yes. I have to find Ben,' she said.

'Is that really a good idea?' Nick said.

'Don't try to stop me, Nick. I've had enough of people telling me not to do this. I'm not changing my mind now.'

Nick smiled resignedly at her. 'No, I guess not.'

'Thanks for your help though.'

He gave her some provisions, then she was on her way to Seahouses, in the hope that Ben would talk to her. She'd come to think of him like a little brother during the trials of the previous year. She didn't know if Ben thought she and Si were dead. Would that have been better than thinking they had abandoned him? She didn't know which would be worse. News from England, that had filtered through to them in Amsterdam, proclaimed them as rebels: Silence and Kate Hunter and Chastity Komchenski were outlaws. There was a price on their heads. Another reason Kate had tried to persuade her to wait a little longer before returning to England. But Chas was stubborn. So, here she was following the coast to Seahouses, her hair cut short and dyed brown, a woolly hat pulled down as far as it could go and a scarf covering most of the rest of her face. She had deliberately chosen the colder months to come back as it was easier to disguise yourself. She carried the phone, which proclaimed that her name was Grace Sanderson. Overnight she made camp at the back of some sand dunes and was up on the move again early the next morning.

She arrived in Seahouses late in the afternoon, the following day. It was such a sleepy little village. It seemed so remote from the tech-cities, and yet it was still a working community. Not many of them still existed since most people were too afraid to live outside city walls, although most of the things they feared were just government propaganda.

She approached Ethan and Sarah's house, pausing at the end of the street. Her stomach lurched as Si's words flashed in her brain. You're making a big mistake. You'll just hurt him all over again. Shaking them from her mind, she crossed the road and knocked on the door. Sarah opened it, on a chain.

'Can I help you?' she asked, looking suspiciously at Chas.

'I'm looking for Ben,' Chas said.

No one came looking for Ben. 'Why? Who are you?'

She pulled off her hat and scarf. Sarah showed no recognition. Chas was glad. 'I'm Chas,' she said. 'I need to talk to him.'

Sarah's face bleached. She glanced up and down the street. 'Come in. Quickly!' She pulled Chas into the house.

'We thought you were dead! At least you look different. There's still a live reward for anyone with information on you or Si. Where is he?'

'He's not here. He's abroad somewhere with his mother,' Chas said.

'We heard about the rescue, but we didn't see how you could have escaped capture, so we presumed the worst!' Sarah offered Chas a seat, so she perched on the edge of the sofa. 'Ben's not here right now. He's at Judo with Ethan and the girls. I'm not sure it's a good idea for you to talk to him. It's taken him a long time to come to terms with things and he's just starting to settle.'

'I just want him to know we're not dead and explain why we left him behind. Then I'll go,' Chas said.

Sarah, still standing, folded her arms across her chest. Her face bore the lines of worry and her anxious eyes willed Chas to just go away. 'Why? What's the point in stirring it all up again?'

'He deserves to know the truth,' Chas answered.

'Maybe when the truth causes pain it should just be left alone,' Sarah countered.

'I'm not going to take him away,' Chas said. 'I'll go as soon as I've spoken to him. You'll never see me again.'

Sarah shook her head, her voice raised ever so slightly and tinged with a hard edge. 'So, back to my point about leaving the truth alone. There is no point in hurting him all over again.' She took Chas firmly by the arm and pulled her up out of the sofa. 'You need to go. You're putting this family in danger by being here. I'll give you some food for your journey and then you leave, before Ben gets back.'

They stared at each other for a moment, each willing the other to backdown.

Chas wrenched her arm from Sarah's surprisingly strong grip. 'Just let me have half an hour with him.'

'No! I'll get you some food then you leave.' She went to the kitchen. Chas swore under her breath. She looked around the living room. There were pictures on the mantelpiece of Ben and the girls, laughing together. A picture of Ben and Ethan on the boat and one of Sarah and the girls cuddled up together. Chas swore again.

Sarah returned with some sandwiches and a flask. 'Here you are. Now...'

Chas was already gone.

She hung around in the centre of town where she could see the path to the house. No matter what Sarah thought, she wasn't leaving without speaking to Ben. She didn't have to wait long before she saw them walking towards the house. Ben was laughing with Ethan and his daughters.

Her stomach lurched at the sight of him, obliviously happy, with his new family. It hit her like a sledgehammer. Sarah was right. She shouldn't shake up his world again. It was selfish. One of the girls pointed at something in Chas's direction. The others turned to look. Chas pulled her hat down and turned to look in a shop window. When she turned back they were disappearing along the path.

She hunched her rucksack higher on her back and bowed her head, stuffing her hands in her trouser pockets. 'Goodbye little brother. Stay happy,' she mumbled at her feet. Then, she turned and walked away from Seahouses.

Part one of her return: Fail.

Part two would succeed.

First, she needed to find somewhere to live and fit in. A commune, like the one she had lived in when she met Si, would be ideal. Then she would make enquiries until she found her blood brother. Once he was dead, she would be satisfied.

She walked for a couple of days, keeping away from roads and sleeping rough; first in a dilapidated shepherds' bothy and the next night in a makeshift shelter. It was very cold, but it felt good to be out in the open again. She saw no one as she walked across the wild Northumbrian landscape. It was dark when she reached the edge of a forest. She laughed to herself as she switched on her torch. This was how she had found Si, stumbling through the woods in the dark. So innocent. So naïve back then. A stab of nostalgia made her look behind, as if he might be standing there, with his stupid grin and even stupider remarks, as she held him at knife point.

'Can't you make it just fifty percent dead?' he'd said.

'Don't push me!'

'So, how will you kill me?'

'With my knife.'

'What kind of knife is it?' he'd asked.

'What?'

'I said, what kind of knife is it?'

'A bloody big sharp one, so shut up!'

She almost laughed. They had laughed together many times over the absurdity of their first meeting. She shook the scene from her mind and stepped into the forest.

It had been a while since she had needed her tracking skills, but they were as sharp as ever, ingrained into her psyche. She would find somewhere to make a shelter for the night soon, then keep looking for people. Maybe there would be a commune here, but it wouldn't be wise to stumble upon them at night. She constructed a shelter from branches, blending it into the undergrowth, then climbed inside, curled into a tight ball and slept; knife in hand.

She was washing her face in an icy stream early the next morning, when a male voice from behind startled her.

'You hungry?'

Her hand shot to the knife in her belt, hidden beneath her jacket, and she whirled around. He was a little older than herself, dressed in jeans, a dark hoodie and jacket. He was grinning at her as if she was a friend, but she didn't do friendly. He repeated the question, in his soft Scottish accent, and Chas shook her head.

'I'm just leaving.'

'You don't have to. Come for some breakfast. Not many

fast food places round here.' He was still grinning.

She looked at the wild countryside and found herself feeling foolish under this boy's unswerving stare. 'I can find food.'

'I'm sure you can, but I can offer you something hot and instant. Yeah, fast food!' He laughed at himself.

Why would he invite a complete stranger back to wherever he lived? No one trusted strangers. It was the rule of the countryside.

'Where d'you live? I didn't see any houses for miles last night.'

'In a commune further up into those woods. Are you coming? I really need to get back. Just been emptying the traps.'

She hadn't noticed the bag slung over his shoulder. As he turned, she saw rabbit's feet and pheasant feathers sticking out. He began to walk.

She hesitated. This was what she had been looking for – a commune to join. He paused and smiled at her over his shoulder. 'We're not as bad as the rumours would have you believe. Last chance...'

Picking up her rucksack she walked a few metres behind him. He was lean and muscled and obviously used to living outdoors. He stopped and looked back at her until she was forced to catch up with him. Her knife hand twitched impulsively. They walked side by side for a few minutes in silence. He had that sort of unwashed, fresh air smell about him and Chas suddenly realised how much she'd missed living in the open.

'Bit unusual to see a girl out here, never mind one on

their own.'

'I'm a loner,' Chas said.

'Yeah? Where you from?'

Chas recoiled. Too many questions already. 'Nowhere in particular.'

They walked on. 'Hope you like porridge, cos that's what's for breakfast.'

'Fine,' she mumbled.

'My name's Mish, by the way. What's yours?'

Chas kept her head down, hoping they would be there soon.

'You gonna make me guess then? There's nay so many different names as there used to be before the Rulers. Could still take me a while though.' Chas didn't respond. 'Okay, starting with A. Affable? Amiable? Affluent? Admirable? Articulate? Erm... can't think of any more As. Bs. Benevolent? Beneficial? Beauty? B... B... Boring? Balding?'

A smile twitched on her lips. She shook her head. 'Sorry. It's just that ... I've had some trouble. My name's Grace.'

'Phew! It would ha' taken me ages to get to G. I had some pretty good ones for F...'

Chas looked away from him and smiled.

'You're lucky to get a decent one. Mish is short for Submission. Idiot names. But you get used to them. Wouldn't be yourself wi'out your name, even if it is a stupid one.'

'Guess not.' She glanced at him, thinking of her real name, which she had always hated.

It wasn't long before they reached the commune. Chas

smelt the wood smoke first. As she stepped into the clearing where the shelters were, she had to stop. It was like someone had punched her in the stomach as the sense of déjà vu hit her. She doubled over, thinking she might throw up.

'You okay?' Mish put a hand on her back.

Chas forced herself to stand up and breathe deeply. 'I'm fine. I think it's just relief.'

'Right,' Mish said.

He led her to some logs by the fire where an older woman was stirring a pot of porridge. 'Give her some,' he ordered. Chas was a little taken aback at the harsh way he spoke to the woman. The woman obeyed instantly, not taking her eyes off the pot.

Mish held up his hunting bag. 'I've got to take these to be butchered. Wait here. Enjoy the porridge.'

Chas sat by the fire clutching the warm bowl, but not able to eat at first. Memories of the day she had brought Si back to her commune played out before her. People she had allowed herself to love, rose up in her mind. She saw them busy, laughing around the camp. Then she saw their dead bodies littering the ground after the massacre. Ambi, Emmy, Dis. She made an involuntary noise, like a dog yelping. Her eyes began to water but she pressed the heel of her hand hard into her eyeballs. The woman looked up but didn't say anything. Some children ran over, screeching as they circled around her. When they noticed she was a stranger, they sat down; curious, asking her questions. She was careful how she answered, but the questions weren't too probing, and they distracted her from the memories.

'Grace?' A man spoke behind her. Chas stood up. 'I'm Stuart.' He also spoke with a Scottish accent. 'I'm the leader of this commune. Mish is my...'

'Son. Yes, I can tell,' Chas forced a smile. Stuart held out his hand and Chas took it, remembering that it was probably good protocol to be less frosty.

The children were still milling around. 'Away wi' ye!' Mish barked at them. 'Go find something useful to do.' They scattered without hesitation.

'Are you far from home?' Stuart asked.

She shrugged. 'Don't really have a home.'

'Ah, that's no good. You can stay here. We welcome anyone who needs a home, if you don't mind roughing it and you don't mind mucking in....'

'Don't mind either,' she said.

'Have you got any skills we'd find useful?' asked Mish.

'Yes. I can hunt, track, build shelters, shoot...'

'What kind of shooting?' asked Mish.

'Bow and arrow...'

Mish raised his eyebrows and nodded.

'Look, you don't have to decide immediately,' Stuart said. 'The offer's there, but if you want to move on we won't stop you.'

Chas was puzzled by his openness but decided it must be due to them being quite remote here. She thought of her mission to find Resolution. She wouldn't find him here, but she could do with a place to stay for a while and to figure things out.

She had only meant to stay for a few weeks, to plan her next move to find Resolution, but the weeks turned into months as she realised how much she had missed living in a commune. She was welcomed by the people who lived there. To her mind, they were much too friendly for their own good. She felt bad keeping her identity from them, but it was necessary. She didn't want anyone remembering her association with Si, however remote the chance was out here. She was hunting and trapping for the commune now, as well as teaching the younger children some archery skills. She slept in a hut with two other young women who seemed to accept and welcome her immediately. As the weeks went on she found herself beginning to let her guard down a little and make friends. It was comforting being back in a place like this and part of her wanted to forget the past couple of years and make this her home. But there were things she couldn't let go of.

Mish made a point of being too friendly with her. She wished he would just leave her alone, or even bark orders at her, like he seemed to do with everyone else. Lots of the girls flirted with him, but that wasn't her. He kept coming to her hut when the others were out. It was clear to her that he was after more than friendship. Chas had not brushed him off but tried to keep him at a safe distance. She had an instinct that it wouldn't be wise to cross him if she wanted to stay there permanently, after she had killed Resolution. She was beginning to think that Mish might make a good ally in helping her to find her brother. She had watched him closely around the camp. He was clearly in authority over everyone else except his father and a couple of other village Elders. He expected to be listened to and didn't take any arguing back. Once she had seen him lash out at a man who dared to disagree with one of his orders. But he was more guarded when his father was around and always pleasant with her. She had gone on a couple of hunting trips with him. He was very accurate with a shot gun and knew all the right places to set traps. Despite herself, she began to be attracted to his strength and competence, as well as his toned body. He was very different to Si. But Si was gone, and she had to move on.

Today they were out hunting together again. They'd stopped to eat, sitting on a rocky outcrop with a view across the Cheviot hills. It was breath-taking. 'I wanted to ask you if you might help me with something,' Chas said.

'Sure, if I can. What is it?'

'I have a brother, but I don't know where he is, and I want to find him.'

'How long since you've seen him?'

'About a year or so. He's older than me. His name's Resolution.'

'And you've no clue where he might be?' Mish asked.

'Last time I saw him was in Durham. He was in pretty bad shape and I'm not even sure if he's still alive, to be honest.'

'Sounds drastic. What was up with him? Did he have plague?'

'No nothing like that. He was injured pretty badly. He offended the Rulers and last time I saw him he was in the custody of the law-keepers.'

Mish blew out his lips. 'Anyone who's an enemy of the Rulers is okay by me, but that's a bleak picture you're painting there. What did he do?'

Chas shook her head. 'He failed.'

'I dinna ken,' Mish said.

'You don't need to. It's complicated.'

Mish knew by now that if Grace chose not to tell you something, you'd have a hard job getting it out of her. So, he didn't try. 'Not sure what we can do...'

'We could make enquiries. We could start where I last saw him.'

'And suppose we find him? Do you think he's still in custody?

'Possibly,' Chas said.

What then? Prison visits?'

'Not really what I was thinking,' Chas said.

Mish raised his eyebrows. 'You want us to break him out?'

'Something like that.'

'I don't go into the tech-cities if I can avoid it. Just to trade or buy stuff now and then,' Mish said. 'But I might enjoy a wee bit of espionage. Not sure how we'd get him out of prison though.'

Chas swallowed the last of her food and wiped her hands on her trousers. 'I'd find a way.'

'You're pretty tough, aren't you?' He brushed a strand of hair out of her face and ran a finger across her cheek.

Chas let him touch her, but not for long. 'We should get going.' She made to stand up, but he pulled her back down, gripping her arm and putting his other hand firmly on her neck. He moved in to kiss her. Mild panic rose in her throat and she felt for her knife, but as his lips touched hers, desire overpowered panic and she found herself enjoying it. Her hand let go of the knife and she relaxed. It was only a kiss and if it kept him willing to help her, all the better.

3

December 2067 in Newcastle

'Kate! It's so good to see you!' Nick kissed her on the cheeks and hugged her. Then he turned to Si, giving him a manly thump on the back. 'Si. Good to have you back.' He took them to the waiting car and piled their few bags in the boot. 'You managed to get through customs then? I was a bit worried. Let's get back to mine for some rest, then I'll take you to the plague camp. It's not an easy place to be. I need to brief you both about what you'll see.'

Back at Nick's place they slept for a few hours, then he made them lunch and they listened as he talked about the plague camp. 'There are around 50 people in the camp I'm taking you to, all of them are dying. They know there's no cure, but they come because they're outcasts from the cities. Most don't last more than two weeks once they get to the camp, but they know they'll be cared for by the staff and volunteers.'

'And what are the Rulers doing about the camps?' asked Kate.

'The camps aren't a threat to them. They know people are going to die. In fact, the camps are helping them get rid of the dead. They even give a meagre amount of funding to the camps. Looks good for them on HTV.'

'How many camps are there?' Si asked.

'There are ten in the North East. I visit them all on a regular basis, along with other doctors, just trying to relieve pain, bring more supplies etcetera'

'Well, they're not going to know what's hit them when people start recovering,' Kate said. 'We're going to have to keep it quiet somehow at first, until there are enough people to stand up to the Rulers.'

'I'm not sure people will do that,' Nick said.

Si sat forward and took a sip of his water. 'Surely people will come together against them once they realise what's been happening.'

Nick shook his head. 'They're scared. They just want to disappear, find jobs, get back to living, try to blend in and be useful. You must understand that the Rulers think of them as surplus population, and surplus population is plague fodder.'

'We have to get them to see that if they don't fight back the Rulers will just come up with another scheme to exterminate them.' Si said.

Kate touched his arm as she recognised his agitation growing. 'For now, let's just focus on getting to the camp and starting to administer the NMBs. Nick, are you sure you're happy to help me reproduce more NMBs? It'll be risky. If we're caught...' Her mind strayed to her husband: dead because they had been caught developing the NMBs.

Nick smiled at her. 'Hey, we know the risks. But we want to change things. That's why we're here. And there are more people than you think who will join us, despite what

I've just said.'

'Do you hear anything of Peter Marsden? Or Meg?' asked Si.

'Yes, Peter and I keep in touch. Carefully. He knows you're back. All I know about Meg is that Peter saw to it that she was looked after. He got her a nice place to live.'

That's good. I'd like to see them,' Si said.

'Not sure about that.'

'Why?'

'Peter needs to keep a low profile. He can't risk being seen with you. He's had a rough ride since he helped you and Chas.'

'I'm sorry,' Si said. 'Maybe one day we'll be able to meet. In the future, when the Rulers aren't in power anymore.'

'That'll be a good day,' Nick said, smiling.

'When can we go to the camp?' Kate asked.

'First thing in the morning. Relax if you can for the rest of the day. Build up your strength. You're going to need it.'

The next morning was overcast and drizzling. Si was up before Kate and found Nick in the kitchen, eating toast and drinking coffee. 'Help yourself.' He wafted his toast in the direction of breakfast food left out on the work surface. Si made himself some toast and sat at the table, opposite Nick, who was reading a medical magazine.

'How was Chas when you saw her?'

Nick looked up. 'Fine. Unstoppable, you know.'

'Did she say much?'

'Nope. She didn't want to talk, just slept and then she was gone.'

Si nodded. Ate more toast.

Nick took a sip of his coffee. 'Try not to worry about her. She's a survivor, a fighter even. She'll be okay.'

Si shrugged. 'I know.'

'You've got important things ahead of you. You can't be moping over her now.' Nick drained his coffee and got up. Si bristled, even though he knew Nick was right. He adjusted his thoughts to focus on the day ahead.

They piled into Nick's car. The box containing the NMBs was carefully packed into the boot. Getting through the check point was surprisingly easy using their false identities on their wearables, but there was still a collective sigh of relief when they were through.

'I've never really done all this espionage stuff before,' Nick said. 'I feel sick every time I think of using the false IDs.'

'People have short memories, thankfully. They'll have already forgotten what Si looks like,' Kate said.

'I'm not so sure about that. You know there's still a reward for information about you or an even greater one if anyone turns you in,' Nick replied.

It was a sobering thought; as if they needed another one. The drive took about forty-five minutes, up past the town of Hexham, heading towards Carlisle. When Nick came to a turning, where the magnetised road ended, he pulled the car to a halt by the side of the road.

'This car doesn't take fuel,' he said. 'Anyway, you just can't get it anymore.' We have to go on foot from here. It's only about a ten-minute walk.'

They shouldered their belongings and various supplies, with Nick carrying the box containing the NMBs. No one spoke, each lost in their own thoughts and anxieties about entering a camp where everyone was dying of plague. Kate was sure that the NMBs were going to cure people, but there would be a lot of suffering to face as well.

After a mile or so of walking, the camp came into view over the rise of a hill. It was made up of long grey tents. There were wooden planks laid as walkways over the muddy ground. The place was bigger than Si had imagined. It was surrounded by a flimsy fence with warning signs nailed to it. 'Danger. Plague camp. No unauthorised access.' As they approached the entrance a couple of guards in military uniforms stopped them. Si felt the hairs on the back of his neck stand on end. He looked nervously at his mother. She didn't make eye contact but strode on towards the soldiers.

'Don't worry,' Nick said to Si. 'They won't be a problem, but we need them to keep out unwanted visitors and, sadly, to keep the patients from leaving.'

They recognised Nick and didn't even look at the other IDs because Nick vouched for them.

Kate noticed some military ambulances around the place. 'How do they get here without fuel?'

'The Rulers still have some supplies for off road stuff like this,' Nick answered. 'It's just impossible for the public to get hold of it now. Stops people straying off designated roads too much!'

A few medical people were going between tents. Some wore decontamination suits. A smell of food wafted out of one tent as they passed.

'A lot of the people who work here are volunteers,' Nick

explained. 'Some are paid by the Rulers, but not many, and they only get a pittance.'

'Why would anyone come here of their own free will?' Si asked.

'They care,' Nick replied, simply. He took them to the camp headquarters. It was just another tent that had been laid out as an office. There was a tablet on an otherwise empty desk, projecting a holo-screen of medical information. Other equipment was stacked in neat piles around the tent. Si noticed a camp-bed in the corner and a wardrobe and realised that this must be where the doctor slept.

The doctor in charge was waiting for them. He was a young Asian man in his twenties. 'Nick, good to see you.'

Nick put the box of NMBs on the desk and the two men hugged. The doctor's tired eyes came alive at the sight of them all.

Nick made the formal introductions. 'This is Kate Hunter and her son, Silence. This is Doctor Sharma.'

Kate stepped forward, holding out her hand. 'Pleased to meet you Doctor Sharma.'

The doctor shook her hand. 'It is I who am honoured to meet you, Mrs. Hunter. We have been eagerly anticipating your arrival. Good to meet you all. Silence, I have heard about your struggles. We are grateful for your tenacity.' He made a small bow to both Kate and Si. 'I am very sorry for the loss of your husband and father.'

Kate and Si smiled and thanked the doctor for his kind words.

'We're looking forward to seeing the NMBs in action,'

Kate said. 'They're commonly used abroad to cure all sorts of illnesses.'

Doctor Sharma shut down the holo-screen. 'I know. So much is held back from the ordinary people here.'

'The first step is to get people recovering, then expose the Rulers for what they really are,' said Kate.

'We are grateful for your help,' Doctor Sharma said. He turned to Si. 'Where is your friend, Chas? We have heard much from Nick about her courage too.'

Si shuffled his feet and looked at his mum. 'She's on a personal mission. She decided it was more important.'

'That's a shame,' the doctor said. 'Let's get you settled into your '5-star' accommodation, then you can have a tour of the camp.'

He called out of the tent to a volunteer. She came in. 'This is Sensi. She will show you where you're sleeping.'

They followed Sensi to a tent, where Kate was shown a bed with the women volunteers and medical staff. Si and Nick were taken to another tent, where they were given beds amongst some of the male volunteers and staff. There was very little privacy, just a flimsy curtain separating each bed. There was a small bedside cupboard but no room to put clothes away. It seemed that people had very little and kept most of it in a bag under the bed.

'Do people volunteer here for long?' Si asked.

'Sometimes,' Sensi replied. 'It depends. Some can't take it. We've had a couple of volunteers contract the plague. We have to be very careful.' She turned to them all. 'Come back to Doctor Sharma's office in five minutes and he will take you to look around. You mustn't go anywhere unauthorized, otherwise you are putting yourselves in danger, as well as others. I'll leave you to it and go to see if Mrs. Hunter's okay.'

'I know it's not great living conditions here, but it's not for long,' Nick said as he dumped his bag on a bed.

'It doesn't bother me,' Si said. 'Just makes you realise how amazing some people are that they volunteer to put themselves at risk for others.'

'Yep,' Nick said. 'Come on, not much to do here. Let's get to the decontamination tent and give you the grand tour.'

Kate was already there, talking to Sensi and Doctor Sharma.

'Great. All here,' the doctor said. 'Put these on and let's go.'

Sensi handed them decontamination suits. Si felt like he was about to embark on a space mission and had a sudden urge to laugh. The others were taking things very seriously, which was only appropriate, but this made him want to laugh even more. A picture of Chas came into his head. He imagined her grappling with a decontamination suit and him laughing at her. She would scowl at him.

'Si.' Kate elbowed him in the ribs. 'Hurry up.' Everyone was ready except him.

'Sorry. I'm struggling with this.'

'Here, let me help.' She held him steady as he untangled his legs and started again.

'Thanks,' Si said, glad that the suit and mask were now covering his face. 'Sorry about that. Got distracted.'

Kate raised her eyebrows at him.

The tour of the camp was bleak, to say the least. Doctor

Sharma took them into tent after tent, where row upon row of people existed in varying states of consciousness. In one tent people were able to walk with help, and feed themselves. Some were reading books. There were clearly signs of pain and discomfort, with people exhibiting flu-like symptoms.

'This is the admissions tent,' Doctor Sharma explained. 'Most people come here when they arrive, although some are so bad that they are immediately moved to another tent.'

When they had left the tent, Kate asked, 'How aware are they, when they come here, that they're dying?'

'They know,' replied the doctor. 'They are resigned on the whole. They know there is no cure, but what other options do they have? The back streets of a tech-city? Outside the walls to fend for themselves in the countryside? You know that most of them get sent here from the workhouse when their symptoms become apparent?'

'I know most of them contract the plague in the workhouse,' said Nick.

'That's right,' Sharma said.

'The plague is introduced into their bodies when they seek medical treatment for anything with flu-like symptoms,' Kate added.

'What makes you say that?' asked the doctor.

'When Morgan and I worked for the government, we were working on nano-technology and its use in medicine. At one point, we were taken into a sort of inner circle of scientists employed by the Rulers to work on a certain type of nanobot. This nanobot would be able to infiltrate the body's immune system and attack healthy cells. It was the anathema of everything we believed in. They were making a killing machine. We were horrified. At first, we refused but we received all sorts of threats, including death threats to ourselves and to Si.

We thought of trying to leave, but we thought and prayed about it and in the end decided to keep working there and, in secret, develop the Nanomedibots that would be able to attack the plague cells. It was a tense time as we knew we were under surveillance. We had access to the work others were doing to develop the killer nanobots. The information we gained helped us to prepare the cure. Then we were caught. Si was kidnapped, and we were sent to the Priory.'

'Wow. That's horrific. Can you prove it?'

'Not yet. But I don't think people will need much convincing that this is the truth,' Kate said.

'I think you're right there,' said the doctor. 'The plague is definitely infectious too, though. We've realised that to our cost. We've lost some good people. Hence the extreme precautions we take now.'

'What about the victims who are not resigned to their fate?' asked Si.

'We have some outbursts, some who try to leave, but we have to restrain them. Hence the guards on the gate. We try to help them, mostly with counselling, but sometimes we have to resort to sedation.'

In another tent, Si wondered if the patients were still alive. There was no apparent movement from any of the bodies laid out on the beds. Some had drips in their arms. Even close up, it was hard to spot any movement of the chest.

'Are these people still alive?'

'Barely,' replied the doctor, 'but, yes, they are. They are being closely monitored but there will be death here soon. There is death here several times a day. People are moved here when they are in the last stage of their journey.'

'This tent must be feared,' Si said.

'Yes and no,' said Doctor Sharma. 'By the time people get to this stage they're ready for the end. In fact, they want it to come quickly.'

'Why don't you just put them out of their misery as soon as they arrive at the camp' Si asked.

Doctor Sharma turned to him as if he were an idiot. 'I'm a doctor. First, do no harm.'

Si shrugged. 'In the Netherlands they have assisted dying. It seems merciful.'

'We believe in the sanctity of life,' Sharma said. 'We relieve their pain as much as we can. We care for them. They go quickly at this point, anyway.'

'What happens to the bodies?' asked Si.

'We incinerate them. We try to let relatives know, if there are any.'

There were many tents with people in various stages of the disease: people tormented with raging fever or severe swellings in various parts of their bodies. It was disquieting to witness, especially since they knew that the Rulers were behind the plague.

When they got back to the decontamination tent and had taken off their suits, Doctor Sharma took them to the mess tent for some lunch. They ate in silence for a while, as Kate and Si tried to take it all in. When they eventually began to talk, Kate asked if any of the patients were aware of who she and Si were and why they were here.

'No. We didn't think it wise to get anyone's hopes up at this stage,' Sharma said.

'I believe we'll see high success rates,' Kate said. 'Certainly among those who have just arrived.'

'We need to think about what we'll do with the people who are cured and how we would cope with the influx of people we might get when they hear about the cure,' Nick said. 'What are the chances of re-infection?'

'Once the NMB has destroyed the plague cells it has been programmed to deliver pathogen impersonators into the blood stream, stimulating the immune system to build up defences against another attack. This should cause the plasma B cells to produce enough antibodies and respond quickly and more effectively, should another attack occur.'

Doctor Sharma nodded as Kate explained. 'How have you tested this?'

Si answered. 'Several of us volunteered to inject ourselves with infected cells. We then tested the NMBs on the volunteers. Everyone recovered.'

'How far did you let the disease run before introducing the NMB?' Sharma asked.

'The volunteers were amazing,' Kate said. 'Several of them were prepared to let the plague run for a few weeks.'

'Some were probably almost at the stage of some of your patients in the final tent,' said Si.

Doctor Sharma raised his eyebrows.

'We took it in stages. First, we injected the NMBs at an early stage. The results were almost instant. Then we let people go further, then a bit further. Each time the results were good. People didn't take long to recover. We didn't let anyone go up to the final stages. I wasn't prepared to take that risk,' Kate added. 'I was pretty confident they would be cured up to that point.'

'And no re-infection? Did you test that?' asked Nick.

'We didn't test it, as such, but I'm confident that the plasma B cells are producing lots of antibodies to fight further infection,' Kate said.

'In theory, I should be immune to the plague,' Si said, smiling at Kate.

Nick looked at him, remembering how close he had been to death, when the prototype NMB had malfunctioned. 'You managed to iron out the glitches then?'

'Yes, thankfully.' Kate was also remembering how she had nearly lost Si, after being reunited with him. 'We've made significant developments in the last year, from the first prototype, to what we have now. I encased the NMB in a polymer shell which dissolves after the NMB has delivered its payload to the infected cells. It is then absorbed back into the blood stream and finally excreted from the body. There is no chance of rogue NMBs anymore.' She glanced back at Si.

'It all sounds very positive. This is going to transform things, Kate. The Rulers are not going to know what's hit them,' Nick said.

'The trouble is, when they find out the source of their annoyance, we're going to be in danger. Have you thought of that?' asked Doctor Sharma.

'We've talked a lot about this. We need to convince people to stay here for the time being, not go back to the tech-cities, telling others about the cure,' said Si. 'This is about so much more than just a cure for the plague. This is about revolution. Until we can bring an end to this regime we have no hope of making the cure widespread.'

'Like you say, they'll do everything they can to stop us,' Kate said. 'This is their population controller. It's history repeating itself. They've started with the weakest people, but who knows what plans they have? Think of Hitler, Mugabe, Mao Tse-tung, Stalin, Kim Il-Sung... the list goes on.'

'We have to stop them,' Si said. 'I know there are only a few of us at the moment, but that'll change when people realise what's at stake.' Si hoped this would be true. What if people didn't want to be part of the revolution? What if people were too afraid or short-sighted to join the cause? His mind turned to Chas. Where was she? He could do with her here, fighting with them.

'How many more camps do you have contact with, Nick?' asked Si.

'Ten here in the North.'

'Once the cure is underway here I'd like to go to each of them and implement the same thing. We can train your staff there to work with the NMBs on an ongoing basis,' said Kate.

'We also need to win people over to the idea of standing against the Rulers,' Si added.

There was a pause. Doctor Sharma nodded, taking it all

in. 'This afternoon you can brief the other medics here, Kate and give them some training in how to administer the NMBs. Tomorrow, we'll start to inject the NMBs and we'll see what happens.'

4

It was three in the morning and Chas couldn't sleep. She was sitting on a hill not far from the camp, overlooking the lake. It was a clear night and freezing but she was wrapped up and the cold rarely bothered her. Her mind was awash with plans for finding Resolution and what she would do to him. He had betrayed her and her family. He had hunted her and Si down and tried to get rid of them. She wished she hadn't listened to Si and Kate and had killed him when she'd had the chance. That would have been a lot simpler than this.

Questions pummelled her brain and finding the solutions was proving almost impossible. Mish had agreed to come with her to Durham, to make enquiries about Resolution. If he was in prison it was unlikely that he was still in the city. He would have been moved to the Bastille or to the Priory, and she didn't fancy trying to get back into either of those places. But whatever had happened to him, she needed to find out. The desire for revenge was like ground elder reaching into her being and holding fast. She couldn't get rid of it. An argument she'd had with Si came back to her. They had been sitting by the canal one day in Amsterdam, dangling their feet over the edge, and he had been trying again to persuade her not to go back without him.

'Revenge won't satisfy you.'

'Yes, it will,' she replied. 'Once he's dead, and I know I killed him, I'll be happy.'

'You won't. You'll just be numb.'

'You have no idea how it will make me feel.' She stood up and began to walk away.

'You're right,' he shouted after her. 'But I know this much. You will just be a cold-hearted killer – like him! Like brother, like sister!'

Those words had made her furious because they had disturbed her sense of justification. She hadn't quite been able to shake them, even though she had determined herself to ignore them. She was intent on murdering her brother.

In the morning, she and Mish would go into the city and find out what they could about Resolution. She hadn't told Mish the full story. She had decided to reveal to him as much as he needed to know on the way. Once she found Resolution, she would fob Mish off with some excuse to go it alone. She wouldn't involve him in what she wanted to do. It wouldn't be fair.

She managed a couple of hours sleep before rising, as it was just beginning to get light. People were stirring around the camp.

Mish found her at breakfast. 'Hey. You ready to go?'

'Almost,' Chas said.

Mish was grinning.

'What's up with you? We're not going on a date you know,' she said.

He kissed her forehead. 'Feels like it to me.'

'Well, don't get your hopes up. We're going to ask some difficult questions, take some serious risks and hope we don't get into too much trouble,' she said.

'Sounds like fun!'

He laughed and headed off to speak to his father. Stuart didn't know the real reason they were going into the city. He thought they were going to buy some supplies and suspected that Mish had ulterior motives for taking Grace with him. He was conscious of the boy's attraction to her and when it came to girls, Mish normally got who and what he wanted without too much effort. Grace had managed to keep him at a distance these past few months, which impressed Stuart, but he had seen signs of her weakening.

Mish had an old quad-bike that they still had some fuel for. He got the fuel on the black market and would top it up today. He and Chas would ride as far as possible before it ran out, then they'd have to go the rest of the way on foot.

'I'll see you when you get back,' Stuart said, hugging his son and giving Chas a kiss on the cheek. 'Look after her, son.' He gave Mish a knowing look, then laughed and walked away.

It was not a comfortable journey, riding on the back of the bike. Mish clearly enjoyed the freedom and speed of the quad-bike. She had to hold him tightly around the waist and she was sure he was showing off. When the fuel ran out they pushed the bike into the undergrowth and looked for landmarks to remember where they had hidden it. Mish had a fuel can in his rucksack. Chas had a few supplies in hers, and her knife tucked into a sheath at her side.

The walk to Durham was still going to take them another day or so and they'd have to sleep rough tonight. Without the security of others around them, Chas was wary of what Mish might try on. As they walked, he talked a lot. Chas answered and made conversation, but her mind kept flitting back to her journey to the Priory with Si last year. She suddenly missed him in such a way that it made her feel sick. She didn't want to think about him and tried to push his face from her mind. It would only throw her off course. He hadn't wanted her to look for Resolution and she mustn't let memories of him cloud her judgement and stop her now. She was being sentimental, and she didn't like it.

'Grace! Look out!' Mish cried, diving into some bushes at the side of the road. Chas came to her senses and dived after him.

'What?'

He caught her around the waist and laughed. 'You weren't listening to me. You've been in a daze for the last half hour. Thought I'd get your attention. I'm bored of talking to myself.'

She tutted and prised his arm off her. She half laughed, attempting to hide her annoyance. 'Idiot! I thought something was really up!' She got to her feet and began walking again. Her annoyance was as much with herself as with Mish for not being alert.

'Were you thinking about your brother?' Mish asked.

'Yes.' It was only half a lie.

'We'll find him. The law-keepers'll have a record of him, even if he's been moved on or released,' Mish said.

'We can't just walk into a law-keeper's office and ask to see him, can we? Then, "Oh do you mind if we take him out for a walk?" "No, madam, that's fine. Just bring him back for tea!"'

Mish laughed again. 'Dinna fash! I've got contacts wi' people I trade with. I can ask if they know anything about him. Some of them have spent time in prison.'

Chas was certain that if Resolution was still in prison, he would not be in Durham. He was a political prisoner, not ordinary riff-raff. Would they have sent him to the Bastille? Or the Priory? Another trip to either of those places filled her with dread. Suddenly, she hoped he was still alive and the Rulers hadn't executed him. Anger stirred in her belly. They'd better not have robbed her of her act of closure.

It was getting dark. 'We should find somewhere to get our heads down,' Mish said. They kept walking until they came to a hamlet of deserted houses. 'This should do us.'

Chas was cautious. 'Just be careful in case we're not the only vagrants on the road tonight.'

The doors on most of the houses were not secured. The buildings looked like they'd been empty for a while and ached with loneliness. They pushed their way into one of the houses, finding a couple of chairs and a few bits of kitchen equipment lying around. Chas tried a tap and was surprised to find running water, which was a bit brown, but it would do. There was no electricity or gas, but they could boil it in their water can if they built a fire in the grate. They checked the whole house for other 'guests' but, apart from the scuffling noises of a few non-human guests, it was empty. Upstairs, there were two empty bedrooms, but a night on the ground in sleeping bags didn't bother them. They ate food from their packs and made tea with the water, huddling in front of the welcome warmth of the fire. They would sleep downstairs beside it tonight.

'Will we get there tomorrow?' Chas asked.

'Aye, I think so,' Mish said, tucking into the last of the sandwiches. 'Tell me more about your brother. You haven't told me much about him. What happened?'

Chas shifted uncomfortably. She should have been better prepared for the questions. 'There's not much else to tell really.'

'Were you there when he got arrested?'

Chas thought back to how they had thrown Resolution out of the car at the checkpoint, in order to get into the city. 'No,' she said.

'Why do you want to see him now?' Mish persisted.

'I need to know if he's alive,' she said.

'You were close then?'

Chas was beginning to feel irritated by all the questions. 'You could say that. He's the only link I have left to my family. But I don't want to talk anymore. I think we should get some sleep and get an early start in the morning.'

'Aye. Right,' Mish said, knowing that if she didn't want to talk he couldn't make her and she would just end up getting annoyed with him.

She picked up her chair. 'We should put these chairs against the door in case anyone tries to get in. It'll at least give us some warning.'

'You're very cautious,' Mish said, standing up.

Chas pulled the chairs across the door. 'Haven't you ever

had problems on the road before? Trust me. It's best to assess the risks and take precautions.'

'Yes, Commander,' Mish laughed, making a mock salute.

Chas looked sharply at him. Commander was her brother's title.

'Did I say the wrong thing?' Mish asked, not understanding her reaction.

'No. It's nothing. Forget it,' she said. 'Let's just get to sleep.'

They got into the sleeping bags. Chas was wary that Mish might try something but before she was even settled down, he was snoring. She was relieved.

*

It was well after nightfall, the next day, when they arrived on the outskirts of the city. Being back here evoked lots of memories: Meeting Nick for the first time; being at Peter Marsden's house, not far from here; Si fighting for his life on Nick's operating table.

She and Mish found a secluded spot a little way up river from the city. They made a fire and huddled around it. Mish moved in close beside her as they toasted bits of bread and warmed some cold meat they'd managed to buy from a peddler on the road. She was glad of Mish's company and didn't push him away. He talked about hunting trips and some of the things he and his brothers used to get up to. Chas was half listening.

'Will you take me to some of your contacts first thing?' she asked.

'Aye. They might not know anything straight away of course, but they'll be able to get word to us.'

'Tomorrow?'

'Maybe not. But we could arrange for a message to reach you.'

Irritation stirred in Chas, but she pushed it down.

'Anyway, we should get some sleep,' he said.

They laid side by side in their sleeping bags, next to the dying fire and she turned her back to him. 'Goodnight.'

Mish moved in behind her and began to stroke her hair. 'Don't I get a goodnight kiss then? I was oot like a light last night.'

Her heart began to beat faster. She hoped he wasn't going to try anything on, but she had suspected that he might.

'My turn to be tired tonight,' she said, faking a yawn.

'Too tired for one wee kiss,' he said, turning her towards him. Before she could say anymore his lips were pressing hard onto hers. He was hard to resist when he kissed her like this.

After a few moments, she pulled her head away. 'We really should get some sleep. I want to be alert for tomorrow.'

'Och, You never sleep much,' he persisted.

'Yeah well, maybe I should,' she said, trying to smile. 'Anyway, it's cold and I'm not budging from this sleeping bag.'

'I could climb in with you,' Mish said, suggestively.

'No! You couldn't. Goodnight Mish.' She rolled over and did her best to ignore him. He moulded his body around hers and kissed her neck a few more times, but she didn't respond. Finally, he gave up, seeing that he wasn't going to entice her to let go of the sleeping bag pulled tightly around her body. With a 'hrumph' he turned over and went to sleep.

*

When the check point opened, soon after dawn, they were waiting to get inside the city. Chas's fake ID and disguise had not drawn any attention. Mish knew where he was headed. He had contacts in the markets. Some of these had dealings with the black market and knew people who might have heard of Resolution or be able to find something out.

The market was already full of traders setting out their wares. Some people were already shopping. The stalls were mainly fruit and veg, grown by local people. Meat production and fishing were controlled by the Rulers and products had to be bought in their official supermarkets. There were some stalls selling crafts and household goods too; a few selling bric-a-brac and second-hand goods.

Mish bought some produce and slung it in his backpack. He also bought a fleece jacket and waterproof trousers from a second hand trader. He had brought some clothes that the children from the commune had grown out of, to exchange with the traders. He asked for a woman named Purity.

'She trades on the black market,' Mish explained to Chas. 'She might be a good place to start.'

Purity was a thick set woman with jet black short hair. She looked tough. She was dressed in worn-out clothes that didn't look or smell like they'd been washed for a while.

Although she knew Mish, she eyed Chas warily. Chas stared coldly back at her.

Mish greeted her. 'Hi Pu. How's things?'

'Okay,' she said, looking from one to the other.

'Can we go somewhere to talk?' Mish asked.

She looked at her phone. 'I've got half an hour.' She shouted to an older man. 'Breakfast time, Bernie! Watch me stall. I'll bring you a tea and a bacon buttie.'

They headed to a shabby cafe in one of the back streets. She was obviously friendly with the owner and nodded and smiled at the few other people hunched over cups of tea and big breakfasts. Loud music made it difficult to hear much, so they huddled over a table with their cups of tea and fried breakfasts.

'What you after this time?' she asked Mish, whilst wolfing down a sausage and three rashers of bacon. This was clearly a routine with them both. 'And who's she?' She nodded at Chas.

'This is Grace,' Mish said. 'I'm not after anything black today. We're after some info.'

Egg dripped down Pu's chin and she wiped it with a paper serviette. 'Yeah? About what?'

'Grace's brother. Taken by the law-keepers last year. When would it have been, Grace?'

'December,' Chas said.

'What'd he do?' Pu asked.

'He...' Chas struggled for how she should word this. 'He was on the run at the time he got arrested. I haven't seen him since. His name's Resolution.' Chas knew she'd have to give more away at this point, in order to trace him. 'He was injured when they took him. Badly.'

Pu shrugged and slurped her tea. 'Don't remember anything being in the news.'

Chas fidgeted. 'I think it would've been hushed up. Would've been embarrassing to the Rulers, if it'd got out.'

'I'd need to know more about him. What does he look like How old is he?'

'He wears glasses and he's tall (about six foot two), skinny, blue eyes, like mine and light brown hair. He's in his late twenties.'

'Can you ask around for us, Pu?' Mish said. 'We can stay for a day or two, but then we'll have to get back.'

'Okay. I'll ask around,' she said. 'Meet me here tomorrow. Same time.'

'Thanks,' Mish said.

Chas didn't intend going back to the commune if they found something out about Resolution. She would give Mish the slip and carry out her vendetta. Despite having grown fond of many people in the new commune, including Mish, she was wary of him and didn't want to end up being his possession. She didn't want to wait around another day without being able to do anything productive to find her brother.

'Can we come with you?' she asked.

Pu shook her head. 'I don't know her,' she said, leaning further towards Mish. 'She could be a spy.'

'Ach! You can trust her,' he said, smiling at Pu's cloak-and-dagger attitude. 'She's been living with us for a while now. We're together.' He pulled Chas towards him.

Pu frowned.

Chas pushed him off. 'He'd like us to be. But he's right, you can trust me.' Not strictly true, but she desperately wanted to find Resolution as soon as possible. Waiting around, doing nothing would be torture.

Pu mopped up the last of the egg and bean juices on her plate and drained her tea. 'Come on then. You can work on the stall, then I'll be free to go and find some people who might know stuff.'

'Thanks,' Chas said. It wasn't really what she had meant, but at least working on the stall would keep her occupied.

It was hard work on the stall. Pu had left them with instructions on what to do and under the supervisory eye of one of her neighbouring traders. By the early evening, the traders were packing up. Mish and Chas had been busy all day. Chas was beside herself with impatience. Mish had to keep convincing her that Pu was their best hope, at the moment. Several times he had to stop her walking away and going off on her own to try to find her brother.

Pu came back as they were packing up.

'Well? What did you find out?' Chas demanded.

Pu bristled and looked at Mish. She didn't like being spoken to like that.

He intervened, giving Chas a hard stare. 'Excuse her manner, Pu. She's anxious. What she's trying to say is that she's really grateful for your help and wonders what you've found out.'

Pu sniffed and stuck her hands in her pockets. 'Nothing significant.'

'But you've been gone hours. You must have found out something,' Chas said, trying to control her temper.

'Just because I've been asking around for hours doesn't mean I've found anything significant,' Pu growled.

'But someone must know something!'

'Why?' Pu said, squaring up to Chas. 'Why must they? I found people who'd heard of your brother, but he disappeared at around the time you talked about. No one knows what happened to him since. He'd been chasing those outlaws, Silence Hunter and that girl he was with. You didn't tell me he worked for the Rulers.'

Chas felt her cheeks begin to flush as Pu referred to her and Si. But there was no sign of recognition in her face. Chas's heartbeat slowed as she reminded herself that she looked different now, even though her natural hair colour had been gradually returning as the hair dye faded. She was safe.

Mish frowned. 'You told me he was out of favour with the Rulers.'

'He was, at the end. But yes, he did work for them. I told you he'd failed. He failed to catch Silence Hunter.' Speaking Si's full name made him sound like a stranger to her.

'We all followed the story of him and that girl, but the Rulers made it sound like they'd dealt with them. No one ever knew who the girl was or what they'd done either.' Mish was staring at Chas now. She looked away; began rearranging something on the stall.

'You didn't tell us the truth,' Pu said, grabbing hold of Chas.

Chas pushed her away. 'Get your hands off me!'

Pu came for Chas but Mish stepped in and eased Pu away from her. 'You should have told me everything, Grace.'

'I didn't think you'd help if you knew he'd worked for the Rulers.'

Chas began to pace the ground around the stall, feeling as if Mish could see right through her false identity. 'Law-keepers would know what happened to him. I need to question them.'

Pu laughed. 'You're crazy. He's probably dead by now anyway, if he failed the Rulers.'

'He's not!' Chas shouted.

'Calm doon! People are looking,' Mish said. 'We need to rethink this.'

Pu turned to Mish. 'You need to take her back to your commune and keep her out of trouble. Crazy cow! Next thing you know, she'll be the one getting arrested.'

Chas turned on Pu and shouted in her face. 'I'm not going back 'til I find something out about what's happened to him.'

Pu grabbed Chas by the scruff of her jacket and pulled her close. Her teeth were bared, like an angry dog. Keeping her voice low, she snarled in Chas's face. 'Well, I can't help you anymore. You're an ungrateful, spoilt little bitch.' She let go of her and turned to Mish. 'Keep her away from us. We don't want 'trouble' snooping around.'

Chas wanted to punch her but stormed away instead. Mish thanked Pu and apologised as best he could. He would have to come back and patch things up with her. The market trade was important to him and the commune.

'Grace! Wait!' he shouted, running to catch up with her. She marched on, not stopping when he caught up. 'Grace!' She ignored him. He dropped back, exasperated, but followed her, figuring she needed some time to calm down.

She walked on through the streets of Durham, her mind flicking over ways that she could continue to search for Resolution without drawing attention to herself. The last thing she needed was to be recognised or suspected of being the girl who was with Silence Hunter. And what to do about Mish? Part of her wanted to ditch him, but part of her thought he could still be useful. She knew he was following her because she had seen his reflection several times in shop windows. Turning up a steep cobbled street, she found herself staring at the great cathedral, more by accident, than design. There was an area of well-tended grass at the top of the hill, surrounded by old buildings, with the remains of a castle opposite the imposing cathedral building. The towers were illuminated against the darkening sky, and she remembered Si telling her he'd often come here as a child. She felt a stab of jealousy for a childhood she imagined to be perfect. But then, Si too had been torn from his parents when he was still a child. She wished he didn't keep coming into her thoughts. The doors of the cathedral were open, so she went inside.

She had never been in such a building before. The vaulted nave towered above her, balanced it seemed, on its elaborately carved pillars. She couldn't help but feel awed by the magnificence of the architecture. Religion was not something that Chas thought much about, but she knew that Kate had a faith that drove her to do what she did, and that Si often grappled with his beliefs. Since the Rulers came to power and outlawed religious gatherings, places like this had become museums rather than places of worship,

There were a few visitors wandering around quietly. Chas sat on a chair in the middle of the nave and allowed the stillness to wash over her. She was tired. Tired of plotting, tired of running. She couldn't think anymore. She looked up and sighed. Where would her help come from? Something calm settled in her mind. Was this what prayer was like?

'Can I sit here?'

Mish was smiling down at her, with his stupid, charming boyish grin. She half-smiled back and nodded. He didn't say anything; just sat looking up at the magnificent architecture. After a while, he put his hand over hers. 'Pretty impressive place.'

She nodded.

He squeezed her hand. 'Come on. We need to go and find somewhere to stay tonight. I've got a couple o' options.'

Chas withdrew her hand from his as they stood and walked out together. 'I'm going to keep looking for him.'

'Aye, I ken,' Mish replied. 'But we canna stay longer than tomorrow.'

She shook her head. 'You go back. I'm staying. I came to find out what's happened to him and that's what I'm going to do. I can't go back. Not 'til I know.'

'You might never find out, Grace. It might be impossible, and you'll just have to accept that. It's not safe in the city for the likes of us.'

She laughed. 'They say the city is the safest place. Out in the commune we're supposed to be in danger. But I know what you mean though. I'll be okay.'

Mish stopped walking and held her by both arms. 'I'm not leaving you here.'

She tried to prise his hands off her arms, but he was stronger. 'You don't own me. If I want to stay, I will.'

He sighed. 'I'll help you tomorrow, but we are leaving the next day.'

She remembered his gentle hand in the cathedral. And now his fingers were digging painfully into her arms. 'I've told you, I'm staying 'til I find my brother. You can do what you like.' She gave him a hard stare. 'Now, take your hands off me.'

Mish hesitated, then relaxed his grip. 'I care about you, Grace. I just wonder if you're doing the right thing. You've made a home with us now. If we don't find anything tomorrow, mebbe you need to let him go.'

Chas laughed, ironically. 'That's the one thing I'll never do!'

*

The next day they tried every pub in Durham, asking if anyone had seen or heard anything about Resolution. Some remembered rumours of the Commander being arrested last year, but no one knew what had happened to him. No one recalled seeing him since. Chas wanted Mish to go to the law-keepers to see what he could find out, but he wasn't keen to expose himself to the Law. He hated even crossing the check points to come into the city, always wary that any official channels could turn on him, as a non-city dweller.

Chas decided to go herself. She figured that her disguise

and false ID would be enough to protect her from discovery. Inventing a story about being a law student, doing some research for a thesis about recent political unrest, she approached the desk. The law-keeper on duty eyed her suspiciously when she spun the story and told her that the whereabouts of prisoners was classified. When she persisted, he became agitated and began to ask her lots of questions about herself. It was time to back off. She left, in a rage, before things got difficult.

Mish was waiting for her outside. By her manner, he could see that she had not been successful, but this didn't surprise him. They walked back to their lodging. 'I didna think that would work.'

'Thanks for the vote of confidence,' she said, sarcastically.

Mish ignored her, trying to be patient. 'Let's go home in the morning and rethink things. We're not gonna find anything more here, so you need a new plan and you're in no fit state to think properly right now. You'll come up with something and I'll help you again.'

Chas said nothing.

All evening she was sullen. She tried to think of what to do next, but Mish was right, she couldn't think straight. Anger clouded her judgement. Maybe she would have to come up with a different idea. But one thing was certain, nothing was going to stop her finding out at least what had happened to Resolution. She had to know if he was dead or alive.

Mish tried to distract her, but he sensed her annoyance and backed off. Instead, he thought about how he would persuade her to go back with him in the morning. He wasn't leaving her behind. Grace was different to other girls he'd had. Most of them succumbed to him quickly for one reason or another, but not her. He sensed that she liked him, but she kept holding back. It was frustrating and, at the same time, attractive. He liked her feistiness and enjoyed the challenge of winning her over. They could make a great leadership team together when it was his turn to oversee the village. He would have to play it carefully. He wasn't letting her go. So, it surprised him, the next morning, when she agreed to come back to the commune, without an argument.

5

The NMBs were doing their job. The recovery time of patients injected with them was remarkably fast and there was a joyous atmosphere in the camp. Si, Kate and Nick worked fast. Kate and Nick supervised most of the medical procedures at first, but soon the they didn't need to.

Kate and Si spent time with the recovering victims, explaining the need to stay in the camp for a while and telling them that the Rulers were using the plague as a population reducer. A lot of people were shocked at this revelation. No one had been happy since the Rulers had taken power, but it was hard for people to believe that they were actively killing innocent people, just because there were too many of them. Some recovered patients were keen to help Kate and Si in a bid to revolt against this injustice. Others just wanted to go back to their homes and find any of their family or friends that were left. Some were too scared to join any kind of revolution, and just wanted to get away from the camp as soon as possible. It was impossible to convince everyone to stay in the camp, and they weren't going to force people. As people left, questions would be asked, and information would get out.

It was time for Kate and Si to move on. Nick would take

them to other camps, so they could set up the process of injecting the NMBs there too.

Doctor Sharma thanked them, 'You've brought new life and optimism here.'

'I hope we haven't put you all in danger. It will probably be the first place they come looking for answers once rumours of the cure begin,' Kate said.

'We have lookouts. We'll be ready to leave if we have to. You've gathered quite a following amongst some of the patients here. They liked meeting Si. Many of them were rooting for you when your face was splatted across the news. Meeting you has done them almost as much good as the cure.'

Si and Kate laughed, but doctor Sharma did not. 'Seriously, you could use that to your advantage if you're trying to recruit people to a revolutionary move.'

'Sharma has a point,' said Nick. 'But, we must go. They'll be expecting us at the next camp, and it's a few hours' drive south of here.'

They left the camp, walking at first, then in Nick's car until the magnetised road ran out. When they met another narrow country road and it was time to go on foot again the terrain was moorland and it reminded Si of the surroundings of the Bastille. He shuddered at the thought of that place.

It was a good fifty-minute walk to the new camp, carrying supplies. Si was reminded how dedicated the volunteers were who came to care for the dying. It made him feel sick that the Rulers were prepared to transport people out here and just leave them to die, behind the official propaganda that the government was working to cure the plague. Everyone knew that no one came back from the camps. All the more reason not to become a volunteer. The volunteers and doctors must be open to the idea of revolution. There had to be a way to get enough people together to stand up against the Rulers. All these thoughts swam around Si's head making him think of Chas again. Where was she? The desire to find her grew stronger every day since they had returned to England. But the chances of finding her were remote. She was too good at keeping a low profile; far better than he ever had been. He laughed, remembering the times when she had been annoyed with him for getting them noticed.

The next camp looked very similar to the first one. They were greeted by Doctor Keel and a couple of her colleagues. 'It's great to have you on board, Mrs. Hunter. Come to my office for some refreshment and I'll update you on our situation here.' As they walked she asked them lots of questions about the other camps.

In her office, they were glad of the rest and something to eat and drink. 'We're keen to start the NMB programme,' Said Doctor Keel. 'This technology should be in use for all sorts of things. I believe the Rulers already have it and use it at their private hospital in The Citadel. They just didn't want it in the hands of people who might use it for the common good. And certainly not to halt their source of control and fear.'

'They definitely didn't want Mum and Dad to have it,' Si said.

The doctor looked at Kate. 'No. I know what happened

to you, Mrs. Hunter, and I'm sorry for all you've been through.'

'What I don't understand,' said Si, 'Is why they are actively isolating the plague victims. Surely they want more people to catch it.'

'They only want the right people to get it,' Nick said. 'Their patrols pick people up off the streets. They don't want people to think they're doing nothing to try and stop it spreading. They have to be seen to be doing the right thing.'

Si rolled his eyes. 'That's what it's all about, isn't it? Seen to be doing the right thing, but underneath, doing the opposite.'

Kate nodded. 'That about sums it up. How many patients do you have here?'

'I think it's around the four hundred mark. It changes a little all the time, as you would imagine. The government bring us new victims once a week. People die every day.'

'When can we get started?' Kate asked.

'I'll take you to the quarantined areas later and we can get things set up. You can start as soon as you're ready.'

It wasn't long before Nick, Kate and Si were ready to tour the camp. There were the quarantine suits to get into again, but this time Si was used to them. This camp was just as bleak as the previous one. People in tents at varying stages of dying. The volunteers tended them as best they could, but it was still a harrowing sight. At the previous camp, they had got used to seeing people recovering. Only those in the final stages of the plague had been lost. The lack of hope here was oppressive.

Over the next few weeks Nick, Kate and Si worked with the medical staff and volunteers. Signs of recovery became apparent within days of beginning the programme. Hope began to rise. Si and Kate talked to those recovering about the prospect of standing against the Rulers and met with the same responses as before.

When the time was right, Nick took them to the next camp only an hour from this one. Doctor Karvel greeted them. 'Great to meet you all. We've been eagerly awaiting your coming. I'll introduce you to the staff and volunteers and take you round the camp.'

Si was used to the sights by now, but they never failed to make an impression on him. The thing that got him through the horror of this initial stage in each camp, was the knowledge that soon they were about to change everything for these people.

One evening they were eating in the mess tent. It had been a long but rewarding day. Si had been talking to a lot of patients, including a boy about the same age as Ben who was recovering in the tent named by the patients; 'Miracle Tent.' The boy had been keen to join anyone in bringing down the regime. His mother and father had recently died from plague, and his little sister was currently recovering alongside him here.

'When are we going to confront the Rulers about all this, Mum?' Si asked. 'And how?'

Nick put down his fork. 'You're starting to get a good following, Kate, and you probably need to do something soon, so you don't lose the impact you've made on people so far.'

'I know. There's just so much to think about. I don't really know where to start, to be honest.'

'We could start with protests,' Nick suggested.

'I don't think that will have any effect on the Rulers,' Si said. 'We know they're vicious. They'd crush it easily. We need to think more... subversively.'

'Keep thinking, both of you,' Kate replied. I agree, we need to begin something soon. But, right now I need some rest, then back to the NMBs tomorrow. I think we can move on again from here soon. Everyone seems to know what they're doing. I just want to see some more results. Talk to more of the survivors.'

Si got up to go to the toilet block before going to bed. As he left the mess tent he saw a man darting away. Had he been spying on them? Listening in to their conversation? All his senses went on alert, like they used to when he and Chas had been in trouble. He moved quickly to the corner of the tent to see where the man had gone, but he was too late. It was too dark and he had disappeared into the night. Si wondered if he was making too much of it. They had just been talking about how to get at the Rulers. Maybe this had made him edgy. But if this guy was an informer... Si decided he would talk to his mum and Nick in the morning. He headed to the toilets then back to his tent. Before he went to sleep, he reached into his pack, curling his fingers round the curves of the sheath. He always carried it, just in case. If Chas had taught him one thing it was to be ready to defend himself; to always be on his guard. He put the knife under his blanket, rested his hand on it, and went to sleep.

The next morning was bright and he felt renewed at the thought of continuing the NMB programme. His sense of foreboding had disappeared with the darkness. There was probably some innocent explanation for the man from last night. His mum and Nick were sat outside the mess tent with empty breakfast plates.

'Hurry up, sleepy head!' Kate said, tousling his hair, like she used to when he was a little boy.

He grinned at her. 'It's only 8.30, Mum.'

'Nick and I have been up for hours. We've done three rounds already.' She said all this with a smile.

'No we haven't.' Nick said. 'We've only been up for an hour. Don't let her make you feel guilty. It's actually been nice to sit here with a couple of coffees and enjoy the warm sun.'

As Si ate, Doctor Karvel came in. 'All ready when you are,' she said. 'The team will meet you in the hut to get suited up.'

'Great,' Kate replied. 'Just waiting for this slow-coach.'

'Sorry,' Si said, through a mouthful of museli.

The doctor smiled and turned to go. 'No rush.'

As Si, Nick and Kate got up, Si said, 'Have either of you noticed anyone suspicious hanging around us here?'

Both shook their heads. Nick grinned at Kate. 'Your mum has her admirers of course. Why?'

Si told them about last night.

Kate replied. 'Hmmm. I don't think anyone from the government hangs around here after they drop off plague victims. There's the guards of course. One of them could have been off duty. Let's just be careful.'

They suited up with the other medics and entered the quarantined area. It was another long, yet positive day of injecting the NMBs into patients and talking to the recovering ones. Si was more aware today of the people around him. Those in the quarantine area were all suited up and he kept wondering if the man from last night was one of them. He tried to be aware of who was working alongside him, but it wasn't always easy to tell with the suits on. He couldn't conclude that any person was hanging around them more than anyone else.

In the evening, Kate had organised a meeting of all the staff and volunteers to talk about the plague being a government weapon of mass destruction. The meeting was held in the mess tent after supper. Kate did most of the talking, with some input from Nick. Some people were shocked and found it too hard to believe. However, most of the people were not surprised. When Kate and Nick were confident of people's reactions, they introduced Si. It was part of their plan to remind people who he was and how he had been hunted the previous year by the government. Kate told them how Chas and Si had rescued her from the Priory and how Si had been carrying the prototype NMB, which was why he was being hunted. Si spoke for a short time about the idea of gathering a force to stand up to the Rulers. By this point, most people were fired up in anger and keen to play a part.

Afterwards, people wanted to talk to the three of them, especially Si. They wanted to know more of his story. How had he escaped? What had happened to the girl and boy he had been on the run with? He was a real live hero to them.

He didn't like the limelight much, but he answered their questions, shook hands with them and played his part. He knew that if this inspired people to get involved when the time was right, that it could make all the difference.

When the tent emptied, the three of them had a debrief. 'I think it's going well,' Nick said. 'People are getting angry and that's good. They also see your courage and determination. It inspires them.'

'Thanks,' Kate said. 'I just hope we can do the right thing to make things better for everyone in the long run.'

'We have to strike at the heart of the Rulers,' said Si.

'All this is going to hit them soon,' said Nick. 'We know some of the good news of the cure must have leaked out by now. It's just a matter of time before they realise who's behind this and come looking for us.'

Kate rubbed her hand over her eyes, revealing just how tired she was. 'We need a safe place. Somewhere to escape to when the time comes.'

'I've already thought of that,' Nick said. 'I've been in touch with Peter. He's set something up for us. He has a cottage in the middle of nowhere. There's supplies for weeks if we need it.'

Si looked at Nick. 'Wow. You never said anything.'

'I've only just sorted it.'

Kate touched his arm. 'Thanks Nick. You're a good friend.'

Nick blushed. 'It's all for the cause.'

Si felt embarrassed, all of a sudden, seeing the way Nick looked at his mum. 'Well, I'm done in. I'm off to bed. See you in the morning.'

'Okay son. One more day here then we'll move on.' She squeezed his arm and he gave her a peck on the cheek. 'Goodnight.'

'Night.'

Si headed to the toilets. He had noticed before, the way Nick sometimes looked at his Mum. It looked like more than admiration for her as a scientist. He liked Nick a lot, but he wished his dad were here. He should still be here. He would have been amazing with all the patients and he would have known what they should do to bring down the Rulers. Si felt himself welling up and took control of his thoughts. It was up to him to be the one now who made the plans.

Suddenly, a hand was over his mouth and someone grabbed him from behind, pushing him into the woods beyond the toilet block. Si's heart raced. He struggled but the assailant was strong. His knife was in his pocket, but he couldn't reach it.

'We need to talk,' the man whispered in Si's ear. He pushed Si to the ground and Si reached in his pocket for the knife.

'You don't need that, Si. I'm not going to hurt you. We just need to talk.'

Si looked up. The man towering over him was silhouetted in the light from the floodlights near the toilet block, making it hard to see who he was, but he recognised the voice. 'Temp?'

'Yep.'

'Why the drama? Couldn't you just have come up and talked to me like everyone else has over the last couple of days?'

'It's not that simple. I don't want anyone to know who I am. I'm on the wanted list too for helping you and Chas last time. I try to keep a low profile.'

'You must feel safe here? I mean, everyone knows who I am.'

'Yes. I heard your rousing speeches just now. Your mother certainly knows how to rally people and you didn't do too badly yourself. Don't you think it's foolish though, to be proclaiming yourself a hero?'

Si became angry. 'That's not what it's about. I'm no hero. Mum thought it would help the cause.'

'A fight against the Rulers?'

'Yes.'

Temp laughed bitterly. 'You've no idea.'

'Si stood up. 'Yes, I have, actually. We both know what it's like in the Bastille. I know they're ruthless and I know what they're trying to do here. We have a way to get back at them through the cure.'

'The cure is amazing. Don't get me wrong. I've been working in plague camps for the last six months. I know the horror of it. But the Rulers are more dangerous than you have any idea about.'

'And you know this, how?'

'I just know,' said Temp. 'I just wanted to warn you to think this through carefully. Are you up to this? You and your mother. It's hardly an army, is it?'

'It's a start. People are coming on board. So, if you've got nothing helpful to say, I'm going to bed.'

'Don't tell your mother about me. I'll move on in the

morning.' Temp turned to go. 'I don't want to see you get into more trouble, Si.'

'Too late for that!' As Temp began to walk away, Si said, 'You could help us. If you know so much, you could help us be the force we need to be to end their reign.'

'I've tried it before. That's how I ended up in the Bastille.'

'Try again. We could use your help.'

Temp kept walking. Si followed him. 'Come and meet mum and Nick. If you know something that would help, then why wouldn't you tell us? You're not a coward. I know that.'

Temp stopped. 'I'm not. I'm just not sure I can fight them anymore.'

'You can. We have to. So many lives depend on us. Freedom and hope depend on someone doing something.'

Temp laughed. 'That's why I like you. Optimistic. Not like Chas. Always said she had a surly streak. Where is she, anyway? I haven't seen her here.'

'She's gone,' Si said.

'Where? Dead? Abroad?'

'She helped me rescue my mum and we left the country to develop the cure. But she wanted to come back early. She's after Resolution. She thinks he's still alive somewhere and she wants revenge.'

'Doesn't surprise me. Thought she might have chosen you over her brother, though.'

Si shrugged. 'No chance. Will you come and talk to Mum? Just talk.'

Temp hesitated. Then sighed. 'Okay. I'll come.'

6

The HTV flickered in the darkness. People and scenes danced silently in the corner of the room, like ghosts flitting in and out of the world. The shabby curtains were drawn against the daylight, as always. There was a bed against the wall, neatly made with clean linen. Against another wall were the few cupboards, a sink and microwave that constituted a kitchen. This bedsit was the cleanest one in the building. Its occupant sat at the table, scrolling through news articles on his wearable device – Smart contact lenses. He was dictating notes to his Virtual Assistant. The Smart contact lenses could project his internet content into the air, as holo-images. He could use certain blink patterns, as well as voice commands, to bring things in and out of his vision. This was his daily preoccupation. He had acquired the wearable through his connections in the black market. Most people only had the use of basic wearable Smart phones, which had recently become more accessible.

He kept himself to himself, avoiding the other residents of his building as if they had plague. He was convinced that some of them did have it. Some tried to find out what this reclusive, enigmatic stranger did all day. They would come knocking at his door or try to talk to him on the stairs, but he never entertained them with one word. Once a large muscular man, with tattoos all over his body, had blocked his path and tried to make him talk. But no one here could do that. He was accustomed to dealing with more elaborate obstacles than this. Most of the residents of the tenement were too stoned to notice him and he was able to live in relative isolation.

Resolution's self-imposed task was to keep abreast of government activity and figure out a way to get himself back in favour with the Rulers. He had always been obsessed with getting to the top, being the best, and here he was at the bottom of the pile, again. He was determined that this was only temporary. After his arrest last year, he had nearly died when he escaped from the ambulance that had been transporting him to the Bastille. Despite the blood transfusion they'd given him, he was still very weak. But, he had made it through and found this place to hide out, deciding that his best bet was to stay in Durham. They wouldn't expect him to, and he was vigilant in case of raids on the tenement block, which happened occasionally.

Money had been hard to come by at first until he had been able to access his emergency account, which he had always kept in another name. There were things he needed to go out for and he was disciplined about taking fresh air for thirty minutes each day. So, he took a walk by the River Wear this morning. He loved the fact that his Smart contact lenses could augment the real world and give him information on what was around him, as he walked. He was reading historical facts about the cathedral, as it loomed above the trees on the other side of the river, when he noticed a boy and girl walking towards him. He stopped suddenly because, despite the girl's fading brown hair colour and short style, he immediately recognised her. Trying not to look conspicuous, he sat down on a bench and fiddled with his shoe. As they passed, she was talking to the boy and he recognised her voice. This was unmistakably Chastity Komchenski. He couldn't quite believe it. After all this time, wondering where she and Silence Hunter were, here she was, walking right past him, on the river path, in Durham. That wasn't Hunter with her, but he would be somewhere nearby, no doubt. How had they kept such a low profile all this time? He knew, from reading on the internet and his few contacts, that the Rulers were still trying to find Silence and Kate Hunter. His mind sparked. He mustn't lose her. He had to find where they were hiding out. If he could bring Silence and Kate in, the Rulers would have to reinstate him and forgive his failures.

Resolution followed at a distance.

Chas had finally persuaded Mish to bring her back to Durham for another attempt to find her brother. Although the waiting had been frustrating, it had given her time to think about what she was going to do. Mish had been very attentive to her since they had returned to the commune. It was clear to everyone that they were together now. Chas didn't like the way he lauded it over the others in the camp sometimes, just because he was the camp leader's son. But, she still thought he might be useful in helping her to locate Resolution. So, here they were together. When the time was right she had decided she would tell him what she really wanted to do to Resolution and she hoped Mish liked her enough to assist her.

They were on their way to meet another of Mish's contacts who was putting them up for the night. This person had been making some enquiries and had told Mish he might have something for them. Chas felt a stirring inside her at the thought that she might finally know where to look for her brother.

As Resolution followed them, his mind began to work overtime about what he could do with his sister and Silence Hunter. The Rulers would be pleased with him if he could turn these two in. Even better if they had Kate Hunter in tow. He would surely get his job back, if not a promotion. Whoever this other boy was, he had just got himself into deep trouble.

They arrived at a large, house, surrounded by high fence with a gated drive. It was in a rich part of the tech-city; the total opposite to the hole he lived in. Resolution decided to wait in the bushes there until they came out. One thing was for sure; he wasn't losing her now. He began to search the internet for any recent references to his sister and Silence or Kate Hunter.

The house belonged to Respect Jones (Pec for short), the leader of the black market. He did very well for himself selling black market goods to people at just enough of an inflated price to make good money. He welcomed Chas and Mish into his house, making them leave their dusty shoes at the door. Even before he offered them a drink he asked if they'd like to 'refresh' themselves and showed them to a bedroom with ensuite shower.

'I think he's saying we stink,' Chas said to Mish when

they were alone.

'He's probably right...' Mish said, already removing his shirt, 'about you, anyway.' He laughed as Chas threw her pack at him. 'I'm showering first. Can't wait to feel clean again. Hate travelling.'

Chas sat on the bed. She hated this kind of environment. She felt much more comfortable in the commune and outdoors. She opened her pack and drank some water, then took out her knife. Turning it in her hands, thoughts of being on the road with Si surfaced. He had been a good travelling companion; Funny and sarcastic, but always patient; always giving her another chance. She pushed the thought away before it had time to get to her. She hadn't thought of him in ages. Over the past months, her mind had been too occupied with finding Resolution and fending off advances from Mish when he got too close for comfort. She looked at the double bed. She would be sleeping on the floor tonight then.

After spending the whole afternoon hiding out near the house, Resolution felt stiff. He had been searching the internet. There had been no sightings of Si or Chas in the last eight months. Were the Rulers just giving up? He doubted it. He found several references to himself, which reinforced that he was also a wanted man. There was one recent report of someone claiming to have been cured of plague, in one of the camp. He knew this could not be possible. There was no cure. Not unless...

Kate and Silence Hunter had reappeared. Where had they been all this time? Was it possible that Kate had somehow perfected the nano-technology to cure the plague? Chastity might hold the answers to these questions and he was going to find out. What's more, he was going to hand them over to the Rulers. For the first time in over a year he felt a surge of contentment.

It was getting dark and he realised, with resignation, that they probably weren't coming out of the house tonight. He settled himself as best he could for the long night of surveillance. The old days, staking out places with Knowles, flashed through his mind. Good times.

Inside the house, Pec treated the newly washed Mish and Chas to a good meal. They ate with enthusiasm, not really listening as Pec told them about all the latest gadgets he had acquired and how much he could get for them. Mish tried to ask the odd relevant question here and there, to be polite.

'Thanks for the meal. You said you had some information about Grace's brother, Resolution. Can you tell us what it is?'

'Yes,' Pec said, with a wry grin. 'It comes at a price of course.'

'Of course,' Mish said, glancing at Chas.

She looked with unguarded dislike at the man who had just fed them. 'What's your price?'

'Three hundred.'

Mish raised his eyebrows. 'You know we're from a commune. We don't have that kind o' cash.'

Pec shrugged. 'Take it or leave it.'

'Depends if it's good information,' Chas said.

Pec grinned again. 'It's worth every penny. I've done deals with your brother. He's quite a character. I'd say you're a lot like him, even from what I've seen so far.'

Chas had not expected this. Someone had actually seen him. He was alive: A free man and here in Durham. It seemed too good to be true. She bristled at being likened to Resolution, but remembered, just in time, that she was supposed to be trying to find him for some kind of family reunion. 'I hope that's a compliment.'

He laughed out loud. 'Maybe.'

'Tell me something about him that will convince me you've met him,' Chas said.

Pec pursed his lips and thought for a moment. 'I won't go for the obvious stuff. Let's see. He drives a hard bargain. He doesn't engage in trivial conversation. And... he's 'one hundred percent' certain of what he wants.'

This was Resolution. His catchphrase. Her catchphrase.

'So, what do you know?' Chas said. 'I'll give you fifty percent of the money if you can tell me something useful and the other fifty percent if it leads me to him.'

Mish looked at her. 'You don't have that kind o' money... do ye?'

'I've got money,' she replied.

'News to me,' Mish said.

'I don't tell you everything.'

'Clearly not,' he said, a hint of anger in his tone.

Pec shrugged. 'I'm a bit of a hundred percent man, like your brother. A hundred percent up front or no information. How do I know you'd come back?'

'I keep my word,' said Chas. 'I'm not one hundred percent like my brother.'

Mish looked suspiciously at her, sensing her bitterness,

and she realised that she shouldn't have said that.

She tried to cover it. 'He can be unreliable. That's partly how I lost touch with him.'

'No money, no information,' Pec said.

Chas gritted her teeth, trying to hold back all the things she would like to say to this idiot right now. 'I'll show you the money and give you a hundred and fifty up front. Mish will bring you the rest when we find my brother. You trust him, don't you?'

Pec laughed out loud again; a big guffawing laugh, that irritated Chas intensely. She didn't like being mocked. 'You are definitely his sister. You drive a hard bargain too. Two hundred up front. Show me the money.'

She went upstairs to get it from her pack.

'Here.' She wafted her plastic in front of his face. Although most people hardly used cash anymore, it was still in use for personal transactions. Pec handled a lot of cash in his line of work. He could see the £300 clearly. She gave him two hundred and the rest to Mish.

'Your brother is living in a tenement block along the river, past Prebends Bridge. It's just inside the city walls. Nice place. Drunks, addicts, prostitutes. He's a bit of a misfit.'

'How do you know this?' asked Chas.

'Does it matter? That's where he is. If I'm wrong, I'll give you a full refund. How's that for generous?' He laughed again. 'I don't know the actual flat, just that the building is down there. You'll have to ask his neighbours. I bet he's friends with them all.' Pec sniggered and drained the whisky he was drinking. 'I'm off to bed. Sleep well.' He winked at Mish.

'G'night. And thanks for your help,' Mish said.

Chas muttered something under her breath, but it wasn't 'thank you.'

They went up to their room. Mish stared to undress. 'You must be excited. Tomorrow you might finally get to see your brother.'

Chas smiled. Oh yes, she felt something, but it wasn't excitement. More the thrill of knowing that finally she was going to take her revenge for all the death and destruction Resolution had caused to people she had dared to care about. 'I'm looking forward to it,' she said.

Mish had climbed under the duvet. 'Aren't you coming to bed?'

'I'm sleeping here,' she said, putting a pillow on the floor and pulling the throw off the bed.

'Come on, Chas. It's the best bed we'll get to sleep in for a long time.' He grinned and patted the space next to him. He'd been trying to persuade her for months to move into his hut with him, but she always refused.

'No thanks. I feel better on the floor. I don't like soft stuff.'

'What is it with you?' Mish said, anger rising in his voice. 'We've been together for ages now. I've made you my girlfriend, which gives you standing in the village. All the girls look up to ye. I've gone out o' my way to help ye. Yet you still push me away.' He softened his tone. 'Come on. Let's celebrate tonight.'

'I'm tired, Mish. I'm sleeping here. Goodnight.' As she turned over she heard Mish throw his head into his pillow with an expletive.

*

As they left the house next morning, Resolution was watching. He followed at a distance and it didn't take him long to figure out that they were heading for the flats beyond Prebends Bridge. How had they found out where he lived? There was only one reason why Chas would be seeking him out: Unfinished business. Whoever lived in that swanky house they'd just come from was dangerous. His mind began working out how he could apprehend them. He had missed the thrill of the chase.

The tenement blocks were a pitiful sight. There were three of them, standing in a semi-circle, like tired old men, leaning in to talk to one another. This was a place where people came who were on the brink of being sent to the workhouse. Anything was better than that in most people's opinions. Surprisingly, each block of flats had a security system.

'What are we gonna do now?' asked Mish.

'We need to be patient, ask around when anyone comes out. See if we can work out which one he lives in.'

Resolution watched them from a distance. He had figured out how he would capture her and deal with the boy.

The residents of the flats were very uncommunicative and very suspicious. No one could or would tell her anything about Resolution. Chas was becoming more and more frustrated. A well-built man, with tattoos and piercings everywhere, came out of the building.

'Hey,' she called, undaunted by his appearance. 'Do you know if a guy lives here who's a bit of a weirdo? He keeps himself to himself.'

The tattooed man walked over. He towered above Chas and Mish. 'Yeah, I know him. He don't talk to no one. Annoying little git.'

'Where does he live? I've got business with him?'

'Flat 9a, up three flights, to the right. Mind how you go. He's not nice.'

'Thanks,' Chas said, as the man held the door open for her and Mish to slip inside.

They stood outside flat 9a. This was it. Finally, she was going to take her revenge. Her knife was almost tingling in her pocket. She turned to Mish. 'I want to see him by myself first.'

'I'm not sure you should see him alone, after what they're saying about him.'

'It's okay. He's my brother. He'll be pleased to see me. And anyway, you know I can look after myself.' She smiled and gave him a kiss on the cheek. 'I'll message you when to come back.'

'Okay. If you're sure. Message me if you need me. I won't go far. You know how I feel about you.' He kissed her on the lips and walked away down the stairs.

Chas took out her knife. She was going to kill Resolution right here, right now and do everyone a favour. She closed her eyes and let all the memories bay for blood inside her, like wild animals: Memories of home, betrayal of their family, the decimation of her village, the killing of Aaron, the torture of Kate and Si. She wanted to shout her rage at the door, but she had to take him by surprise. There was no way he would be expecting this. She knocked.

No answer. She tried again then tried the door. Locked of course. Now she did let out a frustrated growl. She would have to wait, in the hope that he wouldn't be long in coming back. She looked for a hiding place.

Outside, Resolution watched as Mish left the building and walked away. This was good. One less to deal with. He felt for the gun in his pocket. No one was around, and he let himself into the block. He knew she was waiting for him and that she would be armed. However, he reached his flat without seeing any sign of her, so he let himself in and waited.

She saw him go in. It was unmistakably her brother. This was it. The moment she had been waiting for, for a very long time. Best to confront him in his flat where no one could see or interfere. She would knock. He would answer. She imagined he'd be cautious, so she would be ready to force her way in once the door was ajar. There would be a struggle, but she would stab him before he had the chance to react. Surprise was key.

She knocked. Twice. He didn't come. So, she banged loudly on the door hoping this would make him unable to ignore it. Suddenly the door opened wide and she nearly fell in.

'Come in, Chas,' he said, pointing the gun at her. 'And leave the knife out there.'

7

Si took Temp to the mess tent where Kate and Nick were still chatting over coffee. 'Hi again.'

'I thought you were off to bed,' Kate said.

'Yeah, but I met someone I know. This is Temp.'

Kate stood up. 'Oh. Hi. I'm Kate. I've heard a lot about you. You saved my son's life on more than one occasion. I owe you a lot.' She shook his hand vigorously.

'You owe me nothing,' Temp said. 'Your boy is full of surprises.'

'This is Nick,' Si said.

Nick stood and shook hands with Temp. 'I've seen you around. Here and in another camp, I think. You want some coffee?'

Everyone sat down. 'Thanks,' Temp said. 'I was hoping no one noticed me, but I've seen you too. You do a lot of good work, doctor.'

'Everyone does. No one's more important than anyone else. And call me Nick.' He handed Temp a coffee.

'Thanks.' Temp sat down at the table with them. I've been helping out where I can in the plague camps since they started. I laid low for a while after getting Si and myself out of the Bastille. I was amazed when I heard you were here.

I must admit I didn't hold out much hope of them getting into the Priory, never mind getting back out again with you. I wanted to see you for myself.'

'Well here we are,' Kate said, smiling. 'We've got a tough job on our hands and it's much bigger than fighting the plague.'

'I know.'

'Temp would be a good person to have on-side Mum. He knows things about the Rulers that could help us.'

'Do you?' Kate looked at Temp. 'We need all the help we can get. What do you know?'

'It's a long story,' said Temp. 'Too long for tonight.'

'Will you help us?' Si said.

Temp sighed and ran his hands through his hair. 'I don't know...'

'I know this might seem like mission impossible to you right now,' Kate added, 'But you'd be a huge asset. If you know things, you could play a key part in bringing down the Rulers.'

'This is going to be big,' Si said. 'We're not going to lie down and give in.'

Nick joined in. 'We've been alerting members of The Way all over the country. The network is big. Everyone has strong beliefs. These people do not give in easily.'

Temp smiled. 'I know. Last year I met someone I used to know, who's since become a follower. He'd risk everything for what he believes in.'

'That's how we are,' smiled Kate. 'We believe in a God who fights injustice and sides with the downtrodden. This is our cause.'

Temp looked down into his coffee cup. 'I've just lost my nerve a bit.'

'You'll get it back,' Si said. 'Just say you'll help us.'

Temp looked at each of their eager faces in turn and nodded. 'I will.'

Si lay in bed, thinking about his mum's and Nick's passion to do right. It was driven by their strong faith. He pondered what it was that was driving him. Did he share their convictions? He wanted to.

*

Dawn was barely breaking, when Si was shaken violently awake by one of the medical staff.

'Get up! You're leaving.'

'What?'

'You're leaving – *now!* Get up. Grab your things. Be outside the mess in 5 minutes.'

The man ran out of the tent. Si was confused, but obeyed. He met Kate, Nick and a few others, outside the mess tent. 'What's going on?'

Doctor Keel answered. 'Our lookouts tell us that a convoy of military law-keepers are headed this way. You need to leave.'

'What about you?' Si asked.

'We'll be okay. Don't worry. We're tough. The people here are on your side. But the law-keepers mustn't find you.'

'Where's Temp?' Si looked around. 'We must take him, Mum. We need him.'

'I'm here,' said Temp, coming up behind them.

'Thank you, Doctor Keel,' Kate said. 'Keep up the good

work here.'

'We will Kate. The NMBs are hidden already and they'll only lay a finger on them over my dead body.'

Si winced and looked at Temp remembering the commune. He prayed a silent prayer that there would be no dead bodies here because of them.

They set off on foot, away from the main entrance route to the camp. They had called Peter and he was sending a contact who would take them to the safe house.

The man was waiting for them on the road. His car was just about big enough to fit them all in. As they drove, he told them about the raid on Doctor Sharma's camp. Sharma and other staff had been taken away for questioning and the camp had been thoroughly searched. NMBs had been found and destroyed and other government doctors had been left in the place of Doctor Sharma and his staff. Informers among the cured had led them to the camp.

'You need to keep a low profile,' the driver said. 'Your false IDs won't do you much good now. Kate and Silence, your pictures are all over the place again. Don't know if they know about your involvement Doctor Reece.'

'Hopefully Doctor Sharma has managed to keep quiet about Nick,' Kate said, looking anxiously at Nick.

'Back to being devious, then,' Si said. 'It's not so bad being an outlaw.'

'We'll lay low for a while and figure out what to do from here,' Kate said, 'But not for long. The point is to cause a stir and get people on board. They need to know more of what the Rulers have been doing.'

It took a few hours to get to the cottage which was out in

the wilds of Northumberland, near the famous Roman Wall. The driver let them in, handing them an old-fashioned key. It was a small, cosy place. There was a log burner in the living room and a good log supply. The cupboards were well stocked, but there was no electricity in this remote area, so the place had a good supply of candles and torches. There was no running water, but the driver showed them where Peter had stored copious bottles of water, in the outhouse. 'Be careful with the water. Use the bottled stuff for cooking and drinking but there's a stream half a mile away. Use the water carriers and get water from there for washing. Mr Marsden doesn't want to draw attention to this place, so please keep out of sight. No neighbours for miles around. Don't use your phones. Keep them switched off. If you need anything in an emergency, use this phone to call Peter.' He handed them an antiquated Smart phone, from before wearable wrap-arounds became more common-place.

'It only has one number and it's Peter's emergency number. I'll be back in a week to restock the place. If you're gone, that's fine. We don't need to know. Leave the key in the house. I have another.'

They made themselves comfortable. There were two bedrooms upstairs in the cottage and a sofa bed in the living room. There was a small bathroom and kitchen downstairs. After some refreshment, the driver left them.

'Please thank Peter for us,' Kate said. 'He's a lifeline.'

It was strange knowing that Peter was helping them again. Si felt a sense of strength knowing that he was behind them. He was an influential man, but how much he could realistically get involved this time was hard to tell.

The cottage was a haven for the four of them and they spent most of the first twenty-four hours sleeping. Adrenalin had kept them going, now exhaustion caught up with them.

In his dreams, Si was back with Chas on the road. They were laughing and chatting. Then they were being chased. Chas turned to defend them.

'Run Si!'

'No!' he shouted, and tried to run back to help her, but his legs wouldn't move. Then he was running away from her, all the time shouting, 'No! No! I'm coming Chas.'

He woke up in a hot sweat several times. Each time he went back to sleep he hoped she would be there. Even if the dream wasn't good, it was worth it just to see her there so vividly alive in his life again. When he went back to sleep there she was again, waiting for him, smiling at him.

'Where've you been? I needed you?'

This was definitely a dream. She would never say that.

'I'm here.' He reached out for her but as he did, she turned into Resolution. His face leered down at Si on the operating table. His mother's voice came next. 'Si, help me!' He was pinned down, kicking against the restraints, but nothing was happening.

He woke again and sat up suddenly. He didn't fancy going back to sleep after that, so he got up and went to find some water. What was happening to Chas right now? Where was she? Did she ever think about him? Or had her stupid obsession with finding her brother consumed her? But one thing was certain: She was gone and the sooner he stopped thinking and dreaming about her, the better.

'Can't sleep?' Kate came into the kitchen and laid her hand on his back.

'Not really,' Si said. 'Bad dreams.'

His Mum rubbed his back absent-mindedly. 'Not good.'

'No. How about you?'

'I've slept really well. But my mind has decided it needs to be active again. It's already trying to figure out what to do next.'

'Yeah. I can't quite get my head round the four of us bringing down the Rulers.'

'I know. It's daunting. But we've set the wheels in motion now. Several camps have the means to keep on curing people and word is out. We can't stop it now, so we have to press forward. When Nick and Temp have had enough sleep, we'll discuss what to do next.'

Si stared out of the window at the hills. Despite the rain and the dull light of breaking dawn, it was so peaceful. Hard to imagine all the suffering going on, when all looked serene outside. 'Tempted to just stay here forever?'

'Hmmm. Feels good right now, but no. People need us. We can make something happen.'

He turned to face her. 'Yeah. I think so too.'

'Are you ready to be the face of a revolution?'

'Sounds weird, but yeah, if it helps.'

Kate sighed. 'I'm not sure I'm ready to risk my only son like this.'

'You did it before. You put the NMB prototype inside me.'

'We panicked. Looking back, it was extremely risky. Foolish. I'm sorry I did that to you, Si. I nearly lost you.'

Kate's eyes welled with tears.

'Hey. You didn't lose me though. I'm glad you did what you did. I think it's probably the only reason that we're both alive right now. And this time, I chose to take the risks. So, no guilt allowed, okay?'

She smiled at him. 'Come on. Let's go for a walk. I need some air.'

When Nick and Temp got up the four of them sat around the kitchen table, eating eggs and bacon.

'What day is it?' asked Nick. 'It's amazing how so much sleep can mess with your sense of time.'

'It's Tuesday,' said Si.

'Right. Wow! Where did Monday go?'

'We slept it away,' Temp said.

'We needed it,' Kate said.

'This is good,' Temp said, through a mouthful of food.

'It is. We've got a lot to thank Peter for,' said Nick.

'I'd like to meet him,' Temp said.

'I think we might have to,' said Kate. 'I've been thinking, and he could be our best chance of making our cause go viral.'

'I thought he couldn't get too involved,' Si said.

'I think we need him. He has contacts,' Kate said.

'If we could infiltrate The Citadel, get close to Zephyr, we could take him hostage...' Si said.

'I'm not sure we could go that far,' Kate said. 'I was thinking of just getting our faces out there on the internet, on Smart notices boards around the cities, in the news. We could stir people's emotions, telling them the truth, then maybe they'll be willing to protest.'

'People are scared,' Temp said.

'Well, let's make them angry,' Si said. 'Make them really angry about what the Rulers are doing to them. Let's get them to believe they can change things. Then they might get behind us. If you're angry you've got the strength to fight.'

Temp nodded.

'So how do we do that?' Nick asked. 'Remember, we still have to spread the NMBs to more camps and other places where people can be cured.'

'The more people are cured, hopefully the more will come on board,' Kate said.

'I hate to put a damper on your enthusiasm,' said Temp. 'But, Zephyr and his cronies aren't going to listen to you. They'll send troops in to destroy any uprising. You've no idea what's going on here.'

'Do you?' Kate asked. They all looked expectantly at Temp. He stood up and walked to the window. 'Tell us what's going on, Temp.'

Si got up and stood beside him. 'You said it was a long story. We've got time to hear it now.'

Temp stared out of the window, still not speaking.

'Tell us what you know,' Nick said. 'It could be useful.'

Temp spoke quietly. 'When I heard about The Way, I thought it was a way of peace. I didn't want to get involved with more struggles.'

Kate went to stand beside him. 'The Way is not always a path of tranquillity and calm. God teaches us to stand up for the oppressed. His peace remains inside us even as we fight for justice. The Teacher said, 'Do not think I came to bring peace, but a sword.' I think he was talking about times like this.'

Temp shook his head. 'I know you're right Kate. I know. I'm just tired of it all.'

'Well help us to end it for good then,' Si said.

Temp came back to the table and sat down. Nick poured more coffee. 'It's clearly painful for you, but, if you can bear it, please tell us your story.'

Temp picked up his coffee and took a sip. 'Okay, I'll tell you who I am and what I know about the Rulers. There's a lot to take in.'

'There's plenty of coffee,' Nick said, smiling.

'First, I should start by telling you that I WAS one of the Rulers. I'm not proud of who I was. I got involved with politics as a boy. I was obviously born before they came to power.'

'I wondered why you were called Temperance, even though you were born before the time of the Naming,' Si said.

'I'll come to that,' Temp said.

'Just let him tell his story,' Kate said to Si.

Temp shook his head. 'It's okay. If anything I say prompts questions, ask them. I was studying politics at university. The terrorist threat was at a peak. There'd been those attacks on major cities going on for months, then that awful attack just before Christmas in London, on Oxford Street in 2030, where thousands died. People were terrified. They were also disturbed by the rise in drug crime, shootings, rape. Not to mention stuff like binge drinking, drug taking, sexual promiscuity and petty crime. It felt out of control.

There was also a growing fear that the State was unable to look after the increasing population. Too many old, too many homeless, too many immigrants, too many disabled, too many without jobs etc.

So, I got involved with a group called The PDI. They were popular at university.'

'I remember them,' Nick said. 'The Party for Decency and Integrity. People liked what they were saying. I remember their slogan – 'Enough is Enough.' And we were all at that point. The country was metaphorically on its knees.'

Temp took a few gulps of coffee. 'Yes. The Party for Decency and Integrity. It sounded so good. But as I got more involved things changed and I realised that this was just a front. I became friends with one of my lecturers, who was one of the top dogs in the PDI. His name was Josef Steele. He's still there as far as I know, but of course, identities are kept secret from the population. The only one you ever see or hear is Zephyr. I'll get to him in a minute. What PDI really stood for was Power, Domination, Immortality.'

'Immortality?' Kate questioned.

'Yes.'

'But how?'

'Keep listening. I got more and more drawn in. My youthful ideals got twisted and my hunger for power increased. Their plan was to win votes, get into power then pursue their goals of total domination of the country, which included their plans to be very wealthy. And they were working on a way to immortalize themselves.

About a year after I joined I had totally forgotten any decent reasons why I entered politics. I was working hard for the party to win them votes. We all changed our names to fit in with the supposedly moral code of the party. Then they changed the name of the Party in '41 to The True Order and won the election in '43.'

'It was my first time of voting,' Kate said. 'I remember being so excited that I was old enough to vote. I was strongly in favour of The True Order. You're right. They sounded like they could solve all the problems.'

'I voted for them too,' said Nick. 'I remember it being a landslide victory.'

'Then everything changed rapidly,' Kate said.

'Yes, by 2047 the Rulers had finished building their new Capital, The Citadel, away from London, in the North where they felt safer. We were all told to move there and to be honest we were really excited about it. It's a luxurious city, as you'd imagine. It has everything you would ever need and all the latest technology.'

'All the stuff they keep from ordinary people,' Si said.

'Yes. The Fortress, as they call it, was based on the designs of the castle at Bamburgh.'

'We've all seen pictures,' Nick said.

'Yes, they use that image to reinforce their powerful status to everyone,' Temp said. 'It's effectively their parliament building but they keep other top-secret stuff there too.'

'Do you remember the executions for treason and opposition party members 'disappearing'?' Nick said.

'Yes, it didn't take us long to show our true colours. We had gained an incredibly strong position. We had power, and domination was following rapidly. But what about immortality? Let's go back a bit. Josef introduced me to

Zephyr in about '39. He was surly and quiet, about my age and didn't appear to like anyone. But Zephyr is no normal human being.' Temp poured himself the last of the coffee.

'I'll make some more,' Nick offered.

'What do you mean?' Si asked.

'The thing no one knows about Zephyr is that he's a clone. He was made with genetically modified DNA strands, taken from several dictators from the last century. He has no true parents. Josef, or Ambition, as he had now called himself, had been educating him since birth. It was no wonder that he was strange. He had no contact with other children as he was growing up. My job was to befriend him. The Rulers are already cloning themselves so that they can 'live' forever.'

'This is immortality then,' Si said.

'Yes. All the live clones are kept under heavy guard in The Fortress. They used people like me as what they call Shepherds – sort of mentors, to the young clones.'

'Wow! That's a lot to take in.' Nick brought the coffee pot back to the table. 'More coffee anyone?'

'Thanks,' Kate said. 'So, what made you change your mind, then?'

'I got married in the year we won the election. It was a pretty amazing year for me. My wife, Asher, was a beautiful person. I didn't tell her the truth behind the party, because I knew she wouldn't have married me. But she was smart. As I became more embroiled in what was happening it didn't take her long to realise where this was going. She tried to persuade me to leave, but I couldn't. I was addicted to the power and I was scared too. Zephyr was cruel. I was his right-hand man, but I knew that if I crossed him or any of the others I'd be dead.

In 2049 my son was born. Asher wanted to call him Truth, so we did. He was a wonderful baby, so happy and giggly.' Temp paused, and they watched his face for a few moments as he relived memories of his son. No one interrupted the moment and when he was ready, he continued. 'Sorry. Where was I? Yeah, he was perfect. However, we soon discovered that Truth had Downs Syndrome. Asher had refused all the tests, despite strong opposition from her obstetrician. At this time Zephyr had begun pushing for eliminating weakness, including before birth. This included anyone who wasn't what they deemed normal. It was almost compulsory to take the test. Zephyr called me into his office one day for a meeting. All the members of the Cabinet were there, including Ambition. I knew it was serious. Zephyr told me I was required to set an example by giving up my son for 'Compulsory Elimination,' paving the way for this to be rolled out across the country. That was the moment I woke up. I was horrified at the monster in front of me. A monster I had helped to create. The monster we were all hiding behind. I told him I wouldn't allow it. I looked around the room for support. I saw mostly stony faces, but there were some who had bowed their heads, ashamed to look at me. No one stood against the monster. Ambition told me I had no choice.'

Kate had her hand over her mouth. Nick and Si listened in stunned silence.

'A time was arranged for them to come and take Truth away. I left that room in a panic. I had to get Asher and Truth to safety. We packed and ran that night. We got to the river. I had a boat waiting to take us out to sea in the hope that we would make it to Europe. The boat was small, and our chances were slim, but it was all I could do in the short time I had.

They caught us. They fired on the boat. Asher was shot and killed instantly. Her body shielded the baby, but they took Truth and me back to The Citadel. I never saw my son again. I was taken to the Bastille.'

'Oh Temp,' Kate said. 'That's horrendous.' She put her hand over his on the table.

'They tortured me, and Zephyr came to tell me that he would break me for betraying him. He told me my son had been eliminated. I felt empty. They couldn't have broken me anymore than I was already. I had nothing to live for and wished they would just kill me there and then. But they didn't. That was what I wanted, and they knew it, so they weren't going to give it to me. The torture was hellish, so, realising they were always going to keep me one step away from death, I began to look for ways to escape. Finally, I managed to do it and ended up in the village where I met you, Si.'

'Did they know who you were, in the village?' Si asked.

'No, but that's why they massacred the village. It wasn't about you. It was more to do with me. Zephyr hates me.'

There was silence for a few moments before Nick laid his hand on Temp's arm. 'I'm sorry about your family.'

Temp hung his head. 'Too many people have died because of me.'

'You have a chance to change things now. Do it for them,' Nick said.

'Did you know Chas's brother?' asked Si.

'Resolution? Oh yes. I knew him – brash upstart. He had ideas far above his station. He loved the title they gave him - the Commander. Made him feel so important. And he hated me because I never gave him any credit. He tortured me at the Bastille. He must have been incensed when I escaped. That's why he would have relished the day when he attacked the village and found me there. He always wanted to be closer to Zephyr. He was jealous of me, and the irony was that Zephyr couldn't stand him.'

'If he's still alive and not in the Bastille himself, I'm sure Chas will find him and deal with him,' Si said.

'He was a dead man walking when he failed to bring you in. Zephyr wouldn't have let that go,' Temp said.

'Chas won't be happy if he's dead already. She wanted to be the one who finished him off,' Si said.

'Pity she's not with us. She could have taken her revenge on Zephyr for denying her what she wanted,' Temp said.

Nick stood up and stretched. 'I think it's time we thought about what to do next. I'll ringing Peter. We need to meet him and find out if he can do anything else to help us.'

8

Chas was furious with herself, as she sat on a chair in the darkened room. Resolution had made her sit on the floor and cuff herself to the heating pipe, as he pointed the gun at her. Then he had stripped her of personal belongings, including her phone.

How could he have known she was coming? There was no spy hole in the door. All she could think was that somehow, he had seen her outside the flats. How stupid she had been. She had become complacent because of her change of appearance and new name. How could she have forgotten that you were never safe. Always in danger.

Resolution looked excited to see her. He was smiling in that that self-satisfied way he had when he had caught his prey. 'It's good to see you sister.' He enjoyed calling her that. He knew it riled her. 'How fortune for me that you just decided to drop in, after all this time.'

Chas scowled at him. 'I wanted to see how you were.'

'Well, here I am. Look at my palace of dreams. Good isn't it?'

'It's what you deserve,' she said.

He laughed. 'Oh no. This is far from what I deserve. I'm sure you think you came to give me what I deserve. But

I'm making my own plans, thanks. You have brought me a golden opportunity to get what I deserve. I'm going to make the most of it.'

An urge to lunge at him and stuff the consequences of a bullet in the gut, overwhelmed her. She just about managed to remain where she was. The last thing she was going to do was give him the opportunity to deprive her of her goal: Her revenge. 'What exactly do you have in mind?'

'Let's not cut to the chase just yet,' he said. 'I want to catch up. It's been a long time, sister. Tell me what's been happening in your world since we last met.'

She rolled her eyes at him and looked the other way.

He stuck out his bottom lip in fake petulance. 'Oh. Don't be like that. Haven't you always wanted a family who are interested in you? And here I am. I'm here. I'm listening. I want to know.'

She needed to think of a way out of here. How long before Mish came back looking for her? She did not want him involved in all this. He would inevitably get hurt.

Resolution seemed to read her thoughts. 'I tell you what. I will ask a simple question and you give a straightforward answer. If you answer me honestly, I will let your friend live when he comes back for you. So, here it is: Where is Silence Hunter?'

'I don't know.'

'Well that's not a good start, is it? So predictable. I said honest answers would buy your friend's life.'

Chas looked at her brother with contempt. 'I haven't seen him for months. We went abroad with Kate. We fell out. I came back, looking for you. That's it. I don't know where he is.'

Resolution seethed. He half believed her, but it wasn't what he wanted to hear. She must know more. 'Did he come back to England? And Kate? Is she with him?'

'I don't know,' Chas said.

Resolution bent towards her and lashed his hand across her cheek so hard her head snapped sideways and bounced off the wall. He came up close to her, his spit in her ear as he whispered, 'Every time you say those three words something worse will happen.' He sat down. 'I will ask you again. Did Hunter come back to England? And is his mother with him?'

Chas was dazed from the double blow of the hand and the wall. Her loyalty to Si welled up like an underground spring that had been bubbling under the surface for months, only now to burst into life, suddenly. She tried to be evasive. 'There was a plan to come back, but I ...' Those three words were about to emerge. 'They weren't ready.'

'What do you mean 'weren't ready?''

'They weren't ready to come back. That's all. They wanted to stay where they were. Who could blame them.'

'What would make them ready to come back?' Resolution pursued. 'The NMBs? Don't treat me like an idiot, Chastity. I've heard reports of plague victims claiming to be cured.' Resolution reared over her, wielding the gun as if ready to strike her with it. 'Where are they?'

'I'm not in contact with them. I cut all ties when I came back. I didn't want anything more to do with them. My own mission, to find you, was all I was thinking of. And here I am. Mission accomplished.' At least this was the truth.

'Not quite accomplished, sister. I have a slight change of plan for you. You came to kill me, right?'

Chas shrugged and nodded.

Resolution sat down at his desk. 'Fine. But, in a sharp turn of events, you're going to help me get what I want.'

'I am not,' Chas said. 'You know I'd never help you.'

'It's non-negotiable and you don't even need to be willing. Now, who is that boy you're with?'

Her stomach lurched. 'He's not important.'

'That's not what I asked. Who is he?'

'He's just someone from a commune I've been living in since I came back to England. He knows nothing. He was just helping me to find you. He thinks there's a loving family reunion going on right now.' She spat the last words sarcastically across the room.

'He'd better not be coming back then,' Resolution said.

'You don't need to bother about him. Just don't answer the door if he comes back. He'll go away.' Unfortunately, Chas didn't really believe that Mish would give up that easily on her.

'We'll see. For now, get down on your stomach.'

Chas was hating every minute of being in her brother's power, but she knew this wasn't the right time to try anything. She would wait for an opportunity. But now, all she was concerned about was that Mish didn't get hurt. She might not want to be his girlfriend, but he didn't deserve to be another of Resolution's victims. She did as she was told, twisting the cuffs along the heating pipe.

Resolution tied her legs together, pushed her under his bed and pulled the covers to the ground. Her hands were still visible, but Resolution pushed the chair in front of them. 'I'm not even going to gag you because if you make a sound when that boy comes back for you, he's one hundred percent dead and you know it.'

'If you hurt him, I *will* kill you,' Chas snarled.

'That's always been your plan anyway, hasn't it?' he laughed. 'So, I've nothing to lose.'

Resolution opened the door and looked around. He picked up Chas's knife from the floor and brought it inside, putting it in his desk drawer. 'Same old weapon. You really must get something more... modern.'

'It's what I know, and I trust it.' As she lay under the bed, she tried desperately to think of a way to save Mish.

Resolution sat in his chair, weighing up what to do about the boy. How much did he know? Would he be a threat? Did he know anything about Silence Hunter?

Mish had gone for a walk by the river. It had been three hours since he'd left Chas. He kept checking his phone for messages every five minutes now. How long should he wait before going in? He was already back at the flats. He didn't have a good feeling about all this, so as soon as someone came out he slipped in.

The knock came as Resolution was checking his wearable for more information on the rumours of plague cure. He kicked Chas, as if to remind her that Mish's life depended on her silence.

'Who is it?' He spoke through the closed door.

'I'm Grace's friend. I've come to get her.'

Resolution opened the door and smiled. 'Hi. Mish, isn't it? Nice to meet you. I always thought Grace was too nice a name for my sister.' He laughed. 'Come in.'

Mish walked in, warily, already not liking Resolution's attitude. He looked around the small, but well-kept bedsit. Everything was neatly in place and clean. The only thing that was slightly messy was the rumpled bed.

'Where is she?'

'Take a seat,' Resolution said, offering Mish the chair in front of where Chas's hands were secured to the pipe. She could see Mish's feet from under the bed, almost touch them. What was her brother playing at? Resolution stood by the door. Mish didn't take the seat.

'So, where is she, then?' he asked, looking around the room.

Resolution shrugged and laughed. 'Search me.'

Mish frowned. 'Aren't you pleased she's finally found ye?'

Resolution smiled. 'Oh, yes. Very happy. She's made my day.'

'So, where's she gone then?' Mish could feel his pulse begin to beat a little harder.

'Where are you from, Mish?'

'How 'boot answering ma question first.' Mish clenched his fists in his lap.

'Honestly? She hasn't gone far. I expect her to reappear any minute.'

Mish relaxed a little bit, even though the man's behaviour was very odd. Chas could be a bit strange, but this brother was even stranger.

'So. You were saying? You're from...?'

'I live in a commune in Northumberland.'

'Ah. My sister always liked that way of life, although it could never suit me. I'm a tech-city man. I like my gadgets and security.'

Mish looked around at the gadgets on the desk. He didn't think there was much security in this building. 'We should all be able to choose the life that suits us,' he said.

Resolution pursed his lips. 'Should we? Doesn't always work out that way though, does it?'

'No. I hear things haven't been so good for you recently. You must ha' done something pretty bad to upset the Rulers.'

Chas winced. Mish needed to keep quiet and leave.

Resolution raised his eyebrows. 'Ah well, fortunes change. I think mine are just about to take a turn for the better though.'

'You mean now you have your sister back? That's great,' Mish said. 'Listen, d'you know when she'll be back? It's just that I want to get going before it gets too late in the day.'

Ignoring the question again, Resolution asked another. 'You say, she came to your commune. Did she bring anyone else with her?'

'No.'

'She didn't have a boy with her? About the same age? Or a woman? A scientist?'

Mish shook his head, confused. 'No. She was alone. I found her out on the hills. Hasn't she already told you aboot what she's been up to? She's never told me aboot another boy.'

'No. She wouldn't. Wouldn't want you to be jealous, I suppose.' Resolution paused and looked out of the window.

He didn't believe the boy knew anything. Chastity hadn't told him anything. He was innocent. But what should he do with him? How much did Chas care about him?

Mish was feeling more and more uncomfortable. He got up. 'Look, maybe I should wait outside. I'll come back in a while.'

Yes. Chas thought. Go. And please don't come back. Just go. Her eyes stung with tears despite herself.

Resolution moved in front of the door. Chas could see their feet. 'So, here's the bad news, Mish. And I'm sorry to be the one to break it to you.' Resolution paused for effect. 'Hmm. My sister has a bit of a cruel streak. Have you ever noticed this?'

Chas bit her lip, imagining what was about to come.

Mish frowned. Where was this leading? 'Not really. She can be hard and stubborn, but I wouldna say cruel.'

Resolution pretended to be sympathetic. 'She's been keeping that one for a special occasion then, and I think this must be the moment. I'm afraid I lied to you earlier. Here's the truth. She hasn't just 'popped out' and she won't be coming back.'

Mish shifted uncomfortably. 'What do you mean?'

'She left about an hour or so ago. She said you'd come for her and that I should tell you, and these are her words, "Tell Mish, Don't try to find me, you pathetic loser. I'm done with you."' Resolution twisted his face into a more grotesque expression of fake sympathy, as he saw hurt flash in Mish's eyes. 'Sorry about that. That's just how she can be. Nice as nice then, BAM! In with the knife.'

'I don't understand. She wouldna do that to me.' As he

said the words, Mish wasn't totally convinced they were true. 'Did she say why or where she was going?'

Chas wanted to scream, to bite his ankle, anything to make him realise he was being lied to. But she knew Resolution would have no qualms about killing him. He would do it. Best to let Mish think she was heartless and live, than die knowing the truth.

'She told me she'd needed you for food and shelter until she could find me. And she said she's bored with you. She's a restless soul. I think her plan was to ditch you all along.' Resolution smiled sadistically.

Mish shook his head. 'No! I don't believe you! Maybe I should call her.' He looked at his phone on his wrist.

'No point. She left hers here.' Resolution picked up Chas's wearable from the bed.

'Why?'

'She wants to be alone. She figured you'd try and contact her.'

'How will she keep in contact with you? She's been desperate to find you.'

'She knows where I am. I'm sure she'll be back at some point.'

Mish was wary. This didn't feel right.

Resolution opened the door. 'Well, you'd better get going. Don't dwell on her too much. I'm sure a good-looking boy like you has all the girls at his beck and call. You'll find someone else. Someone more... predictable.'

Mish didn't move. 'I'm not going without her.'

Chas swore silently. Go you idiot. Please. While you have the chance!

Resolution grabbed Mish and flung him out of the door. 'Just get going, idiot! I know her better than you. She really doesn't want you to come back. If you hang around I might just have to be more forceful.'

Mish resisted Resolution's grip and tried to push his way back into the room, but Resolution twisted him in to an armlock, painfully wrenching his arm. Mish flinched and tried to turn but Resolution pushed his face in to the wall.

'I'm counting to ten. If you're not gone by ten I'm going to smash your pretty little head off this wall so hard you will puke your guts up, if you ever come round.' As if he were talking to a five-year-old, he began to count, releasing Mish from his grip and pushing him towards the stairs. 'One... two...' Mish gave him a black look and tried to peer again into the room. Resolution, looked on calmly, his arms folded across his chest. 'Six... seven... eight...'

Chas heard Mish's footsteps descending the stairs. Resolution waited until he was sure Mish had left the building, then he shut the door. Chas let go of the breath she had been holding.

'You can get out now. Your little lapdog has gone.'

She pulled herself out, calling him some choice names. 'You enjoyed that.'

'I did,' Resolution smiled. 'I could have just killed him I suppose. Would that have been better?' Chas kicked out at him, but he jumped back and laughed, then kicked her in the stomach. She groaned and lay still, trying to get her breath back. 'Sit up on the bed.' He unchained her from the pipes, still keeping her cuffed, and heaved her up. He held her at gunpoint again. 'Have some water.' He put a glass next to her as she struggled to sit up. 'There, see how kind I am to my family.'

She threw the glass at him, but it hit the wall and shattered. 'I hate you! You are *not* my family. I *will* kill you one day!'

He lunged forward and thrust the gun into her temple. 'Not if I kill you first. And that looks more likely at the moment, doesn't it?'

She rolled backwards and thrust her feet into his face, knocking the gun from his hand on the way.

She jumped to her feet. He reeled back and touched his lip, shuddering as he saw the blood on his fingers. His aversion to it never grew any less. 'You little...' She dived for the gun, but Resolution was nearer to it and kicked it out of the way. Then grabbing her by the hair, he wrestled her to the ground again and kicked her. As she struggled to move he grabbed some tape from his desk drawer and taped up her mouth; then secured her to the pipes once more.

'Bitch!' He punched and kicked her several more times. She doubled her legs up, trying to protect herself.

When he had done enough to ensure her silence, he sat down on his chair and dabbed at his mouth with a handkerchief. She moaned softly, and he smiled. 'You're going on a holiday, sister. To the Bastille.'

9

It was raining heavily as a man in an anorak was approaching the cottage on foot, head bent against the rain.

'He's here,' Kate said, opening the back door. She hugged him. 'Come in. Thank you for coming.' Kate took his coat. 'Have a seat. I'll put the kettle on.'

'Thanks. You must be Kate.'

'Yes. Good to meet you at last.' They shook hands.

The others came into the room.

'Peter!' Nick said, giving the man a hug.

'How's it going, Nick?'

'Brilliant! The camps have been transformed.'

Peter nodded. 'Excellent. And Si...' He moved towards him. 'Long time...'

'It's great to see you, Peter.' Si put out his hand to shake Peter's, but Peter gathered him into a hug too.

'This is Temp Alliston,' Nick said. Temp and Peter shook hands.

'I've heard a lot about you, in one way or another,' said Peter.

'Not sure whether that's good or bad,' said Temp.

'Depends who you talk to,' Peter said.

'Well, I've heard a lot of good things about you,' Temp said.

They talked for a while about the camps and how things had been progressing. Peter told them of more raids and unrest.

'We need to get the cure out to more camps,' Nick said.

'And we want to rally people to rise up against the Rulers,' Si said. 'Maybe we should hijack their slogan from the election; 'Enough is enough.''

'I think I should make it my priority to distribute NMBs to as many camps as possible,' said Nick. 'There's not time for us to visit everyone in person, so I was thinking Kate could make a video of how to use the NMBs. Then we could get them transported to the camps. It's not ideal, but there's no way we can get round them all, especially not now.'

'You should talk about the uprising too, Mum. Rally people to join us.'

'We could do that,' Peter said. 'I could organise transport. We could have an encrypted site for the video, which I could turn into a holo-image of Kate, and distribute the password to the doctors in charge of the camps.'

Kate agreed it would be a good idea. 'We'd like to make a public video, revealing the truth about the plague and get it on social media and holoboards in public places. We could tell Si's story and encourage people to protest. Could you get it onto the boards, Peter? I know only government stuff gets on there.'

'It would make a great impact if our faces suddenly appeared there,' Si said. 'And not just as 'the wanted.''

'You'd certainly have their attention if you did that,' Peter said. 'I'll see what I can do.'

Nick spoke. 'Are you sure you're okay with all this, Peter? You were trying to keep a low profile. I know they monitor you carefully since your involvement with Si last year.'

'It's fine. I can get round them. They didn't put me in charge of Technologies for nothing! And besides, I can't sit by and do nothing while you're all working so hard to defeat the Rulers. I'll stay here overnight, then head back first thing to start putting things in motion. Nick, I suggest you come with me and we work together on getting the NMBs out there. Kate, Temp and Si, you stay here a little longer. Make the videos. Do you have wearables? 'Kate and Si held up their wrists with their phones wrapped around them. 'Okay. Film the videos on those, but make sure there are no clues in the background that anyone could trace to here. Keep all GPS turned off. I'll set up a secure messaging platform for us to contact each other. The phone here is secure, so only call me on that for now. When you come here I'll have a look at your phones. I can insert a device to make them less traceable, although nothing is totally secure. Have you been okay here so far?'

'Yes. It's a great place, thanks,' Kate said. 'We have everything we need.'

'I might know someone amongst the Rulers who might just be willing and able to help us get inside The Citadel,' Temp said.

'Someone from your days in The True Order?' Si asked.

'Yes. He and I were friends. Proper friends. He was in that room when they told me what I had to do to my son, but he decided that to speak up there would do no good.

He helped me when I tried to get Asher and Truth away to safety and tried to keep in touch with me for a while, after I was sent to the Bastille. He even came to see me once and tried to get me out, but there wasn't much he could do. His own family would have been in danger and I couldn't ask that of him. I told him not to put himself, or them, in danger because of me. I know he was secretly opposed to many of the ideals of the Rulers.'

'What makes you think he would risk anything now to help us?' Si asked.

Temp shook his head. 'He was a good friend, that's all. He might not even be alive. I don't know, but it's worth a try.'

'What's his name? I might know him or be able to contact him,' Peter said.

'He took on the name Capability. His surname is North, and his name before the Rulers took power was Lance, in case that helps.'

'I'll make enquiries. I don't know of him personally,' Peter said.

They spent the rest of the evening trying to talk about other things, mainly from a time before Si was born, when things were more hopeful and free. Si listened with interest. He wondered if times had really been so different, or were they just being nostalgic? Si sifted through his own memories, from his seventeen years. They weren't pretty. But even there, nostalgia managed to kick in as he remembered good times with his mum and dad before they had been taken and he had been sent to the workhouse, then the Bastille. There was nothing good about those days.

But then he had met Chas. More than ever now he wanted to find her. He knew he would feel so much better if she was here, working alongside him, telling him what to do in her dulcet sarcastic tones. Maybe she would see some of the revolution propaganda, wherever she was. But then, how would she find them, even if she wanted to? Although, Chas being Chas, she would probably find a way.

The next morning, Peter and Nick were ready to leave. 'This should only take a few days. Then be ready to move out. I'll let you know what next,' Peter said.

'Take care,' Kate said, hugging them both.

Nick kissed her on the cheek. 'You too. I know these guys will look after you.'

Over the next few days Kate, Temp and Si worked on the video. Temp became camera man, using Kate's phone. They recorded Kate speaking about who she was and what she had discovered, telling people about the plague and how it was a control device of the Rulers. She told the story of how she and Morgan had developed the Nanomedibot and Si's involvement. Then Si told his story from the previous year, of searching for his mother and father and breaking them out of the Priory. Then it was back to Kate for a plea to rise up and protest against the injustice of what the Rulers were doing. They merged in images from the plague camps and even snippets of an interview that Kate had recorded with a cured plague victim. They overlaid images of the horrors of the camps, with emotive text. When they had finished, they were pleased with the result. Kate also made a detailed medical video for Peter to upload, so that in the camps she and Nick couldn't get to, the doctors could use it to train their staff in using the NMBs.

A few day later Peter contacted them. The phone projected his image into the living room. He told them that Nick had been making plans with various camps for the distribution of NMBs and he was going to visit as many of the camps as possible. Peter had created a secure site to broadcast the medical message about the NMBs and a different one to broadcast the video about the plague. 'You need to come here. I don't want you uploading anything from there. It's too risky. I need to keep that place a secret.'

'Isn't your house being watched?' Si asked.

'Not really,' Peter replied. 'They call in on me unannounced, now and again, but my security gives me ample warning. They take me in for questioning every so often too. Maybe once they're certain you're involved, things will get more intense, but by that time you won't be here anyway. Temp, we need to have a discussion about your friend Capability, but that can wait until you're all safely here. I'm sending a car to pick you up from the nearest road at 22.00 tonight. Walk down to the crossroads, 2 miles down the Western track. My driver will be waiting for you.'

Si waited with a sense of trepidation and excitement, for night to fall. A new chapter was beginning in their lives. He had this sense of being overwhelmed by the enormity of what they were trying to achieve here. He thought back to all the people he admired from history who had changed things for good, and wondered if they had ever felt like this before beginning their task. People like William

Wilberforce, Mother Teresa, Malala Yousafzai and his own mother and father. Had they been scared? Had they mapped out exactly what they would do? Or did things just happen to them and they reacted? What had inspired them? He knew what had inspired his mother and father. The teachings of The Way and the Teacher. Si thought back to the Teacher. Some would say he was irrelevant to the 21st century world they lived in. The Rulers were trying to make him and all religious leaders irrelevant. But Si was beginning to think that he was more relevant than ever.

'You okay?' Kate said, catching him deep in thought.

'Yes. Fine. Just thinking.'

Want to share it?'

Si shrugged. 'Not really.'

'We need to get going soon. Temp's ready. Seems keen to get going and set things in motion. Waiting around makes me more nervous. I just want to get on with it.'

'I'm glad Temp's decided to get involved,' Si said.

'He's a good man,' Kate said.

'Who is?' Temp said, coming into the room.

'You,' Kate said, smiling at him.

'I don't think so,' he said. 'I've not always been one of the good guys.'

'Hey, we've all done things we regret. You've told us all the bad stuff and you walked away from it. This is about now. Moving on,' Kate said.

Temp shrugged. 'Yeah, I guess.'

Si smiled at him. 'Anyway, I only know the good Temp and I believe in him.'

'In that case, I'll try to believe in him too,' Temp said.

'Are we ready?' Kate looked at Si. He nodded. 'In that case, let's get back to the real world and see if we can't kick some of those bad guy asses!'

'You're funny, Mum,' Si laughed.

The car and driver were waiting for them, as Peter had said, and it was after midnight when they pulled up the drive at Peter's house. The door was opened by Harmony, Peter's house-keeper. As soon as she saw them, she ushered them into the house quickly, clearly nervous to have them there. But then she clutched Si in an enormous hug. 'So good to see you again, boy!'

He was taken by surprise. 'You too,' he replied, trying to breathe, as she squeezed the air out of him.

Peter and Nick had come into the hallway. Everyone laughed. Nick hugged Kate, kissing her on the cheek. 'So glad you're here,' he whispered. She smiled and kissed him back.

'There are rooms prepared for you,' Harmony said, releasing Si from her grasp.

Peter beckoned for them to follow. 'Come on, I'll show you where you're sleeping. We'll talk in the morning.'

*

They met in the dining room for breakfast. There was a feast of fresh fruit, croissants, eggs and bacon, laid out for them to help themselves. Si remembered how it had been when he was here with Chas and Ben. Peter hadn't mentioned them, as if he knew it might upset Si. After breakfast though, as Si stood in the kitchen, helping Harmony load the dishwasher, she had no such inhibitions.

'So, where's your young lady then?'

Si shrugged. 'Chas? You know how independent she was. She's off doing her own thing.'

Harmony raised her eyebrows. 'Her own thing? What does that mean?'

Si explained about her coming back to England, early, to look for Ben and her brother.

'Her brother? Wasn't he that Commander? Scary man. What does she want with him?'

'To kill him,' Si said, bluntly.

'Okay,' Harmony raised her eyebrows. 'She is one tough cookie. Sounds like she's asking for trouble.' She closed the lid of the steam dishwasher and set it running.

'That's what she does,' Si said, gazing out of the window.

'You wish she was here,' Harmony observed.

Si shrugged and turned to face her. Harmony smiled, like she could see right into his heart. 'I think they're waiting for you in the lounge. I'll bring coffee through soon.'

The others were already there, chatting about nothing important. 'Okay,' said Peter, as Si entered. 'Let's look at what we've got. Nick and Kate are leaving in an hour or so. They're taking all the NMBs and meeting the contacts who will distribute them to other camps, at a secret location, just south of Durham.' He spoke to his Virtual Assistant. 'Solomon, load encrypted website P65J4321. Lounge only.'

A voice came back, seemingly out of nowhere. 'Certainly, Peter.'

A 3D web page appeared on the lounge wall.

Si was surprised that he had not been aware of the VA in the house last time he was there. 'I didn't know you had this.'

Peter shrugged. 'Standard stuff. The more affluent houses in the tech-cities have it. I tend not to use it so often. I'm bombarded with it at work, so I like my house more old-fashioned, most of the time. Harmony is a much better assistant than Solomon. No offence, my friend.'

'None taken, Peter,' came the voice.

Peter stood up. 'Before she went to sleep, I asked Kate for her wearable and uploaded the videos you made. They're good, but I've made a few techie tweaks to make them look even more contemporary and emotive. I hope you don't mind. Shall we have a look at them?'

Everyone was keen, especially Nick, who hadn't seen them yet. 'Solomon, play Revolution One,' Peter said. The message began, and suddenly Kate and Si were in the room as holo-images. In the background, scenes from the plague camps played. The plea to join the Revolution and rise up against the Rulers came at the end from Si. Peter had made it more emotive, with changes to the light and timbre of the voice in places. It was very clever. He had also edited in melancholy music over the scenes in the camp, then dramatic music to round it all off.

When it finished playing, no one spoke for a while. Si felt quite choked and he could see that his mum did too.

'Well?' Peter said.

'I'd join you,' Temp said.

'Me too,' Nick agreed.

'I'd join me,' Si said, and the others laughed. 'Wow! I

didn't recognise myself.'

You've done a great job, Peter,' Kate added. 'Thanks.'

'You did most of it,' he replied.

'Now, how do we get it out there?' Temp asked.

'That's the next bit. I'm going to do it from a different location. Nothing that can be linked back here. I'll go today, and by tomorrow it'll broadcast on the holoboards of every tech-city in the country.'

'Tomorrow?' Si said. 'That soon?'

'Yes. If you're ready.'

'Kate answered. 'We are. No point in delaying.'

'Won't the Rulers be able to take it down straight away?' Temp asked.

'Good question. They'll try, but I'm pretty good at what I do. It has a rolling encryption code. Difficult to crack, even for the best hackers. They'll get to it eventually, I'm sure, but not until we've got the message out there for a good amount of time. After that, we might need something different anyway.'

'Won't they be able to trace it back to you? They'll know you did it,' Si said.

'They might try to pin it on me, yes. They'll be round here very soon after it goes live, I'm sure. That's why Si and Temp will be gone from here before it goes live.'

'What about you?' asked Si, looking at Peter with concern.

'I can look after myself. They won't be able to prove anything.'

'What about the medical video?' asked Kate.

'That's easy. Simple video, minimal editing needed there.

Nick has instructions for the doctors. They'll be fine. I'm setting up an encrypted messaging app so that they can talk to you if they need any advice. You can access it from your phone. And we can all use it to communicate with each other more securely.'

'What's the plan for you two, after today?' Kate asked, looking to Si and Temp.

'We need to get inside The Citadel somehow,' Si said. 'We need to get to Zephyr.'

Temp shook his head. 'It's more complicated than that. Remember he's just one of several versions of Zephyr. You take out one, they have another, waiting to replace him. We need to get to the source of the immortality they're creating. We need to get to their cloning labs.'

'Will they be inside the city?' Kate asked.

'Yes. I know where they are. They're inside the exclusive hospital in the city. If we could find Capability, he would help us. I know he would. I just hope he's still alive.'

Peter spoke. 'I'm making enquiries. If he's still around, I can find him.'

'I think we should make our way to The Citadel and find a way in. They must let traders in and people who work in the hospitals and other services,' Si said.

'Yes,' Temp said, 'But security is hot, as you'd expect. You're far too high profile to get past any of that.'

'What about invisibility cloaks,' Si suggested, looking at Peter. 'That really helped Chas and me. Do you have any others?'

'I'd thought of that. I've developed the cloak some more since you wore it,' he said. 'I've made suits with the material. Much easier than the cloak to move in. They have slits for eyes and mouth, with a fine gauze covering. That's the only place you may be vulnerable to being seen. But it's a minimal risk.'

'Awesome!' Si said.

Peter smiled. 'I'll show you, later.'

'If our message does its job properly, people will riot, protest, cause plenty of distraction for the Rulers to deal with,' Kate said.

'That'll help,' Temp said.

'Okay. Let's get everything sorted. Kate and Nick need to leave in just under an hour. My driver is coming for you.'

Kate went to her room to get her things together. Si followed her. He knocked on the door. 'Can I come in?'

'Yep.'

He sat on the bed. 'You okay about everything, Mum?'

Kate sat down next to him. 'Kind of. I'm excited about setting more people free from the plague, but I'm nervous about separating from you. It's been wonderful being with you for so long and I'm scared of losing you again.'

'I'm going to be fine. Temp is with me. He's saved me before, remember. And I know how to handle things better now. I can use a weapon if I need to.'

'This is just so big,' Kate sighed. 'You're my son. You're just a boy and here you are starting a revolution to take down the government.' She laughed, wryly. 'It's insane.'

'I'm seventeen, Mum. I can look after myself. And besides, where's your faith? You're the one who's always trusting in God.'

'I know. And I do. But it doesn't make me immune to

bad stuff happening. This is deep corruption we're up against.'

'We'll be okay,' Si said, taking her hand.

'Yep.' She got up and resumed her packing.

'So, you and Nick... what's going on there?' He grinned at her.

She looked at him, quizzically.

'I've seen the way he looks at you,' Si said, smiling.

'Oh!' Kate blushed and busied herself with folding her clothes. 'He's nice. We're just good friends.'

Si raised his eyebrows in a 'Really?' sort of way.

'That's all there is to it,' Kate said emphatically, but she was smiling.

At the front door, Nick and Kate said goodbye to them. 'Shalom,' Nick said.

Si looked at him.

'It means total peace, even in the face of adversity,' Nick explained.

'Good. I could do with that. Thanks,' Temp said. 'Shalom to you too.'

Kate hugged Si very tightly. 'Stay safe.'

'I'll be keeping an eye on him,' Temp said.

'I appreciate it.' Kate smiled and squeezed Temp's hand. Then, they were gone.

10

It was so hot in here. That was the worst thing about being locked up in this room twenty-three hours a day. The temperature of the room was deliberately kept too high. Chas constantly felt thirsty. She was taken out to exercise, for an hour a day, and food was pushed through a hatch on the door. She had a bed and a toilet and there was one small window, too high up to see out of. She had been here a few days and already she was going crazy, longing for fresh air and open space.

Resolution had looked like a little kid receiving the best birthday present ever, when he heard word that the Rulers would talk to him and give him immunity from prosecution. He was to leave her in the Bastille and go to The Citadel for talks with Zephyr. She had planned to escape as he bundled her into his hired car, but he was a step ahead of her.

Driving into the Bastille had brought back memories of trying to get in here to find Si. Now she was trapped here, and no one knew. There was no one on the outside to come for her. She thought about Mish; wondering where he was and whether he was looking for her. How long had he waited outside Resolutions block of flats? Or, had he just returned to the commune and forgotten about her? She doubted that. She had been so wary of him for a long time, but he had been good to her. And when his life had been under threat, she realised she did care about him. However, he was history now. And besides, it was virtually impossible to get into this place. She needed to get herself out. If Si had managed it somehow, she definitely could. There was plenty of time to think whilst locked in the room. She was so angry with herself for having been so close to finally killing Resolution, then letting him get the better of her. And now what? Back to square one. Worse really. Locked in here, there was no chance of getting at him.

Then, there was the issue of Si. If Resolution wanted to use her as bait to trap him, she certainly wouldn't allow that. If she couldn't escape, she would have to find a way to stop him from using her, even if that meant killing herself. When they let the prisoners out for exercise she looked for any means of escape. It gave her a new appreciation for what Si had achieved in escaping from this place - twice. It looked impossible, but then he had been here much longer and kept under different circumstances.

*

Resolution was in The Citadel. He hadn't exactly been welcomed back with open arms. For the moment, he had been given a comfortable room in The Fortress with good food. Zephyr was keeping him waiting for an interview. Resolution was sure he was being watched. He knew there would be surveillance in the room, but this gave him an opportunity to act in ways he thought would impress.

Finally, he was called for an audience with Zephyr and

several of the Cabinet. He had walked through The Fortress many times in the past, but coming back here made him realise again how impressive this building was. Even though it was based on the ancient castle at Bamburgh, it had modern features, like a roof made of shatterproof glass and steel. It was powered entirely by solar energy and wind, as was the rest of the capital city. It towered majestically over every other building in The Citadel, being built on a craggy outcrop, like the castle it was modelled on. It also reached deep underground. There were many rooms and corridors Resolution had never even seen.

But this corridor, he had walked many times on his way to meetings with various people. He had been given a visitor's pass and was being escorted by a security guard. He hoped that soon he would be back in favour and able to move about freely here, as he once did.

He took a seat in the waiting area and the security guard hovered outside the door. Zephyr kept him waiting a long time, playing games with him, Resolution suspected, but he had expected as much and wasn't going to be intimidated or deterred. He had come this far. He was going to make a damned good case for his reinstatement.

'Premier Zephyr will see you now,' said a personal assistant that he didn't recognise.

Resolution walked into the large office where Zephyr was seated at the far end of a long table, with the Rulers around it. There were seven of them, including Ambition Steele, Temp's old tutor, who sat next to Zephyr, being his right-hand man. It was a joke really, Resolution thought. He had never figured out if this clone was just their puppet, or if Zephyr controlled them. He knew that this first clone of Zephyr was certainly in a vulnerable position, because as soon as they thought he wasn't right for the job anymore, they would replace him with another clone. They had several lined up and waiting in the wings. The next one was a young man. And Zephyr knew this. Resolution wondered if this Zephyr ever feared his own demise.

'Take a seat, Resolution,' the Premier said. 'It's been too long.' He smiled ironically at him. 'And you've been causing trouble.'

Resolution hated this bit, but he knew there was no way round it. He prepared to look contrite and grovel, whilst inside, his anger boiled. 'I'm sorry for any trouble I've caused Premier Zephyr. All I ever wanted was to serve the Party.'

'But you failed,' Zephyr said.

'I did. But I never gave up looking for ways to be useful again. That's why I had to escape from custody. I had to prove to you that you needed me.'

'Needed you?' Zephyr laughed. 'We don't need anyone. Everyone is replaceable.'

'Of course,' Resolution agreed, thinking about the Premier's own vulnerability. 'That came out wrong. I meant to prove to you that I could be useful to you.'

'And so, you've captured the girl,' Zephyr said. 'How convenient that she came looking for you. Why would she do that?'

'She's a blood-thirsty leach. She wanted revenge for the massacre at the commune, after Hunter escaped from the Bastille. But now she's yours. She will know things about the Hunters. She probably knows where they are. You know it's them spreading a cure for the plague?'

'Of course we do, and we will stop them.'

'You could use her as bait. Silence Hunter has a soft spot for her.'

'Possibly.' Zephyr was looking bored.

'Let me interrogate her, Sir. Reinstate me as Commander and let me do it. I know I can get Hunter this way.'

'You ask a lot. We need to discuss this,' said Zephyr. 'Wait outside.'

Resolution returned to the waiting area but didn't sit down this time. He couldn't. He paced the floor, making the PA look sternly at him several times. After an hour, she told him to sit down or she would have him put somewhere else.

Eventually, he was called back into the cabinet office. Ambition spoke. 'We have decided to grant your wish.'

Zephyr smiled. 'You could call me your fairy godmother, Resolution.' One or two members of the cabinet sniggered.

Ambition continued. 'You will be reinstated and interrogate the girl. But bring her here. We want her under our close eye. When we have her here, we will draw Silence Hunter to us and hopefully his mother too. If they are curing people of the Plague, then it won't be long before they're inciting them to turn against us. Let's make an example of traitors. We'll show the people that their claims are false and put down any insurrection with a show of public executions for anyone who starts any kind of trouble, and prison camps for those who get involved.'

Resolution looked at Zephyr. 'A good idea, Premier.'

Zephyr nodded. 'Of course. Just one more thing... Commander. We're assigning you a... bodyguard. After all, Chastity is a dangerous female. She has outwitted you before and we wouldn't want you to... get hurt again.'

Resolution winced at the sarcasm.

'Miller will accompany you out of The Fortress, to your new apartment. He will be at your service until you return here.'

So, they didn't trust him not to fail again, but he would prove them wrong. Despite not liking the idea of a 'bodyguard,' Resolution left the room with a grin on his face. He was given a car, an apartment and security access. When he arrived at his new apartment, the latest wearable was waiting for him. The apartment was equipped with a Virtual Assistant, whom he told to order a takeaway from his favourite Japanese restaurant. He sat in an armchair and breathed deeply, feeling restored, apart from his 'bodyguard,' outside the door. That was a niggle.

The Japanese was divine, especially compared to the cheap rubbish he had become accustomed to over the last year, but he didn't waste much time luxuriating in his new apartment. He jumped into his car, accompanied by Miller, and headed straight back to the Bastille. He would earn Zephyr's respect again, so that no one needed to assign him a bodyguard. Nothing and no one was going to take any of this away from him ever again, least of all his sister. He would enjoy watching her hang with the others.

It was late at night when the Commander and Miller arrived at the Bastille. They hadn't spoken much on the journey. Resolution was not going to treat him like a second-in-command, as Knowles had been.

The Master of the Priory made a show of welcome, but to Resolution's satisfaction, he could see that the man was very put out. He'd never liked him, and the feeling was mutual.

'It's good to be back,' Resolution said, with a smile, as he sat down in the Master's chair in his office.

The Master sucked in his lips. 'I've made sure you have everything you need, Commander. When do you want to see the prisoner?'

'I'll talk to her now, then let her stew until the morning. I'll be taking her back to The Citadel.'

'I've been told to give you an escort,' the Master said.

Resolution thought this was totally unnecessary, and yet another indicator that they didn't trust his competency.

The Master took him to Chas's room. 'A visitor,' he announced as Resolution stepped through the door.

Chas didn't move. She was sitting on the bed, her back to the wall, her legs stretched out in front of her. She looked contemptuously at her brother.

'I want to speak to her alone,' he said to the Master and Miller.

'There is a camera in here,' the Master said.

'Obviously,' said Resolution. 'I have nothing to hide. Just leave us.'

The other two left the room.

'I wondered when you'd be back,' Chas said. 'I'm getting a bit too used to this luxury.'

Resolution sat down on the hard chair next to the bed. Chas drew her legs up closer to her body. 'I'm taking you to

The Citadel tomorrow to be interrogated. You'd better be ready to talk.'

'Why? I've got nothing to tell you.'

'I'll find something in that little head of yours that I want, believe me. You will let me in on one hundred per cent of what you know about the Hunters and their plans to bring down the Regime.'

'Well, that will be one hundred per cent of nothing then, because I know nothing. I already told you. I left them behind. If they're here stirring things up, then good for them, but I won't be of any use to you.'

'Oh yes you will. Silence Hunter will come for you and we'll be ready to take him in and put an end to this ridiculous idea of revolution.'

The trouble was that Chas could see it all unfolding just as Resolution predicted. Si was a puppy. She knew he had feelings for her and wouldn't be able to resist giving himself up in exchange for her. There had to be a way to stop this happening. Her mind began working things out. If she could somehow convince Si that she wasn't worth saving. Maybe she could convince him that she had become a traitor. But how could she get him to believe she would collaborate with Resolution? It seemed too far-fetched to be believable. And she would have to convince her brother that she wanted to help him willingly. Virtually impossible.

'He's not worth bothering about. He won't succeed anyway. He's small fry. He only succeeded before because I was with him.'

'So modest, aren't you? We'll see,' Resolution said, standing up. 'Get some sleep. You won't be getting much after tonight.'

When he'd gone, Chas seethed with frustration. She felt helpless and that was the worst thing for her. She had to find a way to escape before Resolution could use her against Si. For the first time in ages, she felt a passionate surge of loyalty to Si and Kate emerging from behind her hatred of Resolution. She had put the hatred first and suddenly she realised she had jeopardised everything Kate had worked for and everything Si and Kate were trying to achieve now. If she'd had her knife on her she might have stabbed it into herself. If she allowed herself to be taken to The Citadel who knows what Resolution would do to her. And not only that, he would take great pleasure in torturing her. She knew that. Would she be strong enough not to beg for mercy? She had always thought she could resist anything, defy anyone, but trapped here, she was no longer sure. One thing she was sure of was that she didn't want to be the bait to lure Si to them. She wanted to help him and Kate. If she could escape and help them to bring down the Rulers, then she would also be defeating her brother. She might have to let go of the desire to kill him herself, or maybe she would still get the opportunity. One thing she was certain of in this moment of clarity, was that her loyalty to Si and Kate was greater than her hatred of Resolution. That gave her some hope.

The next morning Resolution, Miller, the Master and two security guards arrived to take Chas to the waiting vehicle.

'They've laid on a whole entourage for you. You must be very important,' Resolution said, as Chas was handcuffed and led out by the guards.

'Looks that way. You really shouldn't have gone to all this trouble for me though.'

He pulled her back by the collar of her shirt. 'There's not going to be any chance of escape, Chastity. I've made one hundred per cent sure of that. No one is going to accuse me of losing the game this time. No escapees. No runaways.'

Chas was marched to a waiting car. There was another car behind, ready to follow them and one to go before them. He was right. There was no way she could make any attempt to get away whilst surrounded by this lot, cuffed and without a weapon. She sat in the back of the vehicle, desperately thinking of how she could escape before they got to The Citadel. Resolution got into the passenger seat and Miller drove. A darkened glass screen was between her and them. She was glad to feel separated from her brother's presence, even by this small thing.

The only idea she came up with, was to try was to say she needed to pee. She could run fast. That was her only hope; maybe if she had even a short moment, she could run fast enough to get away. Even with cuffed hands and maybe several men in pursuit? It would be harder, but she had to try.

She waited until they were far enough from the Bastille, in open countryside, for them not to turn back. Somewhere with trees would make it easier to avoid being shot. She knew they wouldn't kill her, because they wanted to use her. But she had no doubt they would try to bring her down if she ran.

She banged her forehead on the dividing screen. They

ignored her at first, but eventually the screen went down. 'Stop doing that, Chastity. You'll get a headache. We wouldn't want that, would we?'

'I need to pee.'

'You can wait. It's only another hour or so.'

'I can't wait. I didn't get the chance to go this morning. You'll have a wet seat in here if you make me wait. But if that's what you want; fine.'

Resolution rolled his eyes as the screen came back up. The thought of urine all over the seats of this expensive car, and the smell, was almost as bad as the thought of blood.

'I will do it!' she yelled and began to bang on the screen again.

'Pull over,' Resolution said to Miller.

'Really Sir? She's bluffing. Thinks she can escape.'

'Then she's more stupid than I thought.'

The car pulled over. They were on the edge of the moor. Chas could see a clump of trees about fifty metres away. She could normally run that distance in ten seconds. She would just have to hope that they weren't good shots.

Miller pulled her aggressively out of the car and took her over to a ditch on the edge of the grass. 'Get on with it.'

Resolution stood on the other side of her. She glanced at the trees. Fifty metres.

'I need my hands free to get my trousers down.'

'You'll just have to manage,' Miller said.

'I'm not doing it in front of you two.'

'Get back in the car then.' Miller took her arm and pushed her towards the car.

'Okay,' Chas said. 'Just let me go behind that rock. You can stand right next to it if you like. I need to pee and I'm not doing it for you to watch.'

'No rocks. We'll turn the other way,' said Resolution. 'But Miller is not letting go of your arm.'

Chas cursed under her breath. 'Fine.'

Now what? She began to act as if she were trying to pull down her trousers. Both men were looking away, but Miller had a tight grip. She looked at the trees. This was her only chance. She had to try. As she bent forward, she suddenly bit hard into his middle finger. Instinctively, he let go and she ran.

Ten seconds...

One, two, three, four...

She heard Resolution swear at Miller and shout for back-up. Car doors slammed. With cuffed hands, it was difficult to get the pace she would normally be able to achieve. The ground was uneven, and she was fully aware that she must not stumble. She heard pounding feet behind her and swearing from Miller, but she didn't look back. Her eyes were firmly fixed on the trees.

Six, seven... nearly there. She stumbled but managed to steady herself before she fell.

Several shots rang out. She was still running.

Eight, nine... she could almost touch the trees.

Another shot. And she fell, hitting the ground face first, unable to use her hands. Incredible pain shot through her right thigh. Now it was her turn to swear. She forced herself on to her feet, despite the searing pain, but before she could even drag herself beyond the first tree, Miller was on her, grabbing around the waist. She tried to fend him off by kicking him in the shins, with the leg that wasn't hurt. He stumbled back and she fell to the ground. She tried to get up. The pain! But she must. Miller grabbed her again as the other guards arrived on the scene. Other hands gripped her and before she could defend herself, someone hit her across the temple with a weapon and she blacked out.

Resolution breathed a sigh of relief as the car drove on towards The Citadel. Despite Miller's incompetence at losing his grip on Chas, he had redeemed himself by cleaning up the blood, bandaging the wound and tying a tourniquet around her leg to stop the bleeding, without Resolution having to see too much of it. Chas lay unconscious across the back seat. Not quite how he had wanted to bring her in, but at least he still had her. She should have been called Determination, not Chastity. She would have to have the bullet removed at The Citadel Hospital, which was adjacent to The Fortress, and this would delay things. He was annoyed, but maybe he could use the wound to his advantage when it came to luring Silence Hunter in.

He called ahead to ask for a medical team on stand-by to treat her, hoping he could have all this done discreetly, without Zephyr or the other members of the cabinet finding out. It seemed unlikely, when she was going to be treated in their hospital. He realised he would probably have to explain all this to Zephyr.

They were admitted to the city, where an ambulance was waiting at the check-point. Chas was transferred to the vehicle and Resolution insisted that he go with her. To his constant annoyance, Miller insisted he accompany them too. As the ambulance travelled the short distance, Resolution organised an armed guard to accompany Chas at all times. When they arrived at the hospital, security guards were waiting alongside the doctors and Chas was whisked away.

Resolution's phone was ringing. He cursed. It was Zephyr.

11

Once every few weeks, Ben headed to Newcastle with Sarah and her eldest daughter, Honour, to stock up on supplies from the tech-city. Ben wasn't a big fan of these trips, but went along to help carry things and because Honour wanted him to. Honour, who was the same age as Ben, absolutely loved the city. She loved going clothes shopping in real shops and eating in fancy restaurants, as she called them. Sarah always made it a bit of a treat for them. They had been good friends ever since starting school together. Honour loved the outdoors; climbing trees, making dens, exploring the beach and generally getting dirty. It had been hard for her when Ben's family had moved away, so she was thrilled that Ben had come back to live with them. He was like her brother now.

They had just had lunch in a café and Sarah had a couple more specific shops that she needed to go to for things Ethan had asked for. Then, they were heading to the Bigg Market to buy their supplies. This area of Newcastle had once been known for its clubs and pubs, but since the Rulers came to power, it had been restored to its original purpose of trading in foodstuffs. There were strict regulations on drinking establishments these days and only a few were able to trade.

As they passed the Monument, a louder than usual noise attracted their attention to the holoboard. They stopped to watch as Kate Hunter appeared before them. Ben had never met Kate, but he recognised the name and stood, transfixed.

'Who is it?' Honour asked.

'It's Si's mum. You know, the boy who came with me to your house last year?'

Honour nodded. 'No one ever told me much about them. All I know is that they didn't come back.'

They listened to Kate's story, as did many of the passers-by who had stopped to watch.

'They must have done it. Got her out of the Priory,' Ben said, disbelievingly.

Then Si appeared to tell his story.

'Si's alive!' Ben felt excitement rising. Si was back. He had rescued his mum and he was back to fight the Rulers. As the holo-presentation came to an end, with dramatic music and cheering, people in the street became agitated. A few cheered. Some began shouting abuse at the now blank holoboard. Others were looking around, anxiously, in case law-keepers were coming. A man stood up on the steps of the Monument and began to shout over the top of everyone else.

'If this is true we need to do something. This is outrageous!'

Some people moved away hurriedly, but others shouted in response and one or two others got up on the steps to speak to the crowd.

Sarah began to get jittery. 'Come on, we need to get out of here. It won't be long before the law-keepers are here. We can't get involved in this.' She ushered Ben and Honour away towards the Bigg Market. 'Let's get what we need and get out of town. This is going to cause trouble.'

Ben followed Sarah, but his mind was working overtime. Chas and Si were back. Why had they not come for him? Over the last year, he had come to terms with them leaving him behind and often wondered if they were dead. He had been angry at first; felt betrayed, but Ethan and Sarah had helped him understand why they might have left him, if they had escaped. So, Ben had settled with their family, and although he still thought of Si and Chas, from time to time, he had accepted that they were gone. But this... this had stirred his longing to see them again.

'I can't believe they haven't tried to contact me,' Ben said, as they hurried through the streets.

'Sounds like they're too busy starting a revolution,' Sarah said. 'And anyway, they wouldn't want to drag you back into all the danger.'

'They might at least have sent word or phoned,' Ben said. 'They would know I'd see something like that.'

'Not really,' Honour said. 'You live out of town. They probably wouldn't think you'd see that.'

'You're best out of it,' Sarah said, hurrying ahead of them so that they had to jog to keep up.

'I'd like to see them again though. They were like brother and sister to me for a while. They saved my life too.'

'I know,' Sarah said. 'But they've moved on without you. They left you behind, remember.'

Ben looked at Sarah. There was a harshness to her voice that he very rarely heard. 'Yes, but it was for good reasons. You helped me see that.'

'Yes...well... we've got things to do, then we need to head home. Stop thinking about them now.'

How can I? Ben thought.

At the Bigg Market they shopped for their groceries; all the things their small local shops didn't supply. When Ben and Honour went to a few stalls, by themselves, he said to her, 'I want to join them. I don't think I could stand to go back to Seahouses and just try to pretend nothing's happening. Something big is about to kick off and I want to be part of it.'

'It's exciting,' Honour said. 'And scary. But you wouldn't be able to find them anyway.'

'Maybe not. But I bet I know someone who could tell me how to find them.'

'Who?' Honour said.

'His name's Peter. He helped us last time and he doesn't live far from here.'

'You're not thinking of going there now, are you? Mum wouldn't let you.'

'She can't stop me if I want to go.'

'How would you get there? Do you know the way?'

'I'll walk or hitch a lift or something. It's just outside Durham. I'll find it.'

'Ben, you wouldn't. I don't want you to go.'

'I don't want to leave you Hon, but I ... I don't know. I just want to be with them again.'

'More than with me?'

'Come on, we'll always be friends, won't we? We're virtually brother and sister. I'll be back. I just need to be part of this.'

'You might not come back,' she said.

'I will. Don't be daft.' He shoved her playfully and she shoved him back. He ran, and she began to chase him round the market stalls.

'Hey!' Sarah shouted as they ran past her. 'We're going soon. Get back here.'

They kept going, but were back beside her in a couple of minutes, out of breath and laughing.

She laughed briefly. 'Right, you looneys. I'm ready to leave. Talk is spreading around the market already about the holo-presentation.'

'I'm not coming,' Ben said.

Sarah stared at him. 'What do you mean?'

'I'm going to find Chas and Si.'

She shook her head. 'No, you're not. You're coming home.'

'I'm not. I've made up my mind. I'm going to find them and join them.'

'You don't know where they are,' Sarah said.

'I know where to ask though. They'll be pleased to see me. I know they won't turn me away.'

'They don't want you with them Ben. You're too young.'

'I'm not and they will. I know them. Chas understands me and makes me feel important.'

'And we don't?' Sarah looked hurt.

'I'm not saying that. I just want to see her again. She's

like a sister.'

'So am I,' said Honour.

'Yes, I know you are, but I have to do this.'

Sarah was getting desperate to leave and noticed that people were looking at them, overhearing their conversation. 'You won't see her, even if you find Kate and Si Hunter.'

'Yes, I will,' Ben replied.

'No. You won't,' Sarah said.

Ben looked suspiciously at her. 'What do you mean? And how do you know?'

'She's not with them,' Sarah said.

'Just because she wasn't on the holo-presentation, doesn't mean she's not there,' Ben insisted. 'Of course she's with them.'

'She's not with them. I know it for a fact,' Sarah said, more emphatically.

'How would you know that?' Ben's voice was rising in pitch and volume.

Sarah was regretting saying anything now. They were drawing attention to themselves and she was digging a deeper and deeper hole for herself. But she had to try and keep Ben from leaving. 'Because... she came to see you a few months back.'

Ben was incredulous. 'She came... you saw her?' His voice rose in pitch and volume. 'She came to Seahouses and you never told me?'

'But Mum, why?' asked Honour.

'Keep your voices down,' Sarah said. 'I told her to leave. I didn't want her upsetting Ben.'

Ben was furious. 'I would have been okay! I can't believe you didn't let me see her!'

Sarah tried to touch his arm, but he moved away. 'I thought it was for the best. I was trying to protect you.'

'I don't need protecting from Chas!' he shrieked. 'Where is she, then? Why isn't she with Si?'

Sarah glanced at the people who were now staring at them. 'Ben, calm down. I don't know. She said Si was abroad with his mother.'

Ben began to walk away. 'I'm going to find them,'

'Ben!' Honour called. 'Please don't go. It's too dangerous.'

He stopped. 'I have to Hon. I'd never settle back home.'

Sarah tried. 'Ben, we've thought of you as our son since you came back into our lives. I'm not your mother, but I'm standing in for her. She'd forbid you to walk into danger like this. I'm forbidding you. You can't go.'

Ben looked at her. Her eyes were pleading. He shook his head. 'You can't forbid me! I've got to find them.' Before they could stop him, he ran off into the crowd.

'Mum!' Honour cried. 'Why did you say all that? Look what you've done!'

'I was trying to stop him.'

Honour stared after Ben. 'What are we going to do?'

They watched him disappear. 'Nothing. There's nothing we can do to stop him.' Sarah's face was drawn and gaunt. 'Come on, we need to go home.'

'Go home?' Honour stared at her mother. 'No! We need to find him. I'm not leaving without him. We have to convince him to come.'

'He's gone,' Sarah said, walking away. 'Come on.'

Honour took one last look in the direction Ben had run. Then she turned towards her mother. 'I'm faster than him. I'm going to find him.'

She ran off in Ben's direction, to the sound of her mother's frantic voice behind her, calling her name.

*

It was dusk. Peter, Temp and Si were having their evening meal.

'Mum has messaged me to say all's well at the first camp,' Si said.

'That's great,' Peter said.

'And she says she's heard from some of the other camps who've watched the medical instructions and are going ahead with the treatment as soon as possible.'

'Good,' Peter said.

Temp put his fork down and wiped his mouth on a serviette. 'We're ready to go.'

'Excellent. The car is being delivered for you, in half an hour. I believe the first broadcasts have gone down well today.'

'I saw it on the News,' Si said. 'Some positive reactions.'

'No response from the Rulers yet,' Temp said. 'They'll need to discuss a strategy. Won't take them long though.'

'All the more reason for you to be gone soon. You should have been gone before that broadcast went out really. You've packed the invisibility suits, haven't you?'

'Yes,' Si said.

'And the spare ones?'

'Yes. And I've memorized the address of the woman you suggested we stay with, close to The Citadel,' Si said.

'Good. Sounds like you've got everything then. Make the most of this food. You won't get anything as good as Harmony's roast chicken anywhere else.'

Just as they were finishing the meal, there was an alert from Peter's security cameras and a buzz on the intercom. Peter jumped up.

'Are you expecting anyone right now?' Temp asked.

'They're earlier than I expected. You two need to get to the safe place right now. I've done lots of security improvements since you were last here. Harmony,' Peter shouted, but she was already in the doorway. 'Sorry. Take them to the safe place please.'

'Follow me,' she said. 'Grab your things on the way.'

Peter ran his hands through his hair and went to check his security cameras, thinking on the way about how he was going to handle the law-keepers. He wondered how many there would be and if they'd sent anyone like the Commander to interrogate him. He was surprised by what he saw. A young boy and girl, with hoods pulled up over their faces. Was this some kind of criminal gang, creating a distraction, whilst others tried to break into his house? He relaxed. This was no threat.

He spoke into the intercom. 'Who are you and what do you want?'

The boy lowered his hood, looked directly into the camera. 'Hello Peter.'

Peter recognised him instantly. 'Oh great!' he said, closing his eyes.

'We've come to find Chas and Si,' Ben said.

Peter spoke into the intercom. 'Don't say anymore. Who's that with you?'

'She's a friend. She's okay, I promise.'

Peter sighed. 'Come in then.' The gates opened, and they hurried in.

'Everything's okay,' Peter shouted up the hallway to Harmony. ''False alarm. Bring Si and Temp to the lounge. They'll want to see who this is.'

Peter opened the door and ushered Ben and Honour into the lounge.

'Wow!' said Honour, looking around. 'This is a nice place. I mean really nice.'

'Hmmhm.' He turned to Ben. 'I have to admit to being slightly disturbed by you turning up here. I thought you were living in Northumberland with a family you knew.'

'I am. I mean I was. I'm trying to find Si and Chas. I saw the broadcast in Newcastle earlier today. I couldn't miss the chance to come and see if you knew anything.'

'You walked all the way from Newcastle?'

Ben shrugged. 'It's not that far. I'm used to walking. And we managed to hitch a lift part of the way.'

Peter raised his eyebrows and motioned for them to sit down. 'Under different circumstances I'd be pleased to see you again, Ben. But, it's dangerous for everyone; you coming here. For instance – were you followed? Does anyone else know you're here? Why have you brought this young lady with you?'

'I don't think we were followed and only Sarah, Honour's mum, knows I've come to find Si, but she doesn't know where. This is Honour, by the way – my sort-of-sister. She wasn't supposed to come,' he glared at her, 'but she followed me and wouldn't go back, so I had to bring her.'

'I'll make sure you both get back to your family,' Peter said. 'But it will have to be in the morning.'

'I'm not going back,' Ben protested, 'until I find Si.'

'And I'm not going back if he's not,' said Honour.

Peter sighed and rolled his eyes. 'Okay. I see what I'm up against. We at least need to let your mother know you're safe for now. She'll be frantic. Do you have a phone?'

'Yes.'

'Good. Okay, call her.'

Honour frowned. 'She's been ringing me forever, but I'm not picking up. I don't want to talk to her.'

'You have to. Think how she must be feeling,' Peter said.

Honour pursed her lips, 'I know. I will speak to her, just not yet.'

Ben was impatient for news. 'Do you know anything about Si and Chas? Have you had any contact with them?'

'I think this may answer your question,' Peter said, not able to suppress an upward twitch of the lips. Ben and Honour had their backs to the door and, as Peter was talking, it began to open. Ben turned to see Si walking through the door. They looked at each other in shock.

Si spoke first. 'Ben! What? How?' He looked at Peter for an explanation. Peter just shook his head.

Ben stood up. He'd grown much taller since Si had last seen him and they were almost the same height. 'Wow! Hi. I...' Si ran out of words and moved to hug him, but Ben pushed him away, then, without warning, punched him in the stomach with such force, it sent Si tumbling backwards into Temp, then landing on the floor, gasping for breath.

'That's for leaving me!'

Ben's face was full of anger and hurt. His fists were clenched by his side. Temp stepped forward to stop another blow. 'Hang on there, buddy. No need for that!'

Ben wasn't intimidated. 'He left me behind. I had to do that. But I'm not planning another.' He held out his hand to Si, to pull him off the floor. Si took it and stood, bent over, clutching his abdomen, unsure of what to do next. Everyone looked expectantly from one to the other.

Si looked up and grinned. 'Good punch!'

There was a moment's pause, then suddenly, Ben flung his arms around Si.

'I'm so sorry,' Si said, hugging him back.

'You've got a good six-inch jab,' Temp said, offering his hand. 'I'm Temp. I've heard all about you.'

'And I've heard about you,' said Ben, shaking Temp's hand.

They all sat down. 'This is Honour. She's my sort-of-sister.'

'Hi,' said Honour. 'I'm with Ben, and where he goes, I'm going.' She had a protective air about her and Si couldn't help liking her instantly.

'Okay,' Temp said. 'And where might that be?'

'Back home,' Peter said. 'First thing tomorrow. You've seen Si now. You know he's okay. So you need to go home.'

'I'm not going back there. I want to help,' Ben said. 'I'm old enough and that holo-presentation said you needed people to stand up and make their voices heard against the Rulers. Well, I'm in this with Si and I'm not leaving.'

Peter nodded, in resignation. 'We'll see. At least Honour should return.'

'I'm not going,' she protested. 'Don't try to make me. If Ben can stay, so can I. Equal rights for women!'

'Feisty,' Temp said. 'This young lady has guts. That's what we need.'

She smiled at him in thanks.

'Don't encourage her,' Peter said. 'Think about if she were your daughter.'

'True,' Temp said. 'If she were my daughter, I'd still admire your spirit, but I'd put you somewhere safe and I wouldn't take no for an answer. It's not going to be safe with us.'

'We haven't come for safe,' Ben said. 'We have as much cause to hate the Rulers as anyone else. The plague destroyed my family, don't forget that.'

'It's the kind of passion we need,' said Temp, looking at Si.

'We have to leave very soon. We can't take you with us,' Si said to Ben.

Ben's face fell. 'Why not?'

'Because we haven't figured out what we're going to do yet,' said Si.

'We won't get in the way,' Honour said.

'With all due respect, mighty lady,' Temp said, 'you are very young. We can't go putting you in danger without a good reason, and we don't have one... yet.'

'Can we stay here?' Honour said, looking at Peter.

'Until tomorrow, yes. But if you don't ring your mother, I'm ringing her – tonight!'

'Where's Chas?' Ben looked towards the door, as if expecting her to appear as he spoke. 'Apparently, she tried to see me months ago, but I only just found out. Sarah sent her away.'

Si shifted uncomfortably in his chair. 'We don't know. She's gone her own way. Things have changed. She's not involved anymore.'

Ben looked confused. 'She just left?'

'She's on her own personal mission now.' Si looked at Temp, wondering how much to say. Then he decided to simply tell Ben what he knew. 'You know how badly she wanted revenge on her brother? Well she never got it. We went abroad but she came back to find him, before I returned with my mum.'

'Don't you have her number?'

'She didn't let me have it. She wanted to cut herself off.'

Ben shook his head.

Peter's phone bleeped. 'The car's here.'

Si stood up. 'We've got to go,' He looked at Ben. 'Give me your number.'

Temp and Peter moved to the door.

Ben held onto Si's arm. 'Please let me come Si. I can do stuff. Look how valuable I was when you needed to get into the Priory. And, as you can see, I can fight. I've been learning to box and do Judo in Seahouses.'

Si shook his head. 'What about Honour?'

She stood up. 'I do boxing and Judo too. I'm not scared of anything. I'd be useful.'

Temp looked at them both, then to Si and Peter. 'Normally I'd agree that they should go back home, Peter. But these aren't normal times. I wonder if we could use their help.'

'And her mum? What will we tell her?' Peter said.

'I'll call her,' Honour said. 'She'll worry, no matter what. But I'll tell her I'll message her every day.'

They were conscious of the car waiting. A quick decision was needed. 'I don't think it's a good idea. They're just kids,' Peter said.

'Please,' Ben pleaded. 'I'll only run away again and come to find you.'

Temp looked at Peter. 'Better that they're with us where we can keep an eye on them, than running around causing all sorts of trouble without us.'

Peter closed his eyes and shook his head.

Si made the decision. 'Come on then. Just get in the car. We'll figure it out when we get to the location.'

'Yes!' Honour and Ben gave each other a high five.

'You'll have to leave phones here. They're vulnerable and I haven't got time to secure them,' Peter said to Honour and Ben.

Honour shrugged and handed her wearable over. 'That's my Mum's number. You will call her, won't you?'

Peter nodded. 'Yes, when I've managed to encrypt the phone. You're probably getting me into a lot more trouble with your mum than Si has ever got me into!'

12

The garrulous young physio, who was helping Chas to do her exercises, was not much older than her. Her name was also Grace. She chatted to Chas about what she was doing after work and how much she loved the perks of living in The Citadel. After the first couple of days, she had given up asking Chas any questions about herself, apart from ones that related to her treatment. It was obvious that Chas was an important prisoner, because security followed them everywhere, but this seemed to make Grace feel more important that she had been entrusted with her care. She was itching to know what Chas had done, but Chas was giving nothing away.

Surprisingly, Resolution had not been to see her since she came round. At first, she had thought she was back in the Bastille. But it didn't take her long to deduce that she was somewhere else. She was in a room of her own and she could see guards through the window of her room, but this room was not a prison cell. She could move around with much more freedom than she had been allowed in the Bastille, even though she was accompanied everywhere. At the moment, she could only walk with a frame, or Grace's help. The bullet had been removed and for a while she was on intravenous pain-killers. This had now been reduced to strong oral ones. The physio girl had appeared almost as soon as she had been conscious. One of the few questions Chas had asked her was, 'Where am I?' The answer had not surprised her. She wondered why Resolution had left her alone for this length of time. It certainly wasn't out of compassion.

The physiotherapy was to strengthen the damaged thigh muscle. The exercises were painful, but Chas was glad of them. Here was one perk of the best hospital in the country. Thank you, brother! This would help her to regain her strength as soon as possible. She had to get out of here. She could not allow herself to be used against Si and she knew that it wouldn't be long before Resolution was here to do just that.

As if reading her thoughts, Grace said, 'You're making great progress. You're certainly determined.'

'Thanks,' Chas said.

'I've heard you're having an important visitor this afternoon.' The girl seemed excited.

'Oh?'

'Yes. The Premier himself is coming, with the Commander. You know, the one who was on the wanted list and has now been reinstated?' She raised her eyebrows at Chas, as if to say, I'm sure that's got something to do with you.

Chas said nothing.

Chas lay on her back as the girl stretched out her leg and bent it up to her chest. She chatted away. 'I hope I can sneak a look at the Premier. I've only seen him in holo-broadcasts. Hey, maybe I could hang around and pretend we're still doing physio.' She began to giggle.

'Be my guest,' Chas said, her eyes fixed on the ceiling.

'You must be a pretty special guest here.'

Fishing again Chas thought. 'Yep. I must be.'

Grace frowned. 'I'll see what I can find to make you look... smarter. I'll put a bit of my make up on you. And I know they have a supply of spare clothes here. You look about my size.'

Chas shrugged. 'Go for it. But maybe go easy on the make-up. I'm not really into that.' She liked the girl, despite her being about as different to herself as anyone could be.

'I'll be back in a jiggle. See if you can keep doing that movement.' She waltzed out, humming to herself.

So, Zephyr was on his way here. Why wasn't Resolution coming alone? She began to make plans. If she couldn't escape (which was still her first hope) she would have to convince them that she wanted to work for them. She didn't want to be the pathetic bait to draw Si in. She would have to convince them that she could be of much more use by helping them to infiltrate Si and his followers. A plan was forming in her head as Grace returned to the room with clothes. A long, cream, cotton dress and sandals. Chas never wore dresses. This wasn't practical. She should have thought to ask Grace to bring trousers.

'I don't really do dresses,' Chas said.

Grace looked slightly crest-fallen, then perked up. 'There's always a first time. And what better time to try it than a visit from the Premier. And besides, it'll be easier to cover your wound. Sit here. I'll do some make-up, then you can try it on. I think it'll suit you. I've found some straighteners too, so I can do your hair.'

Chas pulled a face, but didn't let Grace see it. 'Can you get me some trousers to change into after the Premier's been? I'd be more comfortable.'

Grace frowned. 'I'm not sure you would, with your leg, but I'll see what I can do.'

Chas shrugged and allowed Grace to do whatever she liked. The girl was enjoying herself and Chas couldn't have cared one way or the other. As Grace chatted on and on about the excitement of a visit from the Premier, Chas zoned out from her voice and continued to think about how to convince Zephyr that she wouldn't be much good as bait.

At 2.00pm there was a flurry of activity with the guards in the corridor. Grace was still in Chas's room, having made as many excuses as she could think of to stay. In the end, the guards had allowed it. The girl was security checked anyway and they liked her bubbly, flirtatious nature.

When two guards stepped into the room and stood either side of Chas, cuffing her to the bed, she knew Zephyr would be there any moment.

'Is that really necessary?' Grace asked, pointing to the cuffs. 'She's not going anywhere, is she?' She laughed, but the guards were in ultra-serious mode now.

'She's dangerous,' one said.

Grace looked at Chas. 'Really?' She was glad to have found out some juicy bit of gossip about her, at last, to tell her friends over a few drinks tonight.

Chas smiled and shrugged. At least her reputation was still intact.

An entourage of people came down the corridor and waited outside. Then Zephyr entered the room, flanked by two men she had never seen before. Her brother followed, and Chas noticed the smug look on his face. It was strange seeing the Premier in the flesh, when all she had ever seen of him was flickering holo-images. He was taller than she had realised, and his eyes were darker and more piercing than they came across on HTV. She could see that he was older than he appeared; probably in his late thirties, but still a good-looking man. They looked at each other for a few moments without speaking.

Chas decided that it would be appropriate to be flippant. 'I would get up and shake hands, but as you can see I'm not in a position to.'

Grace, who was standing unobtrusively in a corner of the room, stifled a gasp at how Chas spoke to the Premier.

The Premier smiled. 'You've led us on a wild goose chase these past eighteen months, Chastity. But now we finally meet. Let me introduce you to my two top officials. This is Ambition and Zealous. Not many people get to see any of the Rulers. You're honoured.'

'So I am,' she said. Grace stared wide-eyed at these important men. So much to tell her friends!

'And you've met Commander Resolution several times now. Although you keep giving him the slip. Luckily for him, you didn't manage to this time.'

Resolution nodded courteously at Zephyr, but Chas knew he would be inwardly fuming at the implied insult. This made her smile.

Zephyr looked around the room. 'I hope you are making

the most of the excellent treatment you are receiving in the best hospital in the country.'

Chas looked coldly at him. 'Nice to know such medical treatment exists somewhere.'

Zephyr ignore the sarcasm. 'Even though it's very nice to have you as our guest, you must know it's not really you we want.'

'I'm flattered to be a guest of the Premier,' Chas said, holding up the cuffs around her wrists. 'I know you want Si and Kate and everything they've worked for.'

Zephyr moved closer to Chas. 'You're right, of course. And you're going to help us bring them in.'

Grace gasped loudly enough to attract attention. Resolution turned to look at her.

'Why is this girl here?' he interrupted.

'She's the physio,' Chas said. 'She wanted to meet the Premier.'

Grace gave a short nervous giggle and stepped forward. 'I'm overwhelmed to meet you Sir,' she began. Zephyr frowned.

'Get her out of here. She shouldn't be hearing any of this,' Resolution said. Two more guards came into the room and man-handled a frightened-looking Grace outside.

Chas felt sorry for the girl, but she ploughed on with her planned speech. 'I'll help you, but not in the way you think.'

Zephyr raised his eyebrows. 'Oh?'

'I already told the Commander that I cut all ties with Si. Si and Kate abandoned me when they came back to England. We fell out. I didn't want to be involved in what they were doing. I had other plans.' She looked at her brother. He glowered back. 'What they're doing is futile. They're on the losing side and I've had enough of that. I could infiltrate them easily and lure them into a trap. I know you want to use me as bait to draw Si in, but this would be more effective than your plan. You couldn't guarantee they'd take the bait. Si is a lot more focused than you think. And I hurt him, big time. He's angry with me.'

Ambition stepped forward. 'And why would you do that?'

'I just told you, I'm sick of being one of the losers. But I'd want a reward if I get them here.'

Zealous grabbed hold of Chas and stuck his face in hers. 'We don't give rewards to scum.'

She felt like spitting in his face but decided that wouldn't help her cause. Instead, she turned her head away from his rank breath.

'Put her down,' Zephyr commanded. 'She will do what I decide is fit for our purpose.'

'Don't trust her, sir. She'll double-cross you. She only cares about one person, and that's herself,' Resolution said.

Chas glared at him. 'That's right, Commander. And that's why I'm willing to change my allegiance. For me.'

Resolution shook his head. 'She's a liar!'

Zephyr waved a hand at Resolution. 'Back in your cage, Commander. Like I said, I will decide how she will help us.' He turned to Chas. 'The Commander is going to take you to his office tomorrow and you will tell him everything you know about the Hunters, the Nanomedibots and their plan to eradicate the plague.'

Chas shrugged. 'That'll be short then, because I know very little.'

Zephyr took her chin in his hand, almost as if he were going to kiss her. She held his gaze for a few seconds. Then he squeezed hard, making her wince. 'The Commander will squeeze every ounce of information from you, I'm sure.'

He let go of her and led the way out of the room, followed by the other Rulers. Resolution lingered and came close. 'You won't let me down, sister,' he whispered. 'You know what I'm capable of.' He laughed and followed the others.

Chas kicked her good leg out and made a frustrated noise. When she had been uncuffed, she would have been glad of Grace's presence to distract her by talking about trivia. Despite her tough exterior, she felt sick at the prospect of being interrogated by Resolution. She remembered what had happened to Aaron last year and what they'd done to Kate and her husband. And she still didn't know if Zephyr would explore her suggestion and send her to find Si and Kate. Had she been convincing enough? She would have to give Resolution as much information as she could, without jeopardizing their mission. It was true, she didn't know much that could harm them. She certainly didn't know their whereabouts. Now, all she could do was wait until the next day. She turned over and tried to sleep.

Resolution didn't come for her in person. Part way through the next morning, two guards escorted her to a waiting van. She still wasn't fit enough to walk very far, so they bundled her into a wheelchair. The Commander was waiting for her in his 'office.' As expected, this wasn't really an office. It had a large chair in the middle, somewhat like a Victorian dentist's chair, which Chas was strapped into. Next to it were several instruments that Chas didn't think were for painlessly extracting teeth.

'I don't need an audience,' Resolution said to the guards, sending them out of the room. Chas tried not to show how sick she felt. She had eaten nothing that morning in preparation for what might be coming. Resolution smiled at her. 'Answer my questions, fully and correctly, and this won't hurt too much.'

'I bet you've been longing for this moment, haven't you?' she said, glaring defiantly at him. 'Wishing you could get your hands on me and treat me like you treated the rest of our family.'

'People only get what they deserve, Chastity.'

One day, you'll get one hundred percent of what you deserve, she thought.

He sat on a stool in front of her, his eyes level with hers. 'Let's cut to the chase. First question: What are the Hunters' intentions?'

'You already know that. They have the Nanomedibots and they're going to try and cure the plague.'

Resolution nodded. 'Second question: Where have they been so far?'

Chas didn't fully know the answer to this but knew that an answer of 'I don't know' would only incite Resolution to do something nasty to her. 'They were going to the plague camps in the North, but I don't know for sure. Like I said, we fell out.'

This confirmed what Resolution already knew. They had

raided the camp west of Newcastle and had Doctor Sharma in custody. The man was not used to torture and had been very helpful with only a little persuasion.

'Next question: Where are they now?'

What was she to say to this? The honest answer was that she hadn't a clue. If she made something up he would check it out and it would all pile back on her. They'd never trust her. She just had to tell the truth and take the consequences. 'I really don't know. I've not been in contact with them at all for months.'

'I don't know is not the right answer,' Resolution said.

'I'm sure you've checked my phone. You'll know I don't even have their numbers.'

Resolution knew this was true, because all the data had been downloaded from Chas's phone and been analysed. 'You must know something.'

'How can I? I've told you, I've not got any means of contacting them.' She watched him, as he fingered the implements beside him, like a boy trying to choose which favourite sweet to eat next. Her pulse rate quickened. She squirmed in the chair. 'You can't extract something from me that I don't know, no matter how much you hurt me. I told you I will help.'

The perverse thing was that Resolution could possibly believe that; she was after all, his sister, with the same self-serving genes, but he wasn't going to give up yet. He enjoyed an interrogation. 'If you want to be helpful, tell me what else you know.'

Chas tried to think of what to say, that would seem helpful, but wasn't. Then she hit on an idea to throw Resolution off the scent for a while. 'That boy I was with in Durham – Mish. I told him about Si. I told him what they were doing, and he wanted to help. I told him I didn't want anything to do with it, but he did. He went off a few times, by himself, on long journeys and when he came back he was secretive. I bet he knows what their plans are.'

Traitor! It was Si's voice in her head.

Betrayer! Mish's voice was there too.

She closed her eyes and saw them both looking accusingly at her. She opened them quickly. She'd rather look at Resolution and his torture chamber, than at their angry faces.

'Where is this commune?'

She felt sick. She did not want him massacring another group of people, like he had done at her previous commune. She was not doing very well here. This was not how she'd intended it to go. 'In Northumberland. I'm not sure where. It doesn't exactly have navigation coordinates.' She tried to back track a little. 'And I'm only vaguely convinced that he knows anything.'

'I might check him out. Next question: What of this uprising?'

What uprising? Chas knew nothing of this. 'I've not seen anything about it.'

'It has your finger-prints all over it. Silence and his mother made a propaganda broadcast against the Rulers. People are protesting in the streets. Some are swearing allegiance to Hunter.'

This was news to Chas. Good news.

Resolution pressed on with the questions. 'What are they

planning? And how many are there?'

'Let me find them, pretend to join them and I'll find out. Though it sticks in my gut to help you, if this is good for me, I'll do it.'

'You're not going anywhere,' Resolution picked up a tool with a small hook on the end, then a scalpel. She shivered involuntarily. He replaced those and took a hammer-like implement from his tray. He wouldn't cut her and risk any blood.

Chas began to writhe. 'What are you doing? I've told you all I know. And I've offered to help you. I know where they might be.'

Resolution replaced the hammer and placed his hands around her neck. He began to squeeze. Chas began to choke. She managed to splutter, 'Let me take you to them.'

He kept tightening. 'Where are they, sister?'

She could no longer speak. She couldn't breathe, and black spots were beginning to swim in front of her eyes. This is it, she thought. He's going to kill me. He's actually not bothered about my answers. He just wants to kill me before I kill him.

Suddenly, he let go. Self-control, Commander! he said to himself. He sat back down. 'Where are they?'

She was confused. This wasn't how she'd envisaged things. She wasn't sure what to do for the best anymore.

Resolution picked up another of his tools. 'This is your last chance. You say you have no loyalty to Hunter anymore, and yet you hesitate.'

Forgive me Si. 'I hesitate because I really don't know. I'm telling the truth. But I have an idea. They could be using

Peter Marsden's house. Let me go there. I can get on the inside and get information for the Rulers.' She figured that Peter would have something to do with the propaganda and if so, the law-keepers would most likely already be on to him.

Resolution looked contemptuously at her. 'I always thought you'd be a good liar. But you're terrible. You are staying right here. But law-keepers have been dispatched to Marsden's. And, I will find the commune you mentioned.'

Chas closed her eyes. Please God, if you exist, not another slaughter.

Resolution seemed satisfied that she had told him everything. He was disappointed not to use any of his toys on her, but he knew Zephyr would not be pleased if he did too much damage yet. He drew back his hand and slapped her hard across the face. She blinked away the pain and spat at him, missing her target. He grabbed her by the hair and pulled back her head, forcing her face to turn away from his. 'Get well soon, sister,' he whispered in her ear. 'You are going to be on HTV.' Then he sent for the guards to take her back to the hospital.

Back in her room, Chas was distraught. Her tactics for escaping and joining Si had back-fired. She had potentially jeopardized the Hunters' plans and implicated Peter Marsden. Not only that, but she had put more people in danger, especially Mish and the village. Right now, she hated herself and wished Resolution had actually killed her. Tears ran down her face and instead of trying to fight them as she normally would, she let them turn into wracking sobs.

13

Si, Temp, Ben and Honour arrived at the safe house, about five miles from The Citadel, late at night. Esme Shultz was the owner of the house; another member of The Way and friend of Peter's. Peter had told them to leave their car hidden, away from the house. There needed to be as little evidence as possible of people coming and going. Even though she had no neighbours, it didn't do to attract attention by doing anything out of the ordinary.

Esme lived alone, in a large stone-built house. It didn't have the hi-tech security that Peter's had, but Esme had her own ways of keeping out intruders. As they opened the gate marked 'Beware of the dogs' they became aware of the first security measure. Because Esme was expecting them, she had her two mastiffs securely locked in the kitchen, but their warning barks and growls were a decent deterrent. Honour cowered behind Ben, but he coaxed her to the door, reassuring her that the dogs would be locked up.

Esme was in her sixties and didn't look much of a threat to anyone, until she opened her mouth. 'What in God's name was Peter thinking, letting you bring children with you?' were her first words on opening the door.

'We're not children,' Honour said, regaining her courage.

'We're both twelve and we're going to help bring down the Rulers.'

Esme's mouth turned up at the corners, just a little. 'Well, if that's the case, you're welcome in this house. But keep your voice down and come inside.' Having swept them indoors, she added, 'I hope you have a good plan young lady.'

I don't, but they have.' She pointed to Temp and Si. 'We're just going to do whatever they need us to do, aren't we, Ben?'

He nodded. 'I was with Si when he was trying to find his mum. I helped him get the boat to break into the Priory.'

Esme nodded, impressed. 'All of us, in The Way, know about Si's adventures last year. News filters fast through our network. I didn't realise you were *the* Ben. My apologies, young hero.' Esme gave a flourishing bow. Ben wasn't sure whether she was making fun of him. He blushed, the others laughed, and the ice was broken. Esme showed them to the rooms. Si and Ben were sharing.

Ben began to unpack the few things Peter had given him. 'This brings back memories.'

'It does,' said Si. 'I never envisaged this, I must admit.'

Ben lay down on his bed. 'You will let us help, won't you?'

'Of course. I know there'll be something you can do. I'm just worried about Honour. I don't want to put her in danger and I feel bad for her mum.'

On cue, she came into the room.

'Hey, you should knock! We might be getting changed,' Ben said.

She shrugged. 'I want to do as much as Ben. And don't worry about Mum. When this is all over I'll make it up to her.'

Si shook his head. 'Your mum and dad were good to us. We need to get you back to them in one piece. Come on, let's go and talk to Esme and Temp.'

They found them in the kitchen, where Esme was preparing some supper and Temp was stroking the two fearsome looking dogs.

'Wow!' Ben leapt over to stroke them, but Honour held back. Si remembered how Ben had fallen in love with Aaron's dog, Elvis, and how badly that had ended.

'Meet Kurt and Brigitta. My late husband's family were Austrian, and these are the names of his grandparents.' Esme chuckled. 'They're just like them in character too. Kurt is more placid and Brigitta is stubborn as a mule at times. If I didn't know better, I'd think the old pair had been re-incarnated!'

Honour stood close to Si. 'They look scary.'

Esme smiled. 'That's good. They're meant to. And they can be when I need them to be. But they are very, *very* obedient. Not like the original Kurt and Brigitta! They'll only do what I tell them to. So don't be frightened of them, unless you're going to attack me.'

Honour smiled, nervously.

'Come and stroke them,' Ben said, already rubbing his face in their fur and hugging them like long lost friends.

Temp encouraged her. 'Here, stand next to me.'

Tentatively, Honour approached the dogs. One was now lying on its back while Ben rubbed its stomach and the other nuzzled in to Temp's legs, as he scratched it behind the ears. Honour stretched out her hand and copied what Temp was doing. 'Not used to dogs, eh?'

She shook her head but kept on rubbing Brigitta behind the ears. The dog pushed her head up against Honour's hand.

'She likes you,' Ben said.

After breakfast they discussed a plan to break in to The Citadel, to try and find out more about the cloning and how the Rulers intended to use it.

'What about the plague?' Ben asked. 'I thought you wanted to find out how to stop it.'

'We do,' Temp said. 'But it's all tied in together. The immortality of the select few and the enforced mortality of the unimportant.'

'Si's face is all over HTV,' Esme said. 'I don't know how you're managing it, but your call to revolution is being broadcast every hour. It's countered by the Rulers' own broadcast, of course, damning you and all those who follow you. They say you're spreading lies and they're showing footage of all they have done, in setting up the plague camps and 'caring for the dying', as they put it. They're pretending to be glad of the cure, but condemning the call to rebel.'

'We know they're liars and so does most of the population,' Si said. 'Mum called me and told me that people are protesting on the street. Many are refusing to go into the workhouses and some people have raided a workhouse in Halifax and set the inhabitants free. People are becoming bolder.'

'I heard about that,' said Esme. 'But I also heard on the

news that, as of today, the Rulers are cracking down. Law-keepers have been given the go-ahead to make examples of the rebels. This afternoon, they're broadcasting live hangings in several cities where rebels have been burning effigies of Premier Zephyr and where people have attacked government buildings.'

Si stood up. 'What can we do? We can't let them do that.'

'It was always going to happen,' Temp said. 'There's nothing we can do for them now. We have to keep to the plan.'

Esme looked uneasily at Si. 'Actually, they're saying that if Si and Kate turn themselves in, the hangings won't go ahead.'

Si cursed and paced the room.

'You can't do it, Si,' Ben said.

Temp laid a hand on Si's shoulder. 'He's right. You have to look to the bigger picture.'

'Well at least we should stop broadcasting our message for the time being. We can't be responsible for loads more deaths.'

'It won't make much difference whether you stop the broadcasts now or not,' Esme said. 'So many people have seen them. I think you should make another. A fresh one. Show compassion but also strength. Let them know you won't give in to their threats. The people need to know you're strong.'

'They're more likely to say I'm a heartless little upstart and how could I possibly think I could defeat the Rulers?'

Temp took him by the shoulders and made Si face

him. 'Some will think like that, but most will be glad that someone has made a stand. You need to inspire them. Call these victims martyrs.'

Si looked at Esme. She nodded. Ben said, 'I think it's a good idea.'

'Me too,' Honour said.

'Okay. I'll talk to Peter about it, today. Meanwhile, we need to find a way into the city.'

'I'm waiting on communication from Peter,' Esme said. 'He's made contact with your old friend, Capability. We're trying to arrange a place for you to meet him in the next few days.'

'He's still there then?' Temp said. 'I'm relieved. I had a horrible feeling he might be dead. Although, I'm not sure why he would still be involved with the Rulers. He hated them as much as I did in the end.'

'Can we trust him?' Si asked. 'Why would he still be there if he hated them? Wouldn't he have got out, like you?'

'Peter is meeting him. He's going to try and get an idea of exactly that,' Esme said. 'We've not really come across him before. He clearly keeps himself to himself. So, he might not want to get involved, even if he is sympathetic.'

'Is Peter going to tell him about me?' Temp asked.

'I think that's the plan.'

'That should be a good test of where his loyalties lie,' Temp said.

Ben looked up from the dogs. 'So, we just have to wait?'

Esme stood up. 'Yep. I suggest you all get some rest and let me feed you up.'

'Do you think they'll go ahead with the hangings?' Si

asked.

'Yes,' Temp said. 'They want to squash the rebels.'

Si was still pacing the room. 'Let's work on that new message this afternoon. I can't just sit around doing nothing, while people are being strung up.'

'What can we do to help?' Honour asked.

Si thought for a moment. 'Someone needs to take the video and I could do with someone helping me to write the speech. Any good at English?'

'She gets straight A's at school in everything,' Ben said.

'Cool. You can help me then. Any good at persuasive writing?'

Honour beamed. 'I'm good at debates in English.'

'Okay. We'll make this the best speech you've ever written. Come on.' Si and Honour went back to Si's room to get started.

Ben stood up. 'Can I take Kurt and Brigitta out for a walk?'

Esme smiled. 'With me, yes. Come on.' She moved to get the dogs' leads, at which signal they leapt to their feet, tails wagging.

'How far to walk to The Citadel?' Temp asked.

'About six kilometres,' Esme said. 'Why?'

'I'm going to have a look and a think about how we're going to get in, using the invisibility suits.'

Esme clipped the leads onto the dogs' collars. 'I think you should keep away for now. If they see someone snooping around...'

'They won't see me. I'm going to test out one of the suits.'

When the others had gone out and Honour was engrossed in writing the speech, Si couldn't help himself: he had to see if the Rulers would really execute the rebels. He commanded the HTV to come on in the lounge and found a news channel. He had managed to avoid seeing any executions since he had been forced to watch them during his time in the workhouse and then the Bastille. The gruesome memories were etched in his brain. A reporter was at the scene of one of the hangings. She stood in the centre of Sheffield, surrounded by a mob of people. No one was making a sound. It was eerie. The crowds were subdued, everyone looking ahead. Then the cameras panned to the place they were looking. On a platform at the front, five bodies hung from a scaffold: four men and a woman. This was a live news cast. It was all over. Law-keepers stood at strategic points around the crowd, with tazers pointed towards the people.

Then a holo-image of Premier Zephyr was projected onto the platform, to speak. The reporter said, in hushed tones, 'This speech is being broadcast at every hanging this afternoon.'

'I am your Premier and this is a sad day for our country. A day that should never have happened. These people were incited to violence and extremism against our nation. We cannot let this go unchecked. For your safety, we must stop people who want to destabilize our society and undermine the values we have fought hard for. But these, you see before you, are mere pawns in a bigger game. The real ring -leaders are still out there. You know who they are.' The camera zoomed in on the face of the Premier, then images of Si and Kate appeared next to him, making Si jump at seeing himself on the platform. 'Silence Hunter, Kate Hunter. You have caused the deaths of these people. You incited them to violence, based on a lie. If you had turned yourselves in, these people need not have died. More will die if you continue to spread lies about the Rulers and the plague. Turn yourselves in now. We implore you.'

Then, as if it was staged, a few people around the crowd began to shout, 'Traitors! Traitors!' The lone voices seemed to multiply and before long the single chants had turned into one big unified chant. 'Traitors!'

'Off!' Si yelled at the HTV. The holo-images disappeared. He pounded the furniture and began to roar in frustration.

Honour came running in. 'What is it?'

Si shook his head and slumped down on the sofa, his head in his hands.

'What's happened?'

'They did it. They hung them. And they blame me.' He looked up as unwelcome tears streaked his face. He brushed them aside.

Honour sat down and put an arm round him, like she would have comforted her little sister. 'That's all the more reason to get this video made.'

Si stood up. 'We can't let them get away with this.'

'Get away with what?' Ben entered the room, closely followed by Esme.

'I just saw the hangings and everyone chanting for me and Mum to turn ourselves in. I have to speak to her.'

'Get that message made first,' Esme said. 'I daren't contact Peter while he's in The Citadel, but he said he would call me tonight. We can speak to him then about broadcasting your video. You have to counteract their message with one of your own. Strength and hope.'

'Come and read the speech, Si,' Honour said.

Si followed her to his room and sat on the bed to read what she had written. Her words were full of passion, sincerity, strength and hope. 'Wow! You are an amazing writer. I couldn't have put it this well. It's just what Esme was talking about.'

'I think we should maybe change some bits and put something in about your pain at seeing the hangings today. I've said you wished you could have stopped them, but more people will die if the Rulers are allowed to continue with their lies. We could put a bit in here, about how you felt when you saw the hangings. Maybe you should go and read it to the others. See what they think. You'll need to memorize it too.'

Temp wasn't back, but Esme and Ben were in the kitchen, having a drink. Ben was sitting on the floor with the dogs. Si read the speech out.

'That's brilliant,' Ben said. 'I told you she was a star.'

Honour smiled at him.

Esme nodded. 'Clever girl. You need to practise it now, Si. Put all your heart into it: pain and passion.'

'Tell us when you're ready and we'll record it,' Ben said.

Si went away to rehearse. His anger helped him to focus, and speak with conviction. As he was rehearsing, his phone rang, and Kate's face appeared on his screen. He answered, and a holo-image of his mum appeared in the room.

'Hi son. Did you see them?'

Si nodded. 'It's horrendous.'

'We're lying low for a while. We daren't go into any camps just now. The Rulers have posted guards on all of them. Nick is trying to work out a way for us to get the NMBs through without arousing suspicion.'

Si told her about the video.

'That's a great idea. We need to hit back. People don't know what to believe but we have to do everything we can to keep them with us. We've had some amazing support and I'm pretty sure who most people believe.'

'But what about that chanting today in Sheffield?'

Kate shrugged. 'Plants in the crowd. And fear. You'd probably shout for your own surrender if you had tazers pointed at you.'

Si nodded. 'True.'

'What's happening with getting into The Citadel?'

Si told her about Peter's meeting with Capability North and what Temp was doing.

'Okay. Keep me posted. I just wanted to make sure you're okay. Don't blame yourself for today. It's heart-breaking but this is not our fault. The Rulers are to blame. Remember that.'

Si smiled faintly. 'Thanks Mum, I'll try. I'll let you know when we're on the move.'

When Si appeared in the kitchen, an hour later, he felt as ready as he could, to give his speech. Ben was going to record it on Si's phone. They went back to the lounge, where Esme made him stand in front of a neutral wall that gave nothing away about his location. Honour stood to one side, with the speech in her hand, ready to prompt if needed.

His palms were clammy, so he wiped them on his jeans. Then, he cleared his throat, indicated to Ben, and began.

'Today the Rulers carried out another cruel and vicious attack on your liberty, and I am devastated by what has happened. My heart goes out to families of those who bravely gave their lives today. The Rulers did not take their lives. They gave their lives for something they believed in passionately: freedom from tyranny. These people were martyrs.

The Rulers are trying to blame me and my mother, but we are breaking through their lies and presenting you with the truth. The truth is, that they are deliberately killing off the poor and defenceless with this manufactured plague. We are stopping them with the cure. You are already seeing evidence of it, as people return, for the first time, from the plague camps. This cure comes at a price, though. Not one of our choosing, but one imposed by the Rulers.

Today the price has been the lives of those martyred in our city centres. Tomorrow it could be me. But I am willing to risk everything for this. Are you? We ask you not to be intimidated by this violence against innocent people. Let's stand together and break the power of this corrupt regime.

Stay strong.'

Ben stopped filming. They watched it back and did a few takes, but finally decided to go with the first one. 'It's the most passionate,' Ben said.

Si agreed. 'But this time, no effects, music, nothing. Just stark. Raw and real.'

'It just needs a bit of editing, then it's done.' Ben took Si's phone and went off to work on it, followed by Honour.

Si wandered back into the kitchen, where Esme had begun cooking a meal. 'Temp's been ages. I hope he's alright.'

She didn't look up from the ingredients she was chopping. 'He shouldn't have gone. He should've waited for Peter to get back to us.'

Si sat down at the table. 'When will that be?'

She shrugged. 'He just said tonight sometime. Let's hope this Capability person works out to be what you need him to be.'

Si watched her chopping the vegetables. She was the least revolutionary-looking person he could think of. 'Why do you do this, Esme?'

She turned around, knife in hand, and paused. 'Why wouldn't I? Most of my generation can remember a time before this lot took over. And most of us have pain to bear from the scars of the regime. This lot have set Zephyr up as god. We want freedom for your generation and the generations to come.'

Si asked, 'Do you know about the cloning? Did you know Zephyr is a clone?'

She shook her head. 'Not 'til Temp told me about it last night. It makes the whole thing even more sinister.'

The dogs, who were lying in their beds at the other end of the kitchen, began to growl. Esme and Si looked out of the windows. Brigitta rose to her feet and began to snarl at the door. Kurt followed.

Ben poked his head around the door. 'What's wrong?' Honour followed, staying a step behind him, uncertain of the snarling dogs.

'I'm not sure,' Esme said, clutching the knife she was using. 'I can't see anyone. Get upstairs, all of you. Kurt, Brigitta – to me.' The dogs came, obediently, one to each side.

Just then, the door opened by itself. The dogs crouched and began to bark. Si, Ben and Honour didn't move. Suddenly, a bodyless head appeared.

'Temp! You scared the pants off us!' Si said.

Esme sent to dogs back to their beds. 'Off!'

'Sorry,' Temp said, laughing. 'I couldn't resist trying it out on you.'

Esme frowned. 'You're lucky my dogs are so well behaved.'

'I only did it because I know they are,' Temp replied.

Honour came towards Temp. 'Those suits are so cool!' She stretched out a hand, expecting to be able to put it straight through the air underneath Temp's head. Instead she felt his chest. She proceeded to feel around him, as if she were searching him.

'I'm still here,' he said. 'This is just an illusion: a scientific cloaking device.'

'Can we wear them?' Ben said.

'You can try them on, yes. It's not too uncomfortable. The only problem is, you have to be almost naked underneath, to get into them, so excuse me while I go get some clothes on. Then I'll tell you about my visit to The Citadel.'

'Did you go inside?' Si asked.

'I did. Give me a few minutes.'

When Temp returned, food was ready, and they sat to

eat. Esme was clearly not impressed that Temp had been in The Citadel, even in the invisibility suit. The others had heard lots of rumours about the Rulers' city and wanted to know what it was really like in there.

'It's more hi-tech than other cities. Everything is brand new. Nothing from the past.'

'It was built specifically for them when they took power,' Esme added.

'But the fortress is based on Bamburgh Castle isn't it?' Honour said. 'We learnt about it at school.'

'Yes,' Temp replied. 'It's an impressive building: definitely fitting for a seat of power. It's actually built from Northumbrian Stone. The Rulers 3D copied the stone. It was constructed in an almost impossibly short timescale. I've been inside it many times in the past. Everything is high-tech and high security.'

Ben and Honour looked at Temp, imagining what The Fortress was like. Si had heard some of it before, when Temp had told them about his earlier life.

'What's the rest of the city like?' Ben asked.

'There are magnetised vehicles everywhere. No one walks anywhere. Everything is pristine and luxurious. Every need, want and whim met.'

'Do people live there?' asked Honour.

'Oh yes. But only those important to the Rulers and only those who are wealthy supporters of the regime. It's an exclusive club. But that's also why it's small for a city.'

'How can we get in?' Si asked.

'There are four gates to the city. All heavily guarded. I held on to the back of a delivery truck. Easy. These suits are brilliant. You really are invisible. You don't feel it at first, until you take some risks and realise that no one can see you.'

'The dogs knew you were there though, before you opened the door,' said Honour.

'Yes. Animals have much keener senses than us. We'll have to watch out for that.'

Esme bent to stroke Kurt, who had crept near to her after the meal. 'You can't fool a dog.'

'What else should we know about?' asked Si.

'There's a big medical facility and hospital.'

'Is that where the cloning takes place?' Si asked.

'Some of it,' Temp said. 'But the live clones are kept in The Fortress. There are underground tunnels between the hospital and The Fortress.'

At that moment, Esme's phone rang. It was Peter. An image of him, sitting in the back seat of a car, materialized just above her arm.

'Hi all. I've got good news. Capability North has agreed to meet Temp and Si outside The Citadel.'

'That's great,' Temp said.

'He suggested a place, but I said no. I think we need to be careful you're not walking into a trap. He seems genuine, but let's keep control. Esme, where do you suggest they meet? I'll call him tomorrow with the location.'

'There's an abandoned farmhouse, about a mile up the road, then turn left up a track. He'll have to walk, which will make it easier to escape if you need to get away.'

'I'm sure he's trustworthy,' Temp said, 'But I agree, we should be cautious.'

'Okay. Tomorrow at ten,' Peter said. 'How are the young stowaways?'

'We're fine,' Honour said, grinning and pulling Ben towards her.

'Your mother is spitting feathers!' Peter said. 'I think I'm more scared of her than the Rulers at this point in time.'

Honour laughed. 'She'll forgive me, when I get home. And you, of course.'

'Peter grimaced. 'Not so sure about that. She's really worried about you and threatening to do horrible things to me, if I don't make sure you're safe and return you to her asap.'

'Well, I'm not going back,' Honour said, pulling her most defiant face.

Si changed the subject, before it turned into an argument, pulling up his sleeve and began activating his phone. 'Peter, we have another video to broadcast as a response to the hangings today.'

'I saw some News footage on the HTV in the car. Awful. Send it to me. I'll upload it now. I'm on my way home. I'll call you tomorrow to see how the meeting went.'

'Thanks,' Temp said.

Si sent the video and Esme began clearing the table. 'So, you are another step closer to bringing down Zephyr and his followers.'

'A positive step,' said Temp, standing up to help her. 'If anyone can do anything for us, it's Capability. I still believe he's a good man.'

'But is he still a brave one?' Si said.

14

Chas was still berating herself for handling the whole situation badly, when Grace came to see her the next morning. The young physio stopped suddenly, as she came into the room, her hand to her mouth. 'What happened to you?'

The bruises on Chas's face were coming up purple and black where Resolution had hit her. She bruised easily.

'The Commander,' Chas said. 'He decided to give me VIP treatment.'

Grace moved forward and looked closer at Chas's face. 'Ow! Have they given you anything to put on them?'

'I'm okay.' Chas had been offered cold compresses and arnica for the bruising, but she had refused to use them. She didn't think Resolution would use her to make the HTV appeal to Si, with her face black and blue. He wouldn't want the population seeing that she had been treated badly.

'I can treat those,' Grace said, already on her way to find something. 'I can't believe they've left you looking like that. It's shocking.'

'Really, it's no big deal. It doesn't hurt, and I've had much worse,' Chas said. 'Shouldn't we just get on with the physio?'

Grace turned. 'Okay. If you're sure. How's the leg feeling?'

'It's a lot better. I can walk without holding on to anything now.'

Grace smiled. She clearly loved seeing people recover with her help.

'That's impressive. Come on then. Let's see.'

Chas pushed herself off the bed and hobbled across the room.

'That's good. Really good. You've been doing the exercises.'

Chas nodded. She wanted to build up her strength as quickly as possible, so she could think of a way out of here.

'Shall we go a bit further today?' Grace suggested.

This was good news to Chas. A bit further would give her some idea of how she might make it out of here. She could do with finding a weapon too. They walked slowly down the corridor, Chas deliberately making it look like she was still far too unfit to try anything. She actually felt that it wouldn't be too much longer before she could make a move to get out of here. Carefully, she made a mental note of each door, asking Grace where certain passages led. When they got back to the room, she asked questions about The Citadel, disguising them within questions about Grace's life outside the hospital. The girl was in her element, describing to Chas the places she liked to hang out with friends and some of the sights of the city.

'I'm so lucky to be able to live here. My parents are well respected citizens and they passed all the background checks, so I was lucky enough to get an interview for this job straight out of college. I get to meet all sorts of people through my job, famous *and* notorious.' She smiled playfully at Chas. 'But I've never met the Premier 'til I got involved with you. That's gone down in my journal.'

Chas smiled. 'And is this hospital near the centre of the city?'

'Yes. Right next to The Fortress,' Grace said. 'It's a huge building. Much more than a hospital. Lots of top secret research goes on here. I don't know what it is, obviously. I've tried to find out, but it really is hush-hush. You have to have special clearance to go into the research wings.'

'Do you know much about the plague?' Chas asked. 'Do you ever get people with plague here?'

'No! No way! Plague doesn't touch anyone in this city. And that's another advantage of living here. No fear of plague. They're really careful about people coming in. Everyone is screened for any signs of it at the gate. Even if they come here regularly. Even you would have been screened.'

'Reassuring!' Chas said sarcastically. 'So, you don't know much about it then?'

'The plague? All I know is that it kills people outside the city and there's no hope if you get it. But I've been seeing all that stuff on the news recently about that boy, Silence Hunter. Do you remember him from a year or so ago? Everyone was on the look-out for him. And now he's reappeared with his mother, who's a scientist, and she claims to have a cure for the plague, using nano-technology.'

Chas didn't reply. She was wondering whether to tell

Grace anything about herself. After all, if Resolution had his way, Grace would know soon enough who she was. And Chas had chosen the name Grace as her false identity. Could this be a sign that Grace could be someone useful? But then, where would a sign come from? Si would say from God, maybe.

'Do you know who I am?'

Grace shrugged. 'They told me your name was Chastity and that you could be dangerous. Hence the guards. Nothing else. They don't think people like us need to know much.'

'My name is Chastity Komchenski. Does that ring any bells?'

Grace frowned. 'Not really. What kind of criminal are you? Are you famous? I've not liked to ask. You seem pretty nice to me. I can't see how you could be so dangerous.

Chas laughed. 'Oh, I'm dangerous when I want to be.'

A hint of fear passed across Grace's face, but her thirst for gossip got the better of her and she sat down on the bed. She glanced at the guards outside the window and whispered, 'Tell me more.'

'I'm Silence Hunter's girlfriend.'

Grace's face suddenly came alive with recognition. 'No! Really? It was you they were after? Wow! I remember now. They never got a picture of you though, did they? Oh wow! So that's why he's interrogating you. The Commander. You really are a big name. Are you in on this plague cure thing? I don't understand what the big deal is. I'd have thought The Rulers would welcome the cure.'

Chas nodded. 'If they wanted a cure, they would, right?

But they don't want it. They created the plague.'

Grace shook her head. Her eyes widened in shock. 'No!'

'You really have led a sheltered life,' Chas said. 'It's too much detail to go into the whole story, but it's true. Si's dad was killed because of what he and Kate developed, and she was in the Priory. We broke her out.'

'Wow! From the Priory? That's impossible, isn't it?'

'Pretty much. Now I've told you all this, you're going to have to decide what to do with it. You could ignore the implications and just think of yourself and how great this gossip is going to be in the bar tonight, or you could do something heroic yourself. You could help me get out of here.'

Grace looked horrified and Chas realised she might have just made another big mistake.

'I don't think I could get involved. It's too risky.' She stood up and moved away from the bed.

Chas laughed sarcastically. 'You're right. Too risky. You should just run off to your shallow little friends tonight and share your gossip.' She laid down and turned away from Grace.

'I'm helping you get better. I can't do anything else. You can't expect me... I hardly know you.'

'Just go,' Chas said. 'I think you're done here.'

Grace picked up her coat and left.

When she'd gone, Chas heaved herself up to a sitting position. She had called herself Si's girlfriend. She hadn't thought of herself as that since she left Amsterdam and she wondered if Si would even want to know her again. In some ways, she hoped not. At least then, when Resolution made his appeal for Si to come for her, he wouldn't care enough to risk everything. She hoped he wouldn't, and yet, she hoped he would. What would happen if she couldn't get out of here? She had to get out and she had to do it tonight, before Resolution had the chance to force her to make that video.

At night, the corridor was quiet, but her guard would still be there. She had to figure a way to get past him. She could do with a weapon too. Her knife and few possessions had been taken. She moved slowly around the room looking for something she could use, but there was nothing in this room. Perhaps she could squeeze toothpaste in his eyes, knee him in the balls and run. Well, hobble... She laughed at herself, but this was actually her best bet.

She would wait until late, when the place was the least busy, then she would attempt to get out, somehow. Even if it turned out to be futile, she had to try. But now, it was time to get some rest.

When the door to her room opened, she was in a deep sleep. A hand shook her, and she sat bolt upright, nearly knocking the person on the floor.

'Get up. I'm getting you out of here.' It was Grace.

Chas shook her head. 'Eh? What time is it?'

'It's only five thirty. I told them I had to come back for a second session today, because you were doing so well, and I'd been told to get you fit as soon as possible.'

Chas flinched. Perhaps Resolution had said something to Grace.

'I'm going to take you to the pool. I told them we need to do some aqua therapy. We can get you out from there. My boyfriend has a car waiting in the main car park.'

This time it was Chas's turn to be amazed. 'You're full of surprises!'

Grace smiled. 'Not so shallow, eh?'

'Clearly not,' Chas said, with a little upturn of the lips. 'The guard will follow us, won't he?'

Grace helped Chas to her feet. 'I'll try and shake him off. Are you sure you're ready for this?'

Chas took some steps away from Grace and glanced through the window at the guard. 'I've been trying to figure out the best way to squirt toothpaste in his eyes and run!'

Grace giggled. Then she saw Chas was serious. 'Oh my goodness, you have, haven't you? Looks like I came just in time. That would never have worked.'

Chas smiled. 'I think your plan is slightly better.'

Grace took Chas into the bathroom and produced some outdoor clothes from her bag. 'Put these on then put the towelling robe over them.'

'Where's the swimming costume?' Chas asked.

Grace looked confused. 'You're not actually going in the water.'

'I know, but it has to look like I escaped, not like you planned this. It should look like you intended to get me in the water.'

'Okay, I'll go get one.'

'And those clothes... get rid of them. Where would I have got them from?'

'You're going to run in a swimming costume?'

'I'll think of something.'

Grace returned ten minutes later with a swimming

costume. They made their way slowly from the room and, as Chas had predicted, the guard began to follow.

'It's a long way to the pool, so I've arranged a wheelchair.' Grace looked at the guard. 'Maybe you could push it?' Chas sat down in the chair.

The guard took the handles. 'Isn't it electronic?'

'I thought you should be in charge, that's all,' Grace said, smiling flirtatiously.

'Hmm.' He pushed the chair along several corridors, down three floors in the lift and along more corridors to the pool area. Chas realised she may never have found her way out.

As they approached the door for the pool area, Grace said to the guard, 'We'll be about an hour. Do you want to wait out here or come back for her?' She leaned in conspiratorially, whispering, 'I don't mind if you want a break for an hour. You know I'm used to her by now. She's not going to cause any trouble.'

The guard looked at Chas in the wheelchair. 'Okay. I'll be back in an hour.'

Grace smiled winningly at him.

Chas stood up and Grace helped her into the pool area. 'You're good at that.'

Grace grinned. 'Plenty of practice.'

The pool area was on the first floor. There were large windows to the outside along one wall. Chas noted the fire exit.

'Listen, I think for your own safety, you should let me make it look like I overpowered you and escaped.'

Grace looked uncertain.

'You love your job, right?'

Grace nodded.

'If they think you helped me, you'll never work again. You'll be an outlaw. If I knock you out, it will look like you're innocent.'

'Knock me out?' Grace looked horrified.

'I can do it so that it doesn't hurt. Promise. You won't come round for a while. I'll leave you where the guard will find you. You'll have some marks on your neck, so it looks authentic, but they'll fade.'

Chas could see she was scared. 'What about my boyfriend?'

'I don't know. Hopefully we can get away without anyone spotting us, so no one will know he was even here. And I'm going to need your clothes. That okay?'

Grace frowned anxiously for a moment, then shrugged. 'I've come this far. Okay. Let's get it over with. He's outside in the main car park. Go down the fire exit and turn right at the bottom. Follow the wall round and you'll come to the car park. The car registration is ZZ52 KUP. Red mini. Hi name's Aspiration, but he calls himself AP. It's getting dark. Hope you make it.'

Chas smiled at her. 'I won't forget this. Thank you. Now, give me your uniform and trousers.' Grace stripped down to her pants and T-shirt. Chas put the clothes on, then stood behind her. 'This won't hurt. Try not to tense up.'

She put pressure on Grace's carotid artery, cutting off the blood flow. Grace struggled a little at first, but Chas had a firm grip on her and talked gently to her until she became unconscious. Then she guided Grace's unconscious body to the floor and made for the exit. The door opened easily, and she was outside. At the bottom, she turned right, but as she peered around the corner of the building, she saw more guards at the entrance. The car park was in sight. There were lots of cars in it. She cursed under her breath. She needed to find Grace's boyfriend quickly. She began to walk calmly across the road to the cars, hoping she wouldn't be recognised.

'Stop!'

She looked behind her. The guard was running down the fire escape. She cursed again. There was no way she could find Grace's boyfriend now. She tried to run. Pain shot up her leg, but that wasn't going to stop her. She was outside, and she was not going back.

Other guards from the entrance had joined the pursuit. Chas reached the cars and began to weave in and out of them, trying to dodge her pursuers. Just then, a car up ahead turned on its lights and reversed backwards at great speed. It was a red mini. It sped away. She wanted to shout at him to stop, but she knew it would only endanger him and Grace. Cursing, she tried harder to run, but the pain in her leg was worse. There was a lot of shouting from her pursuers and some of the people in the car park were staring at her. She was not far from the car park entrance, but there was a barrier with a guard on it. He had seen what was happening and started in towards her. She dodged the other way, ducking down behind cars, but the place was swarming with guards now. Frantically, she looked around for a way out, but they were closing in on her. One of them grabbed at her shoulder. She lashed out, wishing she'd brought the darned toothpaste. He held on to her as she tried to turn and poke her fingers into his eye sockets or knee him in the balls, but he was too quick for her in her current state. Within a few seconds, three guards were on top of her and everything went black.

*

'Why, why, why?'

As she came round, back in the hospital bed, Resolution was sitting in the chair opposite her. Her heart sank.

'How did you think you were going to get out of the city? You've no idea how good the security is here. The guard who was supposed to be keeping you under close surveillance has been executed. I've doubled the security.'

Chas felt sick. She was desperate to know what had happened to Grace, but she daren't ask, for fear of arousing suspicions about her.

Resolution seemed to read her mind. 'The physio girl was distraught. You traumatised her. She thought we were going to execute her as well. She asked to be reassigned. There will be no more physio. I've waited long enough. Tomorrow we make the video to draw Silence Hunter here. As soon as I have him, his mother will come easily.'

She sat up. 'I won't do it. You can do what you like to me, I don't care anymore, but I won't help you capture Si.'

Resolution stood up and moved to the door. 'We'll see, sister.'

Chas lay down and closed her eyes, trying to blot out the whole thing. She wished she could just die now. Then she wouldn't have to think about any of this anymore.

Early the next morning, guards came for her. They took her to a room in The Fortress where Resolution was waiting. 'Good morning Chastity.'

She didn't even look at him. Her mind was made up to not speak one word. She would let him do whatever he wanted, to her, and hope that she could take it. His capacity for cruelty was large, she knew that. She hoped she wouldn't scream or beg. If she couldn't kill Resolution, maybe her only revenge would be silence, when he needed words. Then maybe her own death would have to suffice for his. A lingering doubt made her worry that he wouldn't let her die.

The guards cuffed her arms and ankles, to a chair in front of a camera and autocue. 'You can wait outside,' he ordered them. Then he turned to Chas. 'Ready to begin? This will be very easy. I have a script prepared. You just need to read it. A bit of feeling would be desirable, but if you can't muster any, it doesn't really matter. All we need is your sweet pleading face and the right words. Your devoted boy will do the rest. He won't be able to resist. He's too ... nice.' Resolution laughed and turned away from her, to an HTV on the wall. He spoke to someone on his wearable. 'Is everything ready?'

'Yes Commander,' The voice replied.

He turned back to Chas and looked at her for a few moments, without speaking. He shook his head, slowly. She watched him, keeping her features neutral and her eyes focused on the hard lines of his angular jaw. 'Let's begin, shall we? I assumed you wouldn't cooperate in order to spare your own life. I do have some admiration for you sister, I have to admit. But, you too have your weaknesses. We all do.' He looked away. Chas knew he was thinking about his fear of blood. 'Yours is that you care about people. You love. You've tried not to. But you always fall into the trap. Such a weakness. Far greater than mine.'

She felt her stomach lurch and tighten. Where was he going with this?

He saw her fear. 'You're wondering who I'm going to show you, aren't you?'

Chas tried to keep her face calm, but her heart pounded. Who could he have that was important to her. It wasn't Si, otherwise this was pointless. It couldn't be Kate either because, again, this would be pointless. She suddenly thought about Grace. Did he know that she had rigged the escape attempt? For a second, she closed her eyes. Please, no! This was not the moment for her innocent face to appear. Although the girl was a virtual stranger, Chas did not want her torture or death on her conscience.

Resolution waited for her to process this information. 'Now, you can make the video willingly, or I can use persuasion. Your friend is waiting in another room and I can give you a VIP seat via the HTV as we persuade you to cooperate.'

Chas didn't speak, but she wanted to scream, to explode, to self-destruct, so that she wouldn't have to face this.

Resolution lurched forward and dug his fingers into her jaw. 'Answer this question, or I will take your silence as a no. Will you make the video?'

An involuntary whimper escaped her lips. This was impossible. 'Who is it? I want to see them first. Will you let them go, if I cooperate?'

Resolution let go of her jaw. 'Yes. I will let them go. As soon as the video is complete. You have my word.'

Chas laughed. 'For what it's worth. I'll need to see them leave, unharmed.'

Resolution paused. 'No further damage will be done to them. I can't alter what's already done.'

'You've already hurt them?'

'I can't help it if someone resists arrest, can I?'

Chas winced as she pictured Grace's pretty features, bruised and beaten.'

'I hate you,' she screamed, losing her self-control. 'Let me see her!'

Resolution raised an eyebrow and smirked. 'Her? I'm interested in who you're talking about, but another time.' He turned and spoke to the screen. 'Visuals. Room 3.'

Suddenly a holo-image appeared in the room. Sitting in a chair, bound, gagged and badly beaten, was Mish.

Mish! She couldn't speak. How could he be here? Resolution was right. Her weakness was greater than his. She did care about Mish. He looked straight ahead, as if looking at her.

She tried not to let her voice waiver. 'Can he see me?'

'Yes,' Resolution said. 'And hear you. And when he starts to cry out, you will hear him too. He's tough, but not so tough as he'd like to be. He knows who you really are. We went to the commune and arrested him. He knows you led us there.'

The commune. No. Her thoughts raced back in time to Dis and the others. How Resolution's men had destroyed the place and killed everyone. 'What did you do to the commune?'

Resolution shrugged. 'Not important. His father tried to stop us, so he's dead, but apart from that no one else put up any resistance. We left them pretty much as we found them.'

Chas shouted obscenities at her brother, kicking and pulling against her manacles. 'Mish, I'm sorry. I'm sorry about your dad. I tried to save you by sending you away at the flat. I'm sorry I involved you at all.'

She recalled how she had told Resolution about the commune in an attempt to make him think she was changing sides. She threw her head back against the chair and tears rolled down her cheeks. She began to sob. She couldn't stop herself. 'I'm sorry, Mish. I'm sorry.'

She looked up again to see Mish struggling and shouting something, but there was no sound.

'Back to my question,' Resolution said. 'Will you make the video?'

She looked at Mish, who had stopped struggling, trying to discern what he must think of her. 'Yes,' she said, quietly, trying hard to get control of the sobbing. 'Yes. I'll do it.'

15

It was a horrible morning. The rain was lashing down. Visibility was poor. At 09.15 Temp and Si left Esme's house to meet Capability. They had seen the new video on the HTV this morning. Si hoped it would convince people not to return to subservience.

It felt like a long walk, in the rain and up a steep, muddy track. Esme had given them waterproofs, but they were soaked by the time the ruined building came in sight.

'Great! No roof!' Si said. 'I hope he still turns up.'

'He will. I know him.'

The walls of the small building were still intact but there was no upstairs, no windows or doors and no shelter. The place was just a shell. Weeds and grass grew tall inside the building. Si and Temp arrived earlier than the arranged time. No one was there. They checked around the building. There were two exits, which made Si feel safer in case of a quick getaway. He had taken a knife from Esme's kitchen, as Chas would have advised him not to go without some kind of weapon. They huddled down inside the walls, keeping a lookout from one of the empty window frames.

At ten o'clock precisely, a figure in a waterproof coat, trousers and walking boots approached. He appeared to be alone. Although they couldn't see his face, Temp recognised him. 'That's him.'

He made to stand up, but Si pulled him down. 'I think we should stay hidden 'til he reaches us. What if he's got marksmen positioned around here?'

'I trust him,' Temp said, standing up and moving to the doorway.

The man came up to the entrance, lifted his face and grinned, as water dripped off his nose. 'Lovely weather!'

Temp grinned back. Then grasped his old friend in a bear hug.

'It's so good to see you,' Capability said. 'I feared you were dead.'

'I nearly was on several occasions.' Temp drew him into the house. 'This is Si.'

Capability offered his hand. 'Good to meet you. I know a lot about you and your family.'

'Do you?' Si said. 'Thanks for coming.'

Temp looked his old friend over. He had lost weight and had more lines on his face, which made him appear a lot older than his years. 'What are you doing still living in The Citadel? I thought you'd have got out years ago.'

'I couldn't. Same reasons as you. I had to protect my family. I know too much.'

'So why are you willing to help us now?' Si asked, warily.

'My wife died two years ago in a car accident. My daughters are grown up now and I've managed to get them out of the country. They want me to join them, and we've been making plans for me to escape, but when I heard about you, I decided it's my time to stand up for what's right now.'

'Sorry to hear about Min,' Temp said.

'Yeah. Tough times.' He drew a hand over his dripping face.

'What about your son? Excellence, isn't it?'

Capability sighed. 'Sadly, he's very loyal to the Rulers. He has ambitions. He would like to be in the government one day.'

'How old is he now?' Temp asked.

'Eighteen. I don't see much of him. He moved out as soon as he could. He lives in student accommodation. He's studying to be a politician at The Citadel University.'

Temp moved further into the corner, to try and shelter more from the driving rain. 'Does he know about your plans to go abroad?'

'No. I have to keep so much from him to protect the girls. He doesn't know where they are, and he doesn't know that I know. For their safety, and mine, he has to think I'm still devoted to Zephyr.'

'That must be a difficult pretence to keep up,' Si said, trying to weigh up this stranger.

Capability shrugged. Water was streaming off his hood and into his face. He wiped it again. 'It is. But, how can I help you? What are your plans?'

Si looked at Temp. Capability had confided in them about his son, but he was still unfamiliar. Si wasn't sure if they should entrust everything to his knowledge, but he didn't have the chance to express his thoughts to Temp. Temp clearly had no qualms about trusting him. He told

Capability about how they wanted to get to Zephyr and expose the lies told by the Rulers. How they intended to expose the truth about the plague and the quest for immortality.

There was no going back now, so Si added, 'We want to depose the Rulers.'

Capability shook his head. 'Tall order.'

Si shrugged. 'Can you get us into the place where they do the cloning, and can you get us close to Zephyr?'

'I'm not sure how...'

'We have invisibility technology,' Temp said.

Capability nodded his head. 'Impressive. Yes. I can get you into those places. But what are you going to do against all the security, when there's only two of you?'

'If we can get to Zephyr, we could take him hostage and show the people evidence of what's really happening,' Si said. 'My mum says people are ready to follow us. The Way already have a network of people waiting for instructions on what to do next.'

Capability smiled. 'You make it sound simple. Let me get you into the Genetic Research Centre first. It's part of the hospital complex. You need to see what's going on. This is not just cloning, this is genetically modifying human DNA. The implications are enormous. They keep the embryos there, as well as all the clones. There are two successful clones of Zephyr alive at the moment. One is about your age, Si, and the other is a child. The Zephyr clone has been manufactured from a concoction of DNA, carefully extracted and combined from despots of the past.'

'What? You mean like Hitler and Kim il Sung and people

like that?'

Temp nodded.

'That's hideous.' Si said. 'How did they get the DNA from those dictators?'

'I'm not sure. They lead us to believe that Britain is isolated from the rest of the world, pretty much, these days, but they trade with people all over the world when they want something. They have connections with several dubious characters in other governments.'

'Is there a clone of you?' Si asked.

Capability shook his head. 'No thanks. I said I wasn't ready to be reproduced in this way.'

The incessant rain was beginning to get to them all. Si pulled his hood forward and tried to wipe the rain vigorously from his face. 'So, do all the other Rulers have clones?'

'Most have by now, but they're only children, at the moment. There've been problems. A number of the first clones were mutants, with hideous deformities. These were killed at birth. The only one to make it through was the Zephyr who is your age.'

'Wow! This is huge,' Si said.

'Yep. Potentially, this regime could go on forever with the same people in charge, over and over again.' Capability looked at his wearable. 'This weather is awful, and I need to get back before I'm missed. Let's make arrangements to get you in.'

'We can get ourselves in. It's easy with the invisibility suits,' said Temp. 'You just need to guide us to the right places.'

'Tomorrow then. Meet me at the back entrance of the

hospital. Red zone. I'll be in my car, a grey Merc, looking at documents. Same time? 10am?'

'Okay,' Temp said.

'How will I know you're there, if I can't see you?'

Temp thought for a moment. 'I'll tweak the wipers on your car. You still have those, I presume?'

Capability laughed. 'Yes. I like to drive my own car, and I like wipers. I'm old-fashioned. I don't think many of us really liked the driverless car idea. See you then.'

'Si shook his head and grinned. 'Nope. You won't see us, but we'll see you.'

'Of course.' Capability laughed again, shaking hands with Si and hugging Temp. 'So good to have you back, my friend. So good.'

'Likewise,' Temp said.

They watched him trudge away across the sodden grey landscape. 'We've laid our cards on the table now,' Si said.

Temp nodded. 'Yep. Can you trust him?'

Si shrugged. 'You obviously do. So, I guess I do. We have no choice now anyway.'

When they arrived back at Esme's house, the first thing she made them do was strip most of their dripping clothes off, on the doorstep. Then it was hot showers for both of them. Ben and Honour were keen to find out what had happened. Esme sat them all down, with cups of hot chocolate, coffee, sandwiches and freshly made cookies. Si and Temp related all that Capability had said.

'When can we come with you to The Citadel?' Honour asked.

'You won't be going at all if I get my way,' Esme said.

Honour scowled at her.

'We have to wait and see what we find out tomorrow,' Si said. 'There's no point in risking anything we don't need to risk.'

'When do you think Peter will call?' Si asked Esme.

She looked at her phone. 'Soon, I'd imagine. He'll be keen to know what the outcome of your meeting was.'

'What's happening on TV? Are the broadcasts still getting through? Any news on reactions from the people and the Rulers?'

Esme nodded, refilling her coffee. 'The video is still going out. Every hour. The Rulers have put out their own contrary message, but they haven't found a way to stop yours. They're saying you're a liar and a dangerous criminal. And they're now showing interviews with plague victims, at death's door, claiming they took the cure and it made them worse. They've also got people saying they've been injected with the plague by your mother!'

Si banged the table with his mug. 'What?'

Honour put her hand over Si's arm. 'Don't worry Si. Only idiots will believe them.'

'It's confusing people, though,' Ben said, taking another cookie.

'The sooner we can get evidence of the cloning and the plague manufacture, the better,' Temp said. 'We could do with Kate and Nick here. They're the ones who know all the science.'

Si looked at Esme. 'Maybe we should get them here. Can we do that?'

She shook her head. 'It might not be wise to have you all

in one place.'

'Good point,' Si said. 'Maybe Peter will have an idea of where they could stay and be in reach of The Citadel.'

'When he calls, we can ask him,' Esme said. 'Not much to be done 'til then. I suggest you all go twiddle your thumbs for a while. I've got some cooking to do, unless anyone wants to help?'

Ben leapt over to the two mastiffs, who began licking him as he stroked them. 'Can I take the dogs out?'

Esme smiled. 'You're good with them. They like you. But it's pouring still. Wait 'til later. It's no fun trying to dry them off when they get sopping wet.'

'I like cooking,' Honour said. 'I'll help you, if you like.' She and Esme began to chat over the ingredients.

Si and Temp went into the lounge to talk.

'We need to take photos and video evidence tomorrow. Can we do that with the suits on?' Si asked.

'It won't be easy. We'll have to expose the wearable. It's a risk we'll have to take though.'

Si switched on the HTV. 'Let's see what's going on out there.'

He found a news channel and they watched as reporters gave various accounts of reactions to the contrasting broadcasts by Si and the Rulers. There was still unrest on the streets, but most people, as predicted, were confused. The Rulers were promising to come down hard on those who 'breached the peace' as they put it. On the hour, Si's video broke through the normal broadcast.

Kate phoned. She wanted to know about the meeting with Capability. Si told her what he'd said and that it might be a good idea for her and Nick to come soon and get into the Genetics Research Centre themselves.

'Be careful Si. I know the invisibility suits are good, but you're still vulnerable.'

'We will, Mum. I'll talk to you again tomorrow, after we've been in there.'

Just then, Ben came running onto the lounge. 'Si. Come quickly. Harmony is on the phone.'

Si and Temp went back to the kitchen, where Esme was projecting a holo-image of Harmony from her phone. She was crying. 'They came for Peter. He made me hide, but they ransacked the house and took him away.'

Si slumped down on a chair. Temp closed his eyes. 'Do you know where they took him?' Esme asked.

'No. I only just ventured back into the house and he's gone. That's all I know.'

'What can we do?' Si asked.

Harmony sniffed. 'I don't know. I'll contact Eric. He's going to be furious.'

'Let us know what happens,' Esme said. 'Be careful, Harmony.'

Harmony nodded and disappeared.

'Are we in danger here?' Si asked.

'It depends what they are prepared to do to him. He's an important guy. He's tough though,' Esme said.

Si stood up. 'He's not invincible. They can be persuasive.'

'They won't care about his status, if they think he has information,' Temp said.

'How many invisibility suits do you have?' Esme asked.

'Four,' Temp said.

She stood up and paced the kitchen. The dogs pricked up their ears and became alert, sensing her tension. 'I think you should all go into The Citadel tonight. Only because the children might actually be safer there, for the time being. No one will think to look for you there and you'll have those suits on. Just until we can be sure if Peter has talked or not.'

'What about you and the dogs?' Ben asked.

'I'm okay. We can leave here for a while. We've got somewhere else to go.'

Temp looked at Honour and Ben; clearly in a dilemma. 'Okay. If that's our only option, we'll have to do it. I'll show you all how to put on the suits.'

Honour jumped up. 'Yes!'

Everyone gave her stern looks, so she soon sat down again, sheepishly.

'It's not a game, Honour,' Ben said.

'I know. I'm sorry. I just want to do something useful.'

'Hmmmm. And exciting,' Si said, half smiling.

She grinned.

Temp turned to Esme. 'What will you do with our stuff?'

'You've not got much. I'll take it with me. Go get it all together now. We'll eat. Then we need to leave.'

Ben headed to Honour's room, after grabbing his bag. 'Don't sound too keen, okay?'

'She was stuffing her things into her bag. 'Sorry. I'm just glad we're going with them. We wouldn't have been allowed to go if this hadn't happened.'

'Yes, but it means bad things are happening to Peter.'

'I know. I'm sorry. I didn't mean to...'

'Never mind. I don't know why I was worried about you. You like to stare danger in the face!'

Honour laughed and made Kung Fu movements. 'Ha!Hoo! Ha! Ya! I'll wup their little asses!'

Ben laughed. 'Too many books, Honour!'

Si appeared at the door. 'Come on you two. Food's ready.'

As they all sat down to eat, the mood was sombre. Even Honour, despite her excitement, kept her mouth shut. No one said much and soon it was time to leave. Si's phone rang. He looked at his wrist. It was Kate. She was pale and drawn.

'Si. Are you near a TV? Switch on quickly if you can.'

They moved to the lounge and Esme commanded the HTV to switch on.

Suddenly, an image of Chas flickered into the room. Si and Ben gasped simultaneously. She was handcuffed to a guard on either side. Her empty eyes stared straight ahead as if she was reading an autocue. She was in the middle of a speech.

'...Inciting people to riot and disturbing the peace. Silence Hunter, give yourself up to the authorities. There is no truth in the rumours of a cure for the plague, or that the Rulers deliberately started the plague. Give yourself up, Silence. If you don't do this within 24 hours, your punishment will be my public execution in the Plaza of The Citadel, tomorrow at 7pm. I fully confess to being a criminal and I deserve to die. The Rulers will show mercy in exchange for your surrender.'

The image of Chas was replaced by a news reporter. 'A disturbing image of the girlfriend of the outlaw Silence Hunter. She was on the run with Hunter over a year ago. If Hunter doesn't get this message, and turn himself in within the next day, we will be watching an unprecedented execution, live, this time tomorrow evening, from The Citadel itself.'

Si slumped down on the settee, his head in his hands, his elbows on his knees. He didn't often swear, but several expletives tumbled from his lips. Ben sat down next to him, in shock. Honour saw him swipe a tear from his cheek.

'I don't understand,' Si said. 'How is Chas mixed up in this so suddenly?'

The others stared at him, also in shock, not knowing what to say next. The image of Kate was still open on Si's phone. Ben stood up and began to pace around, throwing his hands up in the air. 'We have to do something. We can't just let them kill her.' He looked at Temp, because Si wasn't responding.

Temp shook his head. 'What can we do? Do we hand Si over, then watch them execute them both? Because that's what they'll do. They're not going to let her go, are they?'

'They might. To save face,' Ben said, desperately.

'They don't need to "save face." They rule with terror. That's all they need,' Temp said.

Honour began to shout. 'Well, you can't just do nothing.' She sat down next to Si. 'What are you going to do, Si?'

He still didn't respond, so Honour shook his arm. 'Si!'

Ben knelt down beside him. 'Si. This is Chas. We love her. You love her. You can't let them kill her.'

Esme watched them all. 'There's more at stake than just your friend's life, Ben. Si and Temp, Kate, Nick, Peter ...you and Honour, me, we're all risking our lives for something much bigger here.'

'We need to think carefully,' Kate said. 'Esme is right.'

'But... you can't just let Chas die!' Ben shouted, pleading. He shook Si. 'You can't Si, please!'

'Stop it, Ben.' Temp pulled him away from Si, but Ben struggled free of Temp's grip. 'We have to think it through.'

Si stood up as if to leave the room. 'Where are you going?' Ben grabbed his arm.

Si shook him off. 'I need some space.'

Kate began to speak to him. 'Not now, Mum!' And he ended the call.

He bounded up the stairs and into the bedroom he'd been sharing with Ben. He slumped on the bed.

No! No! No! No!

This couldn't be happening. Chas was miles away, trying to find her brother and kill him. How was she now involved in all of this? How was she suddenly presenting him with a horrible choice? Her life or the Revolution. Or maybe it wasn't a choice at all. Maybe Temp was right. If he gave himself up that would be the end of both of them. And even if they let her go, should he jeopardize the whole operation to possibly save her life?

If it was just about him and her, of course he would hand himself in. All this time he'd wanted to see her. Wanted her to be here, one hundred percent involved. But not like this. Now he wished she was hundreds of miles away.

He became aware of his wearable vibrating and remembered that he had ended the call to his mum abruptly. He answered it and Kate appeared in the room. 'What shall I do, Mum?' Tears began to run down his face.

'I don't know, son.' Kate's eyes filled with tears at the sight of his distress. 'Nick and I have just been talking, trying to think of a way we could get her out. I guess there's a possibility of rescuing her with the invisibility suits and the contact with Capability. It's slim, but she risked her life to help you save me. She's a stubborn little madam, but I don't feel right abandoning her to her fate, even for a greater good.'

'You think we should try to get her out?'

'Yes.'

'What about our plans?'

'Put them on hold. She's important to you. To us.'

'What if they catch us?'

Kate shook her head. 'I can't think about that. We'll get you out. Things are happening. The Way is assembling lots of supporters. People are ready to risk their lives, Si. You've inspired them. And she's part of that, even if she doesn't want to be.'

There was a knock on the door. Then Esme's voice. 'Si? We have to leave.'

Si ended the call and opened the door. 'Let's go. We're going to get her out.'

Esme looked doubtful but smiled and squeezed his arm.

Ben and Honour were thrilled, but Temp was not so sure. 'I'm not convinced she'd want you to, Si. Really. She'll think it foolish. Didn't you see her face? The blank look. She's resigned to her fate.'

'I know she'll call me all the names under the sun, but I can't resign her to her fate. I'd like to hear her call me a one hundred percent stupid, foolish, big bloody idiot.'

16

Chas sat in a cell, replaying the events of the last twenty-four hours over in her head. When she had finished making the video that would lure Si to The Citadel, she saw them unchain Mish, who had been made to watch as she recorded the message for Si. She had asked to speak to him in person but had been refused. The guards had escorted him out of the room. A few minutes later, she watched on another camera to see them release him onto the streets of The Citadel. He had looked up at the imposing structure for a few moments, then turned, pulled up his hood against the rain and walked away. The last she had seen of him was as he rounded a corner, out of sight of the camera. There was no guarantee that he wasn't already back in custody. She didn't trust Resolution, but she had had no option but to give Mish the only chance she could.

Now, she had to wait. Wait for Si to come handing himself in, or making a rescue attempt, as she knew he would if he had seen the broadcast. She'd rather wait for death. In a few hours she could be hanging from the noose in front of thousands of people. That would be a relief, under the circumstances, except for the pain of course. She wasn't looking forward to that. Her stomach churned at the thought and she tried to breathe away the feeling of nausea that rose in her throat.

If only Si wouldn't see the video. She'd rather die alone than wait for him to be captured, because then, at some point, when he was of no further use, he would die too.

Time to reflect was agony. She tried to sleep, but that was impossible. For the first time in her life she tried praying. She had spent time with the followers of The Way in Amsterdam, but had never joined in any of their Gatherings. They were so convinced that their God was helping them. Would he help her, an unbeliever? She didn't want anything for herself, so maybe he would listen. 'God, if you're there, do something to stop that idiot from coming here.' She paused. 'Save him.' She looked up at the ceiling. It didn't feel like anything could escape from this cell, not even her mumbled words. 'Please,' she added.

*

Resolution was also waiting. Waiting for Hunter to come, as it was almost certain he would. The hanging would go ahead at 7pm as planned, if Hunter didn't come. The Citadel was being primed for a high profile hanging. It would attract a big live crowd, as well as an audience across the country.

It was a risk to only give twenty-four hours response time. If Hunter didn't come, he would have no choice but to hang Chastity and then he'd have to think of another way to lure Hunter, without the bait of his sister. But he cast that thought aside. He would come. Resolution knew it.

Zephyr had called him in to a meeting. He walked up the

corridor to the Premier's office. There was no waiting in the outer office this time.

'Sit down, Commander. Drink?'

Resolution nodded, and Zephyr poured him a whisky from the decanter on his shelf. He handed it to the Commander and sat behind his desk. 'So, you have confidence that your video with the girl will lure Hunter in?'

'Yes sir. It may even bring both Hunters.'

'Zephyr sipped his drink. 'Then we can end this whole damn business of the Nanomedibots and get back on track with diluting the population.'

'Yes sir. What do you want me to do with the girl when we have the Hunters?'

'Get rid of her. Not publicly, of course. The people have to think we honoured our side of the bargain.'

Resolution nodded. 'I am happy to deal with her, sir.'

'Although, she might be useful again, if the Hunters prove stubborn over the Nanomedibots,' Zephyr said. 'Do you think I should attend the execution in person, if it comes to it?'

'It would lend gravitas to the situation,' Resolution said.

Zephyr sat forward, resting his elbows on the table. 'Yes. Organise an armed guard for me. A speech might even be in order.'

'An excellent idea, sir,' Resolution said. He knew Zephyr liked the sound of his own voice, although he also knew that it would be one of the Rulers who would write it for him. Zephyr was only their mouth-piece, despite what he liked to think.

'You may finally have redeemed yourself, Commander,' the Premier said, getting up from his chair and showing Resolution to the door.

'Thank you, sir.' Resolution basked in the light of praise from Zephyr. He was edging his way closer to where he wanted to be.

'Update me every hour today. I will keep the Rulers informed. If the boy turns up before the hanging time, we will bring him and the girl out as traitors and I will make a relevant speech. We will make something of our mercy towards her, without allowing that she might go unpunished. You only said she would be shown mercy if he turned himself in, not that we would let her go.'

'Indeed,' Resolution agreed.

He returned to his office to oversee how thing were going with the setting up of the execution platform. There was no word of Silence Hunter yet. It was just after midday.

*

Ben and Honour had never seen anything like The Citadel before. They had both been inside numerous tech-cities, but none compared to this one. Ben couldn't take his eyes off the vehicles, all brand new, silent. It was hard to know they were coming. Everyone was well coiffured and smart. The streets were clean and there was no graffiti. A discreet law-keeping force was visible on every street and all the major buildings seemed to have security guards at the doors.

The strangest thing by far though, was getting used to

being invisible. It was very disconcerting to look down at your own body and not be able to see it. Honour was loving it. She kept saying things to Ben about how cool it was, much to Temp's annoyance. Finally, he pulled her aside.

'Look, you have to be quiet! You're putting us in danger.'

Honour looked sheepish. 'I'm sorry.' She kept silent after that.

Si and Temp were tense. They had entered The Citadel, easily, in their invisibility suits and found somewhere inconspicuous to sleep. Now, it was the day of the execution and they were on their way to keep their appointment with Capability. Because Temp knew his way around the city, he had made a map of how to get to the hospital from the gate. Each of them had memorized it last night, in case they lost one another. Ben and Honour held hands to try and stay together. Honour was afraid of getting lost, despite her exuberance at being invisible. It would have been quicker to take public transport, but they had to remember that even though they could not be seen, they could still be felt if anyone bumped into them.

They knew that they were looking for a grey Mercedes. Temp had told them to rendezvous at the Blue Zone sign in the car park, far enough from the Mercedes to be safe if anything went wrong. He would approach it alone first, to make sure all was well. If it was, he would ask Capability to get out of the car and stretch. This would be their signal to join him.

Si was very nervous. He knew that the clock was ticking on the execution and he didn't know whether Temp was really behind the idea of a rescue. They had talked about it last night, as they huddled in a doorway, shivering. Temp didn't think they had much hope of rescuing her and he wasn't prepared to let Si hand himself in. Si hoped Capability might have some ideas.

Capability was sitting in his car, pretending to go through some work on his tablet. He wasn't really looking at the words on his screen. He kept glancing up, even though he knew he wouldn't be able to see them coming. Ten o'clock came and went. He kept watching his windscreen wipers wondering if he could possibly have missed Temp's signal.

At 10.10 his fears were allayed, as he nearly jumped out of his skin when his wipers lifted up and slapped against the screen, seemingly of their own accord. He looked around, expecting to see something, but was impressed even more with Peter Marden's technology when he could see nothing. He wound down his window and Temp's voice said, 'We made it.'

'Good,' Capability said, keeping his eyes on his tablet.

'Unfortunately, things haven't gone according to plan. Peter's been arrested and with this execution we couldn't leave the kids behind. So, there are four of us.'

'Okay. We'll deal with it,' Capability said. 'Are you all here?'

'I hope so. I told them to wait at the Blue Zone sign for a signal.' Temp said. 'It's difficult to tell if anyone's there.'

'Quite!' Capability said. 'Amazing suits.'

'Peter is a clever man. I told the others you would get out of the car and stretch and that would be the signal that they should come over. Then open the back doors as if you're looking for something. We'll tell you when we're all here.'

'I hope they're here, otherwise I'll have to do a lot of stretching.' Capability got out of the car and stretched for a few seconds. He then opened the back doors and looked inside. Then he opened the front.

'I'm in,' Temp said, and Capability closed the door.

He sat in the driver's seat and they waited. In a few moments the car jiggled slightly as Si's voice, from the back seat, said, 'I'm here. Any sign of Ben and Honour?'

'Not yet,' Temp said. Even though it was useless to look for them, they all found themselves scanning the car park. Within a couple of minutes, Si felt bodies climb in next to him. 'Move over. We're here,' Ben said.

'Don't shut the doors,' Capability said. He went round and closed the doors himself, then started the car.

'Thank you for this,' Si said, as they exited the car park.

'Where are you taking us?' Ben asked.

'Well, I was only expecting two, so I was going to take Temp and Si back to my apartment. It's near The Fortress, overlooking the river. You okay with that? There's a lot of extra security around today, because of the execution. Zephyr is making a speech from the platform, apparently. He thinks it will make an impression on the masses if he's there in person. There was a Rulers meeting last night. They're confident you're coming Si.'

'What else could I do?'

'I think you could have stayed away. I know she's your friend, but this is going to end everything if you get caught. A lot of people will have given up much, including their lives, for nothing. They're not going to follow someone who caves in to emotional blackmail.'

Si said nothing. He looked out of the window to see The Fortress already in view. It was impressive. He compared it in his mind to the real Bamburgh Castle that he'd seen with Chas on their way back from Holy Island. It had only been a brief glance from a distance, but if it was as big and imposing as this, it must have been a sight to behold when it was the seat of power in Northumbria. He thought of all Chas had done for him back then, despite her own pain and anger. He knew he couldn't abandon her.

Capability pulled into an underground car park, behind remote-controlled gates. Inside the car park there was no one about, so they climbed out of the car and followed him into a lift up to the 5th floor, where he let them into his apartment. Once inside, Capability spoke to his Virtual Assistant. 'Capria, close blinds, switch on heating and boil hot water for tea.'

'Working on it,' came the reply. Si, Ben and Honour weren't used to VAs, even though they had seen the technology now and again at Peter's house. Si had seen it when he and Chas had been sold to Kahn, not long after they had first met. VAs were only used in tech-cities and weren't as common as they had once been. Only those with money to spare had them.

'You can get out of those suits now,' he said. 'It'll be nice to finally see who I'm talking to. There's my bedroom for the young lady, and another here for the rest of you to change in.' He opened both doors. 'There's an en-suite in both rooms if you want to shower or freshen up. I'll be in the kitchen with refreshments when you're ready. There's spare clothes for you gents in the wardrobe. Erm... Honour, I didn't know you were coming so...'

'Don't worry, I can wear anything that kind of fits. I'm not fussy.'

'Okay. Well just rummage in my wardrobe and see what you can find. I can get you something more suitable at some point if need be.'

'Thanks,' said Temp.

The doors closed, and they began to peel themselves out of their suits. It was funny watching half bodies appear out of nowhere and Ben couldn't help laughing. 'It's so weird, being invisible!'

'Yep,' Si said. 'But the suits are much more secure than the cloaks Chas and I used last year.'

'Really tight though,' Temp said, peeling his off like a wetsuit.

'Yeah, it's good to get out of them for a while,' Si said. 'But not for too long maybe. We need to decide what we're going to do about Chas.'

Temp didn't say anything.

Ben looked from Si to Temp. 'I know we don't want to risk Si getting caught, but we can't leave her to die. Si could stay here. We could go for her.'

Temp was pulling off the thin layer of clothes he had on underneath the suit. 'Let's get showered first, then we can talk to Capability about it.' He headed into the shower and instructed the VA about temperature.

'He doesn't sound very positive about helping Chas,' Ben said, sitting down on the bed.

Si walked to the window and peered out of the blinds, over the river. It was an idyllic spot. 'I know. I understand why but, well... I'm with you. We have to try. I can't bear this waiting around. I just want to find her.'

'If Temp's friend won't help us and Temp agrees with him, we'll have to go on our own,' Ben said.

'We can't take Honour,' Si said. 'She has to stay as safe as possible here.'

'I agree,' Ben said. 'We might have to gag her and tie her up to make her obey though.' He grinned at Si.

Si raised his eyebrows. 'Hmmm.'

When they had showered, they found Capability in the kitchen-diner, also overlooking the river. Everything was pristinely clean and ultra-modern. The kitchen had all the gadgets you could imagine. There was fresh coffee, juice, pastries and toast waiting for them on the breakfast bar. They hadn't eaten since they left Esme's, the night before, so the food was very welcome.

'Sorry, there's not so much, I was only expecting two people.'

'This is great,' Ben said, through a mouthful of cinnamon swirl. 'Thanks.'

Capability smiled at him, then turned to Temp. 'I was planning to get you into the Genetics Research Centre, but the course of events over the last twenty-four hours has changed that. We can't go anywhere until this execution is over and The Citadel calms down again. It's not just the security. The place is buzzing with people. It seems like everyone is coming out for the big entertainment. Hangings are rare in The Citadel.'

'What do you mean, we can't go anywhere? We have to try and get to Chas,' Si said.

'There's really nothing you can do,' Capability said. 'I'm sorry.'

'That's defeatist!' Si said. 'You haven't even given it any thought.'

Capability looked at him, sardonically. 'Is that what you think? I've been awake all night thinking about it.'

'Well we need to think harder,' Si threw back.

'With the invisibility suits we could get to her,' Ben said.

'Possibly, possibly not,' Temp said. 'Remember you're still physically present.'

'You'd still have to get through the crowds. And even if you managed to get to her, how would you get her away?' Capability added.

'Can't you get us to her before the execution? You must know where she's being held?' Si said.

'I do. She's in a high security cell in the Fortress. No way they'd let me near her. The place is a maze of secure corridors and only certain people are granted the access codes. The Commander is back in charge of all that and he's not letting anyone near her.'

Si stopped eating. 'The Commander? Do you mean Resolution?'

'Yes.'

'He's alive then?'

'Yes, he was the one who brought your friend to The Citadel. She was badly wounded. Gunshot to the leg.'

Si ran his hands through his hair. So, she had found him,

and it obviously hadn't gone to plan. That must be how she had ended up here.

Capability poured himself another coffee. 'The Commander used her as his means of getting back into Zephyr's good books. I don't think any of the Rulers trust him, but he's useful for now, so he's back in authority.'

'Have you seen her?'

'No. She's being kept in isolation. Like I said, the Commander has been almost possessive about her.'

'She's his sister,' Si said.

Capability raised his eyebrows. 'What? Really? I didn't see that coming. His sister? Poor girl. What has she done to upset him?'

'Long story. But getting involved with me only made it one hundred percent worse,' Si said, using the phrase that was common to both Chas and her brother.

'If no one else is prepared to go and you can't risk Si, then I'm prepared to try and get her,' Ben said.

'And me,' Honour added.

'Er... no. That won't be happening,' Capability said, looking the two twelve-year-olds up and down. 'You'll get yourselves killed. It's bad enough that you're here, but at least I can keep you safe until we get you out of here. When I take Temp and Si to the Research facility, you two are staying here.'

They both began to protest, but Temp silenced them.

'Hey, I'm with Capability on this. You are staying put. End of. If we need you I'll come back for you.'

Ben glanced at Si, who was saying nothing. Honour pulled a face and filled her mouth with more toast.

'So, what do we do now?' Temp asked.

'You stay here today. You rest. I've got to go out. I have to show my face at the Ruler meeting this afternoon and stay for the execution.' He looked at Si. 'I'm sorry Si. I really am. I wish I could do something.'

'You could try,' Si said, shaking his head. 'When Temp was trying to escape, all those years ago, it was dangerous, but you helped him.'

'I know,' Capability said. 'But this is different. It's not that it's dangerous. It's more that it's impossible to achieve the outcome you need.' He looked at his wearable. 'Look, I have to go now. If there is anything that I can do, I promise you I *will* do it.'

Si nodded. Ben could not look at Capability. His eyes had filled up and he didn't want anyone to see it.

'Do not go out of this apartment. Ask Caprica, my Virtual Assistant, if you need anything. I'll be back late, I imagine.' He picked up his tablet, car keys and jacket, then left.

When he had gone, Si stood up and began pacing. He went to the window and peered out from behind the blinds. It looked so peaceful along the river. He could see The Fortress about half a mile away. 'Where will the execution take place? Near The Fortress?'

'Temp came and stood beside him. 'Yes, there's a plaza in front of it, designed for such purposes as big rallies and...' his voice trailed off and he laid a hand on Si's shoulder.

Si turned towards him. 'I'm not going to stay here and let her die without a fight, Temp.'

'No. I didn't expect that you would,' Temp said, resignedly.

Si walked back to the breakfast bar and drummed a teaspoon on the surface. 'Don't try to stop me.'

Ben stood up beside him. 'I'm with him.'

'And me,' Honour said, jumping off her stool. All three of them looked at her and Temp rolled his eyes.

'You won't be able to stop her,' Ben said wryly.

Temp sighed 'What do you have in mind?'

Si stopped tapping the spoon. 'Maybe we could infiltrate the crowd. We can't use the invisibility suits. As you've said before, people can feel our presence and it would only draw more attention. We need to blend in, be inconspicuous, and therefore invisible. However, one of us could wear the suit and stay close to someone else, so that when we push into the crowd no one thinks anything of it.'

'Then what?' Temp asked, shaking his head, doubtful that this could be a plan of any merit.

'We create a diversion in the crowd, draw the guards, leaving as few as possible for us to get past. The person in the invisibility suit, gets up onto the platform, taking them off guard. Before they realize what's happening, frees Chas and runs. That person has another suit for Chas to get into as soon as possible, then we're out of there.'

Temp strode back to the breakfast bar and banged his fists down, making the cutlery jump. He leaned into Si's face and spoke angrily. 'Don't be ridiculous! Never going to work!'

Si didn't flinch. 'It might.'

'No. The law-keepers will have her heavily guarded. There's no way...'

Ben broke in. 'If we create a big enough distraction...'

'There'll be so many law-keepers, it won't make any difference,' Temp said.

'What if we caused some kind of stampede?' Honour said. 'If the crowd looked like they were going to invade the platform, that would get their attention.'

Temp threw his hands up in the air and walked away. 'You're all being ridiculous, but what did I expect, bringing a bunch of kids to The Citadel? In fact, what was I thinking? I must be totally and utterly mad!' He slumped down on the sofa in the open plan lounge.

'I think it's worth a try,' Honour said.

'But how could we get the crowd to riot?' Si said. 'Temp's right. No one is there for a fight. They're spectators. They're there for the gore. And the people who live here probably like living here. Why wouldn't they? They're not going to jeopardize that for any reason we can think of, are they?' It was his turn to bang his fists on the breakfast bar. 'And yet, I can't do *nothing*!'

'Me neither,' Ben said.

'I could create a distraction,' Honour said. 'I'm really good at screaming and I could hurl some pretty awesome abuse!'

'They'd just arrest you, or shoot you,' Temp said from the sofa.

There was silence for some time as they sat with their thoughts. Si was horribly conscious that it was mid-afternoon already. Time was eking away and they were no closer to rescuing Chas.

Suddenly, he stood up. 'I'm going. I'll think of something. You can come with me or you can stay here.' Then he turned to Honour. 'Apart from you. I want you to stay here. Two reasons: if it all goes wrong, which is a distinct possibility, you have to get out of The Citadel and find Esme. She told us where she was going. Also, I don't want to deprive your mum of her daughter. I'm too scared of her.' He tried to smile.

'No way! I'm not staying here,' Honour protested.

Ben looked at her and put his hand on her arm. He had a big brotherly look in his eyes, even though he was no older than her. 'No one doubts your courage and commitment. But you have to do what's most useful to the plan. We *need* you to do this.'

She turned away and emitted a low growl. Ben almost jumped back.

Si was collecting things together. He searched Capability's apartment for a weapon. A gun was what he really wanted. He pulled out drawers, pulled down boxes from on top of wardrobes and out from under beds.

Temp came into the bedroom. 'Stop it, Si,' Temp said, grabbing his arm. 'You're making the place look like it's been burgled. It's not fair on Capability.'

Si pulled away from Temp's grip. 'Well, so far I'm not impressed with his idea of helping us. Leaving Chas to her fate, without even trying, is not my idea of help.' He kept searching. 'Anyway, Honour can tidy it up. It'll keep her out of trouble.'

Temp started to gather his things. 'I'll come with you. If you're going to get yourself caught I might as well be there to try and do something.'

Si smiled wryly at him. 'Thanks.'

'Capability might not have a gun,' Temp said. 'Or it could be in a safe somewhere. You might have to resort to something sharp from the kitchen.'

'You mean a big, bloody knife,' Si said, grinning, as he remembered what Chas had called her weapon, when she brandished it at him on their first meeting.

Within ten minutes they were assembled in the lounge area. Si had the invisibility suit half-on (which looked very peculiar, giving him a torso with no legs). He hadn't found a suitable weapon that could be concealed usefully in the suit. Somewhere in the back of his mind, he made a mental note to discuss design modifications with Peter someday. He had the other invisibility suit tucked into his T-shirt. Ben was wearing a black hoodie he had found in Capability's wardrobe. Temp was wearing one of Capability's dark coats, with a baseball cap covering his face. Both Temp and Ben had weapons concealed about their person. Honour was standing with her arms folded, wearing the darkest scowl on her face.

Ben smiled at her and moved to hug her. 'Don't worry sis, we'll be fine.'

'Pah!' was all she said, turning away, but not before Ben saw the worry etched in her features. 'We'll be back, I promise.'

'You can't promise that!' she snapped.

Temp looked from one to the other. 'She's right, you can't.' He looked doubtfully at Si.

'Remember what your part is in this,' Si said to her.

'Yes,' she scowled.

'Promise you'll do it, if anything happens to us?'

'I promise,' she said.

'Capability will help you, 'Temp said. 'Right, let's go.'

Ben hugged Honour and put his hand on the door handle to open it. He pulled and twisted hard, but the door was locked.

Si tried. Then he swore. 'He's locked us in!'

Temp tried. 'He knew we wouldn't do what he said.' Then he said to the VA, 'Caprica: Open door.'

The voice from the Virtual Assistant replied. 'Door access denied. Locked to voice command of Capability North.'

'Open the door!' Si shouted, rattling the handle in frustration.

There was no reply. Several expletives escaped his and Ben's lips.

'What are we going to do now?' Ben asked, frantically. 'There's no other way out.'

'There's a balcony,' Si said, moving towards the sliding glass doors that looked out from the lounge over the river. 'We might be able to climb to another balcony and get out from there.' He pulled back the blinds and tried the door. Locked. He looked for a way to open it.

'Caprica, open balcony door,' Temp said.

'Door access denied. Locked to voice command of...'

'Yeah, we get it!' shouted Si, banging the window.

Honour had been searching around the apartment.' Hey, there's a vent up there.'

They went into the kitchen area and looked to where she was pointing. Near the ceiling was a small air conditioning vent.

'It's tiny,' Ben said.

'No way I'll get through it,' Temp said.

Si looked at Ben. Both of them were skinny. 'Ben and I might be able to get into it.'

'If you can get up to it,' Honour said.

Si looked around. 'Come on, we'll drag that table over,' he said. 'I'll put a chair on it and climb up.'

They built a small tower on the table under the vent, then Si and Ben climbed onto it. The vent was screwed to the wall. 'Find a screwdriver,' Si said, the urgency in his voice, growing more palpable by the minute.

Tense minutes ticked by as they ransacked the apartment again. 'Here!' came Ben's triumphant cry as he wielded the small tool at Si. They climbed back up on their podium and within minutes the vent was off. Si hoisted himself in. It was tight, and there was no room for him to turn around to help Ben. Ben, not being as tall as Si, struggled a little, but with Temp's help, he managed to wriggle in behind Si.

'Be careful!' Temp called into the shaft, as the feet disappeared from view. Si heard and thought of his mum. He hoped she was praying for him right now, and that God was listening and felt like helping them, as Si really had no ideas how they were going to rescue Chas. He prayed the most popular prayer in his arsenal: 'Help!'

The ventilation shaft led to a maze of narrow tunnels. It was very hard work, belly-crawling through them. They were dusty and made them cough and sneeze. Ben kept bumping into Si's invisible legs and getting a face full of foot, until he got used to how far to keep back.

'How do we get out of here?' Ben said.

'I'm looking for a grill that looks like it leads to a

communal area. Oh, hang on, I've got one.' Si removed the panel. 'We'll have to lower ourselves down and jump. It's not far.'

They were soon standing side by side in an empty corridor. 'You'd better pull that suit all the way on now,' Ben said. 'You look weird. Just keep hold of me and I'll follow you.'

They made it out of the building and looked around. The river was just up ahead, and The Fortress loomed on the other side. There were a lot of people heading towards it. Ben followed as Si pulled him in the direction of the crowd. All the time his mind was racing, trying to think of what on earth he was going to do. They reached the river and began to cross a bridge with the crowd. There were no vehicles about in this part of The Citadel, as many roads had been cordoned off. The law-keeper presence, as predicted, was significant.

Si saw a gap in the crowd and pulled Ben hurriedly towards it. Then he lent towards him and whispered, 'If things go wrong, do not acknowledge either Chas or me. You have to get back to Honour and Temp. Understand?'

Ben nodded, almost imperceptibly.

'Promise me. Say it.'

'I promise,' Ben muttered from behind clenched teeth.

When they got across the bridge the crowds were being herded along the embankment of the river. It was hard to see where they were going as the mass of people was becoming thicker. Ben tried to keep enough gap between himself and other people, so that they wouldn't bump into the seemingly empty space that was Si. When they reached the plaza in front of The Fortress they could see the platform but the crowd that had formed was already huge. Si stopped, seeing the scaffold and noose on the big screen, flanked by law-keepers. His stomach lurched. Ben looked up at the screen and made a quiet groaning sound.

The atmosphere was like that of a rock concert. All around them people were chatting excitedly, as if they were awaiting the arrival of a big-name band. Street vendors were selling fast food and beer. But everywhere he looked there were law-keepers wielding guns. A reminder of the ominous nature of this outwardly festive occasion. Si pushed forward and Ben, still holding onto him, lurched with him. They pushed through the crowd, provoking annoyed looks and comments directed at Ben.

'Sorry. Sorry. I'm trying to get to my friend...' Ben kept saying.

Some people pushed him back and tried to block his path. Si lost his grip on him a few times, but each time, he stopped and grabbed Ben's arm once again. It was hard work pushing through the crowd, but finally they reached the front. Si's heart raced. Soon he would see her for the first time in over a year. How many times had he imagined being reunited with Chas? But the scenarios he had played in his head had not been like this. This might be the last time he ever saw her if things went wrong. And how could they do otherwise? He still had no real idea of what he was going to do.

17

The Rulers were gathered inside The Fortress. As always, Resolution thought, away from any real danger. They were in the meeting chamber, which was set up for a function. The side tables were covered with starched white tablecloths and food was laid out in silver serving dishes. Two wine waiters poured copious drinks for the Rulers, as they mingled and talked about the coming execution as if it were a big football game they were eagerly awaiting.

In their meeting, earlier this afternoon, Zephyr had told them what he would say to the people, and received their approval, with a few tweaks from the most senior Rulers. Resolution was present as commander-in-chief and organiser of the whole operation. He had informed them that everything was ready, a crowd was already gathering, and things would go according to plan. They were irritated that Hunter hadn't appeared and handed himself in yet, but Resolution reassured them that there was still time. He had all the security guards, at The Citadel gates, on alert for Hunter and anyone who might show signs of being part of a rebellion. Several arrests had been made already but hadn't proved helpful. Resolution was still certain that Hunter would show up.

Capability was trying to stay calm, although his pulse raced. Knowing he had Si in his apartment was making him sweat and he hoped he didn't look as guilty as he felt. There was a break in proceedings and the Rulers had gone their separate ways to find refreshment, with instructions to return to watch Zephyr give his speech on the HTV. Capability followed Resolution down the corridor, hurrying to catch up with the Commander's stride.

'Are you confident the girl will be a big enough lure for Hunter?' Capability asked, as he drew alongside him.

Resolution didn't even turn to look at Capability. 'Of course.' He kept on walking.

'Where is she now?' Capability asked.

'She in a high security cell. I'm just going to pull her out now and get her to the platform.'

'Right.' Capability swallowed hard. He was remembering Si's desperation to help his friend. 'Can I be of any assistance?'

The Commander stopped at a lift and turned curiously on Capability. 'No. Why would I need help from you?'

As Capability groped for an excuse, thinking he'd made a mistake, his son came up behind him, hurrying along the corridor. 'Father!'

The lift doors opened and both men stepped in holding the door for Excellence North. He stepped in. 'Glad I caught you.' He nodded to Resolution. 'Commander.'

Resolution nodded back. 'How are you, Excellence? I hear you're following in your father's footsteps.'

'Literally,' Excellence laughed, as he stepped into the lift.

'Into politics,' Resolution said, with no hint of a smile.

'Yes,' Excellence said, becoming serious immediately. 'This is a big day for you, Commander. I'm sure Hunter will come. It's very worrying with all this anti-government propaganda going around. If you get hold of the Hunters, you can quash it.'

Resolution nodded.

Excellence turned to Capability. 'Father, I was wondering if you're going to be out there when they hang the girl? It's just I was hoping for a good vantage point with some of my friends.'

Capability kept his face blank, despite his disgust at his son's callousness. 'No. The Rulers are all staying in the meeting chamber.'

Excellence shrugged. 'Pity. I'll just have to push my way to the front of the crowd.'

Resolution smirked. 'A thirst to see justice meted out, have you?'

'Justice?' Capability said, before he could stop himself. He groped for words to cover his blunder. 'I mean... it's not only justice, is it? More a show of the ultimate power of the Party.'

Resolution smiled to himself, thinking more personally of his revenge against his sister. 'Justice is sufficient.'

'Of course it is,' Excellence said, looking askance at his father.

Resolution looked at the boy, sensing his enthusiasm for the Party and for power. 'I tell you what? You want to get a good view?'

Excellence nodded.

'You can come help me with the prisoner, if you like. Your father just offered, but I think you'd do nicely.'

The boy's eyes gleamed. 'Really? Great. I'd love to.'

Capability jerked his head back. He didn't want his son, corrupted as he was, taking part in this. He still had some hope that he may be redeemable somehow. 'I thought no one, except you, was allowed to be near this prisoner.'

Resolution shook his head. 'You misunderstood me. No one is allowed near her without my say-so.'

Resolution smirked, sensing Capability's discomfort. 'I don't think you should come. The other Rulers wouldn't approve if I gave you preferential treatment.' He stepped out of the lift as it came to a halt below ground level. Capability could only watch as Excellence followed, like a hungry wolf-cub. The Commander led him through a maze of corridors and security doors. Excellence had never been in this part of The Fortress before and was agog at how efficient and secure it seemed. 'How do you not get lost down here?'

'I know this place very well. I've spent a lot of time here.'

'Better when you're the gaoler though eh?' Excellence gave a short laugh and at once realised that Resolution didn't have a sense of humour. The Commander turned on him with vicious eyes and not a word. It was enough to make the boy stammer an apology. 'I'm sorry, Commander. I didn't mean... that is... I know you've been outlawed and I... well, I'm sorry.'

Resolution fixed him with a steely glare. 'I've never been a prisoner of the State and I've no intention of being one.

This is my domain.'

'Yes of course,' Excellence said. 'I'd like to learn more about it. I admire you, Commander. I have always looked up to you and thought you were right to pursue Silence Hunter. Not your fault what happened. You're the best person to be in charge of operations to bring in enemies of the State. Everyone knows that. Otherwise, they wouldn't have reinstated you now.'

Resolution's ego was suitably boosted by the boy's obsequiousness, and he released the boy from his fierce stare. 'Your adulation is duly noted.' He was beginning to think that Excellence North could be a possible replacement for Knowles, with the right training. He would have to find a way to test his devotion to the Rulers over all other loyalties.

They had arrived at the door to Chas's cell. Resolution looked in through the one-way glass to see her sitting with her back against a corner and her eyes closed. He released the door lock. The door slid open with a hiss and Chas looked up to see her brother and another man enter. She didn't speak. There was no point. She was ready to face her fate, and her only hope now was that Si would not come and give everything up that he and Kate had worked for. Or worse still, risk everything in a futile rescue attempt. It was clear to her that whatever happened, she was going to die today.

She had expected her brother to come alone for her with some last vindictive words of personal hatred, but with this other person here that wasn't going to happen.

'Get up,' Resolution said. 'It's time.'

Chas did as she was told, and Resolution secured her hands behind her back.

'You can take her out,' he said to Excellence.

The boy moved forward, a look of surprise in his eyes. He took Chas firmly by the arm and led her out of the cell. Resolution walked ahead. Chas was aware that Excellence was not much older than her. He was tall and dressed in a smart suit, but too young to be one of the Rulers, she thought. He had sharp, well defined features and walked with a confident stride. She surmised that he was Resolution's new side-kick.

They got into the lift. Chas could feel her heart thumping. Despite her determination not to show any fear, she was afraid. Afraid of the feeling of being strangled; the panic of trying to breathe. Afraid of how long it would take. Afraid that she would beg them not to do it. No, she wouldn't beg. She'd ask them to cut out her tongue before she would beg mercy from her brother.

He was not looking at her. He had that air of certainly about him. He couldn't be one hundred per cent certain that Si would come, but he was one hundred per cent certain that he had beaten her and she would never take her revenge on him now. That irked her, but she had come to terms with it and made a fragile peace with herself. She wondered if he feared that Si wouldn't come. Would he still go ahead with the execution today if Si didn't appear? He would have to; or lose face.

She had one last card to play. But when to do it? She wasn't certain that he would let her speak outside, in front of the people, so she decided to play it now, in front of this young apprentice. She was standing shoulder to shoulder with him in the lift.

She leaned up and whispered in his ear. 'You do know that the Commander is my brother, don't you?'

The boy pulled back, startled, both by the revelation and by the fact that she had spoken to him. Resolution noticed the jerk of his head.

'What is it?' he asked.

Chas was smirking.

'She just whispered some nonsense to me Commander, nothing important.'

Resolution narrowed his eyes at her. 'What nonsense?'

Chas said nothing.

'It's quite alright, Commander. I don't believe her.'

Resolution shouted 'Stop!' and the lift came to a halt. He launched at Chas and grasped her throat. She laughed in his face as his grip tightened. 'Go on, kill me now!' she croaked.

'Commander!' Excellence put his hand on Resolution's arm.

'What did she say?' Resolution hissed. His grip tightened around her throat and little lights began to blink in her vision.

Excellence tried to stop him. 'Commander, you need her for the execution, remember. She said nothing important.'

'Tell me what she said,' Resolution barked, without loosening his grip.

'She said you were her brother.'

Resolution loosened his grip and threw Chas's limp body

against the wall of the lift. She sank to the floor, grasping her throat, fighting for air. 'Bitch!'

Excellence was taken aback. 'Commander, it's nothing. I don't believe her. I...' He stared at the Commander who was trying to get a grip on his temper.

'She's a troublemaker.'

'I know,' Excellence said. 'No one would believe her, it's a ridiculous lie.'

'Indeed,' Resolution said, cursing himself for his reaction and stepping back to smooth down his uniform.

Excellence leaned down to pick Chas off the floor.

'It's true,' she croaked. 'His name is Komchenski, like mine. He's an illegal immigrant.'

Resolution remained calm but thrust his face right into Chas's. 'Be quiet. No one is listening.'

'He is.' She looked at Excellence and saw that she had made an impression on him. 'Check him out before you work for him.'

Resolution slapped her so hard that her head ricocheted off the wall and she lost consciousness. Excellence caught her to stop her falling again. He didn't know what to say.

'Move. Floor 12,' Resolution ordered the lift. Then he said to Excellence, 'We'll take her to my office and revive her. We only need her conscious enough to stand for the execution. You can stand next to her and hold her up, if necessary.'

Resolution saw that the boy was taken aback. 'It's a tough business dealing with outlaws. You have to be ruthless at times. If you've not got the stomach for it, best find out now. I had high hopes for you. I was thinking you might like to work alongside me.'

Excellence stiffened and tried to erase any shock from his face. 'I... I'd be honoured to work with you, Commander. I... I'm fine with it.'

Resolution nodded. 'And keep her rambling nonsense to yourself.'

'Of course,' Excellence said.

It was no hardship to him to hoist Chas over his shoulder and carry her the short distance to Resolution's office. Inside, Resolution checked the time. 18.15. He needed to have her outside on the platform by 18.45. He still had enough time. Excellence laid Chas in a chair and went to get some cold water. Resolution checked in with his security for sightings of Silence Hunter or any word from him or his mother. Still nothing. He was beginning to show signs of stress. He knew he had behaved stupidly in the lift. If Hunter didn't come, he would have to think of another way to stop him and Kate and the growing revolution that was getting out of hand.

Excellence returned and splashed cold water over Chas. She shuddered, and he slapped her cheeks to keep her alert. She groaned and looked around her. 'Am I not dead yet? When are you going to get on with killing me?' she moaned. 'Just do it, will you?'

'Here, drink this,' Excellence handed her a glass of water. She sipped from it as she came round more fully. Her head throbbed. Resolution snatched the glass from her hand.

'Gag her,' he said to Excellence. 'I'm not risking anymore of your deluded outbursts. You will be dead within the hour, if Hunter doesn't come to save you.'

'And if he comes?'

Then you won't die today,' Resolution said.

'But I will die soon. You're not going to let me go.'

'No. You're right about that. You will die conveniently behind closed doors and no one will be any the wiser, or even care.'

Excellence tied the gag over her mouth before she could speak again. But she was finished anyway. There was no point anymore.

They led her out of The Fortress to a platform in front of the building. The grey sky had gone dark, as it was still early in the year, but the area was floodlit, and a huge crowd had gathered to watch. People cheered as she was led to the centre of the platform, where a single noose hung from a scaffold.

Si gasped audibly when he saw her. Ben swore, and his fists tightened into a ball. Everything, in both of them, wanted to leap up onto the platform and take out as many law-keepers as they could to rescue her. Si could barely breathe, as his pulse raced. When should he make his move? Even in the invisibility suit, would it be possible to get her away without either of them being shot?

Chas felt as if she had stepped back in time. For some reason she thought of Marie Antoinette walking her final steps to the guillotine. The days were long gone when most people thought that capital punishment, and indeed making a public spectacle of it, was barbaric or inhumane. The people had voted it back when they voted the Rulers into power. She felt her stomach tighten and tried not to look at the noose. She breathed deeply.

Excellence led her to the scaffold and stood beside her, holding her arm. Resolution stood at the other side of her. She glanced at him, noticing the look of satisfaction on his face, as he surveyed the crowd. She wished she wasn't gagged so that she could burst his bubble and tell him that he hadn't won anything. Si had clearly not come for her. Her brother's plan to lure him had failed. She felt a stir of satisfaction at that and pushed aside a shadow of hurt. She was truly surprised that Si had not come. She thought he would have handed himself in a lot earlier. Maybe he was wiser than she gave him credit for, unless he was planning a last-minute rescue. She hoped not. There was no way he could get her out of this. Sweat began to form on her brow. The large screens projected close -up images of her across the crowd. Aware that people could see her facial expressions, she tried desperately not to show how afraid she was.

She scanned the sea of faces. It was then that she saw him. Ben! At least she thought it was him. He was alone. How could he be here? She looked again, trying not to stare. It was Ben, at the front of the crowd. He was looking straight at her and he knew she'd seen him. Was Si here? She couldn't see him. What was Ben doing here? She saw the grief in his face and had to turn away to stop her own tears from welling up. But she was grateful that at least she might have the face of someone she loved to look at in her last moments.

There was another roar from the crowd as The Premier stepped out onto the platform, heavily guarded by many law-keepers. He quickly moved behind a bullet-proof screen. Even here in The Citadel they were taking no chances. The cameras focused on him as he began his speech.

'People of The Citadel and of Great Britain, I address you as your faithful Premier, leader of the Rulers. We are living in difficult times, where people are stirring up hatred against our beloved regime. A regime of peace-keeping and a return to true law and order. There are those who would destroy our sense of order and bring chaos and lawlessness back to our streets. We will not allow this to happen. We will protect our law-abiding citizens from those renegades and outlaws. To that end we will bring severe punishments on those who join any rebellion and especially on those who lead it.

This woman, Chastity Komchenski, is an illegal immigrant. She has exploited our good-will. She helped Silence Hunter evade the authorities in 2066. She helped Kate Hunter, a subversive and dangerous criminal, escape from the Priory. She has recently worked behind the scenes, with the Hunters, on a campaign to undermine the Rulers and cause anarchy. She must be punished.'

His speech was punctuated at various points with waves of agreement and cheering from the crowd. Suddenly, a great roar went up, laced with distinct cries of 'traitor!' 'hang her!' and 'execute her!'

'When are you going to do something, Si?' Ben hissed, during one of the crowd outbursts. 'You can't leave it much longer.'

'I know!' Si said. Should he move now while all eyes were on Zephyr? This was his last chance.

The Premier held up his hand and began again. 'However, we declared that we would be merciful to her, if the main instigator of this rebellion handed himself in to us today. We would have commuted the death sentence to life imprisonment if Silence Hunter had turned up. Sadly, for Chastity Komchenski, he has no loyalty to his friends. He is a coward! He has not come, and her time is up. But hear this, we will find the rebels and they will be executed. Every last one of them.'

Another louder cheer went up from the crowd. Suddenly, Si broke free of Ben and began pushing his way through the crowd, nearer to the scaffold. In all the uproar no one really noticed an invisible presence pushing past them. Ben held his breath. This was it.

Zephyr held up his hand for the crowd to quieten down. A threatening silence fell.

'Execute the prisoner!' he commanded.

Another cheer went up.

Excellence and Resolution moved Chas into position on the raised platform, under the noose. Her palms were sweating and her legs felt like they would give way at any moment. She tried hard to control the trembling and the urge to whimper. Resolution placed the noose around her neck and removed the gag. She bit her lip hard, tasting blood, to stop herself pleading for mercy. Tears escaped and rolled down her cheeks. Resolution spoke calmly to her. 'We will find Hunter and give him an even more painful death than you.'

Chas took a deep breath and mustered all her anger. She looked steadily into his eyes and spat. 'Goodbye brother!'

He said nothing, no one had heard her above the roar of the crowd. He stepped off the raised platform, wiping his face with a clean handkerchief from his pocket.

She looked across at Ben. There was no disguising the fear in her eyes now, but she couldn't hold his gaze; it was too painful. Ben looked around frantically for Si. He looked back at Chas, hoping any moment to see her whisked to safety by an invisible force.

'Stop it! You can't kill her!' he screamed. People around him gave him funny looks.

'Hey, man! You a supporter?' said one woman.

'Stop!' Ben yelled even harder.

'You want to join her?' another person laughed, making strangling sounds and miming a noose around his neck.

Ben raise a fist to hit the man, when a hand came over his mouth and he was dragged backwards and down into the heaving mass.

Chas looked again for Ben, but he was gone. Had she imagined him? She closed her eyes and prayed. 'Please make it quick.'

Si was almost in front of the hanging platform. The people he barged out of the way couldn't see him and just put the jostling down to the crowd becoming excited. He wasn't going to get to her in time to save her. He'd left it too late. Frantically he began to peel the invisibility suit off his head and down his chest.

'Stop! I'm here! I'm Silence Hunter!'

The people around him began to gasp and call out to the authorities, as half a person began emerging from the invisibility suit.

'He's here!' shouted one man. 'Silence Hunter!' Several people joined in.

One of the law-keepers on the platform noticed. He hurried to Resolution. 'Sir!' He pointed to where the shouting was coming from. 'It's Hunter! He's here.'

The crowd gradually grew silent as the people around Si grasped hold of his half-emerged body and heaved him onto the platform. The cameras focused on him, as a torso with no legs lay sprawled on the platform at the foot of the scaffold.

Resolution and Excellence gawped at the sight. 'Arrest him!' Resolution commanded.

Law-keepers swarmed all over him.

'You have to stop the execution now,' Si shouted. 'I'm here. You made a deal. Take me instead of her.'

The Premier held up a hand and the crowd fell silent. Zephyr spoke. 'The Rulers are true to their word. We made a deal. We will not break it. Remove the noose.'

Resolution stepped back up to Chas and took the noose from her neck. He had such a look of self-satisfaction on his face that Chas wanted to punch him. The law-keepers pulled Si to his feet, looking incredulously at his non-existent legs.

'Take the prisoners away!' Resolution commanded.

Law-keepers stepped up and took hold of Chas. She looked across at Si and he at her. Their eyes met.

'Idiot!' she shouted.

Then they were led away in different directions.

18

Kate and Nick watched the events unfold on the HTV from Peter's safe house. It was too risky for them to be out in the field in person right now. The work with the NMBs was being continued by the many people who were now trained up to administer them.

Kate cried out as Si revealed himself and was led away by the law-keepers. She put her hand to her mouth to try and hold back the torrent of emotion. Nick put his arm round her. His face was white. 'Hey, it's okay to let it out,' he said soothingly.

Kate turned her face into his chest and sobbed.

'We'll find a way to get them out,' Nick said, stroking her hair. 'You have so many people behind you now. They're not going to be fooled by Zephyr's nonsense about peace and order.'

Kate came up for air, her face red and blotchy. She rummaged for a tissue from her sleeve. 'They were cheering, Nick. They are fooled.'

'Only the people in The Citadel. Only because they want to be. Ordinary people are with you.' He brushed wisps of hair from her face.

She sat up and blew her nose. 'But we don't know what

they're going to do to them now. We don't know if they'll just kill them anyway.'

Nick sat forward, his shoulders hunched. 'We don't know,' he said quietly, 'But I think they'll want to question Si and...'

'You mean interrogate and torture him,' Kate said, stifling another sob.

Nick sighed. He knew what Kate had been through in the Priory, when the Rulers had been trying to extract information from her about the NMBs. Morgan, her husband, had died in there. Then Si had been interrogated and experimented on, to try to find out if he knew anything of the NMBs. They knew what it was like to fall into the hands of the Rulers. There was nothing he could say that would ease her mind, and he knew it.

'We'll rally the people to go in after him. We can attack The Citadel.'

Kate laughed. 'What with? Our bare hands?'

'No...' he trailed off. What did they have? Peter, their only source of technology and potential weapons was in custody too. He stood up. 'We can find weapons. On the black market. We'll find a way.'

'Kate flung her wet tissue on the floor and searched her sleeve for another. 'Where were the others when Si threw himself at the Rulers just then? Temp, Ben, Esme... Why did they let him do it? Alone.'

Nick shrugged. 'Who knows what could have happened to them. They've not been answering their phones for days. They could be in prison now for all we know. We need to leave here and go back to Peter's. Find Harmony and

Peter's friend Eric. They'll be able to help us. Maybe Eric can get Peter released.'

'Not after that display of invisibility technology,' Kate said, indicating the HTV, where news footage was replaying the moment that Si had revealed an invisibility suit. 'That's going to point straight back to Peter.'

Nick nodded. 'Still, I think we have to leave here and try to get Peter out. He's our best chance.'

*

Temp and Honour sat in silence, in Capability's living room, trying to take it all in. It was a long time before either of them spoke. The broadcast had been stopped as Si and Chas were led away.

Temp stood up and went to the window. He laid his head against the glass. Honour didn't know what to say, but she wanted to break the silence. 'What do we do now, Temp?' She went over to stand beside him.

He looked at her and she saw tears in his eyes. 'I don't know. I just don't know.'

Honour bit her lip to stop any tears escaping her eyes. 'I wonder where Ben is. I didn't see him.'

'Let's hope he's safely blending into the crowd and keeping his mouth shut.'

'He'll come back here, won't he?' Honour said, trying to reassure herself. For the first time since she had followed Ben, she felt an urge to run back home to her mother.

'He will, if he can. It might take a while for him to get back here in this crowd.'

They stood in silence again for a long time. They could

see the crowds moving and dispersing along the banks of the river.

'Your friend Capability could get them out,' Honour said.

Temp shook his head. 'I don't know what he can do. I hope he can help us.' He turned to Honour and put his arm round her, but his smile was not very reassuring. 'We'll do our best to get them out of there, although God knows how.'

'At least they're still alive,' Honour said. 'Chas would be dead now if Si hadn't shown himself.'

'Yes,' Temp replied, wondering how long they had, before they were both dead.

*

Ben had struggled hard against his attacker and taken down a few other people in the crowd in the process.

The assailant had dragged him away, apologising to people. 'I'm getting him out of here. I'll deal with him.'

The person had marched Ben as far from the crowd as he could manage, with Ben's arm twisted half way up his back, as if he was being arrested. Now he was pinned against a wall in an alleyway, still trying to lash out, crying and shouting.

'Stop!' the boy said. 'Be quiet!' But Ben continued to shout and struggle. He shook Ben hard. 'Shut up! Were you trying to get yourself lynched too?'

Ben crumpled against the wall and let the tears come. As his body slowly slid down the wall, the boy let go of him.

'She was like a sister to me!' Ben sobbed. 'And she saw me

in the crowd. I know she did. She looked straight at me.'

'You knew her?' the boy asked.

'Yes,' Ben said, wiping his running nose on the sleeve of his hoodie. 'I just said so, didn't I?'

The boy crouched down. 'What's your name?'

Ben looked up at him. 'What's it to you?'

'I knew her too.'

Ben eyed him, suspiciously. He was about Chas's age, maybe older. He was dishevelled and bruised. He did not look like he belonged in The Citadel.

'Ben,' The boy said suddenly. 'You're Ben, aren't you?'

Ben's hand hovered over his knife. 'How do you know?'

'She told me about you. My name's Mish. She was living with me in a commune in Northumberland until a few weeks ago.'

'Why are you here?' Ben asked.

'They kidnapped me from the commune and used me to persuade her to make that video, to lure Si here,' he said. 'Then they threw me out.'

'They just let you go?' Ben said, even more suspiciously. 'They don't just let people go.'

'Well they did. I don't know why. I guess I wasna much use. I didna ken anything aboot who she really was, or what she was up to. They tried to find out, believe me. She'd told me a false name and that she was looking for her brother, Resolution. She said she had a younger brother too, called Ben. She didn't talk aboot her past very often, but it always made her smile when she mentioned you.'

'I'm not her real brother,' Ben said.

'Maybe not flesh and blood,' Mish replied, smiling, 'But

you mean a lot to her.'

Ben wiped his snot-covered face and looked up at Mish. 'Why didn't they eject you from The Citadel?'

'I dinna ken. Probably wanted me to see the execution. And, let's face it, they were never gonna give me a lift home.' Mish sat down next to Ben.

'Why did you grab me?'

'I could see you were gonna get arrested if you didna pipe down. You were going against the flow: Everyone shouting for her to die and you shouting for them to stop. I mean, it didna look good.'

'Yeah well, maybe I didn't care. I couldn't see Si and I had to try and do something. They were on the verge of hanging her.'

'At least she's still alive, thanks to Si,' Mish said.

Ben nodded. He was grateful to have seen some of what happened when Si revealed himself, before Mish had dragged him away completely.

'But how long they'll stay alive, who knows?' Mish shook his head. 'I dinna trust Zephyr to keep his word. Did you and Si come here alone?'

Ben wasn't sure whether to tell this boy about the others, or keep quiet. He could be anyone. Mish saw his uncertainty.

'Look, I need to help. Chas is important to me. She's my girlfriend.'

Ben was shocked. 'She can't be your girlfriend. She...' He was going to say that she was Si's girlfriend, but he had never really understood their relationship. He'd just always wanted them to get together.

'She what?' Mish asked.

Ben shook his head. 'You didn't really know who she was though.'

'No. She called herself Grace. I'm just getting used to the fact that she wasna who I thought she was. There's a lot I need her to tell me, but I get why she was keeping her identity secret.'

'What about your commune? Don't you want to know what happened to them after you were kidnapped? They did awful things to Chas's...'

Ben stopped. This was probably not a tactful thing to say.

'O' course I want to know. And I'm going back, as soon as I know Chas'll be okay. They beat my father, I know that. I know they're capable of hideous crimes. It's a long way back there, but I'll go as soon as I can.'

Ben chewed his lip, uncertain what to do. He knew he must get back to Capability's house, but he didn't want to take Mish. 'I've got to go. I need to meet some people. I'll tell them about you and maybe they'll meet you.' Ben looked around at the alleyway. It was secluded and no cameras here. 'If they're okay about it, we'll meet you here, tomorrow at 9am.'

'Okay,' Mish said. 'I'll be here.'

Ben stood up. 'Don't follow me.'

Mish sat on the ground, his back to the wall. 'I won't. I'll wait here 'til you're gone. Promise.'

'I'll be watching for you,' Ben said. He started to walk away, then stopped and turned. 'Oh... thanks. For stopping me, I mean. I promised Si I would keep a low profile.' He grinned ruefully, shrugged and turned out of the alleyway.

He made his way through the dispersing crowds. It was night time, but the street lights were powerful in The Citadel. He passed some cafes and bars where people were standing outside, having excited conversations about the last-minute reprieve and 'Silence Hunter's invisible legs', or 'Silence Hunter's floating body.' Everyone had certainly been well entertained. When he reached Capability's apartment block, he realised he hadn't thought of how he was going to get back in. He waited until a woman opened the door and squeezed up behind her. The doors were opened by facial recognition and voice command. The woman jumped.

'Hi. Sorry. Didn't mean to scare you. Can I squeeze in behind you? My dad's blocked me from getting in. He's a bit mad with me for going to the execution today, so he locked me out. But I really need to pee.' Ben danced around and grinned.

The woman looked him up and down, clearly thinking him a harmless child. She smiled. 'Go on then.'

'Thanks,' Ben said and shot up the stairs, rather than going for the lift with her.

'Hope you get there in time and make it up with your dad,' she shouted after him.

He got to Capability's apartment. Again, he knew he couldn't get in unless Capability was back. He banged on the door.

'It's me, Ben,' he whispered loudly, into the wood.

Honour's voice came back. 'Ben! Temp, it's Ben! We're still locked in. Capability's not back.'

'It's okay. I'll just hang here 'til he comes and hope no one kicks me out. Did you see the execution?'

Temp was at the door now, too. 'Yes. It's a huge mess. Don't know what we're going to do now! We'll have to see what Capability says when he gets back.'

'At least she's alive,' Ben said.

'Yes, that's one positive,' Temp said.

'And you're okay,' Honour said. 'I was so worried about you when Si got taken. I thought they'd find you. I didn't think you'd be able to keep quiet.'

'Yeah, well that's another story.'

'Wait 'til you get inside before you tell us,' Temp said. 'The place is riddled with CCTV.'

'I know. I hope Capability comes back soon,' Ben said. 'I really do need to pee.'

*

Capability was still in the Rulers' chamber with the others, waiting for Zephyr to return. He was reeling from Si's appearance and from his own son's proximity to the execution. He had seen the gratification in his face as he stood there with Resolution, assisting that thug to send Chastity to her death. If he had been alone now, he could have wept, but his face had to remain neutral. All through Zephyr's speech, the Rulers had babbled on about their dominion over the country. Zephyr was no more than their puppet; their mouth-piece to the masses, and they were very pleased with the dictator they had created. They enjoyed their anonymity and power. Surprised exhilaration flashed around the room like a bolt of lightning, at Si's appearance.

They had him now, even though, at this late stage in the proceedings they had resigned themselves to this being an exercise in frightening the rebels, rather than catching Silence Hunter. Resolution was on the receiving end of rare adulation now, rather than the mumbled criticisms that were usually shot his way.

Capability was used to faking his reactions to blend in with the other Rulers. How he loathed it. He wished he had got out years ago, but he'd always held on to hope that he could save Excellence from himself. Today that hope had been snuffed out. But he still couldn't leave, not until this was over. And how would it end? He couldn't tell.

The door opened, and Zephyr strode in as the room erupted into cheers and clapping.

'Bravo, Premier!' Ambition Steele clapped Zephyr on the back.

'Your speech was effective and well received,' said Zealous, coming alongside Ambition.

Zephyr raised a hand and silenced the room. Even though the Rulers controlled him, they showed him respect as their leader. 'Thank you, gentlemen. A most welcome turn of events with Hunter making his appearance at the eleventh hour. Although, it appears only half of him showed up.'

At this, the room erupted into laughter again.

Ambition motioned for the waitress to bring a drink for Zephyr. 'Let's celebrate our victory tonight and reconvene in the morning to discuss our next move. I'm sure Commander Resolution will join us then. He finally got something right!' Everyone laughed. Ambition raised his glass. 'To Premier Zephyr and our continued rule.'

The rest of the Rulers raised their glasses and toasted Zephyr. The Premier mingled and chatted to groups and individuals. Time was ticking away. Everyone was in jubilant mood and the alcohol was flowing. Capability couldn't leave too early as it would look odd at the very least. He was just wondering if he could fake a migraine when Zephyr came to talk to him.

'You must be very proud of your son.' He sipped from his glass of champagne and looked expectantly at Capability.

'Capability took a large gulp of his. 'Of course, Premier. Excellence has always had ambitions to rise up to be a great politician like yourself.'

Zephyr smiled sardonically. 'I see the Commander has taken him under his wing though.'

'Yes,' Capability said, frowning, knowing that Zephyr was not fond of the Commander. 'I'm not so sure that's the best direction for him to be taking.'

Zephyr smiled. 'Possibly not. Although, I may have to concede to the Commander on this one, if he has decided to take the boy as his assistant. We owe him some small reward, after the feat he pulled off today.'

'Yes, of course,' Capability agreed, feeling a helpless ache in the pit of his stomach.

Zephyr put his hand on Capability's arm. 'You don't look too good. Is anything wrong? You must tell me if I can do anything.'

This was his opportunity to escape. 'I'm delighted that things have worked out today, Premier, but if you will excuse me, I do have one of my migraines coming on.'

Zephyr faked concern. 'What a shame. I expect we will be

celebrating here well in to the night. But you must go and rest if you need to.'

'Thank you. I want to make sure I'm fit to be here in the morning for the meeting.'

'More important than all this frivolity of course,' Zephyr nodded. 'You are a dedicated man. We will see you at nine.'

'Thank you again,' Capability said and made his way to the door.

As he reached it, Ambition stopped him. 'Leaving so soon?'

'Migraine,' Capability said. 'I've chatted to Zephyr. He said I should go home and rest for tomorrow's meeting.' He felt like a school-boy who had just got the headmaster's approval to go home sick.

Ambition eyed him with clear distain. He had been suspicious about Capability since the mysterious disappearance of his daughters a few years ago. 'Did you enjoy today's entertainment?' he persisted.

'Yes,' Capability tried to keep his voice light. 'Yes... it was surprising. And very good news for us.' He really did have a headache coming on now. 'I must get off now, Ambition, get my pain killers and rest.'

Ambition smiled mockingly and decided to let him go. 'I hope your migraine goes away.'

'Thank you,' Capability said and hurried out before anyone else could stop him.

He got in his car with a sigh of relief and drove back to the apartment. His thoughts turned to those waiting there and suddenly he was angry. He wanted to know how Si had got out and what Temp thought he was playing at, letting the boy do such a reckless thing. Part of him though, admired Si's courage and loyalty to Chastity. She must mean a lot to him, to jeopardize everything he and his mother had been working for.

Finding Ben slouched on the floor by the door to his apartment did not help his mood or his headache.

'What the hell are you doing here?'

Ben stood up. 'Waiting to use the bathroom.'

'Get inside,' Capability said, opening the door.

Honour had been talking to Ben through it and hastily moved away as she heard Capability's voice. Temp readied himself to try and explain things to his friend.

Ben ran in, straight to the bathroom as Capability headed to his medicine cupboard, without a look towards Temp or a word. Temp followed him. He waited for Capability to swallow his medication.

'I'm sorry.'

Capability looked at him and raised his eyebrows. 'Really?'

'Yes...' Temp grimaced. 'And no. I couldn't have stopped him. He was determined.'

'You could have. He's a boy. You're older and stronger. I thought I'd made it impossible for anyone to get out.'

'Maybe older, but probably not stronger. And I admit, I helped him. I would have gone myself, only...' He gestured towards the air vent. 'Got too fat in my old age!'

'Capability looked up at the vent and his lips twitched. 'Oh, I see. Hmmm. What's done is done. The boy is determined. God only knows what is happening to them right now.'

Ben came into the kitchen, followed by Honour. 'Can you get them out?'

'Hold on. First of all, how did you get back here? Were you followed? Did anyone see you with Si?'

'No one followed me. I made sure of it. And no one saw me with Si.' He kept quiet about his display of support for Chas. 'I met someone in the crowd, though. A boy who claimed to know Chas.'

Temp shook his head. 'Someone claiming to know her? And why did he speak to you?'

Ben squirmed, realizing he might have to tell the whole truth. 'Okay, I admit, I shouted for them to stop, when it got to the point where they were about to hang Chas. Si had disappeared...' they looked at him ironically. 'Well, you know... he had left my side. He was trying to get to her, but I thought he was going to be too late.'

'So, you shouted out? Great!' Capability felt his anger rising.

'Everyone was shouting. No one heard me. Well, no one except this boy who came up behind me and dragged me away. I thought I was being arrested.'

'Ben!' Honour exclaimed. 'You could have been, you idiot.'

'Who was he? And where is he now?' Temp asked.

'He told me his name was Mish and that he was Chas's boyfriend. They'd been living in a commune together.' Ben related the whole story to them.

Temp looked very uneasy but said, 'It could be true. It sounds like the kind of thing she would do. But he could be a plant.'

'Will you meet him?' Honour asked.

Temp looked at Capability. He shook his head. 'No. We've got enough to deal with.'

'He might be useful,' Temp said. 'We should question him. I'll go, with Ben.'

Capability took in a deep breath. 'I don't think it's a good idea. What good could it do? I don't know what I can do for Chas and Si, but I'm going to do everything I can.' He looked at Ben and Honour's hopeful faces. 'That was my son, with the Commander, on the platform. I feel like I've lost him, but I'm not going to stand by and let them have Si and Chas as well if I can help it.'

Temp put his hand on Capability's shoulder. 'Thank you, old friend. I know we've put you in a lot of danger.'

'Capability smiled. 'It's about time I climbed out of my comfort zone. Now, if you'll excuse me, I've got to lie down and shift this migraine. I've got to be back at The Fortress for 9.00am. I'll see what I can find out then. Get some sleep, if you can.' He turned to Ben and Honour. 'And no going out of this flat. I'll release the doors from my command, but you have to promise me.'

They nodded, sheepishly, glancing at each other. 'There's no point in going out anyway,' Ben said. 'But I don't think we'll sleep.'

'Just try,' Capability said. He patted Temp on the back and headed to bed.

*

'So here we are again,' Resolution said to Chas, as he and

Excellence stood in the cell with her. 'Still alive. Good old Si. I knew he wouldn't forsake you.' His words dripped with sarcasm, like sewerage from a broken pipe.

Chas closed her eyes. 'What have you done with him?'

'He's tucked up in a cell for the night, just like you.'

'And what are you going to do with him tomorrow?'

'That depends on him,' Resolution said. 'You were bait and now he is bait. We will have Kate Hunter and her comrades soon and this whole business will be finished.'

'And me? What are you going to do with me?'

Resolution took her face in his iron grip and squeezed. 'What I'd like to do and what I'm allowed to do are two different things. Goodnight Chastity.'

He left, followed by Excellence, his eager little pup.

She was angry with Si for predictably showing up, and yet, at the same time, she had been ecstatic to see him, not least because he had saved her from the noose. But not only that. Even in the grip of pumping adrenalin, she was surprised how much she had missed him. She couldn't show it out there, of course, and the word 'idiot' had just escaped from her lips. She regretted it now. What was he feeling right now? Had they hurt him yet? And what had he achieved, except a reprieve for her and how long would that last? If she was Kate she'd be furious with him. But, knowing Kate as she did, she knew she would only be worried out of her wits and determined to get her son back.

She heard noises outside the cell. Voices. Footsteps. One of them was her brother's, but she couldn't make out what he was saying. Then the door to the next cell opened and the noises moved inside. She assumed they were putting Si next door. Knowing he was there was no great advantage but brought her some slight relief.

'It was good of you to turn up,' Resolution said to Si.

'You knew I'd come,' Si said.

'Well, yes. You are very predictable. Chastity did her best to resist making the video. She knows you well.'

'What are you going to do with me?'

'I'm sure you know what we want, and you are just a small, but admittedly, significant part of it. We will get to your mother and when we do she will be punished and the Nanomedibots destroyed once and for all. I'm sure your uprising is already dying away.'

Si sat down on the bench and gave Resolution a hard stare. 'Or maybe you've just thrown kerosene on the bonfire.'

The Commander didn't bite. 'We'll speak again tomorrow. Goodnight, Silence.'

When Resolution and his side-kick had gone, Si was glad of the sudden quiet. They had stripped him of his invisibility suit and found the other one on him. All he was left with was the pair of shorts and T-shirt he had been wearing underneath. He was annoyed with himself for revealing the invisibility technology and losing two of the suits. He knew he had put Peter in serious danger. And what for? The word 'idiot' rang in his brain, and he saw Chas's face as they dragged her away. What had he hoped for? That she would fling her arms around him or declare her undying love for him? No, of course not. 'Idiot' was the mildest thing he should have expected from her. However, she was alive. At least, he hoped she was still alive. He didn't actually know that for sure. He closed his eyes and leaned back against the wall. What had he done? What would his mum be thinking right now? But even now he knew he couldn't have lived with himself, if he had just watched her hang from a rope on HTV.

Just then, he heard a knocking on the wall opposite. At first, he thought it was just someone banging around in the next cell and then it became more definite and persistent. He went to it and knocked back. The knocks came back in an exact echo of the pattern he had just tapped out. He knocked another pattern and the person responded. Someone was trying to communicate with him. A surge of hope welled up in his gut. It must be Chas.

She echoed his knock, hoping that somehow she was communicating that she was glad he was there.

He slid down to the floor, sitting with the side of his face to the adjoining wall. She lay on her bench, next to the wall, with her hand touching it.

Both of them fell asleep.

19

Resolution had been summoned to report to the Rulers' meeting at 9 am. He walked into the room on the dot of nine, to find them all assembled around the meeting table, Zephyr at the head, flanked by Ambition and Zealous.

'Sit down, Commander,' Zephyr said, smiling. The rest of the Rulers greeted him with the usual stony faces. 'We want to congratulate you on the success of your plan and eagerly await your ideas for what might come next.'

'Thank you, Premier. I will be interrogating Hunter this morning and finding out as much information about the whereabouts of Kate Hunter. Then I will personally lead the operation to retrieve her.'

Zephyr nodded. 'And where are Hunter and Komcheski now?'

'In my most secure cells. I have taken on Excellence North as my second-in-command. He's there now. A snap decision, yesterday. Call it instinct.' He made a brief nod in Capability's direction. 'I needed someone to replace Knowles. The boy is eager and ambitious. I hope this will meet with your approval, Premier.' Zephyr nodded and waved his hand dismissively. 'And his father's, of course.' Resolution looked at Capability, as did the other Rulers.

'I'm sure you are very proud of your son and supportive of his career move,' Zephyr said to Capability.

'Of course,' Capability said, smiling at Zephyr. He had regained control of his composure from last night, but his pulse still raced with the knowledge of who he was harbouring in his apartment.

Ambition narrowed his eyes. 'How's the migraine?'

'It's much improved. Rest and pain-killers were all I needed.'

Zephyr directed their attention back to the Commander. 'See what you can get out of him today and re-interrogate the girl. She may know more than she's letting on and with Hunter here, under your scrutiny, she may be more inclined to talk. We want to know locations of anyone associated with the traitors and get them brought in. Especially ringleaders. Ambition, get on to the Priory. Marsden is there. He's clearly involved, looking at those invisibility suits. I want you to go there in person and see that he is interrogated thoroughly. And I want to know why we haven't got this technology in our arsenal yet? How long has he been keeping this from us?'

Ambition was clearly not impressed at the thought of leaving the security and luxury of The Citadel. 'I think we should send the Commander. He has more experience in the field and I'm needed here.' He looked to the other Rulers for support.

Zealous spoke up. 'I agree, Premier. The Commander would get much more out of Marsden. He could go, after he's interrogated Hunter and the girl.'

Zephyr rolled his eyes. 'Yes, yes, he can go. But I want

you up there today, Commander. Once you've questioned Hunter and the girl, we can deal with drawing in his mother and the rebels.'

Resolution was not happy at being sent away from the heart of the action, but he couldn't do anything about it. 'Very well, Premier. I'll get on with the interrogations immediately.'

'Let's reconvene tomorrow at ten. Keep me informed as things develop,' he said, looking at Resolution.

'I'll contact the Priory and tell them to prepare Marsden for a visit from the Commander,' Ambition said.

Capability followed Resolution out of the room. He had to try to speak to Si somehow. 'Commander, may I have a word?'

'Yes,' Resolution said, not stopping. 'Walk with me.'

'It's about my son.'

'Go on.' Resolution didn't look at Capability.

'I wondered if I could speak to him. I want to make sure he is fully committed to this slight change in career path.'

'You mean becoming my assistant? I'm sure he is.'

'Never-the-less, I would like to talk to him.'

'I'm sure he will call you when he's ready,' Resolution said.

'I'm not so sure. He doesn't really talk to me much.' It pained Capability to have to confess this to the Commander and to virtually beg for an audience with his own son. 'Can I just have five minutes alone with him now? I'm happy to go to where he is posted, and I won't take up too much of his time.'

They came to the lift. Resolution smirked, as he turned to

Capability. 'I will give you five minutes. I know you're not happy about it, but he won't change his mind for you.'

'I am absolutely fine with his decision, Commander,' Capability said, trying to keep the sadness from his voice. 'I won't try to change his mind. He makes his own choices.'

Resolution nodded. 'I'll take you to him, then I have some things I need to set up, on the twelfth floor. Excellence will accompany you off the cell floor.'

Excellence was standing guard by the cells of Chas and Si. He stiffened as Resolution walked towards him with his father trailing behind. 'Commander.' He saluted. Resolution smiled. He liked the boy's dedication.

'Your father wishes to speak to you. When you are finished, escort him back to the lift please.'

'Yes Commander.'

'I will be back for Hunter soon. Have him ready. You can accompany me whilst I interrogate him.'

Capability tried not to wince. He knew that an interrogation from the Commander was more like torture than anything else. Excellence's eyes gleamed with eagerness.

When Resolution had walked away, Capability said,' How are you son?'

'I'm very well, father. What brings you here?'

'I wanted to find out if you're certain that you want to be the Commander's right-hand man?'

Excellence laughed. 'Of course I am. This is an opportunity I could never have imagined, just thrust upon me by chance.'

'But what about your political ambitions?' Capability

said.

'This can only help them,' Excellence replied.

'What about your studies? How will you finish your degree?'

A shadow of annoyance passed across Excellence's face. 'I don't know right now, but it's early days with the Commander and so much has happened in the last twenty-four hours. We haven't had time to discuss it yet. I'm sure I'll find a way. Or maybe I won't even need to complete it.'

Capability shook his head. 'This could lead you in the wrong direction. Have you thought about that? You know Resolution has been in and out of favour with Zephyr.'

'But he's in now, and that's all that matters,' Excellence said. He turned away, impatiently and looked through the panel of one-way glass in the cell door. 'Is that all father? I'm busy.'

'Yes, I see that,' Capability said. 'Who's in that cell?'

'Komchenski is in this one and Hunter in the next one.'

'Can I look?' Capability asked.

Excellence moved aside. 'Go ahead. She's like a caged lion. She never stops pacing the floor.' He moved aside and looked into Si's cell. 'Whereas Hunter hasn't moved from that corner.'

Capability peered into both cells. He had seen holo-images of both of these young people before but seeing them in the flesh brought it home to him, even more, that he must get them out of here somehow. He thought of their friends waiting for news back at his flat. At least now he could say he had seen them and that they were still alive. He closed his eyes briefly, not daring to think about what state they might be in in a couple of hours' time. There was nothing he could do for them right now though.

'I presume Resolution told you that she's his sister,' Capability said, turning to look at Excellence.

Excellence looked like he had seen a ghost. He hesitated, wondering whether to tell his father of the incident in the lift. 'He didn't tell me. But she did.' He looked into her cell again. 'Is it really true?'

'Yes,' Capability said.

'How do you know?'

Capability swallowed hard. He couldn't exactly tell his son about his guests. 'A friend told me. Someone I used to know years ago, who once knew the girl.'

'She has to be lying,' Excellence said.

Capability shrugged. He'd planted a seed of doubt and that was good. 'Has the Commander trusted you with access to their cells?' Capability asked.

'Yes, he's given me the DNA security clearance to all secure areas.' Excellence was clearly proud of his new status.

Capability raised his eyebrows. DNA security clearance was only used in the most secure areas of The Fortress, including the complex where the clones were kept. He didn't know if Excellence even knew about the clones yet.

Excellence grinned. 'Well, if that's all, father...' He led Capability back to the lift. 'I'll let you know how the interrogation goes, if you like.'

Capability shrugged. 'I'm sure I'll find out from the meeting tomorrow.'

*

Temp and Ben had gone out, not long after Capability, to meet Mish. Honour was left behind, yet again, much to her displeasure. Ben led Temp back to the place where he had left Mish the day before. They arrived early and waited in the darker recesses of the alleyway. Temp had taken a weapon, just in case.

Just after nine, a boy in a hoodie shuffled into view. He saw the two shadowy figures and stopped. 'Ben? Is that you?'

Ben and Temp stepped forward.

'You came. I thought you might not.' Mish stepped towards them. 'Who's this?'

'My name's Temp. Ben and I are friends of Chas and Si. And you are?'

'Mish. I explained to Ben how I know Chas and how the Rulers kidnapped me and used me to make her do the video to lure Si in.' Mish shuffled on the spot, hands in his pockets. 'Yeah, I'm sorry about that. Neither of us had much choice.'

'No,' Temp said. He looked appraisingly at the boy. 'And now? Why are you still in The Citadel? Why haven't you gone back to your commune?'

'I didna want to leave without seeing the... I mean... I thought it was ma only chance to say goodbye to her. I want to know if my father and the others back home are alright, but first I have to help you get Chas out. I never thought I had a hope in hell of trying to save her. Not like you.'

'We never thought we had one either, but Si had to try, and now they have him too, so I guess we didn't.'

Mish pursed his lips. 'At least she's still alive... probably. Look, I understand you don't know whether to trust me or not, but please let me help you get Chas out.'

'And Si,' Ben added.

'Aye,' Mish said. 'I'll join your cause to bring down this stinking regime, if it helps. I know people back at my commune would join too.'

There was a pause as Temp thought about it. 'We can't take you back to where we're staying, it's too risky, but if you're genuine we can use you to help the cause. One or more of us needs to leave The Citadel soon, to get a message to Si's mother and the others. We could help you get back to your commune and maybe you could help us in the meantime. You can't do much for Chas directly, but helping us would ultimately help her.'

Mish nodded.

'Keep checking this alleyway. I'll leave you a message about when and where to meet us. It won't be long. Where are you staying?'

Mish shook his head. 'I'm just hanging around in dark corners and by restaurant bins.'

'Here.' Temp handed Mish a card. 'This is loaded with some money.'

Ben looked quizzically at him.

'Don't ask,' Temp said. 'Get yourself a room for the night and some food.'

'Thanks,' Mish said. 'I'll keep checking back here every day at this time 'til I hear from ye.'

Temp began walking away. 'Come on Ben.' He looked back. 'Don't follow us. I'll know.'

*

Capability headed back to the apartment to let them know that he had seen Chas and Si. He was twitchy and watchful, making sure he was not being followed. He had been very aware of how Ambition had looked at him and that Resolution clearly didn't trust him.

When he entered the apartment, he was nearly pounced on by Honour. 'Have you seen them?'

He pushed past her and headed to the kitchen. 'Coffee,' he said to his VA.

'Well?' Honour said, dancing impatiently from foot to foot.

Capability took down a cup from the shelf. 'Yes, I saw them. I asked the Commander to take me to the cells to see my son, who was on guard. Where's Temp and Ben?'

'They went out to meet that boy, 'Honour said. 'They wouldn't let me go.'

Capability swore. 'I told Temp not to.'

'You didn't,' Honour said. 'You just said you didn't think it was a good idea. But Temp thought it was. So...'

At that moment the door opened, and they walked in.

'Where the hell have you been?'

Ben ran forward like an eager puppy. 'Did you find out about Chas and Si?'

Capability frowned at Temp. 'I told you not to go and meet that boy.'

'You're not in charge here,' Temp said, calmly. 'I make my own decisions.'

Capability sighed. 'I can see that.' Then he said, 'Yes.

I saw them through the one-way glass in the cell doors. They're in separate cells. Chas looked restless but unhurt. Si was hunched in a corner. I couldn't really see his face. I think he's okay, for now.'

'What are they going to do with them?' Ben asked.

'They're going to let the Commander loose on them, to interrogate them about Kate and the rebels.' Capability went to the fridge and took out some milk. He poured his coffee. 'Want one?' he offered. No one did, so he sat down at the counter.

Ben sat down next to him and Honour hovered close by. 'The Commander's vicious,' Ben said, recalling the times he had seen him in action on their travels. 'Can't you get them out of there before he starts on them?'

'It's not that simple,' Capability said.

'I know it's not simple,' Ben said, raising his voice. 'I'm not stupid. But can you do it?'

'No. Resolution will already have them in his interrogation room, I expect. I need to think.' Capability picked up his coffee. 'Temp, come with me. We need to talk.'

Temp followed Capability into his study and shut the door.

Ben got up and began to pace the floor, frustration oozing out of him.

'We'll find a way to rescue them,' Honour said, trying to comfort him.

Ben wasn't usually sarcastic with Honour, but he turned on her. 'Oh yes? You have a plan, do you? Good. Share it with Temp and Capability, cos they clearly have no idea how to get them out of there.' He flung his arm towards the window, where The Fortress could be seen, looming over the river.

'No need to be like that! I'm only trying to help.'

'Get thinking then, because time is running out for them.' Ben flung himself on a sofa and buried his head in a cushion.

*

Once inside his office, Capability turned on Temp. His nerves were fraying. 'What the hell did you think you were doing, going to meet that boy?'

'I'm sorry, I had a gut feeling that he was genuine.'

'A gut feeling? Oh well then, that's okay because your gut feelings are always right.' Capability stood with his hands on the desk, leaning towards Temp on the other side.

Temp shook his head. 'I know it was risky, but it turned out fine. He is genuine. I believe him, but I was cautious. I think he could be useful outside the city. He wants to join the rebellion. He clearly has feelings for Chas.'

Capability rolled his eyes. 'Oh, and that won't be a problem?'

Temp shrugged. 'Who knows. It could be useful. Loyalty is a strong force.'

'But jealousy is the destroyer,' Capability added.

Temp shook his head and walked to the window, away from the intensity of Capability's anger. 'I think we should give him a chance. I was thinking, we should get the kids out of The Citadel and send them to Kate. Let's tell them it's an important mission, or they'll refuse to go; stubborn creatures. We could send the boy (Mish, his name is) with them. I don't know where Kate is at the moment, so they'd need to contact her first and Esme has our phones, so I just hope she's come home.'

'I'd be happier with Ben and Honour out of the city, I must admit,' Capability said, sitting down in his swivel chair. 'This is no place for children. But this new guy...?'

Temp turned away from the window. 'Mish can probably drive, which would help. And I could do with some means of secure communication with Kate, here in The Citadel. Is there any way to get that?'

Capability sat down and swivelled his chair towards Temp, who had now turned to look at him again. 'I can get that. But do we trust this guy? If he's been in Resolution's grip then released, he's probably being tracked.'

I know. I've thought of that,' Temp said, remembering how the tracking device in Si had led Resolution to destroy their commune when they first met. 'I'll check him over. I know how to remove a device, even if it is rather crudely.'

Capability shook his head. 'Okay, I'm tentatively going to go with your instinct. I hope you're right about him. I can get them out of The Citadel without too much difficulty and arrange for a vehicle to be left for them near Esme's. We should keep one invisibility suit with us, in case we can use it.'

'And what about Si and Chas?' Temp asked, coming to sit in the armchair next to the desk.

Capability shook his head. 'I'm just not sure how to get them out of there at the moment, Temp. They're behind intricate security that I don't have access to.'

'Your son does though,' Temp said.

'Yes, but how does that help? He's fully committed to the Rulers and Resolution's right-hand man now. It couldn't get much worse.'

Temp laid a hand on his friend's arm. 'He's your son. Somewhere inside him there'll be a glimmer of conscience.'

'Somewhere very well hidden,' Capability said.

'I don't know how it could help them really, but it's some kind of link, isn't it?'

'Yes, I suppose so. I have to go back to a meeting in the morning. I'll have more news of them after that and, in the meantime, I'll try to figure out how we can help them.'

'Remember the suits too. Maybe you could find out what they've done with the other two that Si had. If we could get access to them, we'd have more to work with.'

Capability tapped his Wearable. 'I'll make some phone calls to get you a phone and find a way of getting them out of the city tomorrow. You should go and break the news to them. I don't think they'd listen to me.'

Temp smiled. 'Don't worry about it. They're not going to be happy with me either when I tell them we're sending them away.'

*

Temp told Ben and Honour the plan, dressing it up as vital that they go. 'We need you to get to Kate and reassure her that we're doing everything we can to get Si and Chas out. I can talk to her when Capability gets me a secure phone, but it'll be better if you go in person. And they need everyone they can get, on the outside, to help the rebels.'

'Also, you want us out of The Citadel,' Honour said, arms folded and a scowl on her face.

'Yes, that too,' said Temp, with a wry smile.

'I'm not leaving without Si and Chas,' Ben said.

'You have to Ben. Think what they would say to you, right now,' Temp said.

'I just...' his words faded, as he realised that Temp was right. He fought back the tears that were pricking his eyes.

'Yeah, I know,' Temp said, feeling the depth of Ben's devotion. 'It's important that you get to Kate. You know so much. You can fill her in and help the rebels to make plans.'

Ben nodded. 'Okay. I'll go.' He took a breath to steady his voice and made himself focus on the task ahead. 'So, we leave tomorrow? Are you going to get a message to Mish?'

'I'm going to meet him in the morning,' Temp said. 'I want to make sure he isn't being tracked. I'm suspicious of why Resolution let him out to wander The Citadel and didn't fling him out into the wilds somewhere, or just kill him.'

'Can we trust him?' Ben asked.

Temp shrugged. 'We don't know yet, but my hunch is that we can.'

'Does Capability have any ideas for getting Si and Chas out?' Ben asked.

'He's working on it. He'll do what he can. You can depend on that.'

Temp turned to Honour. 'And you, young lady, must promise me that you will contact your mother, who must be frantic having seen all the stuff on HTV about the execution.'

Honour glowered at him. Temp raised his eyebrows in a silent question.

She glowered even more, but Temp wasn't backing down. Eventually she gave in. 'Okay, okay, I promise.'

Later, Temp overheard Honour talking to Ben about their 'mission' and thought she looked happier than he had seen her for a long time. He wondered if the prospect of talking to her mother was actually quite appealing. Ben was quiet. Temp knew he didn't like the idea of leaving The Citadel without Chas and Si, but he also knew that Ben would do anything to help them, and if this was it, he would do it.

20

Excellence dragged Si to his feet without a word of explanation.

'Hey, I was asleep!' Si said. 'An alarm clock would be preferable!'

'Shut up!' Excellence said.

'Charming company you are,' Si replied.

Excellence cuffed his hands behind his back and pushed him out of the cell. 'The Commander has requested your presence.'

Si's stomach did an involuntary lurch at the thought of what Resolution wanted with him. He glanced at the cell next door.

'Who's in there?' he asked.

'Your friend Chastity. She'll no doubt be following you soon.'

'Can I see her?' Si asked.

Excellence just laughed. 'You don't get to make requests in here. You get to obey orders.'

'Like you then.'

'I obey because I want to. Now, be quiet. You're annoying me.'

Si was pleased about that. He looked back, as he was

dragged up the corridor, through numerous security doors. He wished he could talk to Chas, there was so much he needed to say. He hoped she didn't really think he was an idiot.

In the lift Excellence stood facing forwards, holding Si by the arm.

Si decided to annoy him some more. 'So, do you enjoy being Resolution's lacky?'

Excellence didn't look at him. 'I'm not his lacky. I'm his second-in-command.'

'Aren't you a bit young for that? He's just using you. You'll probably find that he'll get someone more experienced soon and you'll be out of favour.'

Excellence prickled, Si could feel it. 'Just shut up, Hunter. You'll have your chance to do lots of talking, once the Commander begins his questions.' He turned to face Si, grinning sarcastically. 'Now, that's when you should really talk and keep talking, if you know what's good for you. The Commander is not a merciful man.'

'Oh, I already know that!' Si said, feeling his stomach clench again.

They stepped out of the lift on to the twelfth floor and marched along the corridor, to where Resolution's office and suite of interrogation rooms were. As they stepped inside, Si had a flash-back to his time in the Bastille, when Resolution had been trying to extract information about the Nanomedibots and doing all kinds of tests on him. He felt bile rise suddenly in his throat and thought he was going to be sick. He swallowed hard, took some deep breaths and managed to keep control.

The Commander stood silhouetted in the light from the window. He turned to face them. 'Good morning Silence. It's been a while.'

'Not long enough,' Si said. His usual sense of humour and bravado was not serving him well right now.

The last time they had seen each other was when they had escaped together from the Priory. Resolution had been shot and Kate had saved his life. Thinking of what was about to happen made Si wish his mother was not such a good person.

'Remove his T-shirt and secure him in the chair,' Resolution said to Excellence.

Excellence uncuffed Si's hands, pulled his T-shirt off and strapped him into a high-backed, swivel-chair, with various implements beside it. He tried not to look at them but focused on breathing steadily.

'You can stay,' Resolution said to Excellence. 'Think of this as part of your training. I may ask for your assistance.'

'Thank you, Commander.'

Si braced himself. He must not give anything away about his mother or the locations and safe houses they had been to. He knew Peter was probably already in custody, but he must try to protect him as much as possible.

Resolution stood in front of him, looking as if he was about to do something that gave him great pleasure. 'So, Silence. Today, it is in your best interests not to live up to your name. The more you talk, the less pain you feel. I'm sure you understand how these things work.'

Si spoke more calmly than he had anticipated he would, going by the churning in his stomach. 'I know you'd enjoy it if I didn't talk much at first, and it will be painful for me to give you that pleasure, but do what you want. I won't tell you anything useful.'

Resolution laughed. 'I admire your sentiments, but believe me, you will talk. I'm one hundred per cent sure of that.'

'You can never be one hundred per cent sure of anything,' Si said.

Resolution didn't reply. He took a thin electronic wand, measuring about ten centimetres, from his tray of implements. He switched it on and it powered up with a blue light coiling its way from the handle to the tip. He turned to Excellence. 'This is a little favourite of mine. I had it specially made. It delivers electric shocks of varying degrees, at whatever point I touch it to the skin. Watch.' He held the wand against Si's thigh for a couple of seconds. Si made a noise through his teeth, trying not to cry out. The shock was painful but brief. 'That's on a low setting, of course,' Resolution said. 'I can turn it up much more. But we will build up gradually to that. Do you want to try it?'

He held out the wand to Excellence, who took it and moved forward. 'What setting shall I use?'

'Up to you.'

Si watched Excellence fiddle with the slider on the wand. He took a deep breath and braced himself. Excellence flicked his eyes over Si's body. 'Now, where to try it?' They were acting like two little boys playing with an exciting new toy.

Excellence touched the wand to Si's earlobe. Si couldn't help but cry out. The pain was intense, like someone had just jabbed a sharp stick into his ear and rammed it right through to the other side. When Excellence took the wand away after only a few seconds, Si's head was still ringing.

Excellence handed the wand back to Resolution. 'Hmmm. Effective for such a small thing.'

Resolution smiled. 'Yes, that's why I like it. Now, to business.' He sat down on a chair with wheels, in front of Si, bringing his face level with Si's. 'First, tell me where your mother is.'

Si said nothing. Resolution sighed. 'I need an answer to this question before I move on, and 'I don't know' is the wrong answer.'

Si smiled at him. 'Then there's no point in me saying anything because I genuinely don't know.'

'Where was she when you last saw her?'

Si kept quiet. Resolution moved his chair back. 'She was at Peter Marsden's, wasn't she?'

Si said nothing and tried not to let his face show that this was precisely where he had seen her last. Excellence pulled Si's head back, by the hair. 'You must enjoy the touch of the Commander's wand. Answer his question.'

Resolution waved an impatient hand at his assistant. 'No matter. Your face betrays you, Silence. So, you last saw her there. We know Marsden is involved. He is currently enjoying the hospitality of the Rulers in the Priory.'

Si's heart beat faster. The Priory, built on the island of Lindisfarne, was one of the top detention centres for political prisoners. He knew how difficult it would be to get Peter out of there. His mind flicked back to the journey by boat, from Seahouses, with Ethan and Chas, and their swim to the island. How they had even managed to get there without drowning, he would never know.

Resolution continued. 'Marsden supplied you with the invisibility suits. We have the two you kindly brought to us. How many more do the rebels have?'

Si didn't know what to say. Should he tell him this one? How could it make any difference? But he had told Resolution he wouldn't talk. He looked at the wand and decided that this information was probably not that useful.

'Two more.'

Resolution smiled. 'There. Cooperation is not too difficult, is it? So, where is your mother and who is with her?'

Si closed his eyes briefly. 'I already told you...'

'Remember,' Resolution interrupted. ''I don't know' gets you another turn of my favourite toy.'

Si closed his eyes and shook his head.

'Last chance...'

Si opened his eyes and braced himself.

Resolution adjusted the power on the wand and held it to Si's chest for several seconds. Si's body jerked as if he was having an epileptic seizure. He gritted his teeth against the pain, but it was too much and he cried out.

Resolution stopped. 'Where are they?'

No answer. The wand was pressed to his cheek for longer than any of the times before. Si screamed as pain shot through his face; it was as if someone was boring a hole through his cheek. Involuntary tears escaped from his eyes and all he could do was hold on until the pain passed. He tried to keep a picture of his mother in his mind. I won't let them get to you, Mum. I've already let you down. I'm sorry.

As the pain subsided he was able to focus again on Resolution. Excellence stood in the background, but Si couldn't make out his features. His long-distance vision was still blurred.

'We will find her eventually, Silence. We have infiltrated several of the plague camps and taken people for questioning. Why prolong the agony? Give me names of people involved. Give me other places they might be.'

Si pulled forwards against his restraints. His voice was weakened, and he had little strength in his limbs, but he mustered every ounce of aggression and croaked through clenched teeth. 'I will *never* tell you where my mother is. I will *never* betray her to you!'

Resolution raised his eyebrows, then calmly stood up and held the wand to Si's temple. He shook his head and turned on the wand. Si's body went into spasms, as pain shot through his head like he was being scalped. A white light filled his vision and he blacked out.

'That's the end of today's session then.' Resolution said, putting the wand back in its precise spot on his implements tray. 'Take him back to the cell.'

'Certainly, Commander.' Excellence undid the straps around Si's arms and legs and picked up the discarded T-shirt.

Resolution had moved to his desk and called up his screen to make notes. He glanced up. 'Do you need some help with him? I can call a guard.'

'No. I can manage, Commander. Thank you.' Excellence threw Si's body over his shoulder.

As he put his hand on the door to open it, Resolution said, 'I've had a thought. Put him in with Chastity. I want them to get to know each other again. We'll question him again when we get back from the Priory and let him watch us use the wand on her, for every wrong answer he gives and every silence he keeps. Then we'll see how long '*never*' lasts.'

When Excellence had gone, Resolution finished his report on Si. He was frustrated that the boy had held out for so long. But he knew that Si had feelings for Chastity. If he had come to save her from execution, he wouldn't be able to sit there and watch her being tortured.

He sighed in annoyance at the thought that he now had to drive all the way up to the Priory on Lindisfarne. However, he would no doubt find it interesting to interrogate Marsden. He would take Excellence with him and educate him in the ways he worked. He was glad that the Rulers had allowed him to drop that imbecile Miller and train Excellence instead. He saw potential in this boy for a future in charge of security. Knowles had been a faithful assistant before his unfortunate death escaping from the Priory, but Excellence could be more than that. He could be Resolution's protege.

He began to make preparations for his journey, beginning with a few phone calls. He planned to leave before sunset.

*

Chas was asleep when the door of her cell opened. She

bolted to her feet, as Excellence entered and dumped Si's body on the floor, leaving without a word.

Chas couldn't quite believe what she was seeing. He looked dead. She bent and checked his neck for a pulse. It was there, beating faintly as if all the life in him had retreated away from the surface. She turned him onto his back to look for signs of injury, but saw none.

'Si, can you hear me?'

There was no response. 'Si.' She shook him gently, then harder. He was limp in her hands.

There was a water jug on the table with only a small, lukewarm glassful left in it. There had been no fresh water brought to her in the last fifteen hours. She poured some of it over his face. He spluttered and coughed. His body spasmed and his eyes began to open. He groaned and tried to focus.

He tried to sit up, but the pain shot through the back of his head like a hammer blow. He lay still. The shape of a person swam in front of his eyes, but he couldn't make out who it was. It didn't look like Resolution. It looked female.

'It's okay Si. It's me.' She cupped his head with one hand and tried to ease him up.

Slowly, he tried again to sit up. 'Chas?'

'Yes. Here take some sips of this.' She handed him the half-full glass.

'He closed his eyes and drank. 'I think I have the headache from hell.'

'What did he do to you? I don't see any marks.'

'He's got a new toy. He just has to touch you with it and

it sends excruciating shock waves through your body.' He drained the glass of what little water they had. 'Thanks.'

Chas helped him to stand and sat him down on the bench. 'Did you tell him anything?'

Si looked disdainfully at her. 'You doubt me? Of course not! I know you think I'm an idiot, but it turns out I'm not such a push-over after all.' He bent his head forward, leaning heavily on his knees, catching his breath.

She smiled half-heartedly. 'Yeah, I'm sorry about that. The idiot thing. I didn't mean it.'

He turned to her and grinned. 'Yeah, you did.'

She caught his smile and smiled back. 'Okay, I did mean it at the time, but not now. I appreciate what you did for me. I have to admit, I was very pleased to see you.'

Si straightened up and looked at her. His eyes held a pained expression and she wasn't sure if it was the headache or a window on his soul. 'How could I have lived with myself if I'd just let you die?'

She looked at him and felt tears begin to prick her eyes. Here he was. Si. She hadn't seen him in over a year. She had thought she might never see him again and had resigned herself to that. She had even tried to make a new relationship work with Mish, to a certain extent. But here he was. Silence Hunter. Her heart was pounding, and she didn't know whether she was going to laugh or cry. She stood up and walked to the door, giving herself time to get control.

Si didn't know what to make of this. His head throbbed a little less now and his thoughts were coming more coherently. He had wanted so much to be with her again and he'd lost count of the times he'd had to push thoughts of her out of his head. And now, here they were, locked together in a space only three metres square.

'Why do you think they've put you in here with me?' she said.

Si shook his head, then regretted it. 'Ouch! I really don't know. Not because they wanted to give us a treat, that's for sure.'

'No.'

She looked around the cell. 'I can't see any surveillance, but I'm sure they're watching us. Maybe they thought you'd tell me some stuff.'

Si looked up at the ceiling and around the walls. 'Yeah, well, they can forget that.'

She came back to sit beside him.

'So, what can we talk about?' he said. 'Can you tell me much about where you've been? I presume you found what you were looking for?'

'Yeah. I joined up with a commune and this guy called Mish helped me find Resolution.' At this point she looked up and spoke louder for the benefit of any cameras that might be hidden in the cell. 'Resolution – *my brother!*' Then she lowered her voice again. 'We found him in Durham, living among the junkies and other undesirables who manage to avoid the workhouse. But my plan went wrong, and he took me. I tried to escape and got shot in the leg. They put me in the hospital here, for a while, then I nearly escaped from there, but they caught me. You know the rest. They made me make the video to get to you.'

'They must have done something drastic to persuade

you.'

'Yeah. Resolution found Mish. It was my fault. He brought him to The Citadel and threatened to kill him.'

'Oh.' Si wasn't sure what to say next. 'So, you and this Mish guy. Are you... I mean, is he your...'

Chas shook her head. She didn't want Si to know how close she had got to Mish, despite her hang-ups. 'He helped me, that's all. He's a good guy. So, what could I do when they threatened him? I couldn't have lived with myself if I'd just let them do it.'

'What did they do with him after you made the video?'

She shook her head. 'They actually let him go. I watched him on CCTV. He just walked away.'

'Wow! That's weird. Is your brother showing mercy these days? Or keeping his word? It's not in character with what I've just witnessed.'

'I doubt it. I wouldn't be surprised if they followed him, or if he's not back in custody or maybe even dead.' She shrugged. 'But I couldn't let him die for me.'

Si nodded. 'Any ideas how we can get out of here?'

Chas shrugged. 'In a box?'

Si looked at her, wryly. 'Oh, you mean dead?'

'Yep.'

'Right. Yeah. That's all I can think of too.'

21

Everyone was up early in Capability's apartment. The air was thick with nervous tension. Temp had left, to meet Mish and check him over for a tracking device. He had taken a small knife and some antiseptic spray, in case he needed to remove anything. If all was well, Temp would meet them at the rendezvous point with Mish. Capability was going to drive them all out of The Citadel, through a checkpoint, where he knew the guards. Ben and Honour would be in the boot of the car and Mish would be trying out one of the invisibility suits. Capability was confident that the guards wouldn't check his car too thoroughly and, if they looked like they might, he knew what they liked in bribes. Rulers often bribed checkpoint guards, if they wanted to bring illegal substances or banned people (usually women) in and out of The Citadel. Capability had a couple of bottles of decent whisky on the back seat, just in case.

Ben was nervous. Honour was excited. They had been briefed that they must find Esme and get in contact with Kate. After that, there wasn't really a plan. They would see what Kate thought was best. Capability had organised a secure device for Temp, so that he would be able to communicate with her, from The Citadel. They needed to get the number to Kate, then she could contact Temp.

'Are you ready?' Capability said, finishing off a glass of orange juice. Honour was already by the door, eager to leave.

Ben came out of the bedroom. 'Yep.'

'You're clear what you've got to do?'

'Yes.'

'If Esme isn't back at her house, wait twenty-four hours. If she doesn't come, one of you needs to come back into The Citadel, using the invisibility suit. Come back here and we'll send a car for the ones left behind. Clear?'

'Yes sir,' Honour said, saluting Capability, with a grin.

*

When Mish arrived in the alleyway, he was startled to see Temp already waiting for him. 'I didna expect you this soon,' he said, moving further into the shadows.

'We think you're probably being tracked,' Temp said. 'Have you felt anything unusual in your arms or legs?'

Mish pulled a face. 'Canna say that I have.'

'Can I look?'

'Aye.'

Mish rolled up his sleeves and Temp felt carefully along his arms for signs of a small tracking device, like the one he had found in Si. Nothing there. 'Roll up your trousers.' Temp felt around his calf muscles and up into his lower thigh. Again, he felt nothing.

'I feel like I'm being frisked,' Mish said.

'You are. I'm sorry but you're going to have to let me examine your upper thighs. It's possible they could have inserted it there.'

Mish shrugged and pulled down his jeans. He felt a bit weird and dreaded to think what anyone would think was going on, if they happened to stumble into the alley right now. But he was keen for Temp to trust him, so he didn't object.

'Nothing,' Temp said. 'You're clear, as far as I can tell.'

Mish pulled up his jeans. 'Cool. So, what happens next?'

'Do you still want to help the rebellion?' Temp asked.

'Aye, that's why I'm still here.'

'Okay. You're going to leave The Citadel with Ben and a girl called Honour. One of the Rulers is taking you in his car.'

Mish pulled back. 'What?'

'He's my friend. His name's Capability and you can trust him. He's going to drive you out of the gates. Can you drive a car?'

'Aye.'

'Good. Capability will arrange for a car to be left for you to pick up, near to the house that Ben will take you to. He'll explain more in the car. We want you to try and get to Kate, Si's mother.'

Mish was surprised by the trust Temp was showing him. 'Okay. Right. And what about Chas?'

'This will help her. These people are rallying others to fight against the Rulers. It puts pressure on them. In the meantime, Capability and I are going to see what we can do from here for Chas and Si.'

Mish nodded. 'What about my commune?'

'If you help Ben and Honour get to Kate, you can take the car as far as possible towards your commune after that.'

'Okay, thanks,' Mish said.

'Come on. Keep your hood up. They know who you are.'

Mish followed Temp through the streets of The Citadel. Temp was also wearing a coat with a hood up, as he wasn't sure if he might also be recognised on CCTV. Thankfully, it was raining, so this didn't look out of the ordinary. People with umbrellas, and hoods up, were on the streets now, going to work.

Temp led Mish to Capability's car. Mish got in next to Ben and Honour and Temp got into the front seat.

'Everything okay?' Capability asked, glancing at Mish in the rear-view mirror.

'Yes. He seems to be clear.' Temp turned around. 'Mish, this is Capability. He's driving you through the gate.'

'But the guards...'

'Ben and Honour will be in the boot and you... well, you get to wear the invisibility suit.'

Temp watched Mish's eyes widen and smiled. 'You need to wear minimal clothes underneath it, so give your stuff to Ben to put in the boot.'

Mish looked at the other two. 'Where should I get changed?'

You'll just have to do it in the back. Ben will help you. I know it's a bit cramped but it can't be helped.'

Mish looked across at Honour, who averted her eyes. He wriggled out of his jeans and hoodie. Ben helped him into the invisibility suit.

As his body began to disappear, he laughed. 'Woah! This

is surreal!'

Ben laughed too. 'Yeah, it's weird. It takes a while before you really believe no one can see you. But people can feel you if you touch them, so you've got to be careful of that.'

Temp turned to them all. 'Okay. I'm going to go back to Capability's now. You be careful and remember the plan. No going off and doing your own thing. Do exactly what we told you. Clear?'

'Yes boss,' Honour said.

Ben gave her a withering look. 'Yes. We'll do what we're supposed to. I hope Esme's back home.'

Temp looked doubtful. 'I hope so too. Just be careful. Stay safe.' He turned to Capability. 'I'll see you later.'

'I'll have to go straight to the Rulers' meeting. I'll be home tonight.'

Temp got out of the car and walked away.

Capability spoke to his car. 'Back seat down.' The backs of the seats slid down, making access to the boot. 'Get in. Hopefully this will be over quickly and you'll be out again soon.'

Ben and Honour climbed through to the boot and lay down. There wasn't much space, so they had to curl up together. Honour couldn't help giggling. 'This is cosy. It reminds me of when we used to play hide-and-seek and we'd find the best places together, so Grace couldn't find us.'

'Yeah, well, let's hope the guards don't want to play, 'cos I think they'd find us easily this time.'

Mish kept looking at himself, at least looking at where he knew his body was. It was the strangest sensation, only seeing the car seat where his body should be. As they approached the gate, the car waited in a short queue to get through. Being a Ruler, Capability had special privileges and could jump the ordinary queue, to a shorter one for VIPs.

The car pulled up in front of the guards at the checkpoint. The window lowered, and the guard peered in. He recognised Capability straight away but still asked for ID. Capability waited, ready to offer the bribe if necessary.

'That's fine, Sir. Have a nice day,' the guard said.

'Oh, I won't be long. I've got a meeting to attend, shortly.'

The guard waved him through. Capability felt himself relax. 'Are you okay in the back?'

'Yes. Aye. Good,' Mish said.

They drove on until they were a good distance from the gate, then Capability stopped the car. Ben and Honour climbed out of the boot and Mish peeled back the head-gear of the invisibility suit.

'Pretty cool, eh?' Honour said, grinning at Mish.

'Yeah,' Mish nodded.

'You'll need to direct me to Esme's house,' Capability said. 'I won't take you directly to it. Maybe drop you half a mile away. She doesn't want a Ruler's car pulling up at her front door.'

Ben had a good memory for places. Capability showed them where the car was going to be left for them tomorrow. 'Just be careful.' Then, he let them out of the car and drove back to The Citadel. He was cutting it fine to be in time for the meeting.

'If one more person tells us to be careful...' Honour said.

'It's only 'cos they care,' Ben said.

'It's more like they don't think we're capable of looking after ourselves,' she said.

Mish had gone behind a bush, by the side of the road, to take off the invisibility suit and change back into his clothes. When he emerged, Ben asked him for the suit. 'I'll keep it in my rucksack.'

Mish handed it over, accepting that he was still not fully trusted. 'So, you two are friends of Chas then?'

Honour replied. 'Ben is. I've never met her. I'm Ben's kind-of sister.'

'You don't think Chas is going to go back with you, when we get them out, do you?' Ben said to Mish. 'She won't, you know. Now she's back with Si. I mean, I'm sorry for you and all that, but she and Si are really close.'

Mish smiled. 'Aye, you've told me that a few times. I get the message. I'm going back to ma commune to find out what happened after I was kidnapped. I'm sure some of them will join us.'

Ben bit his lip, hoping that Mish's commune had not been decimated like Chas's had.

'This is it,' Honour said, as they approached the only house on the road. There was no sign of life. No lights on, or movement.

Ben knocked on the door, hoping to hear the dogs bark. It was silent. His heart sank. 'Let's look round the back.'

They knocked at the back door and tried the handle. Locked, and no sounds from inside.

'If they were here the dogs would have barked by now,' Honour said.

Ben sighed. 'We'll just have to sit round the back here, and wait. We can shelter in the shed tonight, if she doesn't come. Then I'll go back to The Citadel.'

'She said she had somewhere else to go for a while,' Honour said.

'I know. We could just do with her being here, right now. I wish she'd told us where she was going.'

They sat down to wait out the rest of the day in the back garden.

*

Capability made it through the doors of the meeting room at 10.07. Everyone else was seated and listening to Zephyr. All eyes turned to him as he sat down.

'I'm very sorry I'm late, Premier.'

Ambition raised an eyebrow, waiting for the excuse.

'What kept you?' Zephyr said.

'I got caught up in some work before I came out. I just wasn't keeping an eye on the time. I'm sorry.'

Zephyr waved a dismissive hand and resumed his speech. Ambition narrowed his eyes at Capability, who quickly looked away and focused his attention on the Premier. He tried to calm his racing heart, knowing that if he was found to have helped the rebels he would be sentenced to death on charges of treason. He pushed that thought out of his consciousness and tried to pretend that Ambition wasn't watching him. He tuned in to what Zephyr was saying.

'The Commander arrived at the Priory last night and will

be reporting to us as soon as he has interrogated Marsden. I'm wondering if we should have him brought back to The Citadel.' He looked around the room.

'If necessary, yes,' Ambition said. 'Let's wait to see what he gets out of Marsden. In my opinion, the man has committed treason. I've had my suspicions about his sympathies for a while. Why wasn't he executed when he helped Hunter the first time?'

Zephyr cleared his throat. 'He's a valuable man. He's contributed much to the technological development of our society. I decided he deserved another chance.'

Ambition snorted. 'Yes, you decided. It should have been a party decision.'

Zephyr stood up and blazed at Ambition. 'I am your Premier. Don't dare question my authority.'

The other Rulers looked at Ambition. They trod a fine line between controlling their cloned leader and doing what he said. Ambition backed down. 'I was only suggesting that we should all participate in such important decisions, Premier.'

Zephyr sat down slowly. 'And we do, Ambition. But there are some things on which I am entitled to decide myself. I am the Premier after all, am I not?' Zephyr looked around the room.

Ambition shifted uncomfortably in his seat. The other Rulers made assenting noises.

'Good. Back to the business in hand. Marsden will be questioned by the Commander, then brought here for trial. Now, what are we going to do with Hunter and his companion, once we've found his mother and quashed the rebellion?'

'Execute them, of course,' one of the Rulers said.

'I wondered if we could have other uses for them first,' Ambition said.

'Like what?' another Ruler asked.

Ambition leaned forward. 'Our Premier here is made up of DNA taken from great leaders of the past. Men with ambition and a determined thirst for power. This is why he is such a strong leader. With their gene base, he has the best chance of leading us to fulfil our dream of Power, Domination and Immortality.' He looked at Zephyr admiringly. Zephyr nodded. 'In the Genetics Research Centre, they're working on our own clones to perpetuate our existence. It's an exciting thought that we will live on forever, even though this original body dies.'

'But what does this have to do with the prisoners?' asked another Ruler.

'Two things,' Ambition continued. 'One: I would like to clone Silence Hunter and Chastity Komchenski.'

Capability was appalled. 'Why would we do that? They're rebels. Why would we want clones from them?'

'They have many qualities that we could use: Loyalty, determination, perseverance. We could create a whole population of fiercely loyal clones from whoever we chose, using our clones of Silence and Chastity to lead the way. Don't you love the irony of that? Then we'd have even less use for people born the old-fashioned way. We can get rid of them on a bigger scale, selecting only the ones we want to clone and educate to our ways from birth. No parents. We'd have complete control.'

There was a lot of murmuring and discussion amongst the Rulers.

'And what is the second thing?' Capability asked, trying to conceal his despair.

Ambition pulled up a screen in mid-air above the table. 'Watch this. It's footage from the secret camera installed in their cell.'

The Rulers watched as Chas and Si talked. They couldn't hear all of it, as their voices were lowered, but they certainly heard Chas's words when she named Resolution as her brother.

'Why would she say that?' someone asked.

Zephyr spoke slowly and deliberately. 'Because maybe it's true. I always thought there was something I couldn't quite put my finger on about Resolution.'

'Maybe it's true, maybe not,' Ambition said. 'Worth finding out. If she is related to that ruthless ambitious zealot, then her DNA is definitely worth having.'

'And the Commander may have an interrogation of his own to endure, from me,' Zephyr said.

'Who would carry the clones to birth?' asked Capability.

Ambition smirked. 'Who better than Chastity herself. We could implant both embryos into her womb. They could grow like twins.'

There were raised eyebrows and more muttering. 'That's never been done before. It's very risky,' Capability said.

'Indeed. That's why we should use her first. If something goes wrong with the embryos, we can try again. If something goes wrong with the host, then it's no real loss. We'd still have the DNA. We could use other rebel women captives to be hosts as we begin to quash this rebellion.'

There was a lot of murmuring from around the table and nods of agreement. Capability's muscles tensed and his mouth was so dry he felt as though he couldn't speak. He reached for the water jug. He couldn't allow this violation of human rights to happen to Si and Chas. And the implications for the future were horrendous. But he felt so helpless. He had to gain access to them somehow.

Zephyr drew their attention. 'So, we'll make a decision on this,' he looked pointedly at Ambition, 'together. Let's take a show of hands. Who would like to go ahead with this experiment?'

Everyone raised their hand. Capability couldn't afford to stand out, so he also consented.

Zephyr shuffled papers in front of him. 'Fine. We'll wait until the Commander returns and finishes interrogating them. Unless anyone has any other business that will be all for today. I'll keep you informed as soon as I hear from the Commander about Marsden.'

As if being summoned, an image of Resolution appeared on the floating screen in the centre of the table. Zephyr accepted the call and a holo-image of Resolution's face appeared above the table. 'Commander, what can we do for you?'

'Premier, I have just had word from The Citadel law-keepers. You know we injected a tracker into Chastity's friend, Submission, before we set him free? I've had word. He's finally left The Citadel, although no one at the check points saw him leave. He passed through checkpoint five, earlier this morning, at 09.10 hours. We're investigating how he got out unseen.'

Capability's heart leapt into his mouth. He swore inwardly, terrified that they might soon be able to identify the fact that Mish had been in his car.

'And where is he now?' Zephyr asked.

'We have the co-ordinates. He's stopped, not far from The Citadel. Satellite surveillance shows him at a house with two other people. I'll get the law-keepers to keep track of them. Hopefully they'll lead us to Kate Hunter and the rebels.'

'Do you have any evidence that he's linked to them?'

'Not yet, but he was involved with Chastity, so there's a good chance of a link.'

'Yes,' Zephyr said, considering what he had just learned about Resolution's own potential link to Chastity Komchenski. 'Who is he with?'

'Two younger people. Boy and a girl. Silence and Chastity had a boy matching this description with them last year, so I think there's a good chance they could lead somewhere significant.'

'Excellent. Keep us posted. What's happening with Marsden?'

'I'm seeing him as soon as I've finished talking with you, Premier.'

'Right. Thank you, Commander.' The holo-image disappeared. 'Thank you everyone. I'll keep you up to date with progress. That will be all.'

Capability hurried away. He felt sick. He had to get to Temp and warn him of everything. They had to leave his apartment and possibly get out of the city. Temp had said there was no tracker! How could he have missed it? How was he going to help Si and Chas now?

His stomach lurched even more when he heard Ambition calling after him, along the corridor. He couldn't ignore him, that would only make it look worse. He did his best to compose himself, turned and waited for Ambition to catch up.

'You left like a bolt of lightning. Are you alright with my idea? You seem a little... shocked.' There was that supercilious smirk on his face again. Capability felt like scraping it off with his nails.

'I'm fine with your ideas, Ambition. I just think we need to be careful. If word gets out to the general populace, about any of this, it will cause more riots.'

Ambition laughed. 'Really? You worry too much, Capability. Firstly, it won't get out and even if it did, it would be managed in a way that made sense to the people. They won't be told the truth, obviously. And they know that we don't tolerate threats to the regime. They've seen that for themselves these past few weeks.'

Capability smiled, sarcastically. 'Yes. Now, if you don't mind, I've got to be somewhere shortly, so I must get off. Goodbye.'

Before Ambition could say anything else to delay him, Capability quickened his pace. He must get back to Temp. As he turned the corner, he felt a sense of physical relief to be away from the feeling of Ambition's eyes boring into his back. He knew he didn't have long. First, he had to pay a visit to the person who was getting him the phone that couldn't be tracked, for Temp.

He kept checking that he wasn't being followed, but there didn't seem to be anyone tailing him. Beads of sweat trickled down the side of his face. He wiped them away with his handkerchief. This took him back to the time when he was arranging safe passage out of the country for his daughters.

The man was waiting with the device for him. Capability paid him the large sum of money and hurried back to his apartment. When he made it through the door his legs nearly collapsed with relief.

'You look awful,' Temp said. 'What's happened? Did they get away safely?'

He told Temp everything that had been said at the meeting.

'I don't understand about the tracker,' Temp said. 'I know what they feel like. I know where they put them inside people.'

'They're constantly developing these things. Maybe it's a different sort of tracker.'

Temp paced the floor. 'We have to get to them before they lead the Rulers straight to Kate and Nick.'

'We'd never get out of the check-point. They'll be looking for my car soon. You and I will be arrested any minute, if we don't get out of here.'

'We have to do something,' Temp said. 'I should try to get to them in the invisibility suit.'

Capability was rushing around the apartment, gathering things he needed. 'We need to get out of here, now! I know somewhere in The Citadel where we can hide for a while. Bring the invisibility suit and you can go as soon as possible.'

'I'll come back,' Temp said. 'I'm not leaving you to face this alone.'

Capability gripped his shoulder. 'Thanks, old friend. Grab your stuff. Let's go.'

22

Resolution pulled Peter Marsden's head backwards by the hair. He was barely conscious, and Resolution recoiled from the bloody nose and swollen face that Marsden had received from Excellence's pre-interrogation 'discussion'. He really should have told him 'no blood,' but he didn't want Excellence to be aware of his weakness, if he could keep it a secret. He didn't yet trust this boy the way he had trusted Knowles. Excellence looked on like a proud puppy, awaiting his master's approval, but Resolution turned to him, with a look of distaste.

Excellence's expression changed. 'I'm sorry, Commander. Have I done it wrong? I thought you wanted me to let him know that we mean business.'

'I think he knows that, just from our presence here. You obviously haven't seen enough of my interrogation style yet.'

'Sorry Commander. I...'

'Be quiet!' Resolution hissed, letting go of Marsden's hair. His head lolled forwards and he groaned. 'He's no good to me like this, before I've even started. I'll have to wait a few hours, maybe until tomorrow now.' He marched past Excellence and left the room. Excellence cursed his stupidity and followed his master.

'Stay there and guard the room,' Resolution barked, over his shoulder. 'I don't want to see you for a while.'

'Yes sir,' Excellence said, going back to Marsden's room and standing outside the door.

Resolution went back to the temporary office he had been given on arrival last night. He brought up a screen and saw that he had a message from the law-keepers in The Citadel, marked as urgent.

The message was a holo-image of one of his men, telling him that they had traced several cars leaving gate five at the time of Mish's exit. There was a list of owners, none seemed significant, until he saw the name of Capability North.

Could he be involved in some way? Why was he leaving The Citadel just before the Rulers had a meeting scheduled? Resolution contacted his man and told him to check out all the other owners of the cars and check the time of re-entry of Capability's car. 09.44 hours. A short trip and back, just in time for the meeting. Gate five was not near Capability's apartment. Resolution paced the floor, trying to think of a reason why Capability would be mixed up in all this. He knew Capability felt uneasy about his son becoming his new assistant, but that wasn't enough. He recalled the questions about Chas and Si; his wanting to see them. His going to speak to his son whilst on duty in the cells.

He sat at his desk and pulled up all the information he could find on Capability North, going back as far as he could. Gradually it dawned on him just what the connection might be. There were several photographs and reports that suggested he had been good friends with

Temperance Alliston when he was one of the Rulers, before he had absconded. Alliston had connections with Chastity and Silence. He was still out there somewhere, or maybe he was closer than they realised. That must be it. He had to tell Zephyr immediately. This should be another feather in his cap with the Premier. It might soothe the annoyance he knew Zephyr would feel, to hear about Marsden. He would blame Resolution for letting Excellence loose on him. Resolution would question the boy about his father shortly too.

*

Zephyr was furious as he stood in his office, flanked by Ambition and Zealous. He had just finished an infuriating call with Resolution. The man just seemed to trail a string of calamities behind him. It made Zephyr all the more eager to find out if he was related to Chastity. This might be one way to get rid of him once and for all.

Ambition ended a call to the law-keepers who had been sent to Capability's apartment. 'He's gone. We've ransacked his apartment and taken anything that might be relevant. No clue as to where he's gone, though. His car's still there and no sightings of him or Temperance leaving The Citadel.'

'I knew there was something suspicious about the way he's been acting recently,' Ambition said.

'And you didn't say anything?' Zealous asked.

'I couldn't put my finger on it,' Ambition said.

Zephyr tutted and shook his head. 'We should have figured this out ages ago. We knew he was friends with

Temperance all those years ago. We knew Temperance had connections with the rebels. It makes sense.'

Ambition remembered Temp when he was a young, fiercely loyal member of the Party. He had mentored him himself, until it all went wrong with the child. And now Temp's loyalties were fiercely opposed to them. 'Undoubtedly, Temperance is with him.'

'I'm sure,' said Zephyr.

'Law-keepers are on high alert looking for them,' Ambition said. 'If they're still in The Citadel they can't stay hidden for long.'

'They might have some invisibility capability too. That's possibly how they got the boy out of the city,' Zealous said.

'I know. That'll make it more difficult. But, we'll find them,' Ambition replied. 'I'll keep in touch with the law-keepers and do some searching myself too.'

'The sooner we find them, the more we'll know about the rebels. Keep me informed.' Zephyr said, dismissing them.

*

Ben and Honour were amusing themselves with memories and funny stories, from their childhood in Seahouses. Honour could feel the tension emanating from Ben and was doing her best to distract him. Mish was asleep, curled up in the corner of the patio, with his head against the tattered cushion of an old garden chair. Before he fell asleep, he had told them more about the commune and his father. They had played games; I Spy, twenty questions, theme tunes game. But the tension had never really left Ben. Every little noise brought him up sharply, alert for signs of Esme or the barking of the dogs. But there weren't many of these, as this was an isolated place. No one really came this way, unless they had to.

It was getting dark. Honour shivered. 'Shall we go inside the shed now?'

Ben noticed that she was getting cold. They had a little food left and a couple of blankets that Capability had insisted they take with them. 'Why don't you go inside and make it comfy?.' He looked over at Mish. 'He seems okay where he is for now and, to be honest, I want to stay out here as long as possible, just in case.'

Honour sighed. 'Okay, but I don't think she's coming. We probably need to think about going back to The Citadel. We can't find Kate without a phone.'

'Tomorrow,' Ben said. 'We're waiting 'til then.'

Honour shrugged and stood up, pulling the blankets out of their rucksacks. She turned towards the shed, then on impulse, turned and bent over to where Ben was sitting and pulling grass out of the lawn. She hugged him tight. 'I love you, big brother. It'll be alright. Whatever happens here, we'll find a way to make it alright.'

Ben smiled. 'Go on. Get that shed really cosy. I'll join you later and Mish probably will, if he ever wakes up!'

Ben had been thinking about Chas and Si all day. He couldn't help being anxious for them. He knew the Commander could be brutal. They needed to get to Kate and see what the rebels could do to get them out of The Citadel. He couldn't face the prospect of going back to

Temp, defeated. But he had the same doubts as Honour, that Esme was not coming back any time soon.

Mish woke up, rubbing his eyes. 'Sorry. Have I been asleep for long? I'm guessing there's no sign of Esme?'

Ben shook his head.

'Where's Honour?'

'She was cold. She's in there.'

Mish shivered in reaction to Ben's words, despite having been happily asleep for hours. 'Look, it's getting dark. She's not coming, is she? She wouldn't be out in the countryside on her own in the dark. She'd be mad.'

'She's got the dogs,' Ben said.

'Still... Listen, you go inside with Honour. Get some sleep. We can take shifts, keeping watch, if you like. I should be good for a few hours.'

Ben agreed, reluctantly.

*

It was hard for Kate, waiting at the safe house without any information on Si and Chas. Temp's phone just kept ringing out. Esme wasn't answering hers either. They had managed to contact Harmony, who was also in hiding. She told them that Peter was in the Priory and there was nothing Eric could do about it. Nick had tried to assure her that they would think of something, but his words seemed futile.

'We have to go back to Newcastle,' Nick said. 'I think we should call on some of our contacts from The Way to help us. We need to gather those, who are sympathetic to our cause, together now. If we've any hope of bringing the

Rulers down and getting to Si and Chas we have to move quickly.'

'I know,' Kate agreed. 'Where will we go? We can't go back to your flat. They'll have it watched by now.'

'Will they? I'm not sure. They don't know I've anything to do with you, yet.'

'Unless someone from the camps has talked,' Kate said. 'Which is highly likely. They took Doctor Sharma. And we know how they torture people.'

Nick took her hand. 'True, but we also know how people can be amazing at resisting them.' He looked into her eyes, with a smile. She nodded, acknowledging his reference to her time in the Priory; there she had held out, and her husband, Morgan had died, without telling them about Si. She bit her lip, thinking. 'Okay. We'll do it. Let's do our own surveillance on your flat first and if we think it's safe...'

Nick got up and started looking through his contacts. 'I'll get in touch with Pastor Rowley. He can offer us a safe place, if necessary. The members of his group have already been supporting us financially.'

Kate nodded and looked at her phone, willing it to ring and give her some news of Si. She jumped, as if something had bitten her, as it began to vibrate on her wrist. A holo-image of Temp appeared in the room. Nick stopped what he was about to do.

'Temp!' Kate exclaimed, standing up. 'What's happening?'

Temp told her the news on Si and Chas and that he and Capability had had to go into hiding. She slumped back down in the chair. 'We've sent Ben, Honour and a boy called Mish, to Esme's house. But there's a problem. Mish is carrying a tracker. Hopefully not deliberately. I missed it, but he can't be allowed to lead the Rulers to you. Can you get hold of Esme?"

I've tried but she's not answering.'

'Keep trying. I'm on my way out of The Citadel to try and get to them. I've got an invisibility suit, but I'm on foot, so it's going to take some time.'

'Okay. Let me know whatever you find out about Si.'

'Of course.'

*

Ben shivered. He wasn't getting any sleep in the shed: Not like Honour, who was sound asleep. He decided to go outside and keep Mish company. As he opened the door his ears pricked up. He thought he heard a noise round the front of the house. The gate being opened? Then a short bark, swiftly muted by the words, 'Quiet Kurt!'

She'd come!

Mish stumbled to his feet, feeling stiff from all the sitting around in the cold.

'Stay there,' Ben hissed. 'I'll go. They know me. You wake Honour.'

Moving slowly, so as not to startle the dogs, he made his way to the front, but when he got there they were already inside. Now what? Knock? She wouldn't answer. Try to go in? The dogs might attack him. He went round the back of the house again, to peer through the kitchen window. There she was. He tapped on the glass. Esme flinched, and the dogs began to bark.

'Quiet!' she commanded, recognising Ben at once. He virtually fell into her arms, as she opened the back door.

'Esme!'

'Ben!' She looked around the garden. 'Are you alone? Where are the others?'

She motioned for him to sit down. Kurt and Brigitta recognised him too and came to nuzzle their big fierce-looking snouts into his lap. He took some comfort from petting them and spoke to them affectionately. Esme filled the kettle.

'Honour is in the shed, sleeping, and we have a new person with us. Mish. He's a friend of Chas's.'

Esme raised her eyebrows.

'He can tell you his story later. He seems okay.'

'Seems?' Esme frowned. 'Where's Temp?'

'He stayed in The Citadel. He and Capability are going to see what they can do to get Chas and Si out of there.'

Esme gave a snort. 'Good luck there!'

At that moment, Honour and Mish came into the house. The dogs got up and growled again.

'Calm down you two,' Esme said.

Ben held on to them. 'They're friends. It's okay. Sit down, come on.' He pushed the dogs back down and they nestled their heads in his lap once again, still watching Mish and Honour closely as they entered the kitchen.

'Hello,' Esme said. 'Kettle's boiled and there's probably some semi-stale bread in the bread-bin if you want some toast.'

'Thanks,' Mish said. 'I'm starving.' He held out his hand to Esme. 'I'm Mish, by the way: Friend of Chas; enemy of the State.' He grinned.

Esme shook his hand and gave him an eyebrow moment. 'Well, help yourselves to food.' She put a coffee pot on the table and some juice.

'We need to get in touch with Kate and Nick. Do you have Temp and Si's phones?' Ben said.

'Yes, but they're back at the place I've been staying. I'm still not sure if we're safe here. Although I think they'd have probably been here by now, if they were coming.'

'Temp said they were sending a car for me to pick up near here, so I can drive us to find Kate Hunter,' Mish said. 'Capability told me it would be down a side road near the next junction, north of your house.'

'Right. So, we need to call Kate. I must admit I haven't talked to her. I couldn't face the poor woman after what happened to Si. And I was nervous,' Esme admitted.

'When can we go?' Ben asked.

'As soon as you're all finished eating. I just came for a few things. You were lucky. It's the first time I've been back since you left.'

It took them about half an hour to walk to the place Esme had been staying. There was no one else there. It was an empty building, with no lighting or heating, but at least it was sheltered from the elements. The dogs went straight to their beds in the corner. Esme switched on her phone to find several missed calls from Kate. She sighed and called her back.

Kate answered straight away. 'Esme! I've been trying to contact you.'

'Yes. Sorry. I've...' Esme shook her head.

Kate could see the others in the room. 'I've heard from Temp. He told me to warn you. Chas's friend, Mish is carrying a tracker.'

Mish looked from one to the other, as everyone turned accusingly towards him. 'What? That canna be right. He checked me over before he let me come.'

'He told me it must be a different kind, that he's never seen before. They know where you are.'

'Can you do anything about it?' Mish said, turning to Esme.

'I don't know,' she said. 'It depends if I can locate it.' She looked around. 'Damn! That means we're not safe here, either, now.'

'I was supposed to be driving Ben and Honour to meet you,' Mish told Kate.

'Well, you can't do that unless you get rid of the tracker.'

I'll try now,' Esme said. 'Otherwise... well, let's see what I can do.'

*

The law-keepers, back in The Citadel, had seen movement from the tracker and called The Commander. 'Do you want us to move in on him, Sir?'

'Yes. Send a couple of law-keepers to physically stay close, now he's on the move. We don't want to risk losing him and I want people ready to move in straight away, when he leads us to Kate Hunter. Keep me informed.'

Resolution made his way to Peter Marsden's room, where Excellence was still on duty. He smiled to himself at the boy's staying power. He hadn't had a rest for nearly 24 hours now.

'Commander,' Excellence said, standing to attention and saluting.

'How is he this morning?' Resolution asked.

'He's eating and seems a bit brighter.'

'Good. Bring him to the medical facility. I'll be waiting.'

Resolution was determined to find out what Peter knew and how he had helped Silence Hunter. He would certainly gain favour with Zephyr if his information proved valuable. Marsden had always been such a golden boy in the eyes of the Rulers, with his contributions to technological advances. Resolution would enjoy making his fall from the pedestal as painful as possible.

Peter was limping, when Excellence brought him into the room. His face was cut and bruised and one of his eyes was virtually closed. Fortunately for Resolution, he had been cleaned up of all the blood, Excellence had managed to splash around.

'You can go now,' Resolution said to Excellence. 'Have a rest. You've earned it.'

Excellence was surprised. 'But Commander, I thought I should stay and learn from you.'

'Plenty of time for that. Go.' Excellence gave up protesting and left. Resolution turned to Peter. 'Now, Marsden. Let's get down to some proper business. I apologise for that pup's behaviour yesterday. He has no... finesse. Untrained, as yet.'

Peter closed his eyes. 'Just get on with it, Commander. Ask me your questions. Do what you have to do.'

Resolution smiled.

*

'I think that's it,' Esme said. Mish had his shirt off and Esme was poking him, just under his bottom left rib. She had made him strip to his underwear and prodded him, in almost every conceivable place... except the most embarrassing, yet.

'Good!' Mish said. 'I haven't got many places left.'

'It's smaller than the ones Temp knew,' she said. 'Different shape. And they've got it in a difficult place to remove.'

'Can you do it, though?' Honour asked, staring at Mish's chest.

'I don't know. It's embedded almost underneath the rib. A doctor could do it, but I've only got crude means of extracting it.'

'Do whatever you have to,' Mish said.

Esme shook her head. 'It could be dangerous. I've never taken anything out of a place like this before.'

'I won't sue you. Go on. We don't have much choice.'

Esme hesitated then agreed. 'We should go back to my house. I've got first-aid there and it's cleaner. They can find us wherever we are. Come on, we need to hurry.'

Back at Esme's, she made Mish lie on the kitchen table and put on some disposable gloves, which she sprayed with antiseptic. She had sterilized a sharp knife and wiped his skin with the antiseptic. Ben and Honour stood by, with bandages.

'This is going to hurt,' she said.

'Obviously,' Mish said. 'Don't worry, I'm used to pain. No anaesthetic in the villages.'

Honour moved in and held Mish's hand. Ben took the other and Mish gripped them tightly. Esme tried not to let her hands shake, as she dug the knife below his rib, feeling for the small, hard, peanut shape she hoped was the tracker. Mish gritted his teeth and took a sharp breath, but didn't make a sound. Esme inserted her finger and thumb into the incision, which made Mish wince. Finally, she pulled out the small object.

'Got you!' she said, triumphantly holding it up and feeling it pulse faintly in her hand. She put the bloody object carefully on the work surface and turned back to Mish. 'Just got to do up the hole now.' She took some skin glue out of her first-aid box and applied it. 'Probably stings,' she said, as Mish winced again.

'Not too bad,' he said.

She cleaned and bandaged the skin, then picked up the tracker. We need to be ready to move out as soon as I've destroyed this, because they'll know what we've done, and they'll be here quick as you can say roast potatoes!'

Ben and Honour gave her a weird look and she chuckled, mostly from relief that she had found the tracker and not done Mish any harm.

'We're ready,' Mish said, easing slowly off the table.

'Are you alright?' Honour said, still holding his hand.

He smiled at her and took his hand away. 'Aye, I'm fine.'

'I hope that car is where Temp said it would be,' Ben said.

'Me too,' Esme replied. 'Right. Let's find it then I'll kill this thing. Come on Kurt, Brigitta!'

The dogs suddenly began to growl, standing up and moving towards the door. Everyone froze. The law-keepers were here already! Esme instinctively picked up the bloody knife, although realistically she knew it wouldn't help much. She hoped the dogs might hold them off. They began to bark now.

'What are we going to do?' Honour said, feeling really frightened for the first time.

Mish moved in front of Honour. Ben moved beside the dogs.

'Can we get out another way?' Mish asked.

'I doubt it,' Esme said. 'They'll be everywhere. We're going to have to fight. The dogs will be a big help. Arm yourselves.'

She opened the kitchen drawer and they took out various knives. Honour looked terrified. 'I don't know how to kill anyone!'

'Neither do I,' Ben said to her. 'Just wield it around if you have to. It's more of a threat really.'

'Keep near to the dogs,' Esme said, 'and run as soon as you get the chance. Get as far away as possible. Don't wait for me. The dogs will protect me. You just get out of here.'

There was a knock on the door. Esme looked puzzled. 'These dogs will tear you to pieces if you try to come in!' she shouted.

There was a voice from the other side of the door, but they couldn't hear it. 'Quiet!' Esme said to the dogs and they quietened down to a soft growl.

'It's Temp!' came the voice. 'I'm alone.'

'Temp!' Esme breathed a sigh of relief. There was a

visible release of tension from them all as Esme went to open the door.

Temp had stripped the invisibility suit off. He walked through the door, eyeing the dogs warily. They growled at him, but Esme called them off and they went to the corner of the room and lay down.

'I'm so glad you're still here. I had to walk, because the car had already been sent. I didn't know if Kate had been able to get hold of you. Mish has a tracker implanted. Capability found that out at the Rulers meeting. They'll now know he was involved, so he's gone into hiding.'

'Kate contacted us,' Esme said. She held up a small bloody object. 'Here it is.'

Mish pointed to his side.

'I haven't killed it yet,' Esme said. 'I think we need to be ready to leave, before I do. As soon as I do that, they'll be alerted and on us. We thought you were them.'

'The car should be waiting for you. Do you remember where I said it would be?'

Mish nodded.

'We'll leave now,' Esme said. 'What are you going to do?'

'I've got to go back. I can't leave Capability. We'll keep trying to figure a way of getting to Chas and Si.'

Honour flung her arms round Temp and squeezed tight. He was pleasantly surprised by her affection.

The others said their goodbyes and Temp left.

They didn't have to walk far, to find the car. It was exactly where Temp had described. Most cars ran on voice command, but with a key fob as back-up. They found one behind the front tyre. Esme took the tracker and crushed it with a stone.

'It's done. Let's go!'

As they set off, she called Kate. 'We're on our way. Tracker is destroyed. Where are you?'

'We're heading back to Newcastle, to find a Pastor that Nick knows. Meet us there.' She gave them directions to write down, to avoid using the car's SatNav, in case of detection.

'We should be with you in a couple of hours,' Esme said. The dogs were sprawled across Ben and Honour's knees, in the back seat. Even Honour found their warm presence comforting. They were heading closer to home for her and she felt a sudden desire to see her family.

*

They hadn't been gone ten minutes, when the law-keepers broke down the door of Esme's house. After searching the premises and the other two locations where the tracker had been, they reported the disappearance to Resolution. He berated them for being too slow and cursed himself for not having Mish physically followed, from the start. It made him even more determined to get something out of Marsden, who, so far, was resisting giving any information away.

'Sir.' Excellence came into the room.

'I'm on my way to start again on Marsden,' Resolution said. 'What is it?'

'I thought you'd want to know what I've heard from my father.'

Resolution raised his eyebrows. He didn't think Excellence kept in touch with his father. 'Go on.'

'He told me that The Rulers are planning to use DNA from Hunter and Komchenski to make some experimental clones.'

Resolution felt his heart rate increase. 'What? That's ridiculous. Cloning is just meant for the Rulers.'

Excellence nodded. 'I know, but my father rang me to tell me they're also going to be testing her DNA to see if there is a match with the DNA they have on record for you.' He watched Resolution's reaction with interest.

A bolt of fear shot down his spine. If they found out that Chastity was really his sister, they would never trust him and probably worse than that, he would be expelled permanently from his position. Maybe even imprisoned or worse. 'Why would they do that? They didn't hear her accusations!' Suddenly he launched himself at Excellence, taking him by the throat. 'Did you tell someone about her crazy words in the lift? You are the only person who heard her!'

Excellence grasped at the Commander's hands and tried to speak. 'I wouldn't do that. They overheard her in the cell talking to Hunter.'

Resolution released him. Damn her! He would not let her ruin him. If they talked to her, she would tell them everything about their family and they would check it out, as well as the DNA testing which would prove that they were related. He had to get back to The Citadel and stop it.

'We're leaving,' Resolution said. 'Gather our things

and meet me at the car in one hour. Marsden will have to wait.'

Excellence was burning to know if Chastity was really his sister. It seemed obvious to him now, that she must be. He didn't dare broach the subject, as he wasn't keen to have Resolution's hands around his throat again. 'But Sir, won't the Rulers be even angrier if we abandon Marsden?'

Resolution knew they would, but he had to stop them questioning Chastity and taking her DNA. This time he had to get rid of his sister, without it looking like he had done it and he had to think fast.

23

Being reunited with Chas had been something Si had thought about for months, but this was not what he'd had in mind. Waiting in the cell was making them both irritable, as they pondered what the next move of the Rulers would be. There was only so much they could talk about that didn't need to be censored, just in case they were being watched. They couldn't understand why Resolution hadn't been back to interrogate them anymore. Was he keeping them waiting as part of his strategy to break them? Every time someone brought them food, they expected it to be him or his new side-kick, come to get one or both of them.

This morning, the guards came in without food. They didn't say anything, but put Chas and Si back in handcuffs and led them out of the room.

'Any chance you'd like to tell us where you're taking us?' Si asked.

There was no reply.

'Thought not.'

'Don't bother,' Chas said. 'we'll find out soon enough and we've got a pretty good idea anyway.'

They walked, in silence, through the corridors, passing each security check point. Fear squirmed in the pits of their stomachs, as they anticipated what Resolution had in store for them. But it was not Resolution's office they were taken to. The guards presented them to Zephyr himself, flanked by two other Rulers, sat at the end of a large rectangular table.

'Good morning,' Zephyr said, as if they were here for a business meeting. 'Please, sit.' He gestured to the chairs which the guards pulled out for them. 'Take the cuffs off,' Zephyr said. The guards did so, then hovered behind the prisoners. 'Wait outside,' Zephyr told them. As the door closed, he introduced Chas and Si to Ambition and Zealous.

'You may be wondering why I've brought you here to this meeting.' He paused as if waiting for an answer, but Chas and Si didn't speak. He continued. 'We're going to enlist your services in a scientific programme we're trialling. You're going to have DNA extracted and used to make clones of both of you.'

Si and Chas looked confused, but still neither of them spoke.

'It is a painless procedure, you will be pleased to know. You're privileged to be the first people, outside of the Rulers, to be cloned and made immortal.'

'Why would you want to use our DNA?' Si asked.

'You don't need to know our reasons,' Zephyr said. 'You don't need to know much, in fact. You just need to do as you're told.'

'And what if we refuse?' Chas said.

'That's not an option,' Zephyr replied.

'We're not going to cooperate,' Chas said.

'Resistance is futile,' Ambition said. 'You don't have a choice. What can you do about it?' He smiled, as they floundered for an answer.

'What do you intend to do with us when you've stolen our DNA?' Si asked.

'Chastity will become a host for the embryos and you will be our prisoner, until the rebellion is quashed. You will help us bring in your mother and anyone else who has decided to join your cause.'

Both statements left Chas and Si reeling for a moment.

Zephyr leaned forward. 'Now...'

Chas stood up. 'Wait a minute. You expect me to let you impregnate me with a child that you create from my DNA?'

Zealous spoke. 'Sit down, Chastity.' She didn't move. 'I said, *sit down*!'

Si put a hand on her arm and she slumped back in her chair. 'I won't do it!'

Zealous ignored her and continued. 'Not just one child. You will carry both clones. And if anything goes wrong you will do it again, until we get a successful outcome. Because you share the same DNA as one of them, it should make it more viable for the embryos to successfully implant and grow.'

Chas could hardly speak. She felt sick. Effectively, they were going to force her to become pregnant with human beings, who were replicas of herself and of Si. Neither of them could speak. Si reached out under the table and took Chas's hand in his. She didn't protest; just gripped his hand tightly. She was trying very hard to hold back tears of anger and frustration. Her whole body was jittery to get up and run. Her free hand clenched and unclenched, feeling for her knife that wasn't there. But there was no chance of escape.

Si let go of her hand, got up and moved slowly towards the Rulers.

'Go back to your seat,' Zealous said, standing up.

Si ignored him.

'Sit down, Silence, or we'll call the guards,' Ambition said.

Still Si moved towards them. Ambition was about to call, but Zephyr stopped him with a gesture. 'Let him speak.'

Si stood right beside the three Rulers. He leant on the table, his face close to Zephyr's. Ambition and Zealous were alert, ready to restrain him. His voice was more menacing and bolder than Chas had ever heard it before. 'You won't win. People on the outside know about the clones. They know who you are Zephyr. You're just a puppet of the Rulers.' He stood back and looked at them all. 'People know about your quest for so called immortality and ultimate power. Soon they're going to break that power. They're already breaking the power of the lies you've sown into society all this time. Your power is crumbling. And soon it'll be destroyed completely.' He turned and walked back to Chas. As he sat beside her she squeezed his hand under the table again.

Zephyr spoke. 'Nice speech. We've watched your broadcasts. They're good. But it's only words. Words are just tools. You think you have the truth, but truth is what you make it. Lies or truth? Depends on your perspective.

This is the reality we are making; therefore this is truth.'

'This is spin,' Si retorted.

'Enough!' Zephyr commanded. 'Sit down Silence, or I will have you removed. I only need Chastity for the next conversation. If you want to stay with her, sit down!'

Si slammed his hands on the table, but went back to sit next to Chas.

'Now, Chastity, tell us the truth about Resolution.' He looked at Chas, smiling, as if encouraging a child to tell its parent a secret they were keeping.

Chas was taken aback. For a moment, she didn't want to tell them anything. It felt like cooperating and she didn't want to do that. But not to take the chance to tell them about Resolution felt almost like loyalty to her brother. 'So, you have got cameras in there.'

Zephyr nodded. 'Of course.'

'What do you want to know?'

'You claim he is your brother.'

'He is.'

'And why would we believe such an interesting statement?'

'Why wouldn't you? Why would I make that up?'

Zephyr shrugged. 'You clearly despise him and who could blame you? It would be a good way to end his career, to have him associated with you and the rebel cause.'

'I don't want to end his career,' Chas said, leaning forward. 'I want to end his life.'

'Strong sentiments,' Zephyr said.

'He betrayed our family and killed my brother to get his position with you.'

Zephyr looked at Ambition and Zealous.

'My parents got into the country illegally. His surname is not whatever he has told you it is. It's the same as mine: Komchenski. He knew he'd never get anywhere as the son of poor illegal immigrants. So, he betrayed my parents and caused the death of my disabled brother.'

'When we take your DNA we can prove whether you're telling the truth, or lying, about his relationship to you.'

'At least that's some consolation then,' Chas said, sarcastically.

'You're going to be taken to the Genetics Research Centre now. There's no point in waiting any longer. Your DNA will be taken, then I will personally come and show you around the complex where you will live after that, Chastity, while you host the embryos.'

Ambition called the guards back in and gave them instructions. They cuffed Chas and Si again and led them away.

The Genetics Research Centre was part of the hospital complex. As they entered the building, memories of Grace came to Chas and she wondered what had happened to the girl. She only hoped that no one had ever suspected that she had helped in Chas's attempted escape. There certainly was no hope of escape at this precise moment.

The Genetics Research Centre was accessed through a series of security doors. The guards handed Chas and Si over to a woman in a white lab coat. She looked like she was in her forties, slim, with her mousy hair tied back in a neat ponytail. She neither looked hostile or friendly, just matter-of-fact. She asked the guards to remove the handcuffs and showed them where to take Chas and Si. They were led to a booth and made to sit in slightly reclined examination chairs.

'Strap them in please,' she instructed the guards. Then she brought up a screen and began to tap information into it. Si felt like he was back at the Bastille, awaiting some experiment. His skin began to crawl.

'You can leave now,' she said over her shoulder to the guards. 'I'll call you when I'm finished, or if I need you.' She turned to Chas and Si. 'Have they told you what's going to happen?'

'That you're violating our human rights and stealing our DNA?' Si said. 'Yes. They told us that.'

She frowned. 'I mean, do you understand the process?'

Chas laughed, wryly. 'No. Why would we?'

'I'll tell you then. My name is Doctor Nelson.'

Chas and Si looked at each other. She was treating them as if they were her patients and willingly volunteering for this procedure.

'We don't actually want to do this, you know?' Si said, as if she might not have understood this.

'I know who you are,' she said, taking off her glasses. 'You are a threat to the stability of our society. I don't understand the Rulers' logic here, but just as you don't get to choose, neither do I.' She put her glasses back on and resumed looking at her screen for a moment. 'Okay. So, here's the short version of what's going to be happening. I'm going to take small bits of tissue from you, Silence, and cells formed from this will be cultured in the lab. Once a significant number of cells have grown, they will be starved, for a period of time, until the cultured cells leave their normal cell cycle and enter into what is called the Go phase. This allows the cells to be in step with the egg, which will permit normal embryo development. With Chastity we won't need to do that, as the eggs we are using will be hers and contain her DNA anyway.'

'Do we really need to know all this?' Si asked.

'I don't do things to people without their knowing what's happening.' She continued her explanation. 'We will collect egg cells from Chastity and remove the DNA from one of them. A somatic cell (yours, Silence) from the lab culture will be extracted and inserted into one of the eggs. The cloned egg and the natural egg will then start their developmental program, with a short burst of electrical energy. Once the eggs begin to divide, they will be further cultured in the lab for a short time, until they develop into small balls of cells called blastocysts.

The cloned blastocysts will then be inserted into Chastity's womb. If all goes well and the cloned blastocysts implant properly, nine months later, we will have two clones of both of you. Then it's up to the Rulers what happens to them.'

This was too much to take in. Si had never got on well with science at school and it sounded like a lot of gobbledygook to him. However, he did understand that they were going to make Chas pregnant, with clones of himself and her. Effectively, they would be their siblings, but would feel like their children. Then what? What would become of these innocent human beings?

'Why would you do this?' Si said, quietly.

'I'm a scientist. The work is very interesting. But I told

you; I don't have a choice. The Premier is going to show you around the complex where the clones and their carers live. We don't have any other hosts there at the moment.'

Chas felt numb. Pregnant. With children made from her and Si. It was too much to take in. How could she stop it happening? They had to get out of here.

'Do you have any questions, Chastity?' Doctor Nelson took off her glasses again and looked at her with concern.

Chas shook her head, then said, 'How long until you implant the eggs?'

'A week, maybe two. Now, I'm going to take a swab from you, Silence, to extract your DNA. This is the easiest way to do it. If you're thinking of not cooperating I can have you put to sleep and do it anyway.' She shrugged.

Si resigned himself to the procedure and opened his mouth for her to take a swab from his cheek. I'm going to do you too, Chastity. Not for the clone, but for the tests the Premier wants. We can do these quicker if we take the DNA from here, rather than from the egg.'

Chas opened her mouth for the swab.

After the doctor had dealt with both swabs, she turned to Si. 'Okay, you're done. I need to check some things out with Chastity about her cycle and if the time is right, we'll go ahead and take some eggs right away.'

She called the guards in to take Si away.

'Can't I stay with her?'

'No. She won't want you watching, I don't imagine.'

'Chas?' Si said. 'I won't let them take me away, if you want me to stay.'

'She smiled at him. 'As the doctor keeps saying, you don't

have a choice. And besides, she's right, I don't want you watching.'

The guards came, unstrapped Si and led him off. Chas waited for whatever was coming next. The doctor asked her about her period and where she was in her cycle.

'I'm going to give you an injection to stimulate egg production. It works really quickly these days, so you'll only have to wait twenty-four hours before I can take the eggs.'

Chas gritted her teeth, not against any pain from the injection, but in anger at what was being done to her.

'Okay,' the doctor said. I'll see you tomorrow for the egg collection. She smiled at Chas and received a scowl in return.

Chas and Si waited on chairs in the reception area, for the arrival of Zephyr. He was accompanied by Ambition and led them back to The Fortress, into the complex where the clones lived. Security here was even tighter and required DNA clearance.

Zephyr took them on a tour around the complex, clearly proud of what they were doing there. It was at the top of the Fortress, with access to a roof garden. 'Every child and their carer has a private room. When you are a host, you will have one too, Chastity, and all your health needs will be very well taken care of. There is also a refectory, a nursery, a school, games rooms, a gymnasium and swimming pool.'

Chas and Si were astounded at the luxury of the place. Nothing a person could want seemed to be missing, except perhaps their own freedom.

They stopped in the nursery, first of all. There was no

one in it, but it was filled with brightly-coloured furniture and toys, ready to welcome new babies and toddlers. The doctor had told them there were no other hosts, at the moment. There were obviously no other babies either. Chas felt a stab of loneliness at the thought of spending day after day here, on her own, with two babies to look after. Would they give her any help?

As if echoing her thoughts, Zephyr said, 'This is where I grew up. It was rather lonely back then, as I was the first successful clone to be born. There was just me and my host, then a series of carers and teachers, with visits from others as I grew up, of course. In my teens, your friend Temperance and I were good friends.' He looked wistful for a fleeting moment.

'Don't you miss having a mother or father?' Si asked.

Zephyr shrugged. 'You don't miss what you've never had.'

'Wasn't your host like a mother?' Chas asked.

'There was no biological link between the host and myself. She served a purpose in the process, that was all. She stayed only while I was a baby and then she was replaced. I hardly remember her.' Zephyr spoke dispassionately about the woman who had carried him to birth.

Chas wondered if the host felt the same. Maybe she had been forced to have this baby. Had the woman felt any love for this child she had given birth to? Chas was all too aware that there would be a biological link between her and one of the babies. How would she feel about the baby? Would she bond with her? Would they take her away from Chas, while she was a baby? And what of the other child: the one with Si's DNA? How would she feel about that one? Her head swam with questions and fears. This was crazy. They needed to escape from here before any of this started to happen. But how?

Zephyr moved on. They passed through the corridor of private rooms and into the school, where several children, aged between seven and ten, were at work. Zephyr entered the classroom. The children looked up and delight spread across their faces. 'You may greet the Premier,' the teacher said.

The children ran to Zephyr and clutched him like a father. He, in return, hugged them en masse, speaking to each individual. Chas and Si watched in horrified amazement. The children led him to their work places and Zephyr walked around each desk, admiring what they were doing and offering encouraging words. He lingered with one child the longest: A ten-year-old boy with dark hair and eyes like him. Chas and Si realised that this was one of his own clones. He held the boy fondly, around the shoulders, and the child seemed more familiar with him than the other children had been.

'Now children, back to your lessons. I have to show our visitors some other things.'

The children let out a collective groan and Zephyr laughed.

'Will you come back soon, Premier?' the young Zephyr said.

The Premier tousled his hair and smiled. 'Of course.'

As they walked away, Si noticed Ambition looking back at the children and a smaller boy waved shyly to him.

Ambition nodded at his clone, but with no hint of a smile.

Zephyr returned to his tour. 'The children learn how to behave and respect the regime. They are our ticket to immortality, so they are treated to every good thing we can provide for them.'

'You mean, you indoctrinate and spoil them,' Chas said.

Zephyr turned sharply to her. 'We cherish them. One day, they will take our places. The transition will be seamless.'

He genuinely believed that they were giving these children a great life. 'But what if they don't want to take your places?' Si asked.

Zephyr looked at him as if he were being ridiculous. 'It is their purpose in life. They were made for it and they are being taught everything they need to know for it.'

'And they know nothing else. They have no choice,' Chas said, bitterly.

'Less choice and specific knowledge makes these children happy. Boundaries can set people free. They are not unhappy, you've seen that.'

'But you said yourself, you were lonely,' Si said.

Ambition, who had been the silent accompanist until now, spoke up. 'That's enough. The Premier does not have to answer your questions about his personal life.'

But Zephyr was keen to talk and waved Ambition's protest away. 'It's fine, Ambition. Yes, I was lonely at times, but aren't you? Isn't everyone? It doesn't mean I wasn't perfectly content, most of the time. I knew my purpose and I was determined to fulfil it. That was enough. Let me show you to the roof garden.'

It was surreal being shown around this luxurious complex, as if they were potential guests about to book an expensive spa weekend, not prisoners of a despotic regime about to have their human rights violated.

They emerged into bright sunlight and realised that the garden was not open to the air. It was covered by a huge dome, with regulated temperature. The foliage was like that of a tropical greenhouse. There were seating areas and a large grassed area, with playground equipment.

'This is my favourite place. The children love it. And when I was a teenager I spent many hours here, reading and listening to music. The temperature is always balmy and fresh air is purified and pumped in from outside. Even when the sky is cloudy, and it rains, you can pretend you are in paradise.' He smiled and pointed up to the sky. 'There is another layer over the dome to filter out rain noise. And if you miss the rain, you can always stand under one of the plant sprinklers.' He laughed, as if he'd made the funniest joke.

After they had walked around, admiring the gardens, Zephyr took them to the gym and swimming pool. There was a young man in the gym, lifting weights. He had his back to them and headphones on, so didn't hear them come in. His torso was well muscled. Si guessed immediately who he was. He remembered Capability telling them that there were two successful clones of Zephyr and one of them was about his age. The Premier went up to him and waited until he had put the barbell down, then he gripped him by the shoulder. The boy flinched and turned, taking off his headphones. His reaction to the Premier was not as enthusiastic as the boy they had seen earlier.

'Premier. Ambition,' he said, making a small nod of his head. He looked at Chas and Si with guarded curiosity and wiped his face and chest with a towel.

The Premier was smiling at him. 'How are you, Zephyr? You look in fine shape.'

'I am,' the boy said. 'I'm in the middle of my training routine.' He looked impatient to get on with it and irritated at being disturbed.

'We won't keep you from it. I'm just showing our guests around. You know who they are?'

The boy nodded. 'Why are they here?' His gaze lingering on Chas, in particular.

'You've got current affairs at 14.00 hours, haven't you? I'll be coming up to talk to you about interesting developments in this situation.'

The young Zephyr shrugged. 'Fine. Now I'd like to get back to my training, if you don't mind.' He was bordering on rude to the Premier, but neither Ambition nor Zephyr seemed concerned at that.

'Yes, of course,' Zephyr said. 'I'll see you later.'

As they left the gym, Chas felt as if she were being stared at the whole way. She looked back to see the young Zephyr turn to pick up his bar bell again.

Ambition spoke as they left the complex and met the waiting guards. 'So, from almost executed to privileged guest of the state in the space of a week, Chastity. I hope you are grateful and if wise, you will cooperate fully.'

'Oh, I'm in your debt!' Chas spat back. 'I'm eternally grateful that you are going to use my body and my DNA to make more brain-washed monsters for your regime.'

'Careful Chastity,' Zephyr said.

'I want Si with me.'

'Out of the question,' Ambition laughed. 'Who do you think you are to make demands of us?'

'It would help her to have me there. She would be a better host for the clones; calmer. I'm a calming influence on her,' Si said.

'She doesn't need you. She has coped well enough on her own with life,' Ambition said. 'You will go back to the cells.'

'If you don't let him stay with me I'll do everything I can to end the pregnancy. I'll do *anything*!' She stressed the last word, going right up to Ambition.

Ambition pushed her back against the wall and held her there. Si lunged towards him, but Zephyr held him back. 'Then you'll both die,' Ambition said. 'This is an experiment. You are no real loss. We hold all the cards in this game. You have nothing to negotiate with.' Ambition turned to the guards, who were about to intervene. 'Take them back to the cells.'

'Impudent little bitch,' Ambition said as he and Zephyr made their way down to Zephyr's office. 'Are you sure this is a good idea? We'll have to watch her.'

'Yes,' Zephyr replied. 'We will be doing that. She won't stand a chance of jeopardising this experiment.' When they arrived in the office, Zephyr called Doctor Nelson. Her holo-image appeared in the room. 'Do you have the results of the DNA match on Resolution and Chastity?'

'Yes, Premier,' Doctor Nelson said. 'The DNA from

Chastity Komchenski does not have a high enough match in the siblingship test to that of Commander Resolution.'

Both Ambition and Zephyr were stunned into silence for a moment. 'Are you sure?'

'Positive, Premier. There is no shadow of doubt with this test. The DNA has to rate at 1.00, or higher, for there to be any chance that they are related, and it didn't.'

Zephyr nodded, as if he knew what she meant. 'I see. Thank you, Doctor.' He ended the call.

'I wasn't expecting that,' Ambition said.

'Nor me,' said Zephyr. 'You know I've never really liked the man.'

'Why would the girl lie about it?'

Zephyr shook his head. 'She clearly hates him. There's definitely a connection between them. We just have to find out what it is.'

*

Chas hadn't slept much overnight. Her restless dreams had led her to all sorts of babies; terribly deformed or aggressive, or adult faces on baby bodies. There was one dream, where a baby with Si's face was crying and crying and when she went to pick it up, the baby drew out a knife and tried to stab her through the eye. That was when she had woken up, panting and sweating. Si, who was sleeping nearby, had vaguely woken and asked her if she was okay, then gone back to sleep. The next dream had been about giving birth. She was strapped to a table and Resolution was looking down on her, asking her all sorts of questions about Si and Kate and then about their own family. This was in-between the excruciating pain of contractions and pushing. He threatened to kill the babies if she didn't tell him where their parents were. When she woke from that dream she didn't try to get back to sleep, but instead sat hugging her knees, trying to think of a way out of this place. It seemed impossible without weapons and with all the security. But, she'd helped people escape from the Bastille and the Priory, so there must be a way to get themselves out of here.

When Si woke up, she wasn't in the mood for talking. She felt resentful of his seemingly peaceful night's sleep. But that wasn't his fault and she was annoyed with herself for thinking like that. She didn't tell him about her dreams. Si tried to think of reassuring things to say to her, as her anxiety was evident. Everything he said felt trite and received a cold response. He didn't blame her. He too felt helpless and frustrated at not being able to think of a way out. Where were Temp and Capability? Why didn't they come? Was Ben safe? Since his arrest he had mulled this over and over in his mind. He hoped Ben had gone back to Capability's flat, but he worried that he might have done something stupid and been arrested. He could be here in another cell, although he thought this unlikely, as Resolution would probably have used him against Si to gain information. And where was Resolution? Why had the questioning not continued? He wondered about his mother and Nick. What was happening to them? Had they managed to gather a band of people together, who would rise up against the Rulers? They had been confident that the people of The Way were behind them.

But all of these people were far away and of no help to Chas right now. He didn't know how to stop them taking the eggs from her today. He didn't know how to stop them taking her away from him again. And the thought of her carrying babies, that were clones of himself and her, was surreal. He had thought about it a lot, through the night, when she had presumed he was sleeping. It felt like they were about to become parents; yet they were not the parents of these potential children, they were the identical twins, but older. Too much to get his head around. Si went back to thinking about how to escape.

They came for Chas in the afternoon. 'Do you want me to come?' Si asked her.

'I don't think it's an option,' she said, as they put the cuffs on her.

Si wanted to hug her and fight the guards off, but he knew both of these things were pointless. She was stony-faced and quiet. She'd hardly spoken all day. When they had taken her, he let out a loud roar of helplessness.

Chas heard it as she was being led away. She felt a pang of regret that she hadn't been more responsive to his attempts to soothe her today. He was kind and she knew he loved her. But she was too scared to receive it. How could it help them to fall in love now? It would only make their lives even more painful.

When they got to the Genetics Research Centre, Doctor Nelson was waiting for her. She didn't smile at Chas or say anything to try and make her feel better (which Chas appreciated), but there was an aura of tranquillity around her and it had an effect on Chas. Even though this was the moment she had been dreading, she felt the calmest she had felt in the last twenty-four hours.

'This will be a fairly quick procedure, Chastity. I'm going to give you a general anaesthetic, because it would be quite painful otherwise. When you wake up, you might be a little sore and have some stomach cramps for a while, but I'll give you pain-killers which should help.'

Chas lay strapped to the operating table, where the guards had put her. Doctor Nelson lifted her top and put gel on her abdomen.

'This is so I can take a look at what's going on in the follicles that contain the eggs in your ovaries. It will help me guide the needle.'

Chas looked across at the ultra-sound scan on the screen. Despite feeling afraid all day, she found herself fascinated. She had never seen anything like this before. Being able to see inside her own body distracted her for a few moments.

'I'm going to inject you with the anaesthetic now,' the doctor said.

Chas closed her eyes and took some deep breaths. She didn't like needles, so she pictured Si smiling at her, as the anaesthetic began to work. Her eyes fluttered open briefly, in an attempt to hold on to consciousness. She thought that Doctor Nelson was smiling down at her, with tears in her eyes, and felt the doctor stroking her hair. She smiled. This must be the beginning of some weird dream, caused by the anaesthetic.

She woke up in a recovery room, alone, feeling groggy and slightly sick. Within a few moments of opening her eyes, a nurse was at her side, checking if she was alright. She said she was and the nurse went to fetch Doctor Nelson.

They sat Chas up and the nurse gave her some pain killers.

'Take these now,' Doctor Nelson said. 'Once I'm satisfied you're really okay, guards will come and take you to your room in the Complex.'

'Wait. You mean I'm not going back to the cells?'

'No. We have your eggs, so now the Premier wants you treated with ultimate care, so that your body has the best chance of accepting and carrying the embryos.'

'But, I didn't say...' She was going to say that she hadn't said goodbye to Si, but this sounded so sentimental that she stopped herself. What she meant was that she had been in such a bad mood earlier and she didn't want to leave it like that. Who knew when, or if, she'd ever see him again. She bit back tears that unwittingly welled in her eyes.

Doctor Nelson finished her sentence for her. '...To Silence.'

'No, I... yes, to Si.'

The doctor looked at her, over her glasses for a moment, then dismissed the nurse. She took off her glasses. 'I'll see if I can pull any strings to get them to allow him to visit you.'

Chas looked up at her, surprised by the sudden kindness and didn't know what to say. But spending time with Si over the last couple of years had taught her to thank people, even for little things, so she did. The doctor nodded. 'I'm not allowed to give you more pain-killers to take with you, but they'll look after you in the Complex. A team of nurses and carers will be at your beck and call. You've just entered a whole new world.'

Chas raised her eyebrows. 'I'm thrilled!'

The doctor smiled wryly. 'I'll be back to do a final check later and the nurse is around if you need anything.' She turned to leave, but then stopped. 'Don't think of trying to escape, Chastity. Believe me, there is no escape from here.'

*

Si had been pacing the cell for hours, feeling anxious and twitchy. He'd shouted at the invisible cameras, demanding that they tell him about Chas and he was alert to any sounds in the corridor, hoping they were bringing her back. Finally, the door unlocked, but it wasn't Chas. Resolution came into the cell. Si hadn't been expecting him and jumped up from where he had slumped in a corner.

'Where is she?' he shouted.

Resolution strode over to Si, took him by the throat and pinned him to the wall. 'That's what I want to know.'

'Don't you know?' Si tried to keep Resolution's hands from tightening any more. 'They took her to the Genetics place. They're taking her eggs for the cloning process.'

'And the DNA?'

'Already done.' Si realised, all of a sudden, why Resolution was so angry. A smile crept across his face, despite being half-strangled. 'They'll know one hundred per cent who you are now!'

Resolution's grip tightened, and Si struggled. He tried to knee Resolution in the groin, but he was pinned too hard against the wall. He punched him as hard as he could, in the places he could reach, but it was having no effect and he felt himself beginning to lose consciousness.

At that moment, two guards rushed into the cell and a voice came out of nowhere. 'Take your hands off him Commander.'

Resolution hissed in Si's ear. 'Before this day is over, she's dead!' The guards wrestled Resolution off Si and hauled him back out of the cell.

Si gasped for breath, then shouted hoarsely at the invisible voice, 'What have you done with Chas? Where is she?'

There was no reply.

Si yelled, 'He's going to kill her!'

There was no answer.

He choked back an angry sob.

24

Resolution was hauled into Zephyr's office.

'What do you think you're doing?' Zephyr said. 'Why are you back here and what are you doing, trying to kill our valuable prisoner? I've got a lot of questions for you, Resolution, so start talking.'

Resolution hated eating humble pie, but he had no choice if he wanted to try and salvage his career. He could act. 'I'm sorry about Hunter, Premier. He winds me up and I shouldn't let him. I had to get back, Premier, because I heard that Chastity Komchenski had been falsely accusing me of being her brother, an illegal immigrant. I had to get back to refute these ridiculous claims, Sir.'

'You wanted to stop us testing her DNA?'

Resolution felt trapped and fumbled for the right answer. 'No. I... you have every right to do as you wish. I just wanted to make it clear that I am not what she is accusing me of.'

'Then why is she so vehement?' Zephyr was enjoying watching Resolution's discomfort. Like a fish caught on a hook, the Premier held him up to watch him squirm.

'She is a nasty piece of work. She hates me for ordering the destruction of her commune, when Hunter first escaped from the Bastille.'

Zephyr paused. He walked around his desk and sat on the edge, watching Resolution. 'We already have her DNA. We also have her eggs. She is going to make an interesting clone. Useful, I believe.'

Resolution's face blanched, but he had to keep calm. 'Forgive me, Premier but I don't see the point of cloning her and Hunter.'

'It's an experiment, Resolution. I believe we can mould them to our ways and if we can do it with them, we can do it with any clone. Just think, we could make normal means of reproduction illegal and control it completely. No more useless people. Only ones we choose.'

It was an extreme thought that had never crossed Resolution's mind. He didn't see how the Rulers could enforce such a radical policy, but there again, power was power, and they would stop at nothing. 'Interesting idea, Sir.' But he wasn't really interested at all. What he desperately wanted to know was, had they tested Chas's DNA yet, or did he still have time to destroy it?

Zephyr was conscious of the unasked question. 'We have tested Chastity's DNA and compared it to yours.'

Resolution's heart began to race. What could he say? How could he refute the evidence and salvage his career now? 'Premier, I...'

'She is, of course, a liar. It didn't match. But you understand, we had to check.'

Resolution could hardly believe what he was hearing and struggled to keep his composure. He didn't know how this was possible, but he was delighted. 'I understand, sir. I'm sorry that I over-reacted to her lies. She also makes me angry.'

'You need to get control of your temper, Commander,' Zephyr said. 'She is going to be well looked after, for the next few years, here in the Complex, as she hopefully carries the clones to term and nurtures them, whilst they are babies.'

'Yes, of course. What are your plans for Hunter?'

'He will be our prisoner until the rebellion is quashed. You can do what you like with him to gain information and find the rebels. But don't overdo it. I want him alive until this is over.'

'Yes Premier. I will not fail you. I'll find out what he knows and track down the rebels.'

'And find Capability and Temperance. I'm hoping they're still somewhere in the city, but they may have had those invisibility suits and got out. We're working to find a way to make them visible. I also want a debrief on Marsden and what you found out. We should have had access to this technology. He is going to pay for his treachery.'

'I'll need to go back at some point, sir. I'm not finished with him.'

Zephyr nodded. 'Do not put your personal life before the concerns of the state again, Commander. Do you understand?'

'Yes, Premier.' Resolution left Zephyr's office feeling disorientated and elated. He hadn't expected to leave there with his freedom, let alone his job. How the DNA test had come back negative, he had no idea, but he didn't care. He was off the hook.

*

The only thing Si could think to do, as he waited in the cell, was pray. He hadn't prayed properly since before his parents were taken away, but now he was earnestly praying. No words came out of his mouth, but there were plenty in his head. A floodgate had been opened and a torrent of questions, requests, fears and desperation poured out. He felt so helpless, sat there in the cell, not knowing anything about what was happening to anyone. Not being able to do anything was driving him crazy. So, he prayed, and this felt like doing something. It was funny, it didn't feel like empty words. It didn't feel like they hit the ceiling and bounced back this time. It felt like they were the one weapon he could use against the Rulers from here. As he prayed for the others, it felt like his thoughts were able to pierce the ceiling and escape from the Fortress, flying like missiles to where they were needed. His desperation and fear turned to determination and purpose.

When the door to the cell opened, he almost didn't notice.

'Silence, come with me.'

He looked up to see Doctor Nelson standing in the doorway, accompanied by a guard.

'Where's Chas? Is she alright?' he said, jumping up from the bench he was lying on.

The guard put handcuffs on him.

'She's fine,' Doctor Nelson said, as they walked down the corridor. 'She asked to see you and I said I'd see what I can do. She is in the Complex. That's where she'll be staying now.'

Si's heart dropped. They were taking her away from him again. He hadn't thought they'd do it so soon.

'Thank you for letting me see her,' Si said.

The doctor nodded, but didn't say anything else. She had security clearance to the Complex and they walked straight in. She took him to a private room where Chas was asleep on the bed.

'You have ten minutes.' The doctor left the room.

Chas was sound asleep, and he felt guilty waking her up. He sat by the bed, just watching her, for a couple of minutes. He wanted to pick her up and carry her out of there to somewhere safe. Somewhere where they couldn't use her body in their experiment. He stroked her hair and planted a tiny kiss on her cheek.

'Chas.' She still didn't move, and the precious ten minutes was ticking away. 'Chas.' He said it more loudly, this time, and shook her gently.

She stirred and opened her eyes. Then she smiled, in a way he'd not seen for a long time. 'I wish you were really here,' she said, groggily.

'I am.' He twined his fingers through hers. 'I am here, but we only have a few minutes.'

She opened her eyes more fully and struggled to sit up. 'How did you get in here?'

'The doctor came for me. She said I could see you.'

'Wow! I didn't think she'd really manage it. She said she'd try.'

'Are you alright? Does it hurt?' Si looked at her stomach, as if he might see through her clothes and skin.

'I'm fine. And not really. Bit of an odd feeling, that's all, and they've given me pain-killers.'

'How long 'til they implant the embryos?'

'I don't know. Not long I think, a few days.'

Si looked around, wondering if they were being watched or listened to. He leaned closer. 'We have to get out of here.'

She laughed. 'Yeah! State the obvious! But how? Got any genius ideas? Got an invisibility suit stuffed up your shirt front?'

Si smiled, sarcastically.

Chas rolled her eyes at him. 'Well, if you think of anything, I'll be waiting here.'

'Your brother's back,' Si said. 'He came to the cell, looking for you. He didn't know where you were and nearly strangled me trying to find out.'

She raised her eyebrows. 'How did you stop him?'

Si told her about the voice from nowhere, and the guards coming to drag him away. 'I told him about the DNA test. He was like a rabid dog.'

'Well, at least they know who he is now. Maybe he'll be deported. It's not how I wanted to get rid of him, but it's the best I could do under the circumstances.'

The door opened, and Doctor Nelson came back in. 'Time's up.'

'Thank you for arranging this,' Si said.

She nodded. 'The Rulers want to keep Chastity in good condition. I think they might let you make regular visits.'

Si grasped Chas's hand tightly, not wanting to be prized away from her again.

'Come on,' The doctor said. 'We have to go now.'

He didn't know what to say. He felt choked. He let go of her hand and suddenly she grabbed him and hugged him close. 'Get me out of here,' she whispered, urgently.

'Come. Now!' the doctor said, firmly.

As he walked back to the cell, he said a silent prayer of thanks and asked for a way to grant Chas's request.

*

The journey to Newcastle hadn't taken long. Everyone was tense, wondering if they were still being tracked. Mish kept apologising and Esme had eventually got so irritated with him, that she told him bluntly to 'just shut up!'

Kate had given them the address of the Pastor, who was a friend of Nick's. They had decided that it wasn't safe to stay at Nick's flat in Newcastle, so they were hiding out with Pastor Rowley. It hadn't been easy to get into the tech-city unseen. The Pastor had sent some followers of The Way to bribe certain law-keepers, who he knew were susceptible to such things. He had only told them that he was smuggling in two friends from the country, who didn't have ID, for a meeting of The Way. This was a fairly common occurrence for him, and the law-keepers in question were happy to turn a blind eye, for a price.

Esme and the others had found the house in the suburbs of the tech-city, and had entered, having been told by the Pastor exactly what to say at the gates. Nick and Kate were so pleased to see them. They took some time to talk things through. Mish was keen to leave again and get back to his commune, so they arranged for him to be 'smuggled' back out of the gate that evening.

'I promise I'll be back,' he said. 'Once I know my dad and the others are safe, I'll contact you.'

Kate shook his hand. 'Thank you for helping us.'

'Yeah, thanks for stopping me getting into trouble,' Ben said, grinning.

Honour flung her arms around Mish. 'Wish you didn't have to go.'

Mish prised her off him and smiled. 'Ah, dinna fash! I told ye, I'll be back.'

Pastor Rowley had arranged a meeting the next day, at his church, with a few of the Elders. His church met in an office building, on a derelict trading estate, not far from his house. Most of the windows were broken and there was graffiti on the walls, both inside and out. But the church had made the fifth floor as cosy as possible, with a brazier for warmth and boiling water, and a conglomeration of assorted chairs and cushions. They had blocked up the broken panes with black plastic, which also served to keep any light from being seen from outside; it was illegal for religious groups to gather together. At seven-thirty, people began to arrive in ones and twos, and by eight-thirty there were twenty-six people in the room. There was no electricity, but they had brought torches and candles. Several people came to greet them, most recognising Nick, and some recognising Kate from the HTV.

Pastor Rowley called the meeting to order and they began with a prayer. This was alien to Ben and Honour, who had never had anything to do with religion in their lives. They had been taught by the State that there was no God and that was that. Ben had never really questioned it or given it a second thought, until he had met Si. He'd had some interesting conversations, on the road, with Si and Chas, about who God might be, and why anyone would risk so much to follow the Teacher.

After the prayer, the Pastor read from their Scriptures. His voice was filled with passion, as he spoke vehemently.

'Do you Rulers indeed speak justly?
Do you judge people with equity?
No, in your heart you devise injustice,
and your hands mete out violence on the earth.
Even from birth the wicked go astray;
from the womb they are wayward, spreading lies.
Their venom is like the venom of a snake,
like that of a cobra that has stopped its ears,
that will not heed the tune of the charmer,
however skilful the enchanter may be.
Break the teeth in their mouths, O God;
Lord, tear out the fangs of those lions!
Let them vanish like water that flows away;
when they draw the bow, let their arrows fall short.
May they be like a slug that melts away as it moves along,
like a stillborn child that never sees the sun.
Before your pots can feel the heat of the thorns—
whether they be green or dry—the wicked will be swept away.
The righteous will be glad when they are avenged,
when they dip their feet in the blood of the wicked.
Then people will say,
"Surely the righteous still are rewarded;
surely there is a God who judges the earth."

'Who would have thought that King David, speaking thousands of years ago, would prophesy about the times we are living in today. This is a violent Psalm. An invocation to our God to mete out justice on those who oppress us. We follow The Teacher, who some would say was 'meek and mild,' 'kind and gentle,' 'nice and safe.' But, if you read more closely, he was also dangerous and controversial, angry and fierce, strong and extreme. His words were about protecting those less fortunate and condemning those who seek power, whilst trampling on others in order to get it.

He said, "Do not think that I came to bring peace on the earth; I did not come to bring peace, but a sword."

What did he mean? He was undoubtably a man of peace, but he meant us to fight injustice. How shall we fight injustice? We have watched for too long, hiding in secret, as the people of our land cower in fear of the repercussions of the Rulers. We have seen how they turned from their election ideals to corruption, lies and oppression. We have seen how they introduced the plague to get rid of the poorest in our society, and those they deem weak and useless.

Well, now we have a chance to stand up and fight back. With a sword? Maybe, maybe not. But by joining our friends here, in rebellion against the Rulers and gathering as many others as we can, we are standing up for those less fortunate than us. We are standing up for justice and breaking the power of the lies we have been sold!'

The Pastor was becoming more and more animated. He was almost shouting. Having been so used to keeping quiet, for fear of being discovered, some of the people were looking uncomfortable.

‘Are we ready to stand with Kate and Nick? With these young people who have already sacrificed so much?’

There were murmurs of agreement amongst the congregation. They were already risking a lot by being here.

‘Who is with me? Stand up and be counted!’

Everyone rose to their feet without hesitation, despite the fear on some faces.

The Pastor shouted, quoting from the Bible,

“*Break the teeth in their mouths, O God;*

Tear out the fangs of those lions!

Let them vanish like water that flows away!”

People began to clap, and someone started a song. Ben looked nervously at Honour, hoping there was no one patrolling the industrial estate. The Pastor invited Kate and Nick to come up to the front, and tell the people what they had been doing in the plague camps. Then, the others were invited to tell their stories of how they got involved.

After the meeting, there was a buzz of anticipation in the air. Normally people left quickly, eager to get away from their illegal meeting, but tonight everyone wanted to talk to Kate and the others. Some were very concerned about Si, telling Kate they were praying for him. Others were keen to know what they could do to help.

After everyone had left, they returned to the Pastor’s flat, in ones and twos, at spaced out intervals. Kate and Nick arrived first. It was very late and they were tired, but they were happy with the outcome of the meeting. They talked for a while about how they might take things forward.

‘The most pressing thing, I think, is to get to Peter,’ Nick said. 'I've had an idea.'

'He's in the Priory, isn't he?' Honour said.

'Most likely,' Kate replied.

'My dad could help, like he helped Si and Chas,' Ben offered.

Nick nodded. 'We might call on him. But I was thinking that, at the Priory, they won't know my face in association with all of this yet.'

'You hope not,' Esme said. 'Peter may have talked. Or someone from the plague camps.'

Nick frowned. 'Maybe, but just supposing they haven't...'

'It's risky,' Esme said.

'Yes, but hear me out. If I could pose as a doctor, sent by the Rulers to examine Peter, I could try to smuggle him out, because Ben's given me an invisibility suit. Peter could put it on and just walk out with me.'

'How are you going to get them to believe you're sent by the Rulers?' Kate asked.

'Fake ID and documents,' Nick said.

'From where?' Esme asked.

'From me,' The pastor said, grinning.

Nick brought up the holo-screen from his phone and showed them.

'Well, well, a man of many talents,' Esme said, smiling at Pastor Rowley.

'Anything is permitted in the pursuit of justice.' He smiled back at her.

'So, Ben, I want you to take me to Seahouses. Honour can ring her Mum tomorrow and tell her to expect us,' Nick said.

Honour beamed. 'I'm coming.'

'She should,' Ben said. 'We need her to smooth the way with Mum and Dad.'

Kate shifted, uneasily. 'I'm not sure, Nick. A lot could go wrong.'

'Yes, of course it could. But Peter is too valuable to just leave him there. Heaven knows what they've already got out of him, but he can help us so much against the Rulers.' Nick lent over to Kate and took her hand. 'I'll be okay. I promise I'll come back.'

She smiled sadly at him. 'You can't promise you'll come back from the Priory.'

Nick squeezed her hand. 'Tomorrow then, at dawn, Ben, Honour and I will drive up there.

*

Dawn came too quickly for Kate and not fast enough for Honour and Ben. Both were excited about returning to Seahouses, but also about being important to this serious mission.

Nick kissed Kate as he got in the car. 'I'll be back soon. Try not to worry.'

She hugged her cardigan around her and fought back the tears welling in her eyes.

It was still early when they arrived in Seahouses. Honour had spoken to her mum on the way, so both Ethan and Sarah rushed to open the door, when they heard the knock. Sarah gathered Honour in her arms, on the doorstep, and hugged her fiercely.

'Let them in,' Ethan said, 'Come on, get in the house.'

There were tears, hugs and recriminations all round, before anything could be discussed about why they were here. Nick had a lot of apologising to do, on behalf of the adults, for not returning Honour and Ben immediately to them. But Honour stood up for the others. 'We wouldn't let them send us back, Mum. It's not their fault.'

Nick explained what he was going to do. He said it would be best if he drove over to the island. Nothing should look suspicious about his visit. All he wanted from them was a safe place to bring Peter back to. Were they willing to involve themselves with the rebels in this way? It was a big ask.

'Since our daughter and adopted son have clearly aligned themselves with you, and since we helped Si and Chas before, I'd say we're already involved,' Ethan said. He looked at Sarah. 'You can bring Peter back here, if you need to.'

'Don't go back to Newcastle without me,' Ben said. 'If you think you're leaving me behind, like Si and Chas did, think again.'

'Nick grinned. 'I won't leave you, Ben. We need you.'

'Can we come to the Priory with you?' Honour asked. 'You might need some help.'

'You are staying right here, young lady,' Ethan said, looking sternly at her. She rolled her eyes at her dad, but accepted that there was no point in arguing.

Nick set off shortly. It wasn't far to the causeway, and the tide was in his favour. He drove to the checkpoint on the causeway, holding his nerve (and virtually holding his breath). He got through without any difficulty and blew out that breath. Pastor Rowley was clearly practiced at fake IDs. This boosted his confidence for getting into the Priory. He had been rehearsing the back story to his forged identity as he drove.

It was an impressive structure, clearly visible from the mainland. Nick drove up to the gates and waited while they checked his ID. Again, he got through without a problem and as he entered the building, he was greeted by the Priory chief.

He held out his hand to shake Nick's. 'Doctor Carmichael. I'm George McLean, new chief here, since Mark Aspen was removed last year. I understand you've been sent by the Rulers to examine Peter Marsden.'

'That's right,' Nick said. 'This is an impressive place.'

'Thank you,' McLean replied. 'I must admit, I'm curious as to why they would send someone from The Citadel. Don't they think I've got plenty of competent doctors here?'

Nick shook his head. 'I don't understand it either. I'm just obeying orders as you do. You know what it's like. No choice, no matter what we think of the idea.' Nick hoped to appeal to what he sensed was McLean's annoyance with the Rulers. The chief made a humphing noise in agreement. Nick went on, before he could say much else. The last thing he wanted was McLean checking up on him. 'I must say you have a great facility here. I was reading about it before I came. I'd love to have a look around if you have the time to spare.'

He saw the pride in McLean's eyes. 'Sure. I can take you on a tour, although it's primitive compared to anything you have in The Citadel.'

McLean gave Nick a tour, as if he was showing him around a potential holiday destination. Nick made suitably sycophantic comments and watched as McLean puffed up with pride each time. Nick even made him laugh a few times and by the end of the tour McLean had relaxed. 'Well, I'd better let you do your duty, doctor. You only have a few hours until the tide turns, and I presume you're not here for an overnight stay.'

'No, I need to leave today. Pressing matters back at The Citadel. I'd like to work here, one day, though.'

'Really?' McLean looked at him incredulously. 'I'd have thought the luxury of working in The Citadel, with everything you need, would be enough of a pull to keep anyone there, once you've made it. Why would you want to be marooned here day after day, 365 days a year?'

Nick laughed. 'Don't get me wrong, The Citadel's a great place to live and work, but it does get a tad boring sometimes. Some of the complaints I deal with are laughable. And somewhere like this seems more... frontline. You get really interesting people here.'

Mclean snorted. 'You could call them that. Come on, I'll take you to Marsden's room. You know the Commander has been here, torturing him, don't you? I expect that's partly why they've sent you. Between you and me, I don't like the man. It's all well and good keeping these people from doing whatever subversive things they were doing before, but he's a sadist and an arrogant one at that.'

Nick smiled. 'I couldn't agree more.'

They arrived at Peter's room and McLean unlocked it.

'Just let Security know when you're ready to leave and they'll let you out. There's a screen inside the door, so you can communicate with anyone you need to.'

Nick had asked, on the tour, about how closely they monitored the inmates and McLean had revealed that they had cameras in the rooms, but generally they didn't listen in; as the prisoners were kept on their own, so there was nothing much to listen to, except some occasional raving and ranting, which Security didn't much care to listen to.

'I'll say goodbye here, Doctor Carmichael. I've got a lot to do. It was nice meeting you. I'll let you know if a post comes up.' He smiled, shook hands and was gone.

Nick took a deep breath and entered the room. Peter was asleep on the bed, with his back turned to the door. Nick was relieved. It gave him a means of approaching him, without any kind of recognition showing on his face. He touched him firmly, on the shoulder.

'Mr. Marsden, I'm a doctor. I've been sent to examine you.' He hoped his voice would be recognised.

Nick noticed the bruising as Peter opened his eyes slowly. Moving in to help Peter sit up, he whispered, 'Peter. It's Nick.'

Peter turned and squinted at him. There was recognition in his face and a half smile, which he quickly erased. 'Doctor,' was all he said.

'Can you sit up?' He put his arm around Peter's shoulder and slowly brought him to a sitting position, on the edge of the bed. Pain was evident in his face and the stiffness of his limbs.

'Where's the Commander?' he asked.

'Gone back to The Citadel for some reason. Something more urgent came up, I believe. I'm here to examine you.'

Despite what McLean had told him about the cameras in the room not picking up sound, Nick was cautious. He knew they were capable of listening in, and although he felt he'd done a good job on McLean, he wasn't completely sure he had won him over. He pulled out of his bag various pieces of medical equipment and brought up a holo-screen from his wearable. Then, he began to examine Peter and tap information into his medical file.

When he leant in close to listen to Peter's chest, he whispered, 'I've got the invisibility suit. Go to the bathroom and change into it. I'll leave the room, seemingly on my own, but you will be with me. Just touch my arm when you're beside me and hold on to me all the way out. Can you do it? Just answer my next question with a yes or no.' He bent down to examine the muscles in Peter's legs. 'Does that feel okay?'

'Yes.'

Nick reached into his bag. The suit was folded, so that it was invisible in the bag. They had looked inside his bag at the checkpoint, but only seen his medical equipment. He felt for the suit and lifted it out, making it look like he was putting a reflex hammer on the bed. Peter watched where he laid the suit on the bed.

'When I've tested your reflexes, I need a sample of urine, then we're done,' Nick said. He made a show of testing Peter's reflexes, which, thankfully, were fine, then he handed him a sample pot.

'Okay, go and do that now please, then I'm finished.'

Peter shuffled to the bathroom with the suit tucked under his arm. Nick could see that he wasn't moving too well, and from his examinations he knew that Peter wasn't in good shape and needed medical attention, but that would have to wait until they could get him out of here. Peter came back with the sample.

'Thanks,' Nick said, not looking at Peter. 'That's it. I'll be off in a minute, just got to finish my notes.'

'I'm going to shower,' Peter said and shuffled back to the bathroom.

Nick wrote some more notes on his screen, waiting for Peter. After a few minutes, he felt the invisible touch on his arm and called Security to let him out. Peter followed, with a hand on Nick's back. As Nick opened the door, McLean was waiting for him. He hadn't expected to see him again, and his heart pounded just a little more than he'd have liked. He breathed and smiled. 'George. I thought you were busy. You needn't have come back.'

'It's okay. I thought I'd see you out. Everything alright with Marsden?'

They began walking along the corridor, Nick hoping that Peter could keep up with them. 'Well, he's as you would expect after an encounter with the Commander, but he'll live. I've made my report.'

'Do I get a copy of that?' McLean asked.

'Absolutely. I'll be sending it as soon as I get back.' Suddenly, Nick felt Peter's touch leave his arm. He stopped. 'Sorry, I've just thought, I might have left the sample bottle in the room.' He opened his bag and rummaged around. Then he felt Peter touch him again. 'Ah, there it is. Good.'

They continued to walk, Nick trying to keep the pace as slow as possible, by making conversation with McLean, about things he hoped would please and distract him from asking any awkward questions.

At the door, Peter was still with him. 'Right. I'll say goodbye, Doctor Carmichael. Safe journey.' They shook hands once again.

'Thanks. Hopefully we'll meet again,' Nick said, really hoping that they wouldn't.

Peter was out of the building. Nick opened the passenger door, acting as if he was putting his equipment in the car. Then he stood back for a moment, to allow Peter to get in, pretending to admire the view of Lindisfarne Castle, right next to the Priory, and Bamburgh Castle in the distance, across the sea, which would soon cover the causeway and bar his escape. He needed to get going. When he got in the car, he asked, 'Are you here, Peter?'

'Right next to you,' Peter said.

'You are one clever guy,' Nick said, as he drove off.

'You are one good actor!' Peter said, laughing.

They passed through the checkpoints with no difficulty and headed back on the road to Seahouses.

'How are you actually feeling?'

'I'm okay,' Peter said, quietly.

'Resolution is a psychopath. Did you tell him much? No one would blame you if you did.'

'I didn't tell him anything,' Peter said. 'I don't know how much longer I'd have held out though. He's relentless. It's a mercy that he was called away. Do you know why?'

'No. McLean just told me urgent business at The Citadel.

I'm wondering if it's to do with Chas and Si though.'

'I dread to think what he's done to them,' Peter said.

Nick shook his head. 'You should keep the suit on until we get to Seahouses. Ben and Honour are there.'

'Those kids are still with you?'

Nick laughed. 'Yeah. Ben's like a dog with a bone. He's a good lad though and has proved his worth. And his side-kick is fearless and determined.'

'They're so young to be involved in all this though,' Peter said. 'And don't they have school?'

'They're home-schooled, apparently. I agree, they're young, but everyone's affected by the Rulers and they feel strongly about being involved.'

Peter nodded, forgetting that Nick couldn't see him.

Nick continued. 'Things are moving fast, and we need your help to build a force against the Rulers. We're amassing a lot of people willing to stand with us. People from The Way network, all over the country, are joining us and others who've been healed of the plague. We need a headquarters and we need some of your amazing technology to get into The Citadel and The Fortress. The plan is to rescue Si and Chas, kidnap Zephyr and destroy the clones.'

'Nothing too major then,' Peter said.

'No. Nothing we can't accomplish in a day's work,' Nick replied.

'I'll see what I can do.'

'You need some medical attention first, though. We'll call in at Seahouses then head straight back to my surgery. I can sort you out. You should really rest, but there's not much time, if we're going to help Si and Chas. Kate and some others are waiting for us in Newcastle.'

'I'll be fine,' Peter said. 'I'm in good hands. Do you think we can leave those kids at home though?'

Nick laughed. 'Not if they get their way! I'm hoping the parents will put their foot down.'

Peter was sorely in need of some rest when they got to Seahouses. Despite Ethan and Sarah's fears about getting involved, they took care of Peter as best they could. Nick tried to make him as comfortable as possible, until they could get back to Newcastle.

'We're coming with you,' Honour insisted.

Ethan looked at Sarah. He knew his daughter's determination. Honour looked at her father, expecting him to protest.

'Your mum and I have decided that, since you'd be a complete pain if we stopped you, I am coming back with you. We've decided that this is important, and we want to get involved, so I'm coming.'

'Are you sure?' Nick asked.

'Yes. Honour has shown us that it's about time we all stood up for what's right.'

25

It wasn't until the next day that the alarm was raised in the Priory, that Peter Marsden was missing. George McLean was furious with his security team. How could they not have noticed? What were they doing? Why had no one seen that he hadn't appeared on camera in his room for so many hours? Those who had been on duty that day were arrested. McLean knew immediately that it must be something to do with the doctor's visit, but he had no idea how Marsden had got out undetected. He'd been duped by Nick, and he was furious. Moreover, he was terrified of informing Premier Zephyr. He would certainly lose his job and possibly his life. He knew what they'd done to Aspen, after he let Kate Hunter escape. He thought about running himself, but he wouldn't get far. And if he ran, and they caught him, that would definitely be execution. No, he began rehearsing what to tell the Premier. This way, he may keep his life.

Zephyr was furious when he heard the news, and immediately had McLean arrested. He called Resolution, to tell him what had happened. Resolution was also infuriated that he would not have another chance to question Marsden; at the same time he was glad that, for once, he wasn't the one under fire. It made him all the more determined to use Si to root out the rebels. He was frustrated that he couldn't use Chas against him, but Zephyr had told him, in no uncertain terms, that she wasn't to be touched.

Resolution had put law-keepers on alert, looking for Capability and Temp. There were messages going out regularly on HTV, telling people to be vigilant and report sightings of them, billing them as dangerous traitors. Fear had touched The Citadel where, before this, nothing threatening ever penetrated the walls of the capital city.

*

Temp had been restless for days. Waiting was not his strong point. He had been encouraged to hear that Peter had been rescued from the Priory, without much difficulty. They had taken Peter to Pastor Rowley's place. Nick and Kate had only just managed to get a few essential medical supplies from his surgery, before it was raided by law-keepers. McLean had obviously told them everything he knew, once he had been arrested. Able to describe Nick's appearance, it hadn't taken the law-keepers long to work out his true identity. All doctors' records were held centrally by the Rulers. Nick's name and face would now be added to the wanted list.

News that people were gathering behind the rebellion, was also heartening. There were reports of protests in the streets and rioting. Kate had told him that people were pledging support, through members of Pastor Rowley's church; word was coming from some of the camps that, despite the Rulers' raids, people were still getting behind the rebellion. Peter was already working on resources and a place to gather people.

Temp felt powerless, stuck in hiding in The Citadel. He wanted to get to Si and Chas, or be out there with Nick and Kate, working with the rebellion. Capability was scared, but Temp had finally persuaded him to put on the invisibility suit and go into The Fortress, to find out what was going on with Chas and Si. Capability was dubious about the protection the invisibility suit would afford him, but Temp reassured him. Temp wished he could go, but they only had one suit and Capability had all the access codes and knew his way around. He would try to find the other two invisibility suits that had been confiscated from Chas and Si. He had an idea where they would be. More waiting for Temp.

'Try to speak to them if possible. Tell them we're coming for them. It'll give them hope.'

Capability shook his head. 'I'm not sure how I'll achieve that. I don't have access to the cells.' He was half-dressed in the invisibility suit. His legs had already disappeared.

Temp took him by the shoulders. 'You can do this, my friend. You've made your stand against the Rulers. There's no going back now. You've already done so much to help us. No one is going to know you're there.'

Capability smiled at Temp. 'I know. I'm glad you came back, old friend. This was the push I needed to be bolder and finally make a move. I'll do my best. If I don't come back...' He hesitated, blowing out his cheeks. 'If I don't come back within the next eight hours, get out of here. Please get word to my daughters. I've told you where they are.'

Temp nodded. Capability pulled the rest of the suit over his body and disappeared completely.

*

Today was the day that the embryos were going to be implanted into Chas's womb. Resolution felt uneasy about this, despite the odd sensation of knowing that Chas was somehow not his sister. He was still puzzling over how this was possible and determined to find out. He had had no contact with their parents since he had reported them; they had been deported, but he knew where to find people who had known them. When he had the time, he intended to track them down and find out what they knew. However, he had more pressing matters at hand. Today, he intended to break Silence Hunter and find out exactly what he knew about the location of the rebels. First of all, though, he wanted to speak to Chas; to take pleasure in her reaction at the DNA results and when he told her what he was going to do to Si. He had access to the Complex because of his security clearance, but he didn't think Zephyr would approve of him speaking to Chas, so he was cautious.

She was unaware that today was the day of the embryos being implanted. He found her in her room, after an orderly directed him there. The woman hung around, as if unsure whether she should leave Chas alone with the Commander, but he ordered her out of the room.

Chas was sitting on the bed, reading a book she'd found in the library. The days here had been few, but felt endless and she had kept herself to herself, only leaving her room, briefly, out of necessity. When she saw who it was that had come for her, she continued looking down at her book.

'What do you want?' she said, matter-of-factly.

Resolution plucked the book from her hand and placed it on a table, out of reach. She made to get up for it, but he pushed her back, roughly, onto the bed.

'Take your scumbag hands off me!' she said, trying to push him away.

Resolution sat down on a chair, in the corner of the room. 'I'm not staying long. Two things I have to say to you. Number one. Do you know the results of the DNA test?'

'I don't need to,' Chas said, contemptuously. 'You're my brother. The DNA would have proved it. So, why you're still strutting about here, I've no idea.' This irked her badly. He should be under arrest, deported or dead by now.

Resolution smiled superciliously. 'So, you don't know the actual results then?'

She looked at him, curiously, all of a sudden. 'Like I said, I don't need to...'

'Your supposition is false. I don't know how this has happened, but it appears you are not my sister after all.'

Chas looked incredulously at him. 'What? How could you have got at that test to falsify it? Or did you get someone to switch the DNA?' She wanted to tear the smug look off his face, as he sat there calmly, with his legs crossed and his fingers lightly drumming on the arm of the chair.

'I never touched it. I was at the Priory when it all happened. You are not my sister. It's a fact. Your DNA does not have a high enough match with mine in the siblingship test. It has to be higher than 1.00 for there to even be a chance that we are related, and it was not.'

Chas was stunned. All this time she had thought that his dirty, evil blood ran through her veins too. She had no words for him right now. She needed time to process this.

Resolution was pleased at her reaction. 'The second thing.' He came across the room and sat down on the bed right next to her. 'Today, I am going to break Silence Hunter into little pieces. He will not be able to hold out on me any longer. I am going to hunt down the rest of his puny rebellion and kill every person who has dared to join it. Kate Hunter, Peter Marsden and all the others. Finally, I will kill Silence Hunter. I will take my time and enjoy that. Unfortunately, I can't get my hands on you, for a while. But I can wait.'

Her hand went instinctively for her knife, that wasn't there, then she reached to tear at his face, but he was too quick for her. He grasped her wrists and stared into her angry eyes for a moment.

Then he laughed. 'Good luck with the babies.'

She struggled to get free of his grip, but he thrust her backwards and walked calmly from the room, closing the door, just as the bedside lamp smashed against the back of it.

When a carer stepped into the room, a while later, she found Chas curled up in a ball, on the bed. The room looked like a hurricane had smashed through it. The girl gasped at the devastation and hurried over to Chas.

'Chastity? What happened?'

The only reason Chas looked up, was that she recognised the voice.

'Grace?'

'Yes, it's me,' Grace said in her jolliest voice. 'I've been working here ever since... the incident at the hospital. Now, let's get you sorted out.' She helped Chas to sit up and saw that her face was streaked with tears. 'I've just come on duty. What happened here? Did you do this?'

Chas nodded. 'I can't take it anymore, Grace. My brother... at least I thought he was my brother, the Commander, he came here. Told me things that made me so angry and... afraid. And today... do you know what they're going to do to me?'

Grace nodded. 'I heard you were here and what they're planning to do. I couldn't get to see you before now, but I've wanted to come. I thought you could do with a friendly face.' She held Chas's hand, like a child's and squeezed it.

Chas bit back more tears. 'Resolution – the Commander, is going to torture Si. He said he was off to do it, right now. And they're coming to plant the embryos today. Can you help me get out of here?'

Grace looked frightened. She took her hand away. 'I can't. The security here is massive. I don't have any clearance. I have to get the guards to let me in and out. It's impossible.'

'There must be a way,' Chas said. 'You helped me before. You were so brave.'

Grace looked away. 'I know, but it really shook me. They questioned me, and I was so scared. My boyfriend left me...'

'I'm sorry. Can you at least get a message to Si for me?'

'Where is he?'

'In the cells.'

Grace looked even more panicked. 'How could I do that? I can't just wander down there and say "Oh hi, can you give this note to Silence Hunter please?'

Chas shook her head. 'It doesn't matter. Of course you can't. I'm sorry for asking.'

Grace came back and sat on the bed. 'No, don't be sorry. I'll do what I can to help you, while you're here. I couldn't believe it when I heard you were coming and what they're making you do. I'll do everything I can to get you through it.'

Chas nodded. 'Thanks.'

There was a knock at the door. Grace answered it to two guards.

'We've come to take her down to Genetics,' one said. He produced some handcuffs.

'I should accompany her,' Grace said.

'No need,' a guard replied.

Chas didn't struggle.

'I'll be here when you get back. I'll have this room looking lovely again for you.'

Chas didn't respond; just allowed herself to be led away.

*

Resolution had Si in his office. Excellence was with them, watching. Si was strapped to the torture chair, his heart pounding. He steeled himself to resist whatever Resolution was going to do to him.

'Today, you won't leave that chair until you tell me everything you know.'

'Then, I won't leave at all,' Si said, 'because I'm telling you nothing!'

'That's what you think, but you won't be able to hold out forever.'

'Why are you still here?'

Resolution laughed. 'I presume you are referring to the DNA test?'

'Well, I'm not thinking you might have gone on a luxury holiday to the Caribbean!'

Resolution was preparing his instruments. 'It was negative. She's not my sister, as I told everyone all along.'

Si was stunned. 'How did you manage to pull that one off?'

Resolution held up several of his instruments, handling them lovingly, like a child trying to decide which of his favourite toys to play with.

'She told me everything about you.'

'She was lying. She's probably lied to you about lots of things, Silence. Now, enough of that. Let's begin.' He picked up the small implement that had caused Si so much pain the last time. 'I'm going to start with this, as you enjoyed it so much last time, but I have more powerful tools to move on to. And,' he looked at Excellence, 'There's always brute force. That often works a treat. If I need a comfort break, I can always let my second-in-command have his turn.'

Excellence nodded at the Commander and supressed a smile.

Si closed his eyes, terrified that he would buckle. At least he didn't really know much, about where his mother and the others were right now. He thought briefly of her face and pictured her telling him she was with him. This made him almost smile and tears threatened to come. Despite all the circumstances recently, he had felt a renewed inner strength, so he said his most common one-word prayer. Then his mind turned to Chas, wondering what was happening to her. He tried to imagine them, somewhere far away from here, leading a normal life; being happy. But this was an impossible fantasy.

Resolution touched him with the wand and his eyes shot open, his head screaming with pain.

'Shall we begin?'

*

Chas was in a side room, near the operating theatre in the Genetics Centre. Doctor Nelson was with her, and a nurse. She did as she was told, not speaking or resisting, as they asked her to take off her clothes and put the gown on. Doctor Nelson and the nurse were already scrubbed up and in operating garments.

'We need to get you into theatre now,' the doctor said.

The nurse came to help Chas to stand up, but Chas shrugged her off. The operating theatre was the next room along. Chas desperately wanted to bolt, here and now, but there was nowhere to go. She couldn't get out. How could she help Si? Her hand instinctively went to where her knife would have been. It was a long time since she had felt the security of its presence. Suddenly, she had the seed of an idea. There might just be something she could do to help Si.

'Get up onto the table please,' Doctor Nelson said, as they

entered the theatre. Chas looked around, hoping she would see what she was looking for. Bright lights glared down on the operating table in the centre of the room, and beside this was the anaesthetic cart. There were various holo-screens around the room and the walls were lined with drawers and cupboards containing equipment. Various implements were placed, ready for use, on a metal tray near the table. There weren't many needed for this procedure and Chas didn't see what she was looking for.

'Get up onto the table please Chastity,' Doctor Nelson reiterated. The nurse stepped forward to help Chas. This time she let her.

'I'll be giving you a mild sedative to calm you and take the edge off any pain. Afterwards, you will need to lie still for a few hours. I'm afraid I've been told to make sure that happens, so guards will be coming to strap you down. I refuse to let them in while the procedure takes place.'

'Very kind of you,' Chas said, sardonically.

The doctor sighed. 'I'm doing my best for you, under the circumstances. The embryos are very healthy and stand a very good chance of implanting, after the progesterone injections we've been giving you.'

Chas let the doctor talk, trying to block out the noise. It was babble in the background. All she could hear were Resolution's words going around her head. She was not his sister and he was going to break Si. Was he doing that right now? What could she do about it? Everything was spiralling out of control and she had to stop it.

'I don't want a sedative,' Chas said, suddenly. 'I want to be aware of everything you're doing.'

The doctor hesitated. 'It will be uncomfortable, to say the least. You should have the sedative.'

'Please,' Chas said, hoping that her pleading manner would appeal to the doctor's sympathies.

Doctor Nelson shook her head. 'Okay. Fine. I'll be using ultrasound to guide me as I transfer the embryos. You'll be able to see it on the screen here. These are suspended in a drop of culture medium in a transfer catheter. Gently, I'll guide the tip of the loaded catheter through the cervix and deposit the fluid containing the embryos into the uterine cavity. Does that all make sense to you?'

'Yes. Fine. Just get on with it.' Chas continued to look around the room, trying to figure out how to achieve her goal.

'Chastity, are you alright?' The doctor laid a hand on her arm. 'We're all under scrutiny here. No one has a choice. I'll do my best to look after you.'

Chas turned her head to look at Doctor Nelson. There was concern in the doctor's eyes. 'You must have chosen to work for them. Why do you do this? Why do you work for them?'

The doctor looked down, as if embarrassed. 'It's complicated.' She paused and looked at Chas. 'And personal. I'm going to begin.'

The nurse stood by Chas's head, ready to assist. 'Please don't move. If you do, you could injure yourself and I'll be forced to call the guards, who will be in here within seconds. Then we'll have to do it with a bunch of men looking on. Clear?'

Chas nodded. Her stomach lurched, and she took a

deep breath. The doctor began the procedure. The first instrument felt cold and alien inside her. She watched on the screen, as the catheter reached her uterus. It felt strange and uncomfortable, causing cramping feelings in her abdomen.

'Try not to hold your breath. Deep, controlled breaths will help,' the nurse said.

Chas hadn't realised she was. She tried to breathe deeply, but her heart was pounding. She was gripping the side of the table. After what seemed like an age, she watched the catheter withdraw. 'That's it. The nurse will give you some pain-killers. And now, you need to lie still.'

The doctor moved away to type into her screen, as the nurse brought her some tablets. She swallowed them down, then suddenly grabbed the nurse from behind, one arm squeezing tightly around her neck.

The nurse cried out and Chas put her hand over her mouth to prevent her making any more noise. She struggled to pull Chas's arm away, but she was no match for Chas.

Doctor Nelson turned, at the sound. 'Stop that! You can't get away, Chastity. It's pointless.'

'Find me a scalpel. Now!'

The doctor hesitated. 'Why? Don't be foolish!'

'If you call security, I swear I'll kill her.'

The doctor rummaged in a drawer. 'You won't achieve anything by this, Chastity.'

Chas squeezed tighter. 'Hurry up!' The doctor walked to a set of metal drawers and pulled out a sterile scalpel in plastic packaging. 'Take off the cover,' Chas demanded. 'And bring it to me. Then step back right over there, away from any devices.'

'Please don't hurt her, Chastity. It's not her fault and you're not vindictive.'

Chas laughed. 'You don't know me. But I'm not going to do her any damage, if you do what I say.' As the doctor handed her the scalpel, Chas increased the pressure to the side of the nurse's neck and she slipped into unconsciousness. Chas took the scalpel and held it to her own neck, feeling for the artery. She didn't really want to die right now, but threatening to kill herself might be the only way to save Si.

'Chas,' Doctor Nelson used her name in such a gentle way that it nearly threw her. 'Don't do this. Please. I can make this work for you. Please, don't do it.'

'Just stay where you are,' Chas said. 'I'm not doing this because of the embryos. I'll go ahead with the embryo thing, if Zephyr meets my one request. Look, I'm sitting back down.' Chas climbed back up onto the operating table. 'If not, I'll be lying here in a pool of blood, before you can stop me, and those embryos will die with me. Get him on the phone.'

Doctor Nelson called Zephyr, and his holo-image appeared in the room. 'Premier Zephyr, Chastity has...'

Zephyr looked around the room and cut her short. 'I can see the situation for myself, doctor. How this happened you can explain later. What do you want Chastity?'

'Do you know that Resolution is torturing Si this very moment? Did you authorize that?'

'I authorized the Commander to question him, yes. But how do you know any of this?'

'Resolution came to my room earlier...'

Zephyr frowned. He had not authorized that.

'And told me he was going to break Si into little pieces.'

Zephyr flicked his hand. 'A figure of speech. He will do what he can to extract information. The boy won't die.'

'But he'll come close. Release him, or I'll slit my throat and you won't have your fun little experiment with our clones. If you release him, I'll behave myself throughout the whole pregnancy, and I'll do whatever you ask for your clones. You have my word.'

Zephyr curled his lip, ever so slightly.

'If she uses that scalpel, Premier, I don't know if I can save her, and the embryos are unlikely to survive the trauma,' Doctor Nelson said.

'I'll consult the other Rulers.'

'Don't think of sending in security. They won't be quick enough to stop me. And if you don't get back to me, within the hour, you can guarantee, one hundred percent, that I will do it!' Chas said.

The holo-image disappeared, leaving the doctor and Chas at an impasse.

*

Zephyr called an emergency meeting of the Rulers. He wanted Resolution there, too. As the Premier's holo-image appeared in Resolution's room, he could see that Si was almost unconscious. His head lolled forward, and his arms were limp in the restraints. 'Is he dead?'

Resolution shook his head. 'He'll be fine.'

'Are you getting anything out of him?'

'Ramblings. But it won't be long 'til he gives something important away. I'm sure.'

The Premier made a 'hmph' noise in the back of his throat. 'Take a break, Commander. I need you in the meeting room, right now. Excellence can keep an eye on Hunter. Something's happened.'

As many of the Rulers as possible were there within ten minutes, along with Resolution. Zephyr explained the situation to them. 'So, ideas?'

There were various suggestions. 'Let her kill herself,' Zealous said. 'Do we really need her, Premier? It's just an experiment. We could find someone else.'

Zephyr scowled at Zealous. 'I chose her. I want to use those specific clones.'

'You could take more DNA from her and Hunter. Use a different host,' suggested another Ruler.

'No!' Zephyr snapped. 'She has the best chance of carrying these clones and I want to see if she can do it.' Zephyr paused, daring them to challenge him further. He laughed to himself. Not many of them had any real backbone. If it wasn't for himself, Ambition and Zealous, the Rulers would have crumbled years ago. They called him their puppet, behind his back, he knew that, but they still cowered when he barked.

'I have an idea and some of you won't like it.' He glanced at Resolution, then brought up the holo-screen, over the table. Three-dimensional diagrams of cells and flow charts appeared. Zephyr moved through these as he spoke.

'We've been developing a new strain of plague, as you

know, since the Hunters introduced their 'cure' into the mix. It involves our own Nanomedibots carrying the Yersinia Pestis bacterium into the body, and depositing it directly into the lymph glands. The bacterium's defence systems have been modified to make it even more undetectable by these glands; its attack systems are even stronger than before, where it encounters resistance from immune system defence cells. This causes quicker death and less time for intervention from any cure. I think it's time to give it a trial run.' He paused for effect. 'On Silence Hunter.'

The Rulers listened, unsure of where Zephyr was going with this. 'We take some more DNA first, from Hunter, just in case anything goes wrong with the clones before birth, then we inject him with the new plague and send him back amongst the rebels. It's highly contagious. He won't know he has it and he'll spread it without them knowing. He'll be dead within 48 hours, so we have to make sure the rebels come quickly for him. Before Kate Hunter can devise a new cure, half of them will be dead and the rebellion snuffed out like a candle. We can show Chastity CCTV of Silence being released in York or Newcastle or somewhere we know they've been, then she'll settle down and do the job. She gave me her word.'

Resolution laughed. 'With respect, Premier, that is worth nothing.'

'Isn't it? I think it's probably worth more than yours, Commander!'

Resolution bristled. 'Sir, I am one hundred per cent loyal to the regime and to you.'

Zephyr curled his lip and rolled his eyes. 'Loyal maybe,

but a damn fool with it. What possessed you to tell her what you were doing to Hunter?'

Resolution tried to keep calm, even though he was floundering for an answer. 'I thought it...'

Ambition interrupted. 'It heightens his sense of pleasure when he tortures people, to know that he's torturing someone else through it.'

Resolution started to protest but Ambition didn't let him. He stood up and addressed the others.

'With respect to you, Premier, the rebels will be suspicious if we suddenly release Hunter. They won't accept him back, surely.'

'Kate Hunter will. She's not going to ignore her son, is she? We leave him out there and let them discover why. By the time they've figured it out, it will be too late. We'll put it on the public broadcasts that he's escaped. She'll be watching.'

'We should track him,' someone said.

'Yes, but we need to let the new plague do its work before moving in.'

'You could kill half the population if this new plague is highly infectious,' another Ruler offered. 'The first one was... contained.'

'Only people who come into contact with the rebels. They will become pariahs. No one else will dare to join them,' Zephyr said.

Ambition looked at Resolution. 'Does Hunter know where they are?'

Resolution shook his head. 'He's talked about various places. But nowhere specific. I was going to set law-keepers on high alert in Durham, Newcastle, York. These are all places we know he's associated with. I don't think he knows exactly where his mother is, at the moment.'

Zephyr shut down the holo-screen. 'This is going to happen within twenty-four hours. I'm going down to Genetics myself, to talk some sense into that girl. She may have just accidentally inspired our means of ending this rebellion for good. Ambition, get the Nanomedibot containing the new plague and bring it to the Commander's office. Commander, prepare Hunter for his 'escape'. You and Excellence are going to drive him. Where will you leave him?'

Resolution considered for a moment. 'Durham, where Nick Reece's surgery is.'

'Fine. Make him think he's escaped. He mustn't know about the Nanomedibot or the tracker.'

Resolution nodded.

'Zealous, sort out the announcement that Hunter has escaped. Get it out to the public within the hour. Give them plenty of notice that he's coming. Tell them to keep clear; that he might be dangerous. Tell them to report sightings to the law-keepers. The rest of you, I want news of Capability and Temperance. We have to find them. Remember, they may have invisibility technology.'

The Rulers dispersed. Zephyr headed over to the Genetics Centre. He had ten minutes before Chas's hour was up.

26

The nurse had come round and was sitting groggily in the corner of the operating theatre, scowling at Chas. Doctor Nelson had checked her over and she seemed to be suffering no ill-effects of being knocked out. Chas had not let the scalpel drop from the vicinity of her neck, despite the tremors in her hand.

'Are you really going to do this if Zephyr doesn't respond in the next ten minutes?' the doctor asked.

'Yes,' Chas said. 'I told him I keep my word.'

'It's not a good way to die,' Doctor Nelson said.

'Is there a good way?' Chas said.

'In your sleep, when you're old and grey?' the doctor suggested.

Chas smiled sarcastically. 'I don't think I'm going to get the chance to find out on that one.'

'Can't you just see this through Chastity? I told you I'll make sure you're looked after.'

'Do you think I care about being looked after by the Rulers?' Chas said. 'All I care about is Si, right now. I know what a sadist Resolution is. I can't bear him tearing Si apart. He's hurt so many people I love. I can't seem to stop him, and if I can't stop him this time, I might as well get myself away from him and all this, for good.'

Doctor Nelson closed her eyes and took a deep breath. 'Please Chastity. Don't do it.'

'I'm touched by your concern for me, doctor.'

The doctor looked at Chas to discern whether this was sarcasm, but it appeared to be genuine.

'I'm sorry for these innocent lives.' She pointed to her abdomen, indicating the embryos.

The doctor shrugged. They won't know anything, will they? But you will and the people you leave behind.'

Chas shook her head and looked at the clock on the holo-screen. The hour was almost up. 'I've got no one but Si, and he's dead if Resolution isn't stopped.'

There were two minutes left. 'Chastity, please...'

At that moment, the door to the theatre opened and Zephyr walked through, flanked by two guards. Chas stiffened so that the scalpel jerked, and she felt a trickle of blood run down her neck. The guards stood back, as Zephyr spoke.

'Don't panic.' He held up his hands. 'I agree to let Silence Hunter go. 'Everyone in the room looked at him in shock. 'You are valuable to me now. I don't want to lose what I've started. Hunter is not being any use to us and the Commander will likely kill him, before he gets anything out of him. He's being taken to Durham tomorrow morning. If you will agree to be taken back to your room, I will arrange for you to see live footage that proves it, in the morning.'

'I don't believe you,' Chas said. 'As soon as I put this scalpel down, you'll take it all back.'

Zephyr took a step towards her and she flinched. 'Don't

come near me.'

'You told me you would keep your word. I believe you. Now believe me. I will keep mine.'

Chas didn't know what to do. 'I'm keeping the scalpel as my insurance.'

Zephyr nodded. 'Until you see the release images, then you give it back. You will be supervised at all times until then.'

Chas nodded. 'Don't let those guards come near me though, or I might just lash out with this thing.'

Zephyr almost smiled at her determination. 'That's fine.' He turned to Doctor Nelson. 'Doctor, is she fit to move?'

'I think a wheelchair would be a good idea. She shouldn't really walk anywhere, for now.'

'I want the doctor to walk with me,' Chas said.

Zephyr nodded to the doctor.

'That's settled then. You keep your word and I keep mine.'

*

Si was back in his cell, feeling terrible. He had been brought here unconscious, and felt totally disorientated. He could barely move from the pain caused by Resolution's torture instruments. He didn't know why the interrogation had stopped, but he was relieved. How long the reprieve was for, he couldn't hazard a guess. He longed to know about Chas and what was happening to her. Everything inside him screamed to get to her and stop what was going on. He felt so helpless and in pain, that he just lay on the bench with his eyes closed, until he eventually drifted into a disturbed sleep.

The cell door didn't open again until much later. He couldn't tell what time it was, as there was no natural light in there. Excellence came in, with two guards loitering in the doorway. 'Get up!' He hauled Si to his feet and yanked him out of the cell, where the guards put cuffs back on him. Si steeled himself for another session with Resolution. He wasn't sure what he had already told him. He feared he might have said more than he meant to, but obviously not enough if he was being taken back.

However, Excellence led him to a waiting car. 'Where are we going?' Si asked.

'You'll see soon enough,' Excellence said.

'Oh great! A mystery tour, I love those.'

Excellence ignored his sarcasm.

They only drove a very short distance to the hospital. The sky was the dull grey steely colour of pre-dawn. Si was confused and suddenly scared. What were they going to do to him now? Why bring him here?

Resolution came from the hospital and got into the car.

Si looked at him curiously. 'What's going on?'

Resolution was unusually quiet. He offered no explanation.

Si tried again as the car pulled away. 'Where are you taking me?'

Excellence answered. 'Be quiet Hunter, or I'll have to make you. You're irritating us.'

'Oh, I'm so sorry. How inconsiderate of me.'

They drove in silence through The Citadel, towards a gate. Without much of a stop at the check-point, they were out, driving onto the moor. Si gulped back the knot of fear rising in his throat. Where were they taking him? He looked back desperately at the receding city where he was leaving Chas behind.

'I'll come back for you. I promise,' he mouthed.

After a few hours, they arrived at the gates of a tech-city Si recognised. The Cathedral loomed, a deceptively comforting sight, on the hill behind the city walls. He panicked, knowing Nick's surgery was here. Could Resolution have found his mother and the others? Was he bringing Si here, to show him what he'd done to her? He closed his eyes then opened them again suddenly, trying to shake the images of execution from his head.

'What are we doing here?' he demanded. 'If you've hurt my mother, I'll kill you, I swear.'

Still Resolution was silent. They drove through the check-point and stopped, after a few minutes, in a side street. Resolution got out and walked away, around a corner. Excellence was looking at his phone. The Commander was taking a long time, doing whatever it was he was doing. Si was growing more and more anxious. He leaned forward. His hands were cuffed behind his back, but if he tried he might be able to head-butt Excellence and escape. Excellence saw him coming closer in the mirror and whirled round.

'Don't try anything on me, Hunter. I'm too fast for you.' He pushed Si back, with some force. 'I'm going for a piss.' He got out of the car, but Si didn't hear the car lock. Surely, he wouldn't have left it open? He tried the door. It wasn't locked. He couldn't believe it. Excellence wasn't far away, but Si decided that this was his best opportunity to get away. He pushed open the door and leapt out.

He was running. He could see the corner of the street within twenty metres. Running was difficult, with his hands restrained behind him, and he knew Excellence must have heard him. He urged himself on, but before he reached the corner, pain exploded in his back and he blacked out.

Excellence picked Si up and carried him back to the car. He had only stunned him. Resolution was there, putting on a contamination suit. Excellence got into another suit. They were taking no chances. From the box he had brought, Resolution took a syringe, loaded with the latest variation of the plague. He injected Si, threw his limp body out onto the street and drove off.

*

The atmosphere at Pastor Rowley's house was optimistic. It had been all over the HTV channels, that Si had escaped. Kate was on edge. 'How will he find us? He has no idea where we are. And if someone else finds him before we do, they could hand him over to the Rulers.'

'I've got everyone I know from The Way looking out for him, in as many places as we can,' Pastor Rowley said.

Peter spoke up. 'And I have contacts in places near The Citadel.'

Esme had insisted on going home, as soon as she found out Si had escaped, in case he turned up at her house. Even the thought that the law-keepers might already be there didn't put her off. Ben had gone with her, insisting that he could keep her safe, even though he knew that Kurt and

Brigitta would probably do a much better job of that than he could. Honour had stayed in Newcastle with her father and the two of them were out on the streets, looking for Si.

Nick and Kate remained inside, as their faces had been plastered all over the HTV afresh, with the news of Si's escape.

It was mid-morning. They were in the kitchen drinking tea. Kate kept getting up and pacing around. 'We have to find him, Nick. I couldn't bear to lose him again.'

Nick tried to calm her, but he wasn't having much success. She went to the door. 'I need some air. I've got to get out of here.'

Nick stopped her. 'Please Kate. Just wait. There are so many people looking for him. If he turns up, you need to be here.'

She sat down. 'I know. I know. It's just that waiting is the worst. I want to do something.'

Nick took her hands in his. 'I know. Me too. But this is what we have to do, right now.'

She couldn't sit still. She kept getting up and wandering from room to room, asking for news and drinking copious amounts of coffee. Fears and questions filled her head. Nick tried to talk to her about things that might distract her from the worry, but he stopped after a while, knowing it was futile. He pulled up a holo-screen and tried to find news on social media.

Just after mid-day, Pastor Rowley came into the kitchen, a big grin on his face. 'Kate! Look!' He brought up a holo-image from his phone.

It was Si, sitting in a car, with two people from the Way. Kate gasped and choked back a sob. 'Si! Are you alright?'

He was grinning. 'Mum! I think so. I don't know how I've done it, but I seem to have escaped.'

Turn the page to read the beginning of
Part III **Breaking Up**.

Breaking Up

They stood, huddled around the three gaping holes. Only ten people had dared to gather to pay their respects. Fear and grief mingled in a deadly concoction, twisting paralytic tendrils around the group. No one spoke. At first glance they could have been mistaken for standing stones, silhouetted against the breaking dawn.

The rising sun mocked the sombre mood, by shooting spokes of dazzling light across the sky. Kate wished it was raining so hard that her grief might be drowned by the volley of water lashing her face. Instead, she stood nestled into Nick, his arm tightly around her, squinting against the brightness of the new day.

Pastor Rowley had consecrated this makeshift burial ground on the wasteland, near the building they called Church. Other members of The Way were buried here; their graves arranged so as not to look like a graveyard. Each was marked by a slab of concrete, with a small fish symbol carved into it.

Kate shivered, despite the seeping warmth of the sun. Nick had moved to help the other men lift the three shrouded bodies out of the estate car. It was only three days since Si had returned, unwittingly carrying a more deadly, infectious strain of the plague than the one they had encountered. He had begun to show signs of fever within a couple of hours of being reunited with his mother. She had acted fast, but not before several people had hugged him and spent time in his company.

And now, here they were. Three bodies already and

several very sick, in isolation, in the church behind them; including Honour and Ethan.

As soon as she had realised what was happening, Kate had isolated Si and anyone who had been near him, since his return. Then, she had watched as most of them fell sick. The symptoms came on so fast that, before she knew it, the first person was dead.

She suspected that the only reason she and Nick had not succumbed, was because they had both been injected with an NMB before, and this was somehow helping. Si had also been injected, in the trials, in Amsterdam, so Kate was struggling to understand why he had succumbed to this new strain.

All she had thought about and done for the last seventy-two hours, was search for a way to modify the NMBs, in order to combat this new strain of plague. She had not slept at all, despite Nick's attempts to persuade her to have an hour here and there. He had been just as busy, supervising the care of the sick, and trying to prevent more people from being infected.

Kate wrenched her mind away from all that. Just for these few minutes, she was here for the dead: the ones she had not been able to save. Her stomach clenched, and she choked back a sob, as they lowered the first body into the grave.

The second body was lowered into its grave. Tears were now running down her face. She turned her eyes to the third shroud and held her breath. As this one came out of the car, and the men fixed the straps around it to lower it into the hole, Kate's legs buckled, and she sank to the ground, unable to hold back the choking sobs. Nick looked over to Kate, desperately wanting to go to her, but he was holding one of the straps around the body, helping to steady its descent into the grave.

A woman next to Kate bent down and hissed, 'This is your fault!' Then she spat on her and walked away from the mourners, muttering hateful remarks about Kate as she went.

The bodies were in the holes and Nick came back to Kate, helping her to her feet, then holding her close, murmuring what comfort he could think of. 'Ssh! You are doing everything you can. You couldn't have saved him. You couldn't have saved any of these. There's a chance with the others. Ssh! Come on now.'

She buried her head into his shoulder, as someone began to sing quietly. Others joined in, barely above a whisper.

'Yea though I walk in death's dark vale,
Yet will I fear no ill,
For thou art with me, and thy rod
And staff, me comfort still.'

As the hymn faded, Nick moved to help shovel earth into the graves.

'Wait!' said a woman. 'Someone should say something; a blessing or a prayer. The Pastor would have, if...' she choked on her words and looked pointedly at Kate.

A man stepped forward and a hush fell. 'O Lord, we commend these souls into your safe-keeping. Take care of our dear brothers and sister. May they have life everlasting. Amen.'

People began to walk away, but Nick and Kate stood for a few more minutes, looking at the three mounds, neither of them able to say anything to the other.

Finally, Kate looked up at the make-shift isolation ward behind her, and sighed. 'Time for the dead is over. We have to fight for the living now.'

*The story continues
in Part III of the Breaking trilogy*

Breaking Up

For more information and advance orders, go to:

www.monkeyislandpublishing.com

Please review this book on Amazon

Also by Karen Langtree:

Breaking Silence
Knights of the Wobbly Table
My Wicked Stepmother
Fairy Rescuers
Return to Elysia
Angel Small
Angel Small Follows the Star

Musicals by Karen Langtree:

Angel Small
The Rainboat
Go Grace Darling
School for Angels

About Karen...

Karen is a teacher, musician and writer who lives in York, England, with her children and husband. She has been writing children's books for 10 years and has finally made the transition into Young Adult fiction – something she has always enjoyed reading and always wanted to write.

Writing the Breaking Trilogy was a totally different experience to writing for younger readers. She enjoyed doing the research into new technology – something she never thought would inspire her!

The characters have become part of her life and she is keen to explore what they will do next...

Karen loves to hear from readers and always replies to emails. You can contact her at:

www.monkeyislandpublishing.com